CHAPTER ONE
Kat - Trouble with Mercs

"I do know that for the sympathy of one living being, I would make peace with all. I have love in me the likes of which you can scarcely imagine and rage the likes of which you would not believe. If I cannot satisfy the one, I will indulge the other."
— Mary Shelley, Frankenstein

KittKat - Level 38
Near Shellbreak Harbor
Midnight

The night animals were calling. The winter air was bitter cold, but that didn't keep prey and predator from coming out. She wasn't far from the castle, heck its broken towers were visible from the glade. So she waited rather impatiently for the mercenaries to arrive. An hour late already, and they hadn't sent a single message. Kat would give them five more minutes, ten at the tops before she headed back to the castle. The faint sound of a branch snapping caught her attention. She looked up and towards the direction of the noise.

"Took you long enough," She muttered sourly. Her first warning of combat was the lead ball smashing into her head. A chunk of her health disappeared from the critical blow. Kat rocked backward; the costume she wore melting away into the form of her dark armor. Blackened plate-mail wrapped tightly around her body. She cursed as another round whizzed by her.

"A bloody trap," Kat hissed under her breath. Of course it was, she'd been a fool to come out here alone. A second ball slapped against her chest-plate stealing another chunk of life.

"Damn dwarves, can't they fight with honest steel." She cursed drawing her obsidian axe and shield. Three stout little creatures charged her from the bushes. They sprinted towards her drawing short weapons. Two paused long enough to fire another round from their flintlocks. One ball struck the tree she stood next to, the other hit her hip plate. Kat would have loved to get her paws on firearms of her own. The last charging dwarf fired; the lead shot struck her shield taking with it another sliver of life.

"Come on then!" She shouted.

A new dwarf stepped into the small clearing. This one wore no visible armor except a leather smock, and a thick belt laden with tools. He carried with him a large ornate box which he dropped to the ground. As it landed the item started to move, transforming into something. Tiny treads unfolded from the sides as a turret slid up and out of the box. "Oh just great," Kat groused. They had a miniature tank-bot. She'd heard the dwarves couldn't cast magic; instead they had tinkerers and engineers.

"Greater Vampiric Edge," Kat whispered running a hand along her weapon. An angry red glow spread across it just as the first dwarf met her. He dashed towards her with a small axe in hand. It began to glow as the fighter activated his melee skill. A chunk of her life disappeared as he flashed past her. The iron ball braided into his beard flailed about as he turned. Through the mass of facial hair his big pearly teeth glinted as he grinned wickedly.

"Ain't nuthin' personal darling," The dwarf rumbled. That's where he was wrong; Kat was taking this all too personally. She side-stepped his next attack and slashed her axe hard across his torso. Blood from his wound surged up the obsidian axe blade healing her. As she engaged the leader, two other dwarves flanked her. Kat's left side was protected by her black heater shield. She kept it up defensively as she attacked with her axe. The vexed dwarf hammered at her barrier trying to get past the guard. A dwarven crafted short sword rained down on her right side despite her attempts to parry.

Out of the corner of her eye, she noticed a round shape land next to her. She risked a glance. A spiked black ball was hissing, shaking, and grinning up at her with a painted goofy smile. The fuse sputtered once before dipping into the cavity of the device.

"A grenade!" Kat thought diving away just as the ball exploded. Steel shards pinged off her armor like metal rain. The three dwarves gave chase hacking at her armored body. Her health continued to fall rapidly. Using her shield as a crutch Kat levered herself up. Fine then, if she was going to die she didn't need to hold back.

"Asmodeus's Wrath!" She bellowed and a black aura spilled from her armor. The dark, blood-smelling smoke quickly solidified into ebony blades circling her body. The leader lunged at her eager for the kill. His steel axe struck a blackened sword bouncing off. A second blade struck out from the swirling mass slashing the fighter. Blood flicked into the air before being sucked into her armor. Kat's health ticked up a few notches.

"Ain't fair," The dwarf scoffed. Well, the dwarves had their toys and Kat hers.

"Life ain't fair," Kat replied charging the leader. Her health started to increase gradually as the blades did their dirty work. At the same time she attacked the dwarf with her obsidian battle axe. The two dwarves were forced away from her aura as it spun up to full speed. Instead, they fetched ball and powder to reload their flintlocks.

Some thirty feet away the sentry tank came around the tree. It's muddy treads stopped, turret swiveling ominously towards her, and fired another grinning spiked grenade. She dove past the dwarven leader as the shell landed. He too scrambled to get away from the explosive. Kat slashed at his back as he went past making her health go up a few precious ticks. She wasn't going to be the only one taken out today. Her aura wouldn't last forever, and the two pistol-toting dwarves were taking aim. She stood and ran after the leader raising her battle-axe high overhead.

"Unholy Smite," She yelled calling her daily ability and brought the weapon down on his head. A red angry charge spread between her axe and the dwarf.

"N-no..." The dwarf gasped as his health disappeared. The gunfighter's body devoid of life crashed heavily to the ground.

"Nothing personal, darling." Kat mimicked in a sarcastic tone. Three dwarves remained though, and she didn't have an easy escape. Two gunfighters caught up as she turned to face them. They stopped just outside the range of her aura of blades, leveled their pistols, and fired. One bullet was deflected by her mass of black weapons, flicking off into the trees. The other slammed into her, knocking her health into the red. Holstering their guns, they attacked again with melee weapons. Her aura faded, smoke slipping back into her armor as Kat continued to back away. If she could keep a tree between herself and her attackers she might just live. Kat had no hope of taking down another; both were full health, and ready for revenge. Kat's health bar was looking ragged and red. Her axe swung, connected with a dwarven sword. She twisted her wrist deflecting the blow and cut into the dwarf. At least the gun-dwarves weren't as skilled at melee combat.

"Clear space," A squeaky voice commanded. The dwarves bounded left and right. Kat managed to get her shield up just as the tank fired. The cannon round slammed into her, forcibly knocking her back. Thankfully Kat kept her feet—if only barely. She glanced over the lip of her shield and saw the spiked ball sticking to it.

"*Oh fudge,*" Kat thought knowing she couldn't un-equip, or drop her shield in time. She stared blankly at the grenade as it blew. The explosion picked her armored form up and tossed her through the air a dozen feet at least. She had time to reflect that this had been a bad idea. Kathrine let out a quiet sigh. She'd taken one of the dwarves out at least. Kat wouldn't die alone. It had been a good run. She'd made friends, created a guild, and found a lover. Well, 'lover' was a rather strong word for him.

The earth moved to meet her, rubble and stone shot out. Just as the ground neared a white marble coffin breached the soil. The open maw closed over her like a giant shark. A coffin lid slammed down leaving her momentarily in darkness. A few seconds later she tumbled out amid a mass of undead. She never thought she'd be so happy to see a group of zombies and vampires surrounding her. A giant skeletal mage pointed at her.

"You should have told us you were going out." He said in a deep voice.

"It is nice to see you too." She replied holding up a hand. It was true, and she was so incredibly happy to see him just then. He dragged her roughly to her feet. Kat immediately started to feel better now that she was out of combat. Her natural regeneration and the necromancer's aura was patching up the wounds she'd received. The skeletal mage poked her in the stomach with two fingers.

"Negative Energy Bolt," He intoned. A green flash of eldritch energy struck her making all the little hairs on her body stand up. The green glow spread over Kat as her health climbed back into safe territory. By the dark lords, she needed that. The necromancer let go long enough to point his staff past her.

"Attack," He ordered and ten undead rushed the dwarves. The three remaining mercenaries turned to flee into the night. Six vampires quickly circled the trio with their increase speed—not to mention longer legs. They trapped the dwarves between themselves and the zombie pets.

"Protect me," The tinkerer squeaked fumbling for his tool belt. The two remaining dwarves turned to face the undead. Meanwhile, he pulled a flat device from his belt and tossed it to the ground. The fighters fought back to back as the teleporter unfolded. A blue glow lit the round disk as it fully activated. Quickly the engineer stepped atop it and within seconds teleported away. Vampires rushed to attack the remaining two dwarves. The second dwarf shuffled back up onto the glowing device and vanished. The third and final fighter fell a few feet from safety. His eyes turned to the blue device as a sword stabbed down into his back. Seconds later the strange dwarven machine twisted up on itself vanishing among a bright flash of blue light.

At least she'd had an exciting evening, enough to get her undead heart pumping. Moving to the necromancer she leaped up to give him a peck on his exposed cheekbone, not that she was grateful, just because she could.

CHAPTER TWO

Liam - Going Virtual

"I have spread my dreams under your feet;
Tread softly because you tread on my dreams."
W.B. Yeats (1865–1939)

Six Months Earlier - August 25, 2104
California - South San Francisco Bay.

"Hey Jelly, got a minute?" A deep male voice asked. The muscled body—of said question—sat down heavily in the break room chair. He straddled the seat backward, and lazily rested his forearms on it's back. Looking up Liam saw the wide handsome face of Cole Slatko. He searched the other man's expression for any sign of sarcasm, or malice. For years everyone had called Liam by his hated nickname. Many didn't even know his real name; he was just Jelly or Jellyroll. Cole smiled engagingly still waiting for Liam to reply. The former college football player had once been a close friend. It was a relationship that had ended almost a lifetime ago. Back in middle school Liam's weight had ballooned, Cole had put on muscle. Now Liam was an employee in the Slatko family factory. At least the man wasn't Liam's direct supervisor. Not for the first time he wondered why he bothered working at all. It wasn't like he needed the money.

"Cole," Liam said simply; it was enough of a reply for the other to move on.

"Have you heard of Nigmus Online?"

"I have, vaguely, it's that new virtual world MMO," Liam said his words coming out haltingly uncertain.

"That's the one, came out last week. The boys and I have gotten into it recently. Wanted to ask you to join." Cole said his tone still upbeat.

"I don't have the virtual pod," Liam replied his skepticism growing. Nobody invited him out like this, and certainly not Cole and his crew. Virtual pods were the older generation virtual reality machines. Once inside you could see, hear, smell, and feel everything as it happened. Unfortunately, the pods were enormous and expensive. The newest versions though had been miniaturized to the size of a rugby helmet.

"That's fine. We go down to the Pod People Arcade on Second Avenue to play for a few hours." Cole said shifting in the seat. His arms moved from the chair back to the table as he leaned forward. The topic apparently excited the man.

"Join us."

"Why?" Liam asked, "You have plenty of other friends."

"There are five of us, but we need one more for a full group. I'll handle everything, you just show up." Cole continued smoothly. Liam searched Cole's face and eyes for the deceit he'd come to expect from people.

"I don't know, I have errands to run," Liam said feeling something inside twist a little.

"Come on! It's amazing, you should try it once," Cole replied still with that smile of his. Liam tried to remember the last time they'd hung out. God that had been ten years ago. Cole had become a jock and a dick all during high school. College had only served to cement his personality. Liam though considered the other man for a long moment. He suspected something was up, but maybe Cole had discovered some tiny shred of his old self.

"Fine, I think I have time."

"Great, show up at the Arcade at 5 pm. You know where it's at?" Cole asked.

"I can find it," Liam answered. With that Cole stood and left the break room. Liam briefly wondered if he was going to regret this decision. Wendy sat down nearby and scowled at Cole's retreating form, then glanced skeptically at Liam.

"You can not be serious." She said to him. Wendy did have a valid point. Suddenly having Cole ask him to join him and his friends? It did stink.

"I'm hoping there is something decent left inside," Liam replied glancing out the lunchroom door. Cole annoyed quite a few people at work, not just Liam. He was a lazy braggart on his good days. Liam chewed his lower lip in deliberation. He could just skip out, go home, and watch television. For a few moments he seriously considered the idea, but sadly he had given his word.

Still, he'd heard a lot of good things about the virtual pods. They were supposed to be amazing—in some ways better than real life. You could experience the world in entirely new ways. Recent years had brought a resurgence in interest for virtual reality. It would be a nice distraction at least. The clock on the wall chimed signifying the top of the hour, and Liam stood. He washed the plastic food container and put it in his carry-all. Wendy shrugged in a, 'what can you do' gesture.

Liam walked back to his desk to finish the inventory report. At three o'clock he punched out and grabbed his jacket. Going out into the parking lot he got into a rusty half-gasoline, half-electric hybrid. The tiny two-cylinder engine coughed before settling into an ear-splitting whine from a slipping alternator cable. He drove to his townhouse which thankfully wasn't far. The beautiful little one story manor nestled in the lower foothills of California. The estate had been in the family for generations. Tossing his keys into the small bowl, he wandered into the kitchen for a drink, and then back to his room.

Grabbing a change of clothes he crossed the hallway to the master bath. The water came on tepid before quickly turning hot. Undressing he got in before scrubbing clean. After a while, he just stood under the hot water barrage. He dunked his head beneath the spray before letting it beat on the back of his neck. It helped ease the tense muscles there. Finally, he shut the water off and got out. Liam couldn't help but catch sight of his nude reflection. He usually tried quite hard not to look at himself. Liam was over three hundred pounds, and no amount of scrubbing could wash away the extra weight. Before he could turn away, he noticed the look in the reflection. His blue eyes smoldered sullen like a storm front. Far too many years of being overweight had left a mark on him. He pulled a towel off the rack and dried himself before dressing. Armored now he looked back at the mirror thankful that the storm in his eyes was gone. Filling a palm with some cream, he applied it over his face. He shaved quickly—after replacing the blade on his razor—then checked himself in the mirror. Good, next he splashed a little aftershave on before squeezing a dollop of gel into his palm. With the gel, he managed to form his mousy brown hair into something that wasn't a tangle. He was now fit to be seen in public. Leaving the bathroom, he went back to his room to fetch his keys.

Out in the garage, he walked past the old rusty Honda hybrid he'd come home in and got into a green Mazda RX-12. The ancient gasoline powered sports coupe was a relic of the past. One he had paid handsomely to restore to its factory condition. Carbon emission laws ensured he only got to drive it thirty days out of the year. As the smart key turned the engine let out a meaty roar. The music system quaked to life blotting out all noise but classic rock and roll. He smiled to himself. In a world where nearly every car was half-electric, it was nice to hear the purr of the real engine. When he got to town, he parked two blocks down and walked the rest of the way. The Arcade was an old theater that had been re-purposed. He pulled open the darkened doors and went inside.

The pictures on the website hadn't done the gaming club justice. At 5 pm it was nearing capacity. Liam joined the line of people going inside. The windows were blacked out making the interior artificially dark. The floor and ceiling looked like the corridor of a space ship. A fog of wispy white smoke lazily hugged the carpet. Ports and openings leaked out the white fog from dozens of machines. Green and blue neon bulbs artfully provided the ambient light. Hundreds of strange alien characters covered the walls.

One side of the building was sectioned off with frosted glass. Liam could just make out the gaming tables and computers within. Music beat a steady rhythm from the room as the door to that section opened and closed. Liam though became fixated on the rows and rows of virtual pods. There had to be at least three hundred set up to look like cryogenic freezers. Most were full of people, shadowy figures hidden behind opaque white canopies. Liam walked forward until he came to a railed balcony. A second floor below contained even more machines.

"Jelly!" A voice called from the bottom floor. Cole was standing in a small crowd of friends, who waved him down to the lower level. He turned, descending the neon-lit ramp, and passed a dozen people. The gaming cafe was apparently a teenage hangout. Quite a few kids from the local high school were lounging around excitedly talking about the games.

"You're late," One of the men said. Liam didn't know his name but recognized him as part of the welding crew.

"You said five," Liam said to Cole.

"We set up your account. Doug went ahead and skipped all the boring tutorials." Cole boomed patting said man on the back. The wiry little welder smiled and raised a fist.

"We're going to kick this dungeon's ass," Doug said enthusiastically before handing Liam a piece of paper. Account - Jellify with a password that literally was 'Password.'

"Climb into the pod, let's get this started. The place closes in four hours." Cole said pointing to one of the open pods. Six sat next to each other empty and waiting. As the crew passed him, they smiled warmly before a fist punched his arm none too gently. He turned to see the welder grinning at him wolfishly, "We need one more, but this is going to be great." The way Doug said it made the sentence sound like two entirely different topics.

Liam approached the last open pod. The machine was covered in painted alien script with a frosted glass canopy making the person within appear frozen in sleep. Floating inside was an amply padded white seat. He grabbed one of the handholds and climbed in. Slowly the seat settled as the canopy descended. Liam was grateful he wasn't claustrophobic. For a few seconds, nothing happened leaving him boxed into the little white coffin. Something starting up inside the machine, an audible whine made everything slowly fade. First it was the music; the song slowed to a crawl before whispering into silence. Next the semi-opaque frosted glass before him blurred. His vision clouded over by a bright, noisy white. Lastly was the feeling of his body as his fingers and toes grew numb. The sensation of nothing raced up his arms and legs to encompass his torso. It was like he was painlessly dying, which was definitely the weirdest thing he'd ever experienced.

***

Liam - Level 0
Aethon Island - Mothau Crypt <Dungeon>

Liam blinked, taking in the scene that lay before his eyes. He stood in the foyer of a massive underground crypt. When he drew in his first breath, Liam was forcibly assaulted by the smell. Dust and moist earth fought with the overpowering stench of old decay. Along with this, a sensation of cold pervaded everything, like the aura of death had chilled the very air. When he let out the breath it fogged the space before him. Liam looked right then left slowly. Large standing sconces blazed equal distance, each filled with a putrid green flame. In between each brazier was the roughly hewn statue of a skeletal human. Most had been broken or vandalized throughout the ages. The disfigured shapes threw dancing shadows across the walls. About fifteen feet in front of him a stone railing separated the landing from a plummet into darkness.

Laughter behind Liam broke into his reverie. A small huddle of people had just come into the dungeon. The mixed group of armor and clothes was something straight out of fantasy. Four males and one female were all looking at him.

"Holy shit this was so worth it," A warrior said bending over double. The man wore chain-mail with a shield across his back. At his waist, a longsword dangled. Liam had no idea what they thought was so funny but he suspected it was him. He started to close down, his emotions locking themselves up tight in preparation. A leather wearing female fell to the ground clutching her sides. Decayed and brittle bones were crushed as she rolled around laughing. A large well-muscled man wearing half-plate pointed at Liam. His head was thrown back as he laughed like a barking hyena.

"What the fuck is so funny?" Liam asked finally. Instead of his usual voice, it came out so low it sounded like a mountain rock slide. This only caused them to launch into yet another fit of hysterical laughter. A second person joined the woman on the ground.

"Oh god, the best part." The warrior wheezed. "The best part is we didn't even have to pay for his ass." He managed to get out between raucous laughter. Together they gestured towards a large basin near the entrance. Filled with anger and embarrassment, Liam went to look. In the scummy still water he saw a hideous face looking back at him. His skin was greenish yellow with brown splotches. His mouth was massive with lips the size of sausages, and a long set of tusks protruded. He opened his mouth revealing jagged shark-like teeth. A large clownish nose dominated the center of his face. One eye—his left possibly —was three times the size of the other. It made his whole face appear freakishly lopsided. Each ear was malformed but pointed. The final insult was the balding blond hair that barely covered his head in a bad comb over.

"Doug, oh man, you outdid yourself." The plate wearing warrior said.

"What is he?" One of them asked. The man speaking wore blue robes which hid most of the face in shadow.

"I made him a half-orc and ran him over here. You should have seen the aggro train he drew." The girl on the ground said. Finally, she stood brushing the bone dust from her clothes. So that was Doug.

"What did it matter the character was messed up?" Liam thought to himself.

"Are you done?" He asked in that deep bass.

"Almost," The male said still kicking and flailing on the ground.

"Yeah, we only have four hours." Doug reminded them.

"Fine," the man said getting up.

"So what happens now?" Liam asked his voice still a sonorous boom.

"We..." An armored fighter began gesturing to the party, "are going to kill some zombies. You can fuck off."

Liam thought it might have been Cole, but he didn't recognize any of them. "You said you needed a sixth," He said.

"I lied, besides we don't need a commoner." The warrior replied. Collectively the group of adventurers turned away from Liam. They drew their weapons, checked gear, and prepared to assault the dungeon. Having missed the tutorial, Liam had no idea how to do anything. He wanted off this game, out of this club, and back home. Yet he didn't even know how to log out. His hands were empty, and he appeared to be wearing just a set of starter clothes.

The five adventurers formed a small cluster of weapons as they proceeded forward. The three in front were warriors followed by a thief and mage. At least he thought the last man was a spell caster. Liam watched them start across the first bridge to the rest of the level. Quickly they entered combat with the first undead creature on the far side. Their wild cries were ringing out in the distance. Resigned Liam walked across the stone bridge after

them. Halfway over he looked down into the depths. Eddies of
dark mist swirled below; just barely visible humanoid shapes
shambled back and forth. There were easily five levels within
sight, and he admired the dungeon design. A blossom of flame
attracted his attention across the bridge. A small jet of fire was
setting a distant zombie ablaze. The assholes that brought him
here were already leaving him behind.

Liam finished crossing the bridge discovering the destroyed
skeleton. He knelt examining the corpse. The undead creature
was barely more than a collection of broken bones. Most of its
clothes had rotted away except some rusty leggings. One of the
warriors had cut off its skeletal arm at the shoulder. The severed
appendage lay several feet away still clutching a splintered club.
Nothing happened after poking the bones, so Liam stood
glancing around. Cole and the ass-hats were nowhere in sight.
Still, it wasn't hard to follow them. The wake of remains was like
a morbid trail of bread crumbs. At the last landing towards the
back of the crypt, a set of stairs descended. Several steps down a
blackened corpse lay. A helmet sat carelessly discarded next to
the broken body. Liam kicked it sending the object over the edge
and into the darkness below. A few seconds later the metal
clanged as it hit bottom. Dozens of green pinpricks of light
appeared as if he'd flipped a switch. He realized that they were
eyes turning to look up at him. Liam felt a shock of cold fear run
up his spine, which left the hairs at the back of his neck standing
on end. He turned, skipping down the stairs two and three at a
time. He hated to admit it, but he was afraid.

On the landing below was where the crypt truly began. Small
rooms split off at right angles every thirty feet or so. Carved
alcoves lined the walls containing the linen wrapped bodies of
countless dead. In the middle of the room, a brazier burned with
its dark green flame. He'd managed to catch up to Cole and the
group. They were in a preparation chamber hacking at two
skeletal warriors. Doug 'the girl' had two daggers out and was
trying to flank the undead. She launched herself slashing at the
neck of the enemy. Its head came away with a clatter making both

body and skull hit the ground at the same time. Liam concentrated his focus on the remaining creature. A name floated into existence above the skeleton reading [Restless Dead] in bright red blazing letters. He sensed that if he tried attacking any of these monsters, they'd probably kill him. A flame shot from the group consuming the second undead. Quickly they rummaged through the bodies before moving on.

An hour passed like this as Liam trailed behind. He refused to show himself, so he followed after the group in the dark. They made it down another floor before being forced to slow their progress. The further they got the more undead appeared in each encounter. The thief would attract the attention of one or two luring it into an ambush. On the next floor down all the lights disappeared. The braziers became scarce, and far apart; of course the ass-hats had torches. Liam though waited in the darkness watching as they searched another corpse. At first, he was scared to death something would attack him from behind. In the dark, his only guide was the dim glow of the party's lights. This left everything else in nearly complete darkness. The group often skipped side passages plunging recklessly forward. Plenty of monsters were still wandering about. Liam passed a long hallway, and in the dark, a pair of green glowing eyes turned his direction. Slowly it started towards him, and he raced after the group of adventurers.

"How long had it been?" he wondered following after Cole. Liam wished he had a watch or could access the system menu. He hoped it was getting close to four hours so he'd be able to get out soon. The party was nearing the end of the dungeon, and a final stone stairway descended to the bottom floor. Fearful of falling Liam was forced to slide down one step at a time. He sat on the cold stone stairs and slid from one to the next. On the ground floor, he stood rubbing his injured rump. Greenish fire light could just be discerned high above. Cole and his troops were some hundred feet away while Liam lurked well outside the torch-light, and watched the adventuring group huddle. They conversed in hushed whispers next to a set of massive double

doors. On each side half of a skull was carved, the relief joined in the center to form a nearly perfect seam. The little half-time huddle broke apart as each took out a red colored potion. All five drank the red liquid and threw the bottles to the side.

Liam tisked softy, "Litterbugs," he muttered.

As the doors were pushed open an icy draft splashed over him, and he shivered. Liam's green skin goose fleshed from the sudden chill. It was incredible how things could feel so real. His pounding heart was fighting the knowledge this was just a game.

A group of undead creatures came into view as the adventures charged inside. Two [Undead Knights] advanced on the intruders. Beneath each rusted visor eldritch light flared. The guards moved to bar passage into the rest of the room. In the cold darkness outside Liam watched and scratched his nose. As much as he disliked them, he admitted his tormentors were quite good at this. The fighters met the charge soaking up the damage. The wizard in blue robes was doing something in the back of the group. Suddenly the ground was covered in a yellow oily substance making the skeletons slip. Armor and bony bodies hit the ground. The next instant the entire area was aflame including the mobs. That's when Liam caught sight of the decayed lich in all its glory. His name too glowed brilliantly red. [Lich Mothau] raised his bony hands, fingers moving in a strange pattern. A speck of void appeared in the middle of the adventurers. It exploded outward casting the space into complete darkness. All the torches and even the mage-light were extinguished. From his place Liam heard the startled curses.

"How do you like that?" He asked in a whisper. Liam had been spent more than an hour in the pitch black so his eyes were accustomed to the lack of light. A human body came into sight with a mage light sparking back into life. The wizard had the presence of mind to step back out of the field.

"Charge inside!" Someone in the group called. Liam wondered how large the spell area was. Probably it only filled the doorway entrance. The wizard quickly cast a new spell surrounding his body in a shimmering aura. Then he ducked his head and ran into the darkness. Now there wasn't anything to see. Turning Liam glanced around checking if any mobs had wandered nearby. A pair of bright eldritch embers flashed in the distance. Something was being attracted by the fighting which left Liam in a tight spot. Those green eyes seemed to have an uncanny ability to see in the dark. That probably explained why that undead caster had used the darkness spell.

"Fucker, you killed Doug!" Someone bellowed inside.

Liam moved closer to the double doors. A green energy bolt suddenly shot from the darkness nearly hitting Liam. Only the fact he was hiding next to the stone door had saved him. A few seconds later a path of ice raced out of the boss room. Liam's feet froze to the floor, and a health bar appeared in the corner of his vision. It flashed orange, then red, before stopping with a few slivers of life left. The attack hadn't been painful but he felt his feet tingling like crazy. Ice crystals froze his feet to the floor, so Liam couldn't move them in the slightest.

"Ha Lich! What the hell are you doing?" Someone shouted from inside. Liam wondered that as well. Both spells had come damn close to hitting him. He'd almost died from being on the edge of that last one. "Yeah, yeah take it." Someone new shouted. Another bolt of green energy splashed against the door near Liam. If he didn't know better, he'd say the Lich was trying very hard to kill him. Maybe Liam looked like an easy target to the monster.

"Flame Tongue," A voice said from inside followed by the darkness spell suddenly failing. Liam peered cautiously around the door. Four of the five adventurers were standing next to the Lich's body. A wicked rusty longsword impaled the corpse of Doug's thief. Nearby, a fallen torch lay on the floor. Liam didn't feel much pity for the man/woman.

"Well the experience was good, and this ring the Lich dropped is pretty kick ass." The wizard said raising a hand to admire his new jewelry.

"Doug's gonna have to roll another thief though, that sucks," Cole said from near a knight's corpse. He hefted a rusty two handed sword free before dropping the loot into his inventory.

"Why don't we just bring his corpse back to town for a rezz?" Another asked.

"Fuck that. The temple charges a thousand gold for a resurrection. It'll be faster if Doug just makes a new character." Cole replied and knelt next to the rogue.

"Has anyone seen Jelly?" Cole asked after a second.

"Not since the first floor."

"Me either."

Liam ducked back behind the door and prayed that wandering skeleton didn't get any closer. It was moving back and forth in the darkness. Inside the room, he could hear them rummaging about looting the bodies. Slowly the ice covering his feet melted away. He lifted a foot experimentally flexing his ankle. Crystal shards flaked to the ground leaving a puddle of water, but at least he could move again.

"I got Doug's shit, let's bounce," Cole said.

"Why did that pervert make a female?" Another voice asked.

"So he could fondle himself when we aren't looking," Cole replied toeing the dead woman's body.

"I got something he could fondle."

"Gay!" Cole called with a laugh. Liam chanced a look around the doorway. All four held something within their hands. The blue crystals glowed as their bodies started to shimmer. A few seconds later they were gone amid a flash of light.

Moments later Liam was thrust into nearly total darkness. The only light was the distant glow of green fire from above. His fear was amplified by the sound of shuffling from behind him. Those bright undead eyes were moving closer. On his hands and knees, he felt his way around the door into the boss chamber. His knee caught on something hard. Liam reached out touching a bone and identified the remains of one of the guards. He recalled seeing a torch on the ground near Doug's body. Liam could only hope it would work when picked it up. Inch by inch he slid forward feeling his way in the dark. A minute later Liam touched smooth cold flesh. It was a leg he decided as he felt up the clammy stiff skin. They had taken all the equipment which left the corpse wearing just undergarments. Liam tried to remember where the torch had fallen in relation. Moving his hands over the floor he ranged out farther. After a few feet he returned to the corpse to try again. At last, his palm slid over something hard, and when he grabbed it, the torch came alive. It spluttered for a few seconds before flaring. Now he could see at least.

The boss room was small but crammed with items. The middle of the chamber was taken up by a throne. It was made entirely of carved human bones. Large ribs jutted from the top of the chair back like spikes. Skulls of the dead covered the surface all eyes pointed out towards the door. Liam circled the throne several times before moving on. Dozens of iron chains hung from the wall or fastened to the ceiling. In two of the irons, a desiccated corpse hung motionless. Captured prisoners that had died before being turned. A sacrificial altar dominated the back wall. Blood holes were carved into the corners of the slab. More chains lay atop haphazardly as if to restrain and dissect the victim alive. Half spent candles were positioned around the chest-high table, none lit.

Next to the preparation table, a stand held a large blackened tome. It lay open halfway to reveal a strange magical script. The glyphs slowly morphed changing shape and appearance, as if to hide the meaning of the page from curious eyes. Reaching out his big hand he touched the page. The second he did the letters stilled and began to glow with a hellish green color. A moment later a pop-up appeared before his face.

[Do you wish to change classes to Necromancer?]
[Beware the class is advanced.]
[Yes]
[No]

"Umm, that sounds delicious." He thought to himself and pushed yes.

[Warning! Your character will become universally hated.]
[Yes]
[No]

"Pfft, story of my life." He muttered hitting yes again, and a thrumming boom sounded. The glowing letters rose from the page pulsing bright green. They started striking Liam, making his skin tingle hotly. Lifting his hands, he watched the flesh flake away like dry dust. His skin and muscles dripped from white bones. With each echoing boom, more glyphs struck him faster and faster about his body. Flesh fell away from his legs, arms, and torso leaving only a skeleton. The pages of the book fluttered wildly before it started floating upward. A cold chill filled his chest as an orange wisp of energy was dragged from him. His health bar dropped to zero leaving him feeling numb all over. Green chains of energy began to stream from the spell-book capturing the orange mote. It was completely encased in magical glyphs before being dragged into the grimoire. The blackened leather tome slammed shut with the last boom. Slowly the book moved towards him hitting Liam in the chest. When he didn't react it rammed into him again, so reached out grasping the item with a skeletal hand. Dumbfounded Liam just stood there holding the book and the flickering torch.

He turned to go but came face to face with an undead skeleton. Those glowing green unblinking eyes were a burning flame. They flickered softly within the dark recesses of its eye sockets. The creature silently stood there looking at him as if it could see into Liam's soul. It didn't attack or react in any way. It stood for all the world as if Liam belonged here. Just as Liam was about to leap back, his vision began to fade. The light from the torch grew dim, and the world receded into darkness. In the void, a sentence floated.

[Forced logout, please wait.]

CHAPTER THREE

Kat - Experiment

Austin Texas General Hospital
Kathrine(Kat) Ines - Room A23
August 25, 2104
Roughly 2 pm - Earlier that day.

The pain woke her, it race up and down her body like waves of crackling fire. Unending agony was her ever present companion. She wanted to scream, to cry out, Kathrine wanted to die. Tragically the only thing she could do was blink. No, that wasn't entirely true, and she fought to move the fingers of her right hand. Through a torrent of sensation she felt for the call button. As her clumsy digits fumbled for the box it slipped from the bed. The white plastic device slid away from her to hang just out of reach. She blinked back tears of frustration. Nearby machines did the job of caring for a body that couldn't do it itself. Small tubes snaked into her arm, directly into her stomach, and into places she cared not think about. The heart rate monitor started to slowly increase in tempo. The soft beeps were moving closer together as her torment continued. Slowly she felt for the cord that lay near her pinky finger. The white industrial material was slippery, but she dragged it up a millimeter at a time. It seemed to take an age, and all the while pain plunged into her mind like a red hot poker.

The box felt slick as she dragged it into her grasp, then mashed the button with all her ineffectual strength. Kat waited a minute and called again praying Tasha was on duty. To her great relief, the massive black woman bustled into the room. Her usually wild hair was braided into a black cornrow of curls. Kat blinked rapidly at her as the woman neared.

"Are you OK, love?" The big woman said as a warm dark hand pressed to the side of her neck. She was checking Kat's pulse. Tasha never trusted machines to tell her what she could feel for herself. The woman must have just come from eating breakfast in the break room because her hands smelled like frosted donuts and coffee.

"You're in pain?" Tasha asked in a compassionate voice.

Kat blinked. (Yes)

"Dr. Gashiki is on duty right now." She said with a frown. Kat vaguely knew him. The man was awful and never did his rounds checking on the patients. "I'll see if I can't slip past his sleeping body for some of the good stuff."

Kat blinked praying the woman would succeed. Tasha to her credit quickly waddled from the room. She knew the nurse would try her hardest and be back as soon as she could. She was one of the good ones. Still, the fire in Kat's body seemed to reach a peak. The heart rate monitor was spiking with the occasional warning beep. Five minutes passed then ten. She tried not to focus on it, to ignore the pain. Her eyes half closed as she forced herself away into the cage inside her mind. Just when she thought Tasha had forgotten the air nearby was disturbed. Like a riptide receding from a drowned village the torment was gone. It was replaced by a smooth tranquil bliss. Kat looked to her right and saw a syringe pressed into the IV tube. Wonderfully large black fingers pressed the plunger down. Down far so that her world was dulled and muted. The beeping of the machines slowed.

"There you go, love. I'll be back to check on you later. Mr. Forhan had a small accident and I've got to clean up." The sultry voice said. Kat couldn't remember who it was just then but she blessed the woman. The dark angel had descended and taken her away from hell, at least for a little while. The nurse moved to a red box on the wall and slipped something inside. She came near touching Kat's cheek with warm coffee smelling hands. Then the angel departed.

For a long while Kat floated, drifting on a sea of thoughtless time. Any errant notions she might have had swirled off into nothingness. Snippets of memory and dream mixed together. She slept again for a time, catching a nap before the pain resumed. Tasha also returned at some point. Kat limply accepted the administrations as her body was moved and adjusted. Kat didn't bother trying to hold a conversation, not by blinking. Besides she was still floating between heaven and hell. Kat could feel the pain under the surface but it was easily ignored. Cold antiseptic filled the air as Tasha cleaned her body. After feeding her stomach tube the rotund woman laid a heavy blanket over Kat's body. The cloth touching her skin would cause her terrible pain when the drugs wore off, but for now it kept her warm.

"How is that?" Tasha asked looking into her eyes. Kat blinked a special pattern only they two shared, (More drugs, please.) The nurse sometimes gave her enough to last most of a day. Tasha pursed her lips looking sad.

"I'm sorry, hun. Your parents are scheduled to come today." Tasha said her voice full of worry and concern. Kat considered that, then blinked once slowly. It was an acknowledgment but not agreement. She loved and hated the visits from her parents. It was so boring in the hospital that any distraction was welcome. The problem was she needed to be lucid, that in turn meant no drugs.

"Take care, press the call button if you need anything," Tasha said after checking to see the box was still in Kat's grasp.

With that, the woman left the room and Kat was obliged to descend slowly. She had time in the hazy half felt waves of agony to consider. Her life was a pendulum of heaven and hell. In the darkness of night, she often prayed for death, for escape. Especially when she was at her lowest and the pain was at its highest. It left her feeling guilty thinking such thoughts when her parents still cared so much about her. Kathrine was just twenty years old. Still young enough to remember a time when her world had been happy. There were times Kat wished Tasha would accidentally give her a triple dose, to end it in peace. That sometimes happened in hospitals, but not today. Kat took another nap while she could.

Just after eight in the evening Tasha came into the room. The caress of soft ebony fingers over her cheeks roused Kat, and she looked to the rotund nurse.

"Your parents are here," Tasha said before slipping out. Kat thanked the woman for waking her before her parents arrived. She took a few minutes to cage the pain. Her parents didn't need to see that, not from her. She waited patiently for them to arrive.

Kat knew something was different the moment her parents came through the door. Their faces seemed strange like they were torn between conflicting emotions. A third man entered the room and sat down quietly near the door. She didn't recognize him, and he wasn't a doctor here. Her parents broke apart and sat on either side of her bed. Both slid their hands into hers in greeting. Her right hand felt warm and tingled hotly like a sunburn, her mother. Father held her left hand loosely, but it was still a whole different level of pain. An inferno slid up her left side at his touch. Kat did her best to ignore the sensation and blinked in greeting. Mother was fussing with Kat's blanket straightening the thick cloth.

"How are you doing today?" Her father asked. Kat blinked once slowly. (I'm alive).

"I'm glad, are they treating you right?" He asked, and Kat blinked (Yes). She wasn't about to get Tasha in trouble. Kat heard the chair squeak on the tile and glanced at her mother. She'd scooted closer to the bed, and her hands touched Kat's long tousled hair brushing it away from her face.

"Your brother just got accepted to college. He's very excited." She began, and Kat blinked again slowly.

"That was nice," she thought. At least one of them would be

able to do something with their life.

"It's why he couldn't be here today. He's out of state for a few days." Dad said, and she felt the fire in her left hand ease slightly. Dad raised an empty fist to his mouth to cough nervously. "Your mother and I have been talking."

"Dan, we haven't even finished saying hello." Her mother hissed hotly.

"Love, it is important," Dad replied. Her mother scooted closer still, her hands working overtime fidgeting with Kat's gown and blanket. Kat looked to her father and blinked rapidly. Over the years they'd worked out a short system.

Kat blinked twice then three times. (What?)

"We were approached several days ago by a research group. They heard about you and are interested in your case." His voice cracked on the last word, and he coughed again. Kat was both elated and suspicious at the same time. There was no cure for her condition. That was why she was here slowly dying day by day in her personal hell.

"They're a group from VRTek. They research how their technology interacts with the human brain." He said, but the statement sent her mother into a fit.

"No, I changed my mind. I won't let them cut her up, she's my baby." Her mother wailed suddenly.

"Honey," Dad said thickly but she shook her head. Her blond hair flicked about as she shouted.

"No, no, no." She repeated over and over.

"It's for the best," Dad said and the plastic chair clattered loudly as her mother stood. She turned to glare daggers at the man sitting near the door before she fled down the corridor. For his part, the man's face remained passive but alert.

"She's just emotional, and I'll talk to her later," Father offered before picking up her left hand. Pain flared as he lifted it to his lips and kissed her knuckles tenderly. Kat's heart was spinning around in circles like a poodle chasing its tail.

When he looked at her, she blinked rapidly again. (What?)

"Maybe I should let Doctor Gedding talk to you," Dad said and turned to the man. Kat had to admit he didn't look very doctor like. He was medium height with just a little gray in his dark brown hair. He wore a simple business suit and she could tell he was fit. More than fit, the older man put bodybuilders to shame. His neck, shoulders, and arms were well defined. The man stood approaching her right side. Bending down he lifted the chair from the ground and sat next to her.

"My name is Doctor Ben Gedding, and I am the research director for VRTek. Firstly, I want to say how sad I am to hear about your condition. No one deserves this and especially such an attractive young woman. You have my deepest sympathy." The man said in a tone that spoke like honey and milk. His voice had the kind of quality that was easy to listen too.

Kat blinked slowly once. Sympathy didn't help her with the pain. Ben was considering his words for a few seconds. Dad still had her left hand held tightly between both of his own. He was crushing it in his powerful grip, and she wished he'd let go as it was quite distracting.

"We are researching the effects of long-term virtual immersion on the brain. Our team is looking for possible side effects to continual use. That is why I am here. We are searching for willing candidates. Your case of Guillain-Barré syndrome didn't match our criteria at first. Thankfully after talking to your doctor, we were assured your brain is healthy and fully functional."

Kat blinked (How, what?) Ben saw her rapid eye movement and turned to her father.

"She's asking for more details," Dad said and squeezed her hand.

"We have previously done studies lasting ninety-six hours in length. With full-bodied people, they must eventually be removed from the VR to eat and clean. Over a period of four months, this proved to have inconclusive results. So we began to focus on keeping the brain itself alive." Ben stopped and looked at her. "Are you sure you wish to hear this, it is somewhat gruesome?" He asked, and she blinked. (Yes, Yes)

Ben nodded. "Through animal testing, we found a synthetic blood substitute. The nutrient rich NuBlood is dark blue in color. It's quite amazing in that it increases brain activity. Our earliest subject is on his twentieth month. That brings us to the procedure which is somewhat simple in description. You'll be airlifted to our facility where we'll isolate your brain from the body. We thread a tube into your jugular to switch out your blood for NuBlood. Then we chill your body to near freezing. We have a neuro-specialist remove your brain and placed within a sterile plastic cradle. When your EKG readings normalize we introduce you to the specialized VR machine." He said very calmly. It sounded like something out of Frankenstein's laboratory. If it could free her, save her from this nightmare. She'd do it.

She blinked. (Yes)

"Are you sure?" Her father asked and she blinked slowly several times.

(Yes, yes, yes)

"I'll talk to your mother. We have a lot of paperwork to fill out before the hospital will release you." He said leaning forward and kissed her on the forehead which was one of the few places it didn't hurt. He got up and left the room.

"You're a brave woman," Ben said and her eyes found him. She blinked at him twice. It wasn't bravery, not in the slightest. She was a mouse caught in a death trap, any exit was preferable. To his credit Ben seemed to catch her meaning or could read the thoughts in her eyes.

"It's an unknown road to travel." He said and reached a hand towards her but stopped.

"Do you mind?" He asked and she blinked twice. Gently he picked up her right hand with his fingers. Pain slithered up her arm and into her brain like a narrow bladed dagger.

"May I check your condition? Can you tell me does it hurt where I touch you?" He asked and she blinked once. (Yes)

"Here?" He said touching her elbow. Blink; He touched her shoulder through the thin hospital gown. Blink; the lower neck, Blink. His fingertips were warm on her jaw. They were surprisingly soft for a man with such a muscular build. She blinked twice, (No)

"That's good. I think we can help each other. You understand you would become a part of our research team?" He asked looking into her eyes; she blinked.

He nodded before going on. "I will most likely speak with you again before we make the transfer. It will take a week or so for all the gears to move. I'm afraid your father is right. A small forest will be cut down in your honor." He said, and she blinked her acceptance. One of his hands still held hers lightly and she concentrated on it. She wiggled her fingers the smallest bit brushing the inside of his palm. Ben smiled widely, and she felt excitement course through her. He got up and left the room as well.

A week, possibly two. It would be hell again, but she could endure it. There was light at the end of the tunnel. She felt tears beginning to well in her eyes, and Kat tried to blink them away, but they escaped to drip down her cheeks. When the tears hit the corner of her mouth they tasted more sweet than salty.

CHAPTER FOUR

Liam - Reborn dead

"And above all, watch with glittering eyes the whole world around you because the greatest secrets are always hidden in the most unlikely places. Those who don't believe in magic will never find it."
— Roald Dahl

Pod People Arcade
9pm

The world hit Liam like a bucket of cold water. He drew in a ragged breath filling his lungs with the smell of chemical fog and the stink of his own sweat. The sound of many voices reached his ears and his eyes focused. The frosted canopy in front of his face ascended up and away from him. Grabbing a handhold he shifted his bulk and climbed out. He tried to take a step but fell to his hands and knees from a massive dizzy spell. A second later he was retching on the carpet. In the neon lights, the bile looked quite a bit like glowing toxic waste. A girl rushed to his side and knelt.

"Are you ok, sir?" She asked in a compassionate voice. When he looked up he saw the 'Staff' shirt on her slight frame.

"Yes," he rasped in a thick voice.

"Please you should take a seat, there are some couches nearby." She said and reached for him. Taking his arm she tried to help him up. Liam though was so heavy she couldn't do anything other than clutch at his shirt sleeve. Still, the girl kept her face passive and guided him to the rest area. After sitting, he wiped his mouth on a sleeve and closed his eyes. He struggled to calm his mind and still his racing heart. The events of the last hour had him dancing in circles as badly as his equilibrium. He took in a long slow breath before exhaling through his nose. Another few breaths and he detected the scent of strawberry shampoo. One of his blue eyes opened a crack to discover the staff girl standing before him. She wordlessly extended the paper cup. He drained the water inside swishing the liquid around his mouth. He was forced the swallow though, which made him feel a little ill again.

"Sorry about the mess," He said glancing at her.

She had on an impish smile as she spoke, "Don't worry about it, happens all the time."

"Really?"

"Why do you think the carpet is that hideous dark gray?" She whispered holding a hand to the side of her mouth. She smiled again and took the cup back. "Actually it has a name, First-Timers Vertigo." She said, and he blinked in surprise. Waving her hand towards the pods she continued. "It's a bit of a shock the first time you come out. Really you shouldn't have spent so much time in on your initial run—twenty minutes is recommended."

"Am I that obvious?" He asked thickly.

"Sorry, kinda. Your face is all green." She said grimacing in sympathy.

"How did you like it?" She asked and he had to think about that. At first he'd say he hated the experience but that had changed. It had been exciting at the end. Yeah, it wasn't so bad after all.

"I think I might give it another go." He said and the girl beamed.

"Are you with those guys that left earlier?" She asked. "I could credit the account with a few free hours if you're on the membership."

"No, I was just trying it out with them. We're not friends." He said a little sourly.

"Oh," she said seeming to grasp the situation. The girl turned as someone called her name. She made a half-gesture of acknowledgment before turning back to Liam. Her face still seemed mostly kind which he appreciated. "I'm sorry, I have to get back to work. Take your time. The doors don't lock until ten o'clock." She said before turning to go.

"Thanks."

Liam considered the experience he'd just had. It had been terrifying, and memorable, and it made him want to crawl back inside to see what happened next. He knew he was going to have to buy one of those machines for himself. He'd gotten a taste of a new life, and he wanted more. Climbing to his feet he made his way up the ramp. The late fall air that night was unusually dry and hot. Half a dozen people were standing around smoking electronic cigarettes a few feet from the doors. Teenagers not quite ready to pack it in for the night. Liam walked the two blocks to his car and got in. The engine roared to life before he pulled out of the small parking lot and drove home.

Exiting his car he pressed the key code to close the garage. He still felt a light headed but went inside, sat down at his computer, and brought up the Nigmus Online website. It was colorful with pictures of the game world itself layered into the background.

He pulled out the scrap of paper Doug had shoved at him earlier that evening. As he thought the man had spent very little time filling out the details. The account information was blank except a junk email. He changed that so he would control his account. Next he changed the password to something less stupid. He quickly verified that the changes had taken effect by checking his email. Liam added his credit card information and invested in the subscription.

Liam wanted to learn about the world he was about to become apart of. The main website provided very little information but did supply two interesting facts. The first thing he discovered was how to log out. It was such a bloody simple trick, but he doubted he'd ever have figured it out. You were supposed to keep your head still and look up with your eyes. An icon would appear in the lower left corner which was the menu system. The second thing he found out was possibly the most interesting. Everyone started the game as a level zero commoner. It was left to the player to decide what class they wished to play.

More time passed as he browsed the internet. Finally, another tidbit caught his attention. The details on how to change classes was secret. After an entire month of play only five different jobs had been discovered. Fighter, Archer, Thief, Wizard, and Cleric. Each of them had to be unlocked via a special series of actions. Except for Liam, who had just stumbled upon a new class.

Next, he went shopping online and ordered the newest Cerebral-Neural Helmet he could find. Pods were older perfected technology, but they took up space. It was impossible to pull a person from the middle of a simulation with a pod. Doing so was dangerous, Liam though lived alone in an affluent part of the suburbs, so he didn't need a full pod. He opted for the unrestricted immersion helmet. It was a ridiculous amount of money, but he wanted the best experience he could afford. At the same time he ordered a copy of the game to install directly to the Dive Helmet. Liam already possessed a fast fiber optic connection for the necessary bandwidth. Ten minutes later he got an automated message saying his order was accepted. The items would be priority shipped in the morning.

He couldn't wait to get back into the game. Liam felt like there was something special waiting for him in that other world.

***

Liam - Level 1
Aethon Island - Outside New Hearth City
Early Morning

Liam appeared in a graveyard. Small marble tombstones circled like cherubs around the statue of a winged angel. The celestial creature floated amid—but not quite touching—the pool of still water. Little lilies bobbed slowly about on the surface. To Liam's right miniature mausoleums dotted the green grass, stretching away from the protecting angel's gaze. To the left, a trail of white flagstones circled the pool, then meandered toward town. After a second a large pop-up appeared before him.

[Warning! You have died while logged out.]

[This game uses a 'Resurrection' system.]

[You are protected from this until you reach level five.]

[In the future remember that your body will not disappear after you log out.]

[Try and find a safe place to sleep; rent a room at the inn, or an apartment in town.]

[Character Death]

[After level five you will be logged out of your character at death.]

[There will be a one hour cooldown before you can log back in as a ghost.]

[Your spirit will be unable to touch or interact with the world. However, you can show yourself to others in order to secure a resurrection. Your corpse—the vessel for your soul—must be brought to the Goddess's Temple to be raised. Alternatively, a level 15+ cleric may raise the body. The safest solution is to have friends obtain your corpse and bring it to town. You have 24 hours to raise the body before the soul passes on.]

Well shit. That told Liam several things he would have liked to know yesterday. He wondered how he had died. Was he killed by a player, a monster, or possibly by an area of effect spell? He had better figure out the game before he reached level five. The sun poked slightly above the horizon in the distance. The morning dew had already melted off, but there was still a few hours left until noon. As far as he could tell the time matched that of earth. Behind him, the rough stone walls of New Hearth stretched. At the far end Liam could make out the city gate and a road. Tiny figures of people moved in and out with a purpose.

"Damn wolves!" Someone yelled nearby. Liam turned to see a man wearing crudely patched chain-mail popping into existence next to him. His face was set in an angry grimace as he sheathed his sword. Without taking any notice of Liam the man set off directly south at a fast jog.

Liam turned back to the angel amid the water font. Bending over the still pool he looked at himself again. Liam's character was quite a bit different than before. He was a bare bones skeleton without even a scrap of flesh on his body. Liam bent closer to the water to examine his face. It was like some cartoonist had shaped a skull from white silly-putty. His jaw and mouth were enormous, and each jagged tooth was like a sharks. That didn't even count his four inch long tusks. His left eye socket was much bigger than the other. Deep inside his ocular recess's two tiny specks of green flame floated. They were like embers burning on a cold night. In his hands Liam was still carrying a torch and spell book. The torch was totally spent with only a burned end left, so he dropped the item to the ground. The book he would have to carry. Sticking his skeletal hand into his pants brought up a small inventory screen. That was nice, however he only had two slots available, which was likely the contents of both pockets. The first slot contained a large blue gemstone. Removing it he discovered it was similar to the one he'd seen Cole use. Concentrating on the item brought up its description.

Bind Stone -
Activate to bind yourself to a location. It's wise to do this inside a town. Using the gem will teleport you back to your previously bound location. (4-hour cool-down)

Liam needed a quiet place to check out his character for a few minutes. Moving towards a large set of grave markers he sank to the grass. He pressed his bony back into the cold marble before looking skyward. God it was so beautiful out. The colors made the outside world look dull and lifeless. Clouds were still being colored with the multi-hued light from the rising sun. Glancing upward with his eyes he saw a menu icon. He reached up and touched this bringing up a list of options. He selected his character page.

Name - SmellyJelly
Race - Half-Orc/Undead Male
Class - 1 Necromancer

HP - 60 (Con) + 16 (Class Lvl) = 76
Mana - 50 (Int) + 25 (Wis) + 15 (Class Lvl) = 90

7 - Strength (Melee Damage Bonus, Carry Weight.)
5 - Agility (Small bonus to movement speed, feats of dexterity.)
5 - Perception (The ability to hear and see the world around you. Trap Detection.)
6 - Constitution (Duration of Sprinting, Holding your breath, Bonus Health +10 per point.)
5 - Intelligence (Magic Damage, Bonus Mana +10 per point.)
5 - Wisdom (Mana regeneration, Bonus to experience gain, Bonus Mana +5 per point.)
3 - Charisma (Affects shop prices, Bonus to NPC Relations.)

Unspent Attribute Points - 22

Liam sighed at the character name Doug had given him. "*Oh so clever,*" he thought and was glad the man had died. Liam sent a request to a GM for help. He did not want to spend the rest of his short life named SmellyJelly. At least the stupid man had left his attribute points alone. Though, it was more likely Doug had been too busy setting up the joke to bother. Liam let the points be for now and started to poke around. Each of the items he could click brought more information. A pop up helpfully described what each ability stat controlled. He jabbed a bony finger at the necromancer class making another box appear.

"The necromancer has spurned the natural order of life, reaching for power through twisted eldritch magic. Even in death, their knowledge of the arcane continues to grow. If given enough time, enough drive, could a necromancer become a lich? Where ever he treads he shall leave behind a trail of dead and undead. Their appearance can vary in many ways except one. A necromancer's eyes will glow with the eldritch light of undeath."

HP per level - 6
Mana per level - 15
Every five levels the necromancer gains a new bonus feat.

Class Abilities -
Level 1 -
[Paralyzing Grasp] Successfully grappling an enemy will paralyze the living creature for ten seconds. If the grip is broken so is the effect.

Well, that was awesome, being able just to grab someone and paralyze them. After closing out of his character screen, he hefted the spell book into his lap. It was bound in black leather with a brass relief running along the edges of the book. A clasp shaped like a skull held the two sides closed. As he opened the Grimoire, he discovered most of the pages were empty. Apparently all its magical knowledge had been drained transforming him from peon to undead mage. He flipped to the front of the book. The first page contained spell casting instructions.

You can cast a spell by incanting its name or creating a spell macro. To do so, select the spell from the book, then raise your hand in a distinct movement. Higher level spells will require more complicated gestures.

As your power grows so will your knowledge of arcana. Class

specific spells will come naturally to you, but other schools of magic you will need to be copied to your grimoire. You may only have a limited number of these in your spellbook. Take care which spells you wish to learn. When your level is sufficient you may copy a scroll into your grimoire. This will destroy the scroll. After a dozen more instructional pages he found a divider and his first spell.

1st Level
[Negative Energy Bolt]
A putrid green bolt of eldritch energy fired from the hand can damage living creatures. (Note - Negative energy will heal undead creatures. Has no effect on the non-living such as stone golems.)
Casting time - .5 sec
Mana required - 20
Recast - Instant

Underneath this, the page was filled with diagrams and mystic script. He touched the page selecting the spell. The letters started to glow and there was an audible hum. Liam pointed sideways with two fingers held together. After a few seconds, a green light covered his hand before firing from his fingers. There was an electric sizzle as the bolt of energy struck a nearby tombstone. Pretty cool, though he was still without a decent robe or weapon. With his mana it meant he had to kill something in less than five shots or face it unarmed. The next few pages contained utility spells.

[Sense Dead]
Allows the caster to sense the presence of nearby corpses and undead.
Cast time - 1 Seconds
Mana required - 15
Recast - 20 minutes.

[Spirit Lantern]
Casts a small glowing wisp to light the necromancers way.
Lasts for one hour for every ten levels of the mage.
Cast time - 3 Seconds
Mana required - 10
Recast - Instant

Could he go into town and buy a few things? Liam remembered the warning about being universally hated. Trying to get past the guards might be a bad idea, though if he were killed, he'd likely just end up back in the graveyard.

"You requested a GM?" A man asked appearing before him. Liam looked up more than a little startled to see a wide faced human wearing dark blue robes. The red haired man floated a few inches off the ground as if to display his godlike power. Instead of pupils, radiant blue light filled his eyes.

"Yes, thank you for coming so quickly," Liam said.

"It's morning. Things will pick up soon when schools on the east coast start to get out." The man said with a shrug. Liam stood, and the GM eyed his loose-fitting tunic and trousers. What a sight, a undead mage with such lowly beginnings.

"I believe you're the first necromancer I've seen and with such an unusual name." The man said glancing upwards.

"Ah, ha-ha… " Liam laughed lamely. "That's why I requested help. My friends invited me to play the game and we were drinking." Liam lied, and the man frowned tilting his head to the side. His eyes went distant for a few seconds like he wasn't quite there. It was hard to tell since they were glowing so brightly. Maybe he was checking the logs.

"I see, well, considering the name might be offensive to someone I'll change it. What would you like?" The game master asked making Liam think fast. He should have put more thought into this before making the request. He just decided to go with his own name hoping it wasn't taken.

"Liam is fine," He said and the man's eyes were distant again.

"Done, is that everything?" The GM asked, and Liam checked his character screen. Yes, indeed the name was now his own. It was a bit of luck to have it available. He would eventually be Lich Liam. That had an interesting ring to it.

"Yes, thank you. I appreciate the help."

"I'll have the let the higher-ups know the class has been found."

"Why?" Liam asked.

The Game Master smiled knowingly. "There's a reason it used the words universally hated," He said, and suddenly without warning, was gone. Liam was sure now, he'd bitten off more than he could chew.

For a while, he sat considering what the GM had just told him. Slowly it dawned on Liam just how screwed he really was. No auction house, no bank, no inn, probably couldn't take any quests. It was a good thing he was undead or he'd starve out here otherwise. Nigmus Online set him up to fall. Well, he wasn't getting any better by just sitting in the grass. He stood and dusted his loose pants off then started south away from the city. He decided that grouping with a random newbie was likely his best ticket. He pointed to someone near the road and selected "Invite to Party," from the list.

[You may not party with the living.]

"Really Devs!" He yelled up at the sky.

"You hate me too don't you?" He asked but was only greeted with the bland stares of players nearby. That GM hadn't been kidding, he was on his own.

Ten minutes later he slowly walked through a small pine forest south of town. He'd caught sight of a wolf doing its own hunting. The creature's floating name was yellow which probably meant this would end in a short brutal death. Liam took careful aim with his fingers pointed at the creature. The audible hum of magic made the animal pause mid-step, ears flicking around. Then a bolt of greenish energy lanced out striking the animal in the shoulder. The wolf yowled in pain and turned to Liam. With a snarl, it charged straight at him. Aiming again he waited as the magic built. The [Feral Wolf] dodged just as the spell left Liam's finger tips. The green bolt flashed passed and hit a tree making it shutter from the impact. A drove of wilted leaves fell to the ground.

"Crap," he cursed taking a step back. The wolf jumped from ten feet away, and Liam barely got his arm up in time. It's powerful jaws bit down hard taking a chunk of Liam's health. He fired again at point-blank range hitting the wolf in the stomach. It yipped letting go before dancing away, and past a tree. The [Feral Wolf] growled from within the bushes, then for a few seconds, circled Liam looking for a better angle. He braced himself by planting his feet in the soft mossy dirt. With a second deeper snarl the wolf charged from cover. Liam was ready and caught the wolf mid-jump by the throat. The animal stiffened immediately in paralysis. This gave him enough time to fire two bolts of energy into its chest. The wolf went limp in his skeletal hands. Letting go of the corpse it fell lifeless to the ground.

His first fight and he'd managed to win earning a sizable chunk of experience. After poking the body nothing appeared to drop; no coins, or meat, or fancy pelts. Was this going to be one of those games you had to learn butchering? Of course training such a skill would require going into town. Liam sighed in annoyance but left the corpse where it lay. For the rest of the morning he kept at it managing to level several times. There was no doubt he loved the game. The fights were amazing and the spells were wicked cool.

CHAPTER FIVE

Liam - Baby Necro

Liam - Level 4
Aethon Island

Liam wasn't quite in the game yet. He'd logged off briefly for a late lunch and a bathroom break. At the moment he was waiting on the character selection pad. Two people were standing before him. The first was his level four undead necromancer. The second was an elf he'd made last night. Two other pads were empty and waiting for a maximum of four characters.

There were three playable races, or four if you counted half-orc and half-elf. They were the typical fantasy choices; Elf, Dwarf, Orc, and Human with their half-breeds. Not much variety, but maybe in future patches new races would become available.

Part of the reason for making the elf was to test the character creator. It was surprisingly in-depth, and Liam had taken over an hour to finalize the elf. He'd done little more than log in, heck the handsome bastard was still a level zero commoner. Now Liam was torn whether play to the elf or the undead mage. Liam hadn't made the necromancer. It had been a joke, a trick to screw with him. As a half-orc, he wasn't suited to casting magic. The elf, on the other hand, had a keen set of ears and magical affinity. He could regenerate mana twice as fast. If Liam wanted to play a mage the elf, or a half-elf was his best choice.

That was the problem he decided. Playing the elf felt like admitting failure. Like he couldn't hack it, and that stuck in his craw. Liam if anything was a very stubborn man. It was probably why he'd suffered his job at the Slatko Factory for so long. There was another reason, a simple one. He felt a connection with the tall deformed skeleton. Liam knew about getting the short stick in life. For years he'd been a big dumpy guy, and maybe that was why he liked the scary looking necromancer.

He walked towards the elf and knelt at its feet. Putting a hand on the pad caused a set of options spring up. He selected delete, and a pop-up appeared.

[Deleting the character is permanent. All items associated with the player will be erased, including banked items. Are you sure you wish to do this?]

He hit yes. It wasn't like he was losing anything important. The level zero had nothing on him. Liam didn't want to be tempted by the handsome elf every time he logged in. Slowly the character faded. He became ghost-like then disappeared in a sparkle of small lights. At least Liam had been able to go through the tutorial with the elf. Now he knew what the different NPC threat colors were. White names indicated a creature of the same level. Yellow was a slight challenge meaning mobs were between one and four levels higher. Red monsters were extremely dangerous to engage. Such creatures were at least five levels higher than the player.

Liam stood and turned to the undead mage. The seven-foot tall creature was wrapped in a threadbare brown robe which was pick up from yesterday. He still had no weapon to speak of, but at least the robes let him put his giant spell book away.

"Looks like we're stuck with one another," He said to the character. Liam hadn't expected an answer, but the undead mage turned his head at the sound. The tiny green flames in its eye sockets flared briefly. Liam couldn't help but smile a little as he approached. Reaching up he placed a hand on the chest of the necromancer. Immediately his view shifted, turning, and flowing upward towards the undead skeleton. At the same time, everything began to darken as the game logged him in.

The black was all pervasive at first. Liam smacked his head on
something hard as he tried to sit up. He cursed loudly rubbing
his forehead. His dark vision finally kicked in, and he saw the
wood grain of the coffin lid above him. Oh right, he'd crawled
into a casket before logging out yesterday.

He pushed open the lid revealing a monastery cellar. One wall
had collapsed letting in loose rock and soil. Broken crates and old
coffins littered the basement floor. Grasping the sides of the box,
he levered himself out. The ruined building was located near
Mothau's Crypt, which explained the low-level undead
wandering about. Liam stopped near the cellar steps. He wanted
to check over his character before starting out, so Liam pulled the
grimoire from his robes. He unlatched the skull lock, and it
opened with the sound of an angry soul. "Shinu," it whispered at
him as he opened the tome. Nice touch that, every time he
opened the book said 'die' in a random voice. He flicked through
several pages towards the back. Liam had just hit level four,
which gave him another spell to add to his repertoire. Inside the
divider, he checked out the new spells.

Level 2
Disease Cloud - Disease (DoT)
A maligned cloud of foul gas that flows from the caster in a
cone. Affected targets suffer from Acute Hidradenitis
Suppurativa. Boils form about the body then rupture, bleeding
freely, and causing intense pain.

Level 3
Lethargy - (Target Debuff)
Target is weakened, reducing attack speed for five minutes.
Field of Grasping Hands - (Root)
Skeletal hands reach out of the ground to hold fast those
caught inside. Does not discriminate between monster and caster.

Causes no damage.

Level 4
Pain Spike - Direct Damage (DoT)
A single target damage over time spell. It causes muscle cramps and joint pain in the target.

Of all the spells he'd gotten so far [Grasping Hands] had been the most useful. The ability to distance himself from monsters had already proven useful. [Pain Spike] was another interesting damage spell, and hopefully, would stack with [Disease Cloud]. He was still level four, so he could afford to experiment a while longer.

Closing the blackened spell-book he slid it into his robes. Then he pushed off the crate and turned towards the stairs. He was blinded briefly coming up to ground level. Outside it was still early evening, and the dusk sunlight filled the ruined monastery. He paused at the top step, waiting while his vision changed. The gray on black of dark-vision flickered into a vivid pallet of colors. Among the broken pews, a few undead were sitting. The yellow words [Forgotten Mourners] floated above their skeletal heads, and indicated they were a level higher than him.

Eager to get started Liam considered where to head first. The wolves and forest life had gotten him this far. Directly north was New Hearth city, and south was the port. Liam had to be careful of human players. More than once he'd been mistaken for a monster, but thankfully his root spell had allowed him to escape into the forest.

Liam turned east towards the hills, left the undead sanctuary behind, and walked into the trees. After about ten minutes he managed to locate a promising target. About a mile into the woods a goblin camp was hidden within a thick ring of trees. Ten crude pole-tents were constructed around a central fire pit. The smell of smoke and cooking pig had led him here. The goblins were small, standing between three and four feet tall. A dozen wandered around preparing dinner and getting ready to bed down for the evening. Each was green skinned with ridiculously long ears. Liam circled the small group looking for any stragglers. Depending on how smart the goblins proved he might be able to pull several away from camp.

A single goblin was chopping wood near the back of a large tent. Unfortunately, this one appeared red to Liam, so five levels higher, but not more than six. He was certain of that because all the other green skins were even to yellow. This particular male had a huge nose. Pinocchio over there was likely the leader, though he was still too distant to see a name.

Liam considered his options. He would have to get closer to use Disease Cloud, but he'd be spotted before getting close enough. The spell might also catch a few other goblins in it's area of effect, so that was out. Instead, he wanted to try his new fourth level spell. Liam raised a hand pointing at the goblin leader.

"Pain Spike," he said incanting the name of the spell. Magic flowed up his arm in a wave of black and red. A small circular glyph briefly took shape in the air, then a bolt of black shot forward. It stuck the little goblin squarely in the back. The creature yelled in pain before turning in his direction. Pinocchio raised his face skyward and bellowed a shrill war cry. Dinner preparations ceased as every goblin in the area turned at the sound, and all twelve looked directly at Liam.

"Oh balls," he cursed sprinting away. Liam had grossly miscalculated how smart the goblins were. A dozen small feet charged after him. Liam booked it back towards Mothau Crypt. If he got there first, he might be able to lose them in the dark ruin.

A small poorly fletched arrow struck his back. Liam dodged left around several trees before locating the trail. The enraged goblins were still hot on his heels. Liam had hoped they'd lose interest, especially with that wild boar burning back at camp. He had made a big mistake attacking the goblins by himself. It took him a few minutes but he broke out of the trees. Directly ahead was the remains of the monastery, the closest thing to city walls he had. A hundred feet behind him the goblin leader was running towards him. In his little green hands, he gripped the wood axe with murderous intent.

A few nearby skeletons turned at the sound. Liam sprinted for the doors to the ruin, and about halfway there he heard the distinct sound of battle. Behind him the undead started to converge on the goblins. He slowed in astonishment to watch. Apparently, the undead didn't like any living creature which was useful information. All the goblins stopped to attack the undead. Four of the small creatures leapt upon the back of a [Undead Shambler]. They bit and punched at the much taller undead. This was an opportunity Liam wasn't going to let go. He raised a hand to cast a new spell.

"Disease Cloud," He said making a sickly yellow cloud form before him. It flew forward in a cone covering undead and goblins alike. The shamblers took no notice, but boils and lesions broke out across the skin of the goblins. The zombies fought bitterly but the undead were grossly outnumbered. They'd be destroyed soon putting Liam in the same position as before. He needed to stall the goblins while the DoT works its magic.

"Field of Grasping Hands," He incanted aiming at the ground near the goblins. Skeletal fingers punched out of the soil. The goblin chief roared again, and the horde beat at their tiny green chests.

Pointing at the mini-boss Liam cast [Pain Spike] again. The magic built, black glyph flashing, then the bolt slammed into the goblin leader. Pinocchio was knocked to the ground as he continued pounded out a war-cry. Liam turned running toward the ruined monastery as the remaining undead fell. He needed some new help. Cracking open the wooden doors he started to yell inside. The [Undead Mourners] stood from the pews and turned towards the sound. A few in the back started towards his location.

The goblins quickly broke free of the root spell running forward. All of them were damaged, partially diseased, though none had fallen. Liam pointed back toward the mass of goblins with a flat palm.

"Disease Cloud," He said casting the spell again. The cloud engulfed the rushing band and Liam ran inside. He was about halfway down the aisle when the goblin leader came into view, and Pinocchio's health visibly drained with two DoTs. The undead in the pews shuffled towards the living creature.

Eight or nine goblins made it inside before they encountered the Mourners. "This was going to be a close one." He thought. The only escape he had now was down into the basement. He hoped the encounter didn't go that far. Five undead battled against twelve wounded goblins. He pointed to the doors casting another [Grasping Hands]. The spell, unfortunately, drained the last of his mana. He waited watching his energy slowly tick upward. The two groups bit and clawed at one another. Raising his hand, he pointed sideways with two fingers. It was the only spell macro he had. The [Negative Energy Bolt] turned his hand green with eldritch magic. It flew across the pews to strike the goblin leader right in the head.

"Yes!" Liam exclaimed as Pinocchio fell backward. With the leader dead the goblin buff faded, and the undead mourners started to tear the remaining green skins apart. He had just enough magic left to blast one more with an eldritch bolt. To his surprise he found his experience bar go up with each death. It must have been the disease clouds. He'd done enough damage with DoT's to be considered the primary killer. Liam clapped his skeletal hands together happily. He was already a third of the way to fifth level.

"Being a necromancer is awesome!" he thought to himself. Those disease dots coupled with the root meant he could kill several at once. All he had to do was hit the target with a spell and lead it around like a drunken pony. The damage the DoT did would ensure it's attention was fixed on Liam. The root spell would give him enough distance to avoid melee combat. Even if everything went pear shaped he could find a graveyard, and run into a group of undead. They'd help him take out anything extra.

The only problem was in finding a new location to base out of. The monastery ruins were unusually active with people. Players were always fighting around the crypts. He thumped a fist into his other palm in realization. The [Sense Dead] spell would fix that. It detected undead as well as corpses.

"Sense Dead," he incanted and a small circular glyph formed in the air. It flashed once then floated towards his face. The corpses of the goblins began to glow a light blue. The undead nearby looked yellowish in his vision now. He could see them even through walls, objects, and some terrain. Within the monastery cellar, a few undead were lying in the coffins.

Liam paused at the goblin bodies to loot them. Pinocchio had a bloody war-badge on him which was probably a quest item. He also had a handful of copper coins.

"I am rich!" Liam exclaimed holding up the bent and dirty coins. Eagerly he pawed through the other goblin bodies. One dropped a crude short-bow, and a dozen goblin arrows. He had a weapon technically, though its stats were pathetic. Between the dozen corpses, he found fifteen copper in total. Liam straightened and turned away from the monastery. It was time to locate some more prey.

***

It was getting late. Liam had been on for most of the evening pulling monsters, and he was getting tired. Tomorrow was a work day, so he was going to have to log soon, but Liam was so close to level five he could taste it. The bar on his character screen looked full. He could probably swat a botfly and level up.

Liam walked through an evergreen forest higher up the mountain. The cold wind had a nasty bite, and his threadbare robes did little to help. He paused next to a thick fir tree. Liam used it to shelter from the elements as he watched a patrol pass. They were gnolls, hairy hyena looking creatures that walked on two legs. Three of them slowly trudged along a deer trail. The middle creature held a bow while the others wielded spears. Each was yellow and a challenge to take on solo. He needed to separate them, fight them on one at a time.

He pointed with the flat of his palm at the lead gnoll. "Field of Grasping Hands," He whispered as quietly as he could. The black magic built then flashed out hitting the first monster. Hands punched out grabbing furry feet and ankles. The last one though leapt backward out of range, and howled a warning to nearby monsters. The archer started to fire at Liam, while the third gnoll bounded toward him. Excellent, just what he wanted. He aimed casting [Pain Spike] on the charging monster.

Kiting was a useful tactic, which involved the simple expedient of running away. Others would use fancy words like strategic distance. He just didn't want to get near that spear wielding gnoll chased him. His pathetic robes did little against the cold and absolutely nothing against damage. Liam skidded to a stop after a minute of running. He pointed to the ground and cast [Grasping Hands] again.

"Mental note to self; Create spell macro for this tomorrow." He thought as the spell activated. It was a mouthful to say, and a pain to cast in combat. The angry gnoll ran headlong into the skeletal hands sticking fast a few feet shy of spear range.

"Disease Cloud," he incanted summoning a yellow mist over the area, then waited as the monster's health drained.

"Where the hell do you think you are going?!" Liam called after the mob. As soon as the gnoll was free of the root it began running away. Sure it was low life, but Liam was supposed to be the one kiting enemies. He sprinted after monster as it bounded past fir trees. Of course, the beast wouldn't make this easy.

He slid to a stop next to a tree, took aim, and shouted quickly, "Pain Spike!" The black magic caught the retreated monster in the leg. The creature stumbled briefly but continued to run. Liam aimed with two fingers held together. The green [Negative Energy Bolt] built quickly and hit the monster before him. The gnoll stumbled, tried to right itself, before collapsing from the DoT.

That lovely, beautiful, 'Ta— Ting,' sounded next to his ears. He'd just hit level five and was glad for it. Liam was exhausted after his day of grinding. He had just learned that some monsters flee when low life. Liam pulled out his portal stone holding it up. The magic built, and he was transported to a small cottage. Two zombies turned from their human meal to look at him. The [Cannibal Couple] moaned at him in greeting.

"Having a nice dinner I see." He said to the lovers. Liam needed to log and find supper himself. He'd been too fixated on hitting fifth to log off. Liam invited himself to sit down with them, but instead of eating, he wanted to check over any new spells or abilities. As he checked his status screen, a pop-up appeared.

[Congratulations on reaching level five. This message is to warn you that your character is no longer death protected. Be careful taking on too many monsters, and remember to log out in a safe location.]

It was like the game was purposely poking fun at him. He literally couldn't sleep in a safe place. At least his character was improving. His health and mana were both growing by bounds. More importantly, he was glad to see two new spells and a new ability.

Level 5
Suffocation - (Low Damage DoT)
This is a touch attack spell. It causes the target to suffocate for sixty seconds. The affected monster is also silenced for the spell's duration.

Control Undead - (Charm Pet)
Casting this spell on an undead creature will bring it under control of the necromancer. It may only affect undead of equal level or less. Every ten necromancer levels will allow the caster to control an additional pet. One at fifth level, the second at ten, then twenty and so on. Control lasts for one hour.

Very awesome. He was so happy to get a pet spell finally. Now he could bring some undead help with him into battle. He also unlocked a class ability called [Sleep like the Dead] which caused him to mimic a corpse when logged out. That would certainly help him find some better hiding places. Last but not least was his first perk point. It's what let players customize their character. Two fighters could end up with very different builds because of perk points.

He could use the point to upgrade one of his attributes, but that seemed like a waste of a precious perk. With his intelligence and wisdom so high he had several options. [Channel Mana] might be useful, it would regenerate his mana pool faster while resting outside of combat. [Soul Capacity] would give him a larger mana pool though. One perk would let him grind monsters faster, and the other would let him cast more spells in combat. There were also some necromancer options as well. He decided to go for [Eldritch Focus], which gave any negative energy spells a small bonus. Yes, that seemed best, he used an eldritch bolt to finish creatures off a lot.

With that done he needed to grab some chow and crash. Liam walked out of the cabin and around back. On the opposite side, a small wood shack was leaning drunkenly. Wood logs were stacked, and long forgotten by the zombie couple. He crawled behind them. Liam was looking forward to tomorrow, especially that control undead spell. He accessed his menu and logged out.

CHAPTER SIX

Kat - Reborn dead

Location - Unknown
Time - Unknown

There was very little sound. In fact, it was the absence of it that Kat first noticed. She woke slowly, eyes fluttering open then glanced around her surroundings. Kat was in a hospital room but not her own. Not the private room that had been hers for the last three years. Hers had contained exactly eighty-two and a half ceiling tiles, two sprinklers, and one smoke detector. She had counted them many, many times. The modern walls here were bluer than the aging creamy yellow of her suite. It was bigger as well, easily twice the size.

Nearby was a small stand with a pitcher of water and a slim-necked vase. Inside was a small collection of flowers. Next to the stand, a tall stainless steel stool sat. There were no machines, that's what was strange to Kat. No beeping heart monitor, the small kidney dialysis machine was missing as well. The thumping from the diaphragm machine that would fill her lungs once every ten seconds absent too. None of it was present, and fear stole into her heart. It was an ice cold terror that dug its claws into her chest.

A knock sounded on the small white door to her right. Just barely she could see it in the corner of her vision. After a second it opened to admit Doctor Ben Gedding, the man who'd come to collect her. She recalled him arriving with a team and helping to load her into the helicopter. He'd been gentle with her distraught mother. Once again he wore the plain business suit. His bulging muscles threatened to pop the buttons on his vest. He smiled brightly at her as he approached.

"Good afternoon, young lady." He said seating himself on the stool by her side.

"First if I may, are you in any pain?" Ben asked as he settled himself. Kat was mildly surprised by the question. It took her a second to realize that he was right. She felt no pain, none; not even a tingle on her skin. By its very absence, she felt glorious. The greatest drug in the world and tears immediately threatened. Oh God, she would not cry, not yet. She blinked twice, (No.)

Ben smiled at her again. "You should be able to speak now. Nothing is preventing you from doing so."

Could she? What would she say? Should she try for something important? Maybe she could just answer his question. The older man seemed to grasp her dilemma, and smiled again reassuringly.

"Let us start with your full name. Do you know who you are?"

"Kathrine Ines," she said taking herself by surprise. The sound of her own young voice startled her. Kat half expected to blow cobwebs from her mouth. In her shock, she covered her lips with both hands. Astonishment crossed her face again as she realized her hands had moved. Kat brought them away from her face and stared at them. They were perfectly shaped, unlike the withered claws she'd grown used to seeing. Ben was beaming at her like a proud father. She lunged at him wrapping her arms around his thick neck. Her chest sobbed as she struggled suddenly for breath. Ok, she was going to cry now.

"Thank you! Oh god, thank you." She said feeling her heart throb. Kat's chest spasmed in pure joy.

"There, there dear," Ben said patting her on the back. His big hands felt soft and warm. It took her almost a minute to calm herself. All the while she clung to Ben like a drowning woman to a float. Finally, she sat back wiping away at tears that didn't flow. Ben saw this action.

"Unfortunately crying is one of the things that has us stumped." He said watching her. "We can simulate the chest expansion and feeling of pressure behind the brow. Tears though are caused by too many different emotions. Happiness, depression, sadness, even anger can bring tears to a person's eye. Every time we tried people were like water faucets. Crying and hiccups are two things you can't do anymore." He said sounding as if he were truly regretful.

"I'm happy to be alive," Kat said, and the man's face fell.

"It pains me to say this, but I must correct you." He replied before pausing. "The procedure was completed. A doctor put you into medical cardiac arrest. By US legal standards when your heart no longer beats you are pronounced dead. That is why we can perform this research. Your brain is donated to our facility." Despite herself, she felt heavy and leaden. Dead? How could she be dead when she finally felt alive. She was free of the pain.

"I will not lie to you in any way, which is why I am telling you this," Ben said solemnly.

"So I'm in your machine?"

"Yes, Kathrine. Your brain was transferred to its cradle four hours ago. We've been bringing your cognitive functions up to normal levels, and taking careful readings." He continued in a grave voice.

"I want to see," She said suddenly.

"Are you sure? Most of our subjects go to great lengths to forget." He warned.

"You said you wouldn't lie to me," Kat responded a little more hotly than needed.

"I won't, I promise you that." He said withdrawing a phone from his inside pocket. After selecting a number, he pressed the mobile to his ear. "Don, can you go into the cradle room and take a few photos. Kathrine wishes to see where she resides." He said and there was a pause. In the silence, Kat couldn't quite hear the tiny voice on the other end.

"Thanks," Ben said hanging up the phone before turning to her.

"It will take a few minutes for a technician to collect photos. In the mean time may I perform a few routine tests?" He asked politely. Kathrine stared at the man still struggling to come to grips. Dead? The word hung above her like a guillotine, but she nodded slowly.

Ben Gedding did something very odd, and in a strange way it broke the spell on her. Reaching up he pinched her nose and held it. With his palm, he covered her mouth. Kathrine just stared at him in utter stupefaction. Ten seconds went by then twenty as he continued to passively suffocate her. Finally, she felt like she wanted air, and batted at his hand. Ben let go sitting back.

"What did that test?" She asked in confusion.

"Your belief that you still breathe. Memories of it will force your brain to think it needs air." He said moving the stool further down the bed. His hand touched her foot.

"Can you feel this?" He asked brushing the very tip of her big toe with a single finger. At first there was nothing, then after reconsidering she sensed something touch the skin there.

"Yes," She said and he smiled.

"Good, how about this." He said and lowered his hand to tickle the inside of her foot. Kat let out an involuntary squeal and she shifted her foot. Ben tickled her other foot and she kicked her legs laughing. She couldn't help it. It was so different than the pain she was used too. There were so many nerves firing but it wasn't the agony from before, it felt good. Ben's phone rang, and he pulled it from his pocket. Kat got the chance to catch her breath from her fit of giggles. These were the weirdest tests she'd ever heard of. Wasn't he supposed to take out a little mallet and smack her knee?

"Yes, send them to her machine," Ben said then canceled the call. "Can you stand?" He asked her more soberly, and Kat swallowed. Suddenly she wasn't so sure she wanted to see those pictures. The moment of gaiety seemed to shatter before her. The illusion was falling quickly to the floor. Still, she wouldn't back down now. Kat held out a hand which Ben took. Her foot slid from the bed to hang in the air. Slowly she shifted her weight to the edge. The tiles were cool underfoot as her bare feet touched down. Kathrine almost buckled but hung onto Ben's hand tightly. He held her arm but didn't move to support her as she stood. For the first time in three years, Kathrine was able to walk.

He guided her to a flat section of wall. Reaching out he touched the middle panel, and it turned black like a computer monitor. Quickly he found the files on the desktop and opened them. The shock made her step back and her knees were suddenly weak at the sight. Kat almost fell again to the tiles but Ben reached for her elbow. He held her as she stared at the pictures. Within a dark blue liquid Kat could see part of a brain. A white plastic cage surrounded the gray flesh. It was held inside a curved helmet, presumably the VR machine. Her name was printed on a small piece of card stock on the case.

"Are you alright, Kathrine?" Ben said next to her.

"I'm really dead," Kat said in a ghost of a voice. She continued to stare at the disembodied brain in the image. *"Forever dead,"* she thought, Kat would never forget the sight.

"Yes, I'm afraid so." He said sadly, and she turned to look at him.

"What happens now?" She asked feeling the weight of the world on her shoulders.

"That is entirely up to you," Ben replied warming a little.

"What do you mean?" She asked still feeling ill.

"This room is your home machine. From here you can experience anything you desire."

"Why does it look like this?" She asked waving her hand around.

"We decided on this as the default setting, because our subjects always come from a medical environment. It was designed to help keep you calm until a team member could talk to you. It's also, so you will feel compelled to alter it. You can change everything in this room to your preference. The walls, floor, and ceiling you can change or expand. Add any object in our database you wish." Ben said touching the screen they stood next too. A few selections later and the walls turned from hospital white to wood paneling.

"That's it?" She asked looking around the room. Was this her prison cell? She would go mad for sure.

"The world is open to you. You can browse the Internet, read new books, talk to friends—"

"My parents, I can talk to them?" Kat interrupted.

"Of course."

"I want to let them know I'm alright," Kathrine said and Ben withdrew his phone. Once again he dialed a number from his contact list. After a few second he held the phone out to her. Wow, a 'virtual' phone Kathrine realized with delight. She took it carefully and brought it to her ear. There was the sound of ringing before it connected.

"Ines Residence." A rough male voice said wearily. Kat could the quiet depression in those two words.

"Daddy, daddy it is Kat," Kathrine said softly. Her father gasped, choking suddenly.

"Kat, oh god. Kathrine, is it you? Are you alright? Oh sweetie your voice, it sounds so beautiful."

"The pain, is it gone?" Was the next question she heard.

"I'm OK, father," Kathrine said before hearing a shrill cry from the other end. It sounded close to hysterical as the phone seemed to change hands.

"Baby, is it you? You're alive? I prayed so much." Her mother said in a breathless voice like she'd run from across the house to reach the phone.

"It is me, Momma. I'm..." She couldn't use the word alive. That would be lying. Kathrine heard the joyous sobbing from the phone.

"I can walk, and talk, and feel," Kathrine said experiencing just that. Her chest felt so tight it was like a giant was standing on it. She knew she'd be crying too if she could.

"Father and I are coming to see you." Her mother said. Ben made a sad face and Kat looked at him. He must have overheard because he was shaking his head and extending a hand for the phone. Kat could tell he didn't like asking for it back.

"Momma, I'm OK. I love you. The doctors said I have to do

some testing first. I'll call you again soon." Kathrine said quickly.

"No baby, please. I can't believe it is you." Her mother's voice said pleadingly.

"I have to go for now. I'll call you again in a little while." She offered and could hear her mother still crying. "I love you," Kat said rushing to hang up before her courage failed. With great reluctance, she extended Ben's phone back to him. His face was solemn again as he took it.

"We can show you how to make your own phone. It is one of the objects you can add to your room." He said and Kathrine nodded.

"What now?" She asked after he slipped the phone into the inner pocket of his suit.

"Testing first to make sure everything is in order, then I, or another technician will begin showing you how to program your environment," Ben replied and Kat nodded.

"I'm eager to learn," She said.

***

The phone began to ring. Kat shifted on the small couch and reached for it excitedly. Over the past three days, she'd spoken more to her family than her entire twenty years previously. She imagined it was her mother remembering some tiny tidbit of information to talk about. The two covered the familiar ground so many times already, but most likely her mom just wanted to hear Kat's voice again. When she picked up the phone, it's caller ID did not show her parents number. It was Ben Gedding. He could just walk right in if he wanted. It rang again before she accepted the call.

"Hello?"

"Kathrine, it's Ben may I drop in?" He asked pleasantly like he was making a house call instead of checking on a test subject. It was a small gesture that she deeply appreciated.

"Of course," She replied instantly.

"Do you mind if I bring a friend?" He asked next and she

considered. Kathrine was dressed in an extra large t-shirt that fell
to her knee's. She wasn't wearing underwear or anything else.
Why bother with a bra when your boobs are digitally perfect?

"In that case, I need a minute." She said moving towards her
bedroom.

"Would you like me to call back?" He asked in an amused
voice.

"It will only take a second, come in about five minutes." She
responded and hung up. Opening the bedroom door she walked
around the massive plush bed. Kat checked her dresser and
pulled out a modest white dress. She also withdrew a plain pair
of undies before changing. Everything was virtual; it was all just
ones and zeroes, but she wasn't about to let herself go. At least not
in front of company. She checked her hair in the mirror then
added a small clip to the side. Back in the living room she waited,
which didn't take long. There was a knock on the front door, the
one exit she couldn't go through. She'd been waiting just before it
so she could receive her guests.

"Hello, Kathrine," Ben said warmly as she opened the door. He
was in his ever present business suit. Salt and pepper hair
contrasting with his massive bulk. Kat smiled at the older man
stepping back.

"I like what you've done with the place. It's very..." He said
struggling to find the right word. "Retro," He finally added
walking into the small entryway.

"Thank you," Kat said rather pleased. She'd taken hours to
adjust the wall sizes. The next person seemed to materialize in the
air before her door. It was the system drawing his avatar in her
home space. Kat watched in amazement as a small two-foot tall
white rabbit came into being. It stood upright with a slightly
pudgy belly and big floppy ears. What shocked her the most was
the 18th-century suit it wore. It entered with a funny half
hopping gait, and stopped before her removing his impossibly
cute little top hat.

"Madam Ines, it's a pleasure to meet you." The rabbit said in a
polite southern drawl and bowing at the waist.

"This is my old friend Walter Nowel," Ben said from beside her. He was glaring down at the little rabbit obviously not pleased with something. "You told me you had a human avatar," he added pointedly to the little hare.

"And I do, one that I never use," Walter said cheerfully.

The small rabbit hopped forward a foot extending a tiny paw. Kat could have squealed and died from cuteness overload. Instead of shaking his hand she crouched, grasped the small furry creature under the arms, and cradled him to her chest. His white fur was so soft in her arms. Kat pushed her face against the downy hair of his head. Walter curled into her arms and politely kept his hands tucked into his lap. There was a loud cough, and she turned to see Ben looking distinctly unhappy.

"As I said, he is an *old* friend." The man huffed from his place.

"Old in body, not in mind." The rabbit replied still in her arms. He shifted, and she was forced to let him go. His feet landed easily on the floor where he also retrieved his top hat.

"Sorry, you just looked so cuddly." She admitted in embarrassment.

"Think nothing of it." Walter replied easily, and Kat led them both into her apartment.

"Can I get you anything?" She asked.

"No, thank you," Ben replied sitting down on an empty couch.

"A carrot, or a piece of celery if you have any." Walter requested.

"I'm sorry, I have some strawberry pie. It hasn't been very long since I awoke." She admitted.

"Then I must pass, I'm allergic you see. I prefer not to accidentally forget and try one in real life." Walter said climbing into a large loveseat. When he shifted sitting all the way back in the chair, his pawed feet didn't even reach the edge. Kat took the last available seat in the circle.

"Walter and I were just catching up. He works at Dreamshard as a game programmer." Ben said gesturing to his friend.

"That's amazing. I have looked at the source code for some of the items but I'm afraid it's all so far above me. I don't think I'd dare touch it myself." She said admiring the small rabbit on the couch. That must be why he chose that avatar. He could be anything he wanted.

"Thank you," Walter replied brightly and Ben coughed. He was very protective of Kathrine, almost like a second surrogate father.

"Walter knows about our work here. Normally it's very hush-hush, but I've known him for longer than I've known my wife. We grew up together," Ben said with a tone of reminiscence in his voice.

"How long have you been friends?" Kathrine asked.

"Since elementary school. We hated each other at first. As two young and overly bright children we tended to clash. We became friends a few years later after meeting again in high school." Ben replied glancing at the small rabbit.

"That brings us back to why I hoped to meet you," Walter said smiling, and the expression showed of the front teeth of the little rabbit. He continued shortly, "I have a number of key-codes for our new game. I intended to donate some to Ben's research group. As a senior programmer, I was in charge of character classes and skills. I can tell you I had a blast designing each. The melee characters and archers were easy enough. The wizard though took the longest." Walter explained. Kat was instantly excited by the prospect. Wizards and magical sorcery sounded like so much fun.

"The development team kept complaining I made them too powerful, but I told them casters are so easy to kill. You have to offset that by giving them powerful utility." Walter continued naturally excited to talk about his work.

"What kind of game is it?" She asked looking to the little rabbit.

"It's a whole new world. One that is set in a traditional fantasy setting." Walter said excitedly.

"Is it dangerous?" She asked with some nervousness because Kat had enough pain to last her many lifetimes. The question made the little animal sigh regretfully.

"I'm afraid there are many mystical creatures in the game. They are particular about their little slice of the world. Combat is an integral part of gameplay."

"Kathrine if you're worried about the pain you can change the settings. The machine has a hard threshold of five percent, and the default is one percent. That makes a sword cut feel like a fingernail crossing over your skin. If you wish you can even turn the setting off." Ben said pointing up at the ceiling. He seemed to be indicating the machine itself. Kat didn't want to experience pain again but it did sound interesting. She had already started to fear she would become a recluse, sitting in her little virtual prison forever protected.

"I'll give it a try," She said and the rabbit once again beamed. He scooted forward in the chair before hopping down. His little furry tail wiggled as he walked over to Kat. From out of an inner pocket, he withdrew a large black ticket, and on it was a long code printed in gold letters.

"I hope that you enjoy the game. I've spent the last couple of years helping to make this world." He said holding out the little card.

***

KittKat - Level 0
New Hearth City - Aethon Island
Noon.

Kat's foot slipped on the bottom step and she almost took a spill into the water pond. At the last second, caught herself on a marble statue, but she barely noticed as she stared at the world around her. It was like a medieval fantasy come to life. Kat hadn't been expecting much from a game but she was wrong. This, this was so much more. She stood on a raised platform on one side of the plaza. It was where she'd appeared after completing the tutorial. The paved stones under her feet were a cream colored white. Before her lay a wide area and a mass of people congregated. A brass band was playing next to a small spraying fountain. Hundreds of people in a wild assortment of colored garments strolled about. Some danced or stood to watch the performance. The sights, sounds and smells snatched at her attention drawing her eyes from object to object.

A lot of the people wore armor of some kind or another. Kat saw a dozen different swords and shields, and robed players walked along with staffs in hand. A buxom female strolled by wearing the skimpiest leather armor imaginable. Finally, Kat took another step this time avoiding the watery ledge. Moving down into the bustle of people she was quickly swallowed up. Several conversations went on around her as she moved.

"The wizard class is so fun, you have to try it," A tall skinny girl said to her armored companion.

"Way too squishy. Besides, I like the visceral feel of a blade in my hand." The chain wearing male said with a wolfish grin.

"Barbarian," The girl giggled.

"Maybe they do have a barbarian class, that would be fun." The man replied as the two moved on.

Kat was drawn along by the current, and traveled with the crowd like a school of fish. Without a direction, she simply strolled. The open plaza sat next to an equally spacious market place. She smelled the medley of fresh odors from hundreds of stalls. Many sold pastries, fish, slices of meat, or herbal drinks. She bent over a small counter selling glass vials of many colors. Each potion was labeled with its effect.

"You look lost," a voice said nearby. Kat turned to see a red robed man with two companions.

"Can't be lost when you don't have a destination."

"Is this your first character?" A big half-orc asked pleasantly. He was a head taller than the others with mottled gray skin, and little tusks sticking out of his bottom lip.

"My first day," She admitted to the group.

"What do you hope to get out of the game?" The wizard asked stepping forward. Kat noticed he was half-elven just like her. She'd kinda liked the semi-pointed ears and uniquely colored eyes. His were gold colored bordering on orange.

"Oh I dunno, explore the land I suppose," Kat said thinking

about all the new things she could experience. The world was vast and barely touched by others.

"If you haven't picked a class yet I might suggest a paladin. They were just discovered the other day." The red robed wizard said. He stepped closer and his wooden staff clicked on the flagstones.

"The tutorial did say a melee character was easiest to start with," Kat replied.

"Where are my manners," The half-elf said extending a hand. "I'm Deathsythe, and these are my two friends Grayblade and Vasilee."

"KittKat," She replied glancing at their faces. "You guys look pretty powerful." Kat continued noticing their armor and weapons. The two fighters had on a mixed set of chain and plate. The human wore a sword at his waist. Grayblade had a bronze double-headed axe slung across his back.

"No way, we're just a few levels higher. All of us ended up dying in a dungeon and rolled new characters." Vasilee said offering his own hand. His grip was firm, but not overpowering.

"So it's true about when you die?" Kat asked with some trepidation. Everyone had a single life, just one. Death usually meant starting completely over unless you could get a resurrection.

"Corpse retrievals are tough on a new player. Harsh game mechanics to be sure. I think a lot of casual players might be put off. Still the game rewards skilled individuals." Grayblade said shaking her hand next.

"We could use a paladin in the group. If you're interested, we can help you learn the class and level you up some." Deathsythe offered. Kat had been leaning towards a wizard, but the offer was tempting.

"Doesn't that waste your time?"

"Helping a new player is never a waste of time," Vasilee said dismissively.

"Normally the game makes you do fetch quests for money during the first day. Helps people learn the city layout free of danger. We'd be happy to pay for your sword lessons." Deathsythe suggested coming forward and produced a small pouch from the folds of his dark robe. This he extended towards Kat. It turned out to be twenty gold in a purse. "It'll take ten gold to pay for the sword masters lesson. The rest will help buy some starting equipment." The wizard explained. Well, that sold it for her. Learning how to swing a sword might be useful, and she'd be able to get over her initial fear of combat by going toe to toe with monsters.

"I accept your generous offer," Kat replied stepping closer to them.

"Paladins are nice because they can heal party members. Think of them as half fighter and half cleric." The giant half-orc said patting her shoulder. The fighter had a point. Being able to melee and heal herself sounded like a strong character. Today was looking up. It hadn't been hard at all to find some new friends.

CHAPTER SEVEN

Liam - Unlikely Rescue

Liam - Level 10
Mothau Crypt

He hadn't intended to become a player killer. It wasn't his style. Things though sort of happened, and of course he was back where it all started. Liam stepped into the crypt feeling almost nostalgic. Two weeks ago he'd crept through the darkness following people he thought were his friends. Did that say something about him? Well, he was here again. For the last ten levels, he'd stayed away from this place. Not from fear, but he never attacked undead. Liam used them, often as cannon fodder, but he never killed them. So far they were the only creatures in the game that hadn't tried to hurt him. No, curiosity is what drove him here tonight. He was almost positive he knew how he'd change classes. Doubt though had nagged at him enough he'd decided to come and check.

The cold seemed to seep into his bones only moments after entry. He shivered a little wondering again why he felt things at all as a skeleton. The flaming iron pits nearby did nothing to help the chill feeling. Like before the shadows from the stone statues danced before him. Liam advanced inside, and the gnarled bone staff clicked on the stone floor as he walked. His skeletal feet added to the slight noise as he approached the first bridge. Stopping he glanced down into the swirling dark. Maybe he should make this his home for tonight. Find a quiet little alcove and slip inside with nothing but his knickers on. Without a visible name he would look like every other skeleton in the dungeon. It was getting late and he needed to work in the morning. He either had to find a place to sleep or teleport to his usual location. He decided to set aside the problem for now. After crossing the bridge Liam discovered the remains of a destroyed skeleton. It lay broken amid a pile of rags with its head thoroughly caved in. A group was here or had been recently. He doubted he would run into them coming out, because usually, they'd kill the boss then portal home. There was the small chance though. Lifting the staff he carried it so it wouldn't click against the floor. He moved more slowly down from one level to the next. As he descended he encountered several undead that had escaped the party's notice.

"So they weren't very thorough," He thought to himself. He descended several more levels until he came to the bottom floor. Nothing blocked his passage, so it only took a few minutes of walking. Using his bone staff he silently cast [Control Undead] on two level nine skeletons. Both were modestly covered in aged and rusted chain. One though seemed to lack a weapon which was unfortunate. At least Liam was level ten finally. Now he could control two undead at the same time.

"Follow me," He ordered and they shambled quickly behind him.

This far down it was pitch black but thanks to his undead nature he could see well enough in the dark. Unless magically aided most living creatures were blind. Only the dwarves and undead had dark vision. So he was able to quietly walk up on the scene unfolding in the boss chamber. Not that he even needed to sneak. Four people were in the room. Well, three people were attempting to chain the fourth on the alter in the back of the chamber. Liam stopped at the doorway to watch what was going on.

"Damn it, you jerks! Let me go." A woman wearing rather dull half plate spat. She was kicking and flailing like a wild armored wolverine.

"Get in here Deathsythe. She's impossible to keep down." A large half-orc growled. "You're the one that wanted to do this." He said struggling.

"You know my strength score is pathetic. I wouldn't be any use." A red robed wizard said from just out of kicking reach. If Liam had eyeballs, he would have rolled them. *"Deathsythe?"* He asked himself, could there be a more pretentious name. The fact he was obviously half-elf made it all the worse. A second man was doing a much better job of locking up the woman's arms.

"Quite down and stop struggling," The orc growled getting annoyed.

"Or what? You'll kill me!?" The girl hissed, and the half-orc grinned at her nastily. "You helped me the whole day." She bellowed still kicking her legs.

"New players are so gullible." The human warrior said from his place by the alter.

Liam was honestly a little impressed. Other men might have been outraged or furious at the scene. Not Liam, he wanted to applaud. What an evil bastard. Unfortunately, this indicated people were desperately trying to find out how to be necromancers. Countless players had been hounding him for details on the class. Thank god, nobody knew his name, or he'd be drowning in private messages. This player at least was using his head. Did he expect some demon to rise and grant him his immortality? Liam was quite sure he would fail, but it would be a problem to let the wizard live. Deathsythe was entirely too motivated and having more necromancers running around would just make it harder on Liam.

"Why?!" The chained girl on the alter balled.

"Sorry dear, a sacrifice is needed." The wizard said blithely and Liam decided it was time to make his move while they were distracted. Liam pointed at the human warrior. He suspected the man was the stronger fighter. The fact he'd handled the girl's arms so well spoke of his inherent strength. It was important to keep him occupied. Checking to make sure his pets were behind him he whispered, "Attack him." Together all three undead walked into the room. Liam reached the wizard in red robes first, and grabbed the half-elf by the back of the neck. With a satisfying squeak, he froze stiff within Liam's grip. The two undead went past to attack their target.

"Did I hear someone mention sacrifices?" Liam asked in a deep throaty voice. Everyone turned in astonishment at his sudden entrance. Lifting the staff in his other hand, Liam pointed at the half-orc warrior. He intended to cast a spell of holding but the girl did something better. Her foot shot out from the orc's grasp and slammed into his nuts. The large dabbled gray male grabbed his crotch falling backward. Obviously, his mature filter was off, how fortunate for Liam. The human warrior was caught totally flatfooted by the zombies. He was struggling to draw his sword as they attacked him. Liam turned his attention to the wizard who was staring at him out of the corners of his eyes. For someone that was just about to sacrifice a girl to dark gods, he looked terrified by the sudden attack.

"Suffocation," Liam whispered, and a shadowy snake wound its way around his throat and tightened down hard. The wizard once again wheezed as the air left his lungs. It wasn't a very good dot (Damage Over Time) spell, but it effectively muted the target. Liam didn't fight spell casting monsters much. It was partly why he hadn't bothered creating a spell macro for it. That and it was just plain cool to say. Being half-orc Liam was strong enough to shove the wizard towards the wall. Liam was able to maneuver his stiff arms into the hanging wall chains. Now Deathsythe's hands were bound, and he was silenced for the next forty seconds. He wouldn't be able to cast any spells at all. The wizard was just a spectator in the fight, and Liam turned to survey the battlefield.

The human warrior was not having a fun time with the two powerful undead. He'd managed to get his sword out and was using his martial skill to good use, but the fight was one-sided. The unarmed zombie lunged at him grabbing his arm and biting him on the neck. The second undead possessed a rusty sword, and it took the man everything in him to fend off the old weapon.

The half-orc was finally getting up from the ground. He drew a copper greataxe from a back sheath with a vengeful look in his eyes. Liam decided to turn up the fun. He was going to steal a page right out of the lich's playbook. Raising a free hand to form a half moon he targeted the altar. Exploding his fingers outward a little dot of void sprang to life. The next second the room was blanketed in complete darkness blinding everyone in the chamber. Everyone except him and his undead buddies. Liam loved the [Darkness] spell, so useful against mortals.

With a bellowing war cry, the half-orc charged at Liam's location within the darkness. The fighter crossed the room and swung viciously at where Liam had been standing. He though had seen the move and safely gotten out of the way. There was a meaty crunch as the axe sank into flesh. The orc swore and cursed a half-dozen obscenities as he attacked the body before him. The fact he was doing damage was encouraging him. Poor Deathsythe, being chained to that wall made it real hard to block. The fact he was still silenced kept him from alerting his friend, so his death was quick at the hands of the half-orc teammate. Within the darkness, the two undead were easily dispatching the human. Unable to see the blows coming he couldn't continue to parry them. They brought him down in a tangle of claws and teeth. Liam pointed at the half-orc with a free hand.

"Attack him," He said as the undead finished with the human. To his credit, the warrior managed to kill one of them. He was blind fighting by wildly swinging his weapon in the hopes it would connect. Liam decided to try another spell he didn't use often.

"Lethargy," he incanted pointing at the half-orc. The warrior grunted after his next swing. The spell significantly affected his attack speed. This was amplified by the weight of his great-axe. With the remaining zombie's help, and several negative energy bolts the last player fell.

The undead minion turned to the girl on the altar still in

combat mode. Liam pointed at the [Restless Dead]. "Go passive," he ordered, and the zombie stopped. It turned in his direction looking for further instructions. "Stand over there," he said pointing near the entrance. Liam wanted it out of aggro range of the girl but close enough to be useful.

A few seconds after the zombie took its station the darkness spell vanished. This left two torches burning in the room. The previous owners must have placed them there to free up their hands. He wandered closer to the alter. It was much as he remembered except the beautiful armored woman atop. Both of her arms and one leg were chained. Her eyes were wild with fear as she continued to fight and squirm against her restraints. At the sight of the necromancer approaching, she kicked, yowling in terror. She was short, probably five feet tall at most with long jet black hair was flung about in a messy mass of strands. It clung to the chains and hung partly over her face. One eye stared up at him like a big silver coin. She was a half-elf he realized as he caught sight of her slightly pointed ears. That explained her natural beauty.

He wasn't going to calm her down by talking. Somehow he instinctively knew that. Getting close to that foot of hers was also out of the question.

Liam spotted the spell book sitting on the stand near the table, and was reminded why he'd come down here in the first place. Silently he turned and walked over to it. The large grimoire lay half open just like last time. Now though its top pages were blank, which was different. There were no squiggling lines of magical glyphs. He touched the blank page, and nothing happened. Well, Liam was already a necromancer, not like he could expect a repeat performance. Still, he tried getting a response from it by pointed his finger at the book and muttered, "Negative Energy Bolt." The green magic hit the tome making it glow for a second before fading. Nothing else appeared to happen and Liam turned a few empty pages.

"Are you going to kill me or not?" A soft irritated voice said.

"Not," he replied without looking up. He tried flipping to the front of the book only to find every page was blank. Sighing he closed the old lich's grimoire with more questions than answers. If there were no funny squiggles, did that mean it was used up? Was he the only necromancer? That sounded preposterous even to him. There had to be more enchanted spell books out there. Raising a hand to his chin he began to tap at his tusk with one bony finger.

"Hey… hello?! Hot girl on an evil altar. This is the part in the movie where you're supposed to leap to her rescue." The girl said more than a little annoyed. Slowly he turned to look at her. If ever there was a picture fit to print it was the way the raven haired warrior looked chained up.

"The hero in the movie usually gets the girl in the end. Somehow I suspect that isn't going to happen." Liam replied, and she scowled up at him darkly. The fear had apparently abated if she was willing to give him a look like that. Liam supposed he wasn't much of a hero after all.

"Have you calmed down?" He wondered aloud. The girl's breathing was still ragged making her armored chest rise and fall rapidly.

"No, hell no. Get me out of these chains." She said struggling a little again.

"Do I have your parole?" He asked moving closer to the dissection altar.

"What in the world is that?" She asked.

"It means you promise not to kick me in the nuts like the half-orc." He said stopping next to her body. Even covered in cheap half plate, the girl did look incredible or it could have been the way she was chained down. Liam couldn't decide which he liked better. The girl or her helpless innocent body before him.

"That depends on how fast you unlock me."

"I will take that as a yes." He said and bent over her. Liam let her hands go first still leery of getting near her free leg. Immediately she sat up pushing him away. He was glad she hadn't hit him which would have initiated combat, and drawn his pet down on her. He stepped back towards the throne and waited for her to finish unchaining her leg. She threw the offending irons away and stood warily.

"Thanks... I guess." The woman said in an acidic tone.

"Actually I had a pragmatic reason for freeing you. I need a favor." He said, and instantly she sank into a combat crouch. Her hand reached for a sword but didn't draw it.

"I need a fence," He said trying to forestall her attack. She eyed him incredulously. "I can't go into the city. For the last five levels, I've been hoarding my loot. Since you feel so incredibly grateful, I suspect you'd be willing to take on this simple task." Liam said pushing away from the throne. He knelt by the half-orc and opened his inventory. It was mostly cheap crafted gear the city had been flooded with. He pulled out two items that looked worth selling.

"That's stupid; after I reach town, I'll just keep it all." She said her face a long scowl. Her recent brush with betrayal had apparently left a mark.

"You might, I'm holding onto the good stuff for now." He replied and glanced at the undead by the door. The skeleton was eying the woman like it was itching for a taste of living flesh.

"Guard that location," He ordered pointing down the hall. The undead reluctantly shambled off. Liam didn't want to lose control of it while he was busy talking. The girl was still crouched against the altar when he turned back.

"So?"

"Fifty percent," She spit shortly.

"Wow, you have some chutzpah. I save your life, do all the work, and you want half?" Liam asked incredulously.

"Fine twenty-five percent, not that you'd know how much I sold everything for."

"True," Liam replied walking over to the wizard. He rummaged through the inventory finding a nice boss drop. The alabaster ring twisted over on itself in a Gordian loop and looked much like the rest of his finger which was useful.

"So you're him," said the voice from behind.

"Him?" He asked absently as he knelt next to the human

fighter. There was a whole collection of strength enhancing rings and amulets on the corpse.

"The necromancer everyone's been talking about. Those bastards kept blathering on about you nonstop. They said you bought your way into the class." The girl stated in an icy tone. Liam responded with a shrug before standing.

"You can have the stuff on the human. Lots of fighter gear you might like."

The half-elf glanced at the corpse, made a face, but walked over and knelt down. After a few seconds, she swore under her breath. "No wonder the ass was so strong." She said as she fiddled with the inventory screen. He saw a couple of rings slide onto her fingers before she stood again. Liam had gotten out his loot sack and extended it. The leather bag was packed with some of the better magical gear he'd located today. She took it from him before opening it to inspect the contents. Finally, she slid the straps over her head and settled it onto her shoulders.

"So what now?"

"Teleport home, sell it all off, then come meet me in the graveyard outside the city," Liam replied.

"What if you try and kill me after I bring you the money?" She demanded, and Liam sighed. By the gods, her trust was at an all-time low.

"That's why I asked to meet at the graveyard. Guards don't patrol that area so I can safely be there. It is also part of the city so there's no PVP combat inside." He sighed settling his weight on the bone staff. Liam didn't even know her name he realized as she brought out her portal stone, and was gone a few seconds later. Liam cursed his mistake but it was still up to her if she took the stuff and ran though. In the meantime, he had to jog all the way from the crypt to town.

He eyed the corpses of the fighter and half-orc for a short while more. All of the bodies would decay in twenty-four hours including left over items. Their gear was mundane but functional. It would be such a shame to waste it. He turned and yelled down the hall to see if his pet was still under control. A few seconds later a zombie shuffled into the room expectantly. Liam grinned a sharks smile as the idea cemented itself. After collecting the gear from the fallen he handed everything over to his pet.

"Equip all," He said, and suddenly the Restless Dead had a full set of half plate on. In his hands was a large bronze two-handed axe and hanging from its neck an amulet of strength. He patted the zombie on the shoulder affectionately.

"Won't you be a surprise." He said and the zombie eyed him searching for orders. "Guard that spot," He ordered pointing with the staff. The fully kitted out undead went to stand hidden behind the throne. Exiting the boss room, Liam closed the doors after him so the zombie wouldn't wander. Some days it felt good to be bad.

Liam did wait for over an hour after getting to the graveyard. It was late, and he was going to lose sleep for work. He'd have to port to his safe location instead of searching for a place. It was far too dangerous to logout anywhere near New Hearth. Casually he rested against the stone fountain. He was about to give up when he noticed a dark figure approaching from the town gates. The paladin eventually stopped before him.

"Sorry it took me so long, never been to the graveyard." The half-elven warrior said in apology.

"One of the first places I visited." He admitted. A small bag was held out for him and he took his gold. Liam had no idea what he was going to spend it on, but some greedy habits were hard to break.

"Thanks again by the way." She said and he grinned a death's head at her.

"How did you get caught up with them?" He asked, and anger flared in her steel-colored eyes though it wasn't directed at him.

"I was bumbling around the city when they found me. They asked if I was new and I told them yes. They suggested a paladin was a good choice because I could swing a sword and heal." She said sitting down at the edge of the pool. Liam hadn't encountered any paladins yet. He suspected it was another of the recently discovered classes.

"They took me to the weapon master who showed me how to fight. Spent two hours figuring out how to hold a sword. Instead of taking the fighter class they brought me to the chapel. So I signed up with the order and we headed out. It was so much fun, and the levels were going by so fast. After I had hit five, they all suggested we go to the dungeon nearby. Since it was undead I would probably blow through them." She said before looking away. For a few long seconds, she stared into recent memories. Suddenly her armored hand slapped down onto the water making a splash.

"Damn them," She hissed and slapped the water again. With the sun having descended the night sky blanketed the heavens above. A moon hung low like you could almost reach out and touch it. Her pure silver eyes glance at him as he studied her profile. He waited for her to calm.

"How did you do it?" She asked not quite accusingly. Become a necromancer?

"By total accident and no I didn't kill anyone." He said picking a lily from the water. The white flower glistened with dew in the chilly night air.

"Why would you want to be evil, do you hate this world?" She asked.

"I don't hate it, no quite the opposite. When I first appeared in this world, I was standing right over there." He said pointing to the place before the goddess. "It was an hour past sunrise and the view was gorgeous. I stood there for a while soaking it in. I felt free; I felt alive again." He said looking back at her. She was staring at him with suddenly fierce eyes. "Would I be a necromancer again if I had to start over? I'm not sure. It's been tough being on the wrong side of living. You don't have to be evil to be undead. All you do is, not die." He said and she smiled brilliantly at him.

"Do you…" The girl started then cleared her throat. "I mean

would you like to be friends?" She asked and Liam would have frowned if he could.

"I'm sorry, we can't."

"Oh, I see." The girl said morosely. Her hand trailed through the water and picked up a lily of her own.

"It's not that I don't want too. You're the first person I've run across that I haven't wanted to kill. I dunno, there's something special about you too. I can't put my finger on it. Sadly the dead and the living can't mix." He said standing with the use of his staff.

"Try it," He suggested and watched her access the menu. After a few seconds she frowned sadly.

"See."

"At least tell me your name," She said.

"You mean it's not floating above me?" He asked and she shook her head. That was odd. He'd killed two people for sure down in the dungeon. That should have made his name appear above his head with a red halo. It was the universal sign someone had recently been a naughty player. The ring lasted a day, and then it changed to orange. Another day later into yellow before disappearing. You could kill a PK'er without consequence while he had the halo.

"Liam," he said bowing for the woman.

"I expected something scarier like Grimtooth, or Darkveil, or anything with 'dead' in the name." She said eying him from her seated location.

"Best I could do on short notice," Liam admitted with a small shrug.

"I'm KittKat, but I prefer Kat." The girl said standing and extending a hand. Liam took it. Hers was small, dainty within his grasp, but warm to the touch.

"It's a pleasure," He said before turning away. Taking out his portal stone he teleported to his hidden logout spot. He appeared deep under water within a submerged cave. Quickly he climbed into a small side passage and put today's acquisitions with the rest. Turning he flicked a large crab away from his sleeping area before laying down. Finally, he accessed the menu and logged out.

CHAPTER EIGHT

Kat - Leveling

Subject 4 (Kathrine)
Virtual Home Space

Kat fell back onto the triple king sized bed. It was the perfect ratio of firmness and comfort, but of course, it was virtual. Kat was already in her blue silk pajamas and matching top. What a long and eventful day she'd had. The betrayal still felt raw, angrily coiling around her heart. Kat should have known or guessed. How gullible, stumbling into their trap like a lamb to slaughter. She'd been too stunned by what was happening to put up much of a fight. Reaching over she pulled a giant stuffed kitty towards her, and pressed her face into its soft fur. Everything seemed to spill over, and Kat screamed her anger out. The sound was muffled by the pillow, but it made her feel better. Kat squeezed the cat tightly to her chest for a while. It wasn't so bad in all honesty. Kat had known pain, known agony for years. The fear though that had been something new. It was so unlike the knowledge of her slow death by disease. Today her mortal life had suddenly hung on the edge of a knife. That had to be the scariest thing she'd ever been a part of.

She'd seen the necromancer walk out of the darkness like a wraith. His eyes that hellish green color. She was sure he was going to finish the job the wizard had started. Instead, he'd ignored her, actually turned his back to Kat. Then he'd gone over to read a stupid book of all things. That had given Kat time to look at him in the torchlight. Those murdering bastards had told her all about him, but nothing could have prepared Kat for seeing the necromancer up close. He was over seven feet tall with big bones. His skull was malformed even for a half-orc which made him all the more creepy. Her arms tightened on Fluffkins as she remembered the sight. He wasn't bad exactly and had saved her which she appreciated. Though he'd admitted to only needing her help selling his garbage.

"Liam," She said aloud. Not exactly a name for a necromancer. She wondered if he was lonely and Kat wanted to be his friend. In a way, he understood, knew what it was like. The things he'd said had struck a cord in her heart.

"The living and the dead don't mix," Liam had said. Such a sad thing to hear considering her circumstances. Kat decided she'd try and become undead as well. If it took her dying again to see Liam she'd do it.

"Console," She thought, and a small window dropped into her vision. "Summon Datapad," She said and the words appeared before flashing twice. A large tablet appeared in her hands, and she opened a web browser. Kat started a net crawler before typed in the words 'Nigmus+become+undead.' The search didn't bring up results worth looking at. At least the bot would let her know when something promising appeared. Thoughts of the necromancer flitted through her mind again. If she couldn't be his friend she might be able to keep tabs on him at least. She typed in a new search, 'Nigmus+necromancer.' There were several threads on a Nigmus information website. People were speculating on how to fulfill the requirements of the necromancer class change. The last post instantly arrested her attention and she sat up in bed.

Deathsythe - "I was so close to becoming a necromancer tonight. That asshole half-orc necro came out of nowhere and killed me. We need to make a party and hunt him down. At least now I know how to change classes."

Comment - So tell us.

Comment - Totally. You failed so let us try.

Deathsythe Comment - Not until I become a necromancer first.
Comment - Lame.

That jerk! He thought killing her was just a requirement of class change. Kat wanted to reach through her tablet and wring his neck. Her only source of solace was knowing he'd died. Seeing his dead body hanging by the wall chains had been particularly satisfying. Kat signed up for a forum account so that she could post, and started a new thread under Deathsythe's.

UnwillingSacrifice - "Yes, I was there too. You took a level one player and scammed her into following you around. At level five you took said noob to the lich's dungeon so you could sacrifice her. The necromancer stomped you, and your two little buddies at the same time. As I recall you squealed like a pig when he appeared. Just for your information, he let me go. He's a nice guy and did tell me something about changing classes."
Comment - OMG Deathsythe is such a douche bag.
Comment - How did he do it?
Comment - For reals, we want to know.
Comment - What's his name?

Within minutes of the post, her inbox was getting flooded with information requests. People commented on her post over and over. She went back and edited her first post putting the words in big red letters. "No, he didn't tell me the specifics. All he said was that it doesn't require a sacrifice so Deathsythe is a stupid jerk. No, I didn't get his name, the game wouldn't let me send a friend request."

Kat lied about the last part. She did know his name but she wanted to keep that gem for herself. The system might not let him be friends with her but she could probably still send him messages. Sighing she dropped the tablet over the edge of the bed and rolled over. She fluffed the pillow several times before settling back. Lastly, she opened the console and told the VR machine to enter sleep mode. Slowly the room became blurry and indistinct. Now she could rest without being force fed simulation data continuously.

***

It was late morning when she'd roused enough to log into her character. Kat was sitting outside the 'First Steps' adventurer's tavern in which she'd stayed last night. Slowly she composed a private message to Liam.

"Hey if you'd like to talk sometime," She began then stopped herself. After a second she deleted it because it sounded so damn goofy. Kat didn't want to come off as weird, so she tried a different tact.

"Let me know if you'd like to sell more stuff. The free coin is always useful." Kat typed and liked it much better. She didn't appear needy, and it would give her the chance to see him again too. As soon as she hit enter the system informed her the person wasn't online but would receive the message when they logged in. She supposed that was for the best. A group of three low-level players came out of the inn and wandered by her. They opened the little gate that separated the tavern from the street before disappearing. There was always so much activity going on. At any given time thousands of players were entering or leaving the city. When you combined them with the NPC's walking the street, it made New Hearth feel full of life. She took the time to check out her character stats and skills.

Kat had a few daily abilities that came with being a paladin. [Lay Hands] could heal a touched target for a significant amount of HP. Her [Holy Smite] charged her weapon with energy for a single strike. Useful if she wanted to lay the smack-down on something quickly. Her melee abilities had taken the most time to get used too. [Shield Bash] could unbalance a target but it worked best just as an enemy was attacking. Then it would critical the creature and stun it momentarily. She also had [Piercing Thrust] and thank the gods she didn't have to shout that every time she wanted to use it. All she had to do was hold the blade near her body pointed forward. The weapon would glow slightly, then Kat just pushed it forward, and it would do armor piercing damage. Talented players could chain normal attacks with the skills in a combo. At the moment Kat had to stop and consciously use the skill form. Regular fighters also received considerably more of these abilities than her.

Kat couldn't look at what skills she would receive in the future. She would've liked to plan out her character a little more. It would be so annoying to move in a direction with her paladin only to find out it was wasted effort. Her perusing was interrupted by the chat-box appearing in the corner of her vision.

"I want my stuff back," came up on her chat window as a private message. The name she didn't recognize, a person named Riggs. It wasn't Liam, that was for sure. She suspected it might be one of the people that had tried to kill her last night. Obviously, it was someone who knew her name. She decided to take a stab at him.

"Think I'll keep the rings," Kat typed back.

"Bitch, those are mine." Was quickly sent to her and she laughed. She had been right after all. Closing out of her character window she paused long enough to consider her response.

"They look much better on my fingers though," Kat replied then took the time to open her equipment window. She knew from checking the auction that special gear of any kind was rather expensive. The fact magical equipment didn't drop from common enemies made all such items super expensive. Money was only found on humanoid creatures that would naturally be interested in coin. Almost every player was stomping around in plain crafted armor.

"I'll find, and kill you!" Flashed into her chat window.

"You attempted that last night. Grind a few levels little boy then try again." She typed back then waited. She selected his name and saved it to her enemies list. It was similar to the friend list but wouldn't tell her if he was online. If the man happened to come near her she would see his name. After a minute of silence, she shrugged and looked at the new stuff she'd gotten last night. Kat hadn't sold everything Liam had given her. The two strength rings were +1 each along with a set of paladin specific gauntlets. They allowed the wearer to cast [Lay Hands] twice per day. That was coupled with the +1 amulet of faith she'd gotten from the Order. In all, she was feeling pretty good about her gear at just level six. It was time to get her butt moving.

Kat stood from the wooden bench and walked out of the inn's courtyard. The street bustled with activity as players ran by, and she joined the crowd moving towards the south gate. On the way, she stopped at the market square to pick up a handful of weak health potions. Typically hit points regenerated quite slowly unless you used bandages or potions. There was also a food vendor who sold quite a variety of delicacies. She bought two hot pork dumplings for breakfast, which would increase her health regeneration a small amount for two hours. As she walked Kat bit into the pie. The buttered pastry was filled with honey sweetened pork and white cheese. She noticed a little +hp regen icon appear in her periphery then fade. By the time she'd finished breakfast, she was nearing the city exit. Several guards stood around the south gate. They were high-level NPC's, but she could only tell they outmatched her. Their threat levels indicated a massive gap between her and them. One stood on each side of the gate while a third idly wandered about. A guard captain was sitting behind a desk within the gatehouse. Kat stopped just inside the walls as she decided what to do. She considered soloing for the day, but the recent chat with Riggs made her shy from the idea. Being by herself would be just as dangerous as joining a random group.

Cupping her hands to her mouth she yelled, "Looking for group level six paladin." Thankfully it didn't take more than a few shouts. Two people stopped nearby and looked at her. They seemed lowish level with barely enough equipment between them to outfit a single player.

"We could group with you. I'm a cleric, and my boyfriend is a fighter." A tall half-elven girl said. She had greenish hair with twigs interwoven within. The woman was thin as a willow tree, but her assets were over proportioned. The man was average height and handsome in a scruffy warrior way.

"What levels are you?" Kat asked.

"Three," the elf said pointing to herself. "Jack is fourth," she finished slipping an arm around the humans. Kat was mildly relieved by their display. The fact she was higher level than either helped too.

"Can you invite me?" She asked, and a few moments later a pop-up appeared. It invited her to join HackJack's and Evalinn's group. Their names appeared above their heads when she accepted.

"Where should we go?" The cleric asked.

"Lets just pick a random direction, and keep going until we hit water," Kat suggested. The starting city was near the center of a small island nation.

"That's fine with me," Jack said casually.

Since her fellow teammates were still low level she'd have to grind them up a little. Level five was where most characters started gaining any real powers. The cobblestone road came out of the south gate and gently turned southeast. Since it was still morning and the sun was coming up, she decided to turn the group west. That would keep the light out of her sensitive eyes. The foothill slowly dipped down into a low prairie.

"There's an [Adolescent Bear] over there," Jack said pointing. He drew a sword and wooden buckler. Kat caught up to him as she drew her own longsword and shield.

"Let me get its attention first. Bears have big health pools." The waist high bear heard her coming and turned at their approach. As it targeted her the bear roared then charged to meet Kat. Just before it reached her the creature swiped with a blackened paw. She raised her shield blocking most of the damage. A few seconds later Jack was attacking its side.

"Cure light wounds," Evalinn said and Kat felt a rush of positive energy hit her. Her health bar which had been near 92%

ticked back up to full. The bear had done damage, but it was a laughable amount. Kat slashed with her sword cutting at its neck. Jack was on its other side hacking away with gleeful impunity. Kat didn't even bother using any melee skills. Another claw got between the shield and striking her arm, and Kat felt the damage like a butter knife running over her skin. It wasn't painful exactly but let her know she'd been injured. Not for the first time she considered turning the pain threshold off completely.

"Cure light wounds," The cleric called again filling Kat with a tingling warmth. The bear roared its defiance at this then slammed Kat out of the way. It began charging towards Evalinn who squealed in terror. She tried to turn and flee.

"Baby, run this way," Jack called. She panicked though and ran in the opposite direction. Evalinn barely made it a dozen yards though. The bear attacked the cleric knocking her to the ground. She cried out as it bit her face. Kat and Jack caught up hacking quickly with their swords. Kat tried to damage the bear enough to draw its attention again. In the corner of her screen, she could see the cleric's hit points getting decimated. Kat almost used her [Lay Hands] on the girl but stopped herself. Yesterday she wouldn't have thought twice about it. A new selfish side told her the girl needed to die. She'd screwed up by drawing its aggro with all the heals.

"Help!" Evalinn cried out.

"Heal yourself," Jack said as he continued to cut at it.

"I can't it keeps hitting me." She screeched flailing ineffectually. Kat rarely used spells in combat, because her mana pool was so pathetically small that it rarely did any good. At best she could get off three weak heals.

"Cure light wounds," Kat cast pointing at the cleric. Her health ticked up by a few points before a claw came down on Evalinn's chest. A skull symbol appeared next to her party name and she disappeared. Her body was death protected and summoned to the graveyard. Almost at the same time, the bear fell to Jack's blade.

"Bollux," Jack said and looked to Kat. She was annoyed by how the cleric had just wailed like a damsel when the bear was on her.

"Your girl isn't very good at this." She said to him.

"Sorry no, she's not really into games," Jack replied abashed.

"At least she's death protected until five," Kat said turning and jogging east. They'd have to run back to the graveyard to pick Evalinn up. Her health bar appeared again on the party screen.

"Oh god, she's freaking out," Jack said from behind her. "Two weeks and she's only gotten to level three." He said sighing loudly. Kat stopped to stare at him when he said this.

"You've been playing that long?" She asked amazed. Kat had reached level six on the first day, though she'd had massive help from her killers.

"Umm, kinda. Evalinn says she feels bad hurting the critters. So we stay in town mostly, but I haven't minded too much." Jack said jogging past Kat.

"Why?"

"We're in a long-distance relationship. I came into some money so I bought us two VR dive helmets to play together. We have sorta been screwing each other blind since day one." Jack said and Kat rolled her eyes. Just great, she suspected this group was about to end. Ten minutes later they found a crying half-elf sitting on the ground in the graveyard. Jack rushed to her side and knelt putting his arms around her.

"There, there baby." He said tenderly.

"You let me die!" Evalinn yelled punching his back as he held her. Jack silently accepted this and continued to hug his girlfriend. If this was going to continue Kat needed to set the girl straight. She tried to be nice.

"I'm a paladin, so I have cleric spells too," Kat said to Evalinn. The woman's face turned to her a question in her eyes. "Heals cause a great deal of attention from monsters. When you cast them over and over, it almost guarantee's they'll come for you. In the future, you should wait until we get down to half life." Kat instructed the cleric.

"I was so scared, I don't want to do this anymore," the girl said sniffling.

"Sweetness, it's just a game. You'll get the hang of it." Jack tried to soothe. Kat didn't think the cleric was ever going to get the hang of it. She'd frozen up when the bear was mauling her. All she had to do to save herself was attack back a couple of times. She could imagine what would happen when she encountered her first unnatural creature. Kat's suspicions were confirmed a few seconds later. Instead of sucking it up and trying again, Evalinn collapsed as the girl logged out.

"Shit, come on," Jack said and turned to Kat. His face was embarrassed and pleading.

"I have to call her," He said wearily reaching up. A few seconds later his body hit the ground next to the clerics. The party collapsed leaving Kat by herself. She'd just wasted close to an hour killing a single bear. Not only that she'd have to spend more time running back out. Kat was incredibly grateful she hadn't wasted her daily ability, because the cleric would have certainly died at some point during the day. If they were just going to screw around they had plenty of adult social games to play. Standing she left the two unconscious bodies on the ground. Grouping up with those two had been more hassle than they were worth. She wasn't about to wait around. Besides she had no idea how long Jack's damage control was going to take.

She went east this time setting out on her own. Kat would just have to be careful. The terrain ran into the mountains which were a bit higher level. At last, she was able to locate a small goblin village, and the experience was slow all by herself. Even with spells, health potions, and pork dumplings she often had to rest. Kat spent about four hours pulling goblin scouts and runners away from camp. Finally, she leveled up and moved away from the village. Kat was done hunting the same six stray goblins. Besides she'd completed the town quest for getting goblin ears. Now she needed to get some gnoll talismans for the other bounty reward.

Her chat box appeared with a private message. Despite herself, she felt a little flush of excitement at seeing his name.

"Just got your message, I do in fact have more loot to pawn." Liam sent to her.

"That's great, would you like to meet now?" She asked and waited a long minute.

"While I am eager for gold I must be cautious when meeting near a city. The local fauna have been getting aggressive." He typed back. Kat suspected he meant that people were actively hunting him. Liam had made some enemies just by being the only necromancer.

"I'm east of New Hearth up in the mountains right now. I just leveled and could use the break." She typed.

"Congratulations, how do you like being a paladin?"

"We get a horse for free. I always wanted one as a child." She typed.

"None of that lowly walking for you, KittKat rides in style," Liam said and she smiled.

"So?" Kat asked and waited. She sheltered next to a group of boulders for protection. The wind was fierce making the cold cut into her a little sharply. Virtual Reality really got the sensations of temperature pinned down. Kat felt like she was going to end up with frostbite if she stayed here for too long. Her horse was nearby keeping a wary eye out.

"How about I meet you in the wild, and you can mail me the coin. I discovered a post box outside of one of the towns." He typed after a pause.

"Can I trust you?" She asked.

"How direct, I like that. I shall not impugn your purity or life." He typed back and she bit back a laugh.

"Could you roughly handle my purity?" She asked deciding to bait him a little.

"You have me there. I lack any organs of note which makes snuggling difficult."

"There's always the social games," Kat offered.

"With work taking up my day time I prefer doing something that feels productive. Since we are being so direct, can I trust you?" He asked in reply.

"Yes, I'll not turn on you." She typed and meant it.

"I'm glad to hear it. Head North towards the mountain base. Follow it round to the west until you hit the coastal cliffs." He typed and she was surprised. The mobs that far out had to be level twenty, so Liam must have done a lot of exploring on his own.

"Ok, hope nothing kills me," She typed.

"You have that fast horse."

It took almost thirty minutes to negotiate the mountain valleys then skirting larger camps of gnolls, orcs, and goblins. Finally, she came to a bluff that jutted out of the cliff face. It angled about halfway along and narrowed as it curved into the sea. A large dark form was waiting near the end, and she trotted towards it. There was no mistaking the black-robed figure of the necromancer. Kat glanced around looking for danger by quickly learned habit. The view was incredible, especially in the south. The sun was still high over head which let her see for miles. The city of Southport spread itself out in the distance, and tiny ships floated around the harbor.

"Here I thought I wanted to be the explorer," Kat said stopping the horse before the necromancer. He was just as giant and imposing as last time she'd seen him. She slid from the saddle to look up at him.

"I found it was necessary to secure suitable lodgings." He said eying her up and down. That did bring up a question she hadn't thought of.

"Where do you sleep?" She asked.

"A place mortals cannot remain," Liam said in that deep rocky voice of his. She thought of the snow capped mountain they stood next too.

"The mountain top?" She asked but Liam remained silent. Liam would trust to meet her but he wasn't about to tell her where he logged out. It was impolite she supposed and waved off the answer.

"So what do you have?" She asked eager to see his good stuff.

He held out a large backpack which were expensive in their own right. How had he managed to get his hands on one of those? Still, she took it and opened the top. Kat whistled at the gear inside especially for a low-level character like her.

"Where do you find this stuff?" She asked a little annoyed. There were pieces inside that put her half-plate to shame.

"My undead brothers attack any living thing, not just players. Exploring often leads me to find curiously high-level monsters. All I have to do is position a small group of undead before leading the critter into them." He said lifting his big hands in an exaggerated shrug.

"You cheat," Kat said in astonishment.

"I prefer to think of it as assisted leveling." He said with a grin. That totally wasn't fair. Kat wanted some of the pieces inside the backpack.

"If you let me have the fighter gear I'll give you all the gold I get from the rest." She said and he considered the offer.

"Our friendship has blossomed. I think that will be acceptable. Instead of gold can you buy scrolls. I have located a few but my spell book is a little thin.

"Those are kind of pricey," Kat said thinking of all the wizards running around. They died so often that even low-level scrolls were quite expensive.

"I'll let you know what I need," He said in his deep voice.

"OK," She said hefting the backpack up and over her shoulders. She removed the shoulder bag from last time and dropped it on the ground.

"I'll use the auction to get top dollar from these. If you have a list of spells, I can put up buy orders to get them cheaper. It will take longer that way, but I can mail you the scrolls." She said tugging the straps tight.

"Good," He said pushing away from the tree. He stepped towards her and for a moment she froze in terror. Kat forgot to breathe as his massive skeletal body leaned down to pick up the dropped bag. Damn, he was scary up close. All the hairs on the back of her neck stood on end. She briefly wondered what

Evalinn would do if she crossed paths with Liam. Wet herself and log out most likely. He straightened then walked past her leaving the bluff.

"What will you be doing tonight?" She asked his retreating form.

"The same thing I always do," He replied still walking away.

"What's that?" Kat had to yell.

"Try and take over the world," His deep voice boomed from thirty feet away. Taking out her portal stone she activated it. The blue and gold magic took hold of her making the air hum. Seconds later she was standing in the courtyard of the 'First Steps' adventurers inn.

CHAPTER NINE

King Maker

"The strongest principle of growth lies in the human choice."
— George Eliot

Walter Nowel
Virtual Offices of Nigmus Online

Walter removed the virtual phone from his floppy rabbit ear ending the call. Another meeting with the board tomorrow. One of his many duties. He set the device down on his desk and rocked back in the chair. It had been long day, but he truly enjoyed his work. At first, Walter had been a senior programmer for the game. After Nigmus Online had launched he passed most of those duties to concentrate on event management. He was the Grand Game Master for the world. In any given day thousands of minor and major events took place. All of this was carefully choreographed for the perfect experience. That didn't even consider the secrets. Every week the players discovered something new about the game. It was one of the idea's he'd pushed strongly for during the development cycle. That was paying dividends in his opinion. In a way, he'd found the perfect job. Long ago when Walter had been a young man he'd been a pencil and paper dungeon master. Those hours of watching the faces of his friends shaped him. He could still recall the look of wonder, fear, and anger on them as each event unfolded. Walter wanted to bring that same experience to many more.

His reminiscence of friends reminded him of Ben Genning. That old sly rogue was doing extraordinary things. No wonder VRTek had hired him straight out of his doctorate in brain studies. It was nice seeing an old friend doing so well for himself. These thoughts naturally brought him back to the young woman he'd met. Kathrine was her name if he recalled. What a charming young person, and such a tragedy. He wondered about her. Walter had personally invited the girl to Nigmus, so he did feel responsible for seeing how she was fairing. Straightening Walter accessed the floating display on his desk and logged into the system. He had to search for her account for several minutes. The girl had made a character alright and was currently logged in, which was nice to see.

"That's interesting," He said noticing the GM comment attached to her character. Most players went their entire lives without getting one. They could be anything from notes to actions taken.

[Lvl 2 Nebuchadnezzar] Character has been selling goods collected by [Liam] the necromancer. This is a breach of rules between the living and undead forces. This has also given her access to items no low-level character should possess.

"Well, well my dear, you have made some interesting friends already." He said and glanced at her inventory. Almost everything was magical and would get her easily to level twenty. The mention of the Necromancer too was ironic. Walter knew of the undead player of course but in no great detail. *"Was it fate that had brought those two together?"* Walter wondered.

Using his finger, he touched the link for the other player. What he saw astonished him. The character had not one but six GM comments. That was extraordinary, to say the least. The first comment was routine.

[Lvl 1 Callahan] Character requested help with a name change.

[Lvl 3 Fathin] I've been expecting him to spill the beans about the necromancer class. You odd duck. (Was the next comment two weeks later.)

[Lvl 2 Nebuchadnezzar] He's been using undead monsters to fight enemies upwards of ten levels higher than himself. Gaining equipment at a grossly inflated rate. I will ban his account if he does it again.

[Lvl 3 Fathin] No, you won't. The man is going solo without towns and sleeping in caves, and I applaud his ingenuity.

[Lvl 2 Nebuchadnezzar] It's an abuse of game mechanics.

[Lvl 3 Fathin] I don't see it that way. He's found his own party.

Walter was both amazed and a little annoyed. The necromancer was drawing a lot of attention from both players and his staff. The fact he already had several player kills to his name spoke to an innate skill. He too applauded the young man. Walter's annoyance was directed at the fellow GM's. They should not be so focused on any one person. Having so many watching the necromancer might affect the person's playing experience. Quickly he searched for any flags, and the only thing that made him pause was the email change. It had been a random junk mail account but had changed after a few hours to the current one. Walter assigned a level five shadow lock on the account. Only a Game Master of the same level would be able to access his account or character. Walter was the only one on the US Server, which would keep his staff from even being able to locate the necromancer. For a minute he considered going in and lowering Nebuchadnezzar's GM level. The man was showing an unusual interest in the minutia of individual characters. Returning the GM to level one would reduce the powers he could use. That might help him focus on the job of helping players. After consideration, Walter decided against it as being too reactionary.

Walter flipped back to Kathrine's character. He noticed the GM name was the same from the necromancer. There were hundreds of people Dreamshard Studio's employed. So it was no surprise he didn't know the name personally. He added a shadow lock on

Kathrine's account too. Walter wanted to see her have an enjoyable game. Opening up a new floating screen he went into the company costume store. It was a nickle and dime scheme the developers had been forced to add by the board. At least he'd been able to make it so only apparel was sold. There would be no buying your way into great gear. He spent several minutes scrolling through items until he found something he liked. Walter bought it and a dozen Dream Shards with his own money. Next, he opened an anonymous new mail and addressed it to KittKat.

"I hope you are enjoying the game. Please accept this item and some Dream Shards. Head to the Shard Store in town where they sell costumes. It might help cover up that amazing gear you've mysteriously acquired." *wink wink*

He sent the message without signing it. The item he'd attached to the mail would do it for him. That was everything he was willing to do for her. As such a high-level GM he couldn't allow himself to play favoritism games. Still, he hoped she succeeded. He knew full well Nigmus was harsh by design.

Rocking back he allowed his eyes to roam the virtual environment of the office. Over time it had evolved to look more and more like the combat control center of a starship. He stood from the tiny stainless steel desk and walked around to the center of the room. Floating there was a ten-foot diameter holo map of the world itself. The real time image was intricately detailed showing every tiny building. If he wished it he could zoom inside a single room to see all that took place. Just now the blue orb rotated slowly in idleness. Half a million little yellow dots filled the land indicating the exact location of every player on the North American server. The European, Russian, Chinese, and Australian servers each had their unique worlds. Nearly all those pinpoints of life were still concentrated among the four low-level areas. Aethon Island (Humans and mixed), the Wild Forest of Hinthal(Elves), Irondal Mountains(Dwarves), and the Freetark Savana(Orcs) each teemed with life. Walter settled his hands into the holo field and zoomed in on Aethon Island. There surrounding each city thousands of players swarmed to and from the settlements as if a giant ant colony. Glowing patches of light showed the locations of small groups as they fought and leveled. He zoomed out again noticing at a glance the players in other parts of the world. They were the explorers and trailblazers. Even still much of the land was unpopulated, unclaimed.

"Soon... soon, the game would truly begin in earnest." He mused with a little feeling of elation.

***

Orenthal - Level 41
Kraken's Breath Tavern
Shellbreak Harbor - Tramin
9pm

A wood log in the nearby fire pit cracked open violently. Wisps of embers rose up into the air like tiny dancing elementals. Orenthal was alone save for the half-elven server. He admired the way her cleavage deepened as she bent to put the mug of ale down. The tray was tucked under her breasts, supporting them. Her eyes met his and she smiled brightly. She was one of the innumerable AI controlled characters in the game.

"Would you like anything else, sir?" She asked with a girlishly high voice.

"How about you sit in my lap and we can discuss it." He suggested and the girl tilted her head considering.

"I'm sorry I don't think we serve that." The half-elf said still chipper. Orenthal sighed inwardly and waved the girl away. The NPC scripting in the game was childishly stupid. He needed a woman to bed, maybe he could get one of the female players to join him tonight. The half-elf NPC turned with the empty tray towards the door.

His fingers curled around the handle of the beer mug. A perfect amount of white foam floated atop the golden ale. He tasted the cold refreshing body of the drink before setting it down. As the server approached the door there was a swift knock. It opened throwing in the raucous sounds of the main tavern room. A massive armored man stood in the doorway. The half-elf stopped before the paladin coming face to plate-mail chest with the player.

"Pardon me, miss." He apologized and stepped aside for the girl. The paladin held the door open for the server.

"Thank you, gallant sir." The half-elf responded cheerfully and swept past. The paladin wasn't so gallant not to look at her retreating backside. Orenthal noticed the player was wearing the guild mantle. Was it always there, or did he dress up for his superior's benefit? This was the first time they'd personally met. Setting the ale down Orenthal straightened in his seat. The player looked a few levels over twenty. As guild leader he was already edging towards forty, and the only reason he'd come to this fish smelling harbor was for tonight's meetings. He opened the guild page to check the player's identity. Falken was the name and level 21, which was middle of the road for guild members. That was part of the reason he'd called on the holy knight.

"Sir, you asked to see me?" The paladin said coming forward. Falken remained standing at attention opposite Orenthal at the table. He let the man stew for a few seconds so the younger player knew who the leader was, finally though he relented.

"Have a seat," Orenthal said gesturing towards another chair. After an awkward moment, the Paladin took the offered seat. He was big for a human, probably maxed out in height. His helmet was off showing a chiseled square face, and blond locks of hair. The man was the very picture of holy paladin breeding.

"I'm sorry to call you away from leveling," Orenthal said, and Falken brushed away the comment.

"I needed an early break. Besides we were already finishing the dungeon when I got the message." Falken replied easily.

"Good, I have a job for you." The guild leader began casually. This had the obvious effect of piquing the paladin's interest. "There's a particular player I need dealt with," Orenthal said relaxing into the high-backed tavern chair. The man's face frowned then puckered with distaste. Ahh, so he was dealing with a true believer here. He'd have to dance carefully around the player's sensibilities.

"I'm not a player killer," Falken said with some reserve. Paladins were forbidden from murder by their order. Falken it seemed took the sentiment seriously. Now was the hard part.

"No, it's something I think you're suited to. Being a Champion of Light, you are perfect for the job." The guild leader said once again confusing Falken. Instead of saying anything though the knight waited.

"I have sent the occasional recruit out to test the abilities of the necromancer. None of them have reported even a modicum of success." Orenthal admitted feeling that usual itch of irritation creep into his chest.

"You mean the deformed lich?" Falken asked.

"Yes."

"Why? He's just a pet summoner." Falken asked confusion dominating his face.

"Normally I'd agree, but something troubles me," Orenthal admitted lifting the mug of ale to his lips. He took a long drink letting the suspense build.

"What's that?"

"He's the only one," Orenthal said slowly.

"Why is that important?" Falken asked, and the guild leader wished suddenly he could strike the paladin. What a simpleton.

"That means he can think ahead," Orenthal said as if it were obvious. The guild leader had a good sense for the players in the game. It was part of the reason he'd been sending out agents to deal with problems before they became too strong.

"I don't follow, that just tells me he's selfish," Falken admitted. The knight rested an arm on the table and started to tap at the wood with a finger.

"True, but I think its time he died." Orenthal said tiring of the game. There were other people he was to meet tonight. He needed to grab the bull by his horns and point him in the right direction.

"Won't that make me lose my class?" Falken asked.

"That's the beauty of it. Not only will you remove an annoyance but the Goddess of Light will smile upon you." The guild leader said expansively.

"Because he's evil?"

"Exactly," Orenthal said smacking the table with his hand.

"Ok, where is he? I can hunt him tonight." Falken said gaining some interest in the task.

"That I don't know. There are reports he's been seen in the north-west of Aethon Island." Orenthal admitted with a sigh.

"If I recall the monsters there were high teens to low twenties," Falken said with consideration. Such reports were always dubious. Especially the rumors that flew across tavern tables. The latest information placed the necromancer at about fifteen. Another week and he'd be looking to get off the island. Maybe Orenthal could just wait for them to walk into Shellbreak Harbor. Then he'd let the guild members deal with him directly.

"How soon do you want it done?" Falken asked.

"Tonight would be nice, but the necromancer is quite elusive. I understand it may take some time." Orenthal said lifting the mug. Sadly he discovered its contents were empty. He'd have to send for the servant again.

"As you wish, I'll put out a reward for information. Maybe I'll get lucky, and someone will post about him on the Intel forums." Falken said standing from the chair. He paused looking to Orenthal.

"Can I ask, sir? Why does the Lich matter?" The paladin inquired. Orenthal gave him a level stare for a solid ten seconds. "It's just one player." Falken hedged nervously after the pause. For a while, Orenthal considered the problem. He admitted it was more of a mystery than anything, and the necromancer intrigued him. He sensed the man was dangerous. Not for what he'd done, or the little fame he'd garnered. It was exactly because he was so hard to find. Even Orenthal had been unable to pin the necromancer down with his 'gifts' lately.

"He is... not important. I'd do it myself if it were." Orenthal said finally. Falken nodded slightly and turned to go. He opened the tavern room door, but a figure was standing in the doorway. The paladin hissed as he caught sight of the red halo. A short man wearing black leather blocked the door.

"PK'er," Falken spat.

"Got a problem, golden boy?" The smaller man asked with an evil grin on his face.

"Out of my way, murderer." Falken hissed.

"Make me," said the rogue with that wide smile. Combat was forbidden in town. It was impossible to even push another player out of your way. Even with the paladin towering over the small man he continued to smile upwards. Both stood there unwilling to move, but finally, it was Falken that stepped backward. The short black haired assassin stepped past him.

"Pussy..." The other man whispered, and Falken flushed. His hand grasped the pommel of his white great-sword half drawing it. The small man took no notice and entered the room. Orenthal watched the display with some interest. He wondered if the paladin would try and catch the player killer outside of town. After a few seconds, the white-knuckled grip on his pommel eased. Falken strode from the room slamming the door after him.

"Did you enjoy your dominance game?" Orenthal asked as the man slid into a chair. He could see the rogue's name floating above his head. It was a collection of random letters and numbers. Obviously not his first character. He decided to add the name to his enemy list just to keep an eye on him.

"It's the small things in life," the man said relaxing. He set his feet on the table and rocked his chair back on two legs.

"You accomplished the job," Orenthal stated rather than asked. In response, the small assassin pointed upwards towards the halo. That didn't prove anything because quite a few guild members walked around with halos lately.

"Caught him with his pants down. He and his wife were getting frisky in a dungeon." The man said with a merry chuckle. "Hid the bodies in a nearby ravine. He'll not be getting any resurrections." The assassin said after a second.

"Show me," Orenthal ordered and two bloody tokens landed

on the table. He leaned forward inspecting the tags. The name he was looking for was inscribed on one. The other was unimportant. In response, Orenthal tossed a bag of gold coin across the table, which was pay for the job. The rogue likely sold any gear he found on the bodies as well.

"Anything else?" The assassin asked.

"If you're interested I have another name. Low-level paladin still on the island." Orenthal said and the other man extended a hand. He slid a piece of paper across the table.

"Not going to ask about the details?" The guild leader asked the smaller man.

"Could care less, I just need a name." The little assassin said and got up. Even before moving towards the door he slid into stealth. The wooden portal opened and closed silently.

CHAPTER TEN

Liam - Friends

Liam - Level 20
Aethon Island - Overlook Bluff
11pm

It was the smell that he liked about this spot. The salty sea air mixed with the cold draft off the mountain to the north. Liam had heard full orcs possessed a keen nose, so maybe it was the half-orc of his character. He sat on the cliff bluff gazing off at the distant city of Southport. Actually, he was looking at the ships in the harbor. The creatures of the island were no longer proving a challenge to him. The experience he had been gathering had slowed considerably over the last two days. Liam had also been forced to abandon a spot because of wandering parties. Hundreds of players were hunting for bigger and better game. This, unfortunately, brought him into contact with them far too often.

He had a dilemma. How was he going to get off the island? The question ran through his mind for the hundredth time that night. Liam couldn't drown, so a simple answer might be to just walk across the ocean floor. By boat it took two hours, but by foot? It might take an entire night to travel that far. There were fish under the water, low-level aquatic animals. He'd seen them with his own eyes. Were there also giant beasts, krakens, or other monstrosities? One might decide to chew on his bony ass, and that would end his undead career. The second option was by boat. That would mean getting past the town guards, then onto a ship. Somehow he suspected the sailors would also take exception to his stowing away. He'd already been close enough to the ships to know the crews were no pushovers. They'd put up a fight. If he combined the two options that might work. Liam could swim to the boat and cling to the keel under the waves. This still had the danger of him being attacked by creatures in the water though. He sighed. Quite literally he was stuck. Every avenue of thought seemed to go in circles or jerk to a dead end. Resting a hand again on his chin he started to tap his teeth with a bony finger in habit. The soft click-click of bone on tusk helped him think through a problem.

"Hey tall, dark, and handsome." A female voice purred next to his ear. The sound startled him so much he almost fell off the cliff edge. Before he realized it he was reaching for his staff and preparing an attack spell. Then finally he caught sight of his assailant. KittKat was standing only a foot away looking extremely pleased with herself.

"How the hell did you get past the guards." He spluttered seriously annoyed he'd been snuck up on.

"I walked by them," Kat admitted.

"Impossible," He said glancing down the bluff. Sure enough, three skeletal warriors were standing near the narrowest point.

"You said it yourself; they won't attack the dead," Kat replied her voice amused like she knew a secret. Liam looked to her again. The dark raven black hair, the smooth flawless skin. As he eyed her the half-elf turned around in a tight black and white gothic dress. The skirt ended just past the thighs, and two long flaps of cloth ran along the side of her legs ending in points at her knee's. On the extra fabric upside-down crosses were embroidered. Bare scrumptious legs were naturally clad in knee-high black leather boots.

"My eyes must deceive me. You look rather good for being dead." He said and she beamed at him.

"You don't know the half of it," She said slyly. After a few more seconds she relented. Opening her mouth she pointed to a set of fangs where her canines should be.

"A vampire?" Liam asked and Kat smiled.

"Got it on the first try," She said and now he noticed her eyes. They weren't the bright steel he remembered but a dark blood red. That explained how she walked past his minions. He'd been sitting on the bluff for more than an hour, so his control over the guards had long since waned.

"How? I haven't run into any vampires on the island."

"There's one in Southport. You have to join a rogue as he's doing a class quest. Took quite a while for people to figure out how to turn though. I found out a week ago when it popped up on a forum." Kat said shifting her weight. She wore on her hip a stuffed bunny rabbit. It hung from a long white braided cord. She tilted the bunny's head back making the rabbit open its mouth. Her pale hand plunged inside, rummaging about.

"Interesting," Liam admitted both by the news and her strange purse.

"Yep, you have to let him bite you. He'll regenerate all the while he's sucking you dry, so your teammates have to kill him first. It's a bit of a race to see who bleeds out. The kicker, the part nobody could figure out was next. You can't let sunlight touch you for the next three days." Kat said pulling a bright red sucker from the rabbit. She eyed it for a second before sticking it in her mouth.

"Talk about boring," Liam said thinking about the wasted experience he'd miss out on.

"I ended up just logging out, and doing something else during that time. Wasn't about to sit around twiddling my thumbs in the tavern cellar." KittKat said around a mouthful of candy.

"How did you get out of town?" He asked knowing the guards hated undead. Kat pulled the red lollipop out and gestured to her fangs again.

"Vampires must feed on human blood and interact with them, so I can go into town still. There are some big downsides though. Daylight causes such a massive debuff that we become sort of worthless in a fight. Apparently, I also pissed off the Goddess of

Light. When I logged in I got a mess of pop-ups. I have become fallen by allowing myself to be turned undead, so my paladin levels have been converted to blackguard levels." Kat said sticking the sucker back in her mouth. Wow, a blackguard. That sounded pretty cool. He could imagine already how amazing a high-level vampire knight might be.

"That sounds freaking awesome. Are you the first?" He asked.

"Blackguard not hardly, but there aren't many. It's pretty much just a polar opposite of a paladin. Vampires, on the other hand, aren't very popular because you can't group with the living." Kat admitted shifting the candy. The little stick rolled awkwardly from one side of her mouth to the other.

"We can though," Liam concluded as the realization hit him.

"Exactly," Kat said grinning.

"Is that why you did it?"

"Sorta, maybe… Besides how hot is it I can be a vampire? Extra strength, agility, and perception bonuses. Increased regeneration after feeding and dark vision." She said excitedly.

"Do you taste it, the blood?" Liam asked a bit morbidly.

"No, thank god. It tastes like simple syrup and strawberries." Kat responded licking her sucker.

"Don't suppose you can turn others."

"I've heard we can actually, same criteria as before." She said and started to eye Liam in return. Where before she'd always seemed nervous, tonight Kat radiated power. Slowly she walked a circle around Liam looking at him in his necromancer gear.

"Still I'm surprised you found me," Liam said reminded how he'd been snuck up on.

"Not really, I was in town. Someone said they saw undead up on the bluff. Came up here to check for myself." Kat replied.

"Ahh, I must be getting sloppy." He said feeling foolish. Already he was getting lazy about certain habits. That wasn't good. He pictured a vampire rogue sneaking right up behind him. It was a good thing necromancers couldn't be back stabbed —no vital organs to hit.

"I have been looking for you. I want to invite you to my guild."

She said and he laughed. The girl had balls alright, coming up to him like this.

"Gods, the kitten I've come to expect has transformed into a tiger." He said watching her circle him another time.

"Well, can you go into a city to start your own guild?" She asked and Liam conceded she had a point. How would a necromancer even create a clan?

"What's it called?"

"Lawful Dead." She replied with smug satisfaction. He'd seen better names, but he supposed it sort of fit the woman.

"I decided on the name because of something you told me before. Just because were dead doesn't mean were evil." She said and he again nodded slowly to this. The sentiments were relatively close to his own. When the pop-up appeared he accepted the offer. A new guild chat appeared in his message box.

"Welcome to the Lawful Dead. You can suck all you like so long as you don't kill 'em. In short, no player killing or being evil." The message said. He opened the social tab in the menu and found the guild page. Listed was a description of the guild which matched what Kat had just said. Currently, the guild consisted of just two members. KittKat was listed as level eighteen and his own at twenty. A new pop-up appeared telling him he was being promoted to co-leader.

"I appreciate that. Makes me feel just a little better." He said and closed the window.

"It's just you and me for now," Kat said still using her own menu. A few moments later Liam had his first friend. It felt more amazing that he could have imagined seeing a name on that list. He wasn't alone after all. Kat finally finished with her sucker and tossed the little white stick over the edge.

"So what are you doing up here?" Kat asked.

"I was trying to figure out how to reach the next continent, but I think that problem has been solved." He said turning to look back towards Southport.

"How's that?"

"Now that I have a friend who can board that ship, it changes everything. All we need to do is buy a party summon talisman. You hop on the boat. When you get to land find someplace safe for me. A nice undead graveyard would be fine. Then shatter the talisman on the ground. It will bring everyone in your party to you." Liam said feeling tremendously relieved. Here he'd been agonizing over the solution when one presented itself. Once in the new land, they could level together, and Kat would quickly catch up to him.

"Ahh, I see. What were you going to do?" Kat asked curiously.

"Catch a ride under a boat," He replied pointing with the staff to the south. Almost out of sight was a ship heading to the next land.

"That doesn't sound like fun."

"You'd be surprised what I've had to do to survive the last month," Liam muttered a little darkly.

"Tell me," Kat suggested stepping closer. She slipped an arm around his and turned Liam away towards land. So he did, he told her everything. How he started the game. His coworkers fucking him over. Finding the book and becoming a necromancer. Soloing in the wilderness, and using the undead to help him level, and finally searching for an underwater cave to use as his home. He described some of the places he'd logged out in order to keep from being killed while he was offline. Liam spoke for about ten minutes, long enough to wind their way down towards the beach. He didn't do it for her pity, but it felt good to get it off his chest.

***

Liam appeared in a twinkling of magical light. Pieces of a small stone talisman were released from suspension and fell to the ground. He glanced about clutching his gnarled bone staff tightly. KittKat was there in her black dress, and surrounding them were half a dozen undead in a small forest clearing. Their threats appeared even to yellow to Liam. No guards or player assassins immediately attacked. With some relief he eased his grip on the staff. He didn't doubt Kat exactly, but the paranoia was hard to let go of.

Reading his body language Kat frowned. "Did you expect me to turn on you?" She asked in a tight voice.

"I was more worried you'd hop onto land and summon me in the middle of town." He replied.

"I'm not stupid," Kat said a little annoyed.

"I know, I'm sorry. You have to give me more than two hours to get used to the idea of having friends." He said, and Kat sighed with resignation. Liam took the opportunity to drop the overloaded bag he was carrying to the ground.

"Where are we?"

"We're just outside of Shellbreak Harbor on the continent of Tramin," Kat replied easily. She flicked her raven hair back over her shoulder. The salty wind off the sea was quite strong, and Liam thought there might be a storm approaching.

"What's that?" Kat asked pointing to the bag on the ground.

"It's my stash. Thought I would bring everything with me. I highly doubt we'll be returning to the island soon." He said flexing his fingers. All the crap in the bag had weighed him down heavily for the past hour. He'd been unsure when she would use the summon stone.

"Ahh, I forgot you couldn't use a bank. You know the more you tell me, the more impressed I am you managed to survive so long." Kat said coming forward. She knelt before him opening the pack. Liam didn't mind as there wasn't much inside that would interest the fighter. It was all the arcane paraphernalia he'd happened across. It also included all his extra scrolls he intended to inscribe to grimoire when he leveled.

"Shall we start leveling then? I haven't killed anything in three days." Kat said standing up. He shook his head, the first priority was shelter.

"I need to find a place to log out, and store my gear," Liam replied knowing it would take more than an hour to find someplace safe.

"What if I go into town and rent an apartment. We're going to be here for a while." Kat suggested hopefully. The idea of sleeping in a crypt didn't appeal to her very much.

"I can't be in town," he said with exasperation.

"You don't have to be. Once I get a room I'll go inside and summon you. Then you can just set it as your home point. I can lock it so only I'm allowed to open the door." Kat suggested. Liam wouldn't be able to leave the room without being summoned, and Kat sighed at the face Liam made.

"I'm online like twenty hours a day. I'll almost always be around." She said crossing her arms over her chest defensively.

"Won't that be expensive buying so many talismans."

"I haven't had to buy any equipment thanks to you. I think I can just set up an auction bid for as many as I can get." Kat replied and Liam relented. It would be useful not having to take time out of leveling to look for a logout location. An inn also is the perfect place to store any loot they found. Liam was starting to realize the power of having friends on the inside.

"Wait here, and I'll go rent something," Kat said lifting two fingers to her lips. She blew a high whistle and waited. A blue rift of fire crackled open in the air next to the diminutive half-elf. For a few seconds, there was the sound of pounding hooves. Out of the rift a large black horse trotted. From its eyes and mouth flames of hellfire flowed out. Liam recognized the signs of a [Nightmare]. A horse by legend that lived on the planes of Hades. Kat patted its neck before slipping a foot into a stirrup. She quickly hauled herself up into the simple black saddle. Liam couldn't help it, and stepped closer to the demonic animal. Its eyes blazed with the hate of hell as it glared at him. When he tried to pet it the animal stamped a massive black hoof. Fire sprang forth where it struck the ground. Liam wisely stepped back, and Kat smiled down before scratching the horse behind the ears.

"I don't think I'll miss being a paladin, though Mr. Whitefellow was a lovely horse." She said and turned to gallop towards town.

He was left alone in the place, so he amused himself by

checking out the plot. The small graveyard was old and relatively hidden away in the forest. Liam was instantly fascinated. Everything in the world seemed to have a reason to exist. Nothing was haphazardly placed as a set piece. He knelt examining the ancient moss-covered tombstones. The dates on the stones were worn just like the ones on the island. They were obviously old but he couldn't hazard a guess to an exact date. Several undead skeletons wandered by him attracted by a noise in the forest, but they wouldn't walk far from the place of their rest. He turned his attention back to the tombstones. Some of them had inscriptions or the star-cross for the religion here. A few open pits marked where the buried had crawled free of the earth. A former settlement that was abandoned, or possibly an unused cemetery for the harbor. One stone wasn't quite like the others. It was moss covered and partially broken, but the face was blank. An open unmarked grave, how very strange. Since coming to this world, he'd taken an interest in the dead and the little stories they sometimes told. Some were funny, others tragic, still rarer were the vengeful. Here was a tiny mystery and he was intrigued.

Liam tried counting the undead monsters that inhabited the small cemetery. Thirteen, an unlucky number to most. Standing he walked along the rows of stones which numbered more than sixty. Some of the dead remained buried then. For almost ten minutes he tried to figure out who that empty grave belonged too. Finally, he noticed the torn up graves all were missing the cross on their stones. Excitedly he counted the tombstones sans symbols. Fourteen empty graves and only thirteen undead monsters. Liam turned to look at the skeletons again. Their old bones and clothes clung to their fleshless bodies. None appeared to be warriors or even equipped with weapons. Most likely common folk. Dirt and grime still hung from them like they'd recently torn free of mother earth. Moving back to the mysterious fourteenth unmarked grave he crouched.

"Where did you wander off too?" He asked the grave marker. Liam looked down into the hole were presumably the undead had broken out. A wooden box lay mostly buried. Kneeling over the hole Liam looked down. Inside the coffin there was a symbol after all. It was carved into the wood as if by fingernails alone.

"Spirit Lantern," Liam incanted casting the low-level necromancer light. It was the evil equivalent to the mage spell. A little green ball of energy formed over his hand surrounded by a cage. If one looked closely you could see a tiny face in the wisp. He moved it down into the coffin for a better look inside. The box was empty of everything save the small carved symbol. There was no scraps of cloth nor the bones of its owner, and now that the light was on it, the symbol was clearer. A crude skull was drawn. The features were minimalist at best. A half circle surrounded the top of the head with four wavy lines coming out.

"I bought a room, are you ready?" Kat said making a chat box appear. Crap he must have lost track of time. Liam knelt closer and took a few screenshots for later. He'd have to ponder the person's fate another time.

"One second, need to get my bag." He typed back quickly. Going over to the sac he lifted it with some effort. A warning popped up telling him he was overburdened. "Ok," Liam managed to type with the awkward load. Lights began to circle his body as the air hummed. There was a flash of magical power and he was transported.

It was the first time he'd been in such a nice place. The small room was cozy and warmly lit by several flickering lanterns. Much of the space was taken up by a double sized bed, and above it on the wall hung a painted picture of the harbor. The walls were a cream colored stucco and the ceiling made of dark wood planks. Liam walked to the window. A single thick pane of glass separated him from the outside. Already two or three lone beads of water were trailing down. He looked out onto a busy evening street. It was getting late and players were returning to the city to relax. Globes of mage light topped the metal lamp posts along the road. People dressed in casual wear walked about or spilled out of a nearby tavern. There was a spattering of wind and more light drops of rain came down. The storm was rolling in. Next to the window sat a dresser and storage trunk. He opened it noting the massive amount of space it contained. Gratefully he put his burden inside then closed the lid.

"So?" Kat asked when he turned back around. She was standing next to the door with her arms outstretched to encompass the room.

"It's nice," he said and meant it. A lot better than an underwater cave with crabs for company. "Please don't take this the wrong way, but are you sure it's safe?"

"Only I can let people in. While the room is rented I can set the permissions. You are already a full guest. That means you can come and go as you please." Kat said coming closer to where he stood near the window.

"How long?"

"A month was the minimum for a room. We could have rented by the night at the tavern across the street." Kat said pointing past Liam.

"No, this is perfect. It will probably take us that long to out level the monsters in the area." Liam said quickly. It was perfect.

"I'm glad," Kat said sitting down on the bed.

Liam turned to look back out of the window. The revelers were still going in and out of the tavern across the street. Two scantily clad girls were clinging to the waist of a big half-orc. Liam could hear the massive booming laugh of the male. His muscled arms were around their shoulders in merriment. A crack of thunder peeled over the harbor alerting people the storm was arriving. Moments later a wall of water began to fall on the city whipped hard about by the strong winds. Liam could feel Kat's eyes on him and he looked back.

"Thank you, for telling me." She said suddenly and he turned entirely in her direction. She was playing with the pillows on the bed before bringing one towards her. Liam thought it was too bad he lacked certain male organs now. Quickly he sat on that thought. Such ideas would lead no place useful. He was glad to have a friend, and he wouldn't hope for anything else.

"I'm sick," Kat said haltingly.

"Sick?"

"I'm in a facility…" Kat continued pulling the pillow in close. "It's a serious condition, terminal." She went on tightening her grip on the object in her arms. Her face was so sullenly sad just then Liam wished he could comfort her.

"Like a coma or something?" He asked

"Quite a bit worse. I don't want to bore you with the details." She said flicking her eyes to his. Blood red pupils flashed like bright rubies in the flickering lamplight, and Liam could see the hurt inside.

"I'm sorry," He said feeling for the woman.

"Don't be, I'm free now. That's why I'm online quite a lot." Kat said tossing the pillow back in place. Kat jumped to her feet and poked him in the breastbone with a slender finger. Her red eyes bore into him with fierce challenge. "Since you opened up to me, I wanted you to know. Don't go getting sappy on me though. I would hate that." She said and he inclined his head towards her.

"The pity I shall keep, but the friendship you can have." He said in his slow deep voice. Kat smiled at him before reaching up to touch his bony face. It wasn't a romantic touch. More like she was examining his teeth and jawline.

"I suppose you have work in the morning." She asked making it sound more like a statement. He noticed her fingers were cool now, no longer filled with life.

"Yes, but it's Friday. I'll have the weekend off afterward." Liam said.

"Good, I'll start out leveling you otherwise," Kat replied more brightly. That wasn't much of a problem to have really.

"I think I'm going to enjoy conquering this world," Liam said just before lightning flashed overhead, and deafening thunder rolled over the city.

CHAPTER ELEVEN

Kat - Weapon Upgrade

KittKat - Level 18
Tramin Continent - Shellbreak Harbor - The Apartment

It was probably a good thing Kat couldn't do any leveling during the day. The massive debuff's she received from sunlight made doing so suicidal. She tried to tell herself this but she was so bored. It was getting late and Liam wasn't home yet from work. If she left, then died out there Liam would be stuck in the room unable to leave. At worst he'd get cut down the second he left the apartment. Kat had just earned what she considered a good friend. She wouldn't do anything to endanger that. She glanced at him on his side of the bed. As soon as he'd logged off the green flames in his eyes had winked out. For the stillness in his body, the man looked exactly like a dead skeleton. One that wore a blackened spell casters clothes. Not for the first time she'd wanted to check under those robes, because Kat was morbidly curious if he'd been lying to her. Did he have a body under there? She shook her head, that was so weird to even think about.

Oh bloody hell she was bored. Sitting here waiting was slowly killing her. Kat could log off for an hour and check some websites. She'd been meaning to advertise the guild but had forgotten to post last night. Having more members would be nice. Possibly enough to fill out an entire group. Standing she walked over to the window and looked out. The sun was almost down, and the sky was changing colors. With the storm last night the clouds still hanging above were a light purple. They would darken further as the sun sank over the edge of the world. The night would begin soon. At least the game was headed into mid-fall with the promise of a long winter. The days would grow shorter and the nights longer. More time to hunt, more chances to level.

Thoughts of hunting reminded her of feeding. She hadn't yet today, and that was something she could do by herself. Turning she walked around the bed and left the room. Kat's leather boots made clomping sounds as she descended the stairs. A group of players were attempting to haggle with the landlord over his prices.

The old bearded sea dog shook his head several times and drawled, "Price is a hundred gold a month for a single, one fifty for a double sized, and five hundred for a top floor suite."

"That's preposterous, I have sixty gold total from all the leveling I did on the island." A human archer said thumping a fist on the counter. The man had leathers on and a longbow strung over his back. The non-player character didn't respond. The algorithms weren't very smart, Kat knew they often listened for key words.

"Give us a discount, we're new." One of the group pleaded.

"No discounts. You want cheap, go to the tavern. They rent by the night." The landlord said gruffly. Kat felt for the players a little. Even after helping Liam out the apartment had cut her coin purse hard. She could have barely afforded the suite, but that would have wiped her out. Being a spend thrift she'd opted for the double. The three adventurers continued to shout expletives at the NPC before leaving, and she followed them out. The group was already walking across the street toward the tavern. As the door opened music and laughter spilled into the street. Most people tended to hunt during the day, and party the night away. Leveling at night could be exceedingly dangerous for humans who lacked even low light vision.

She turned away and walked further down the street. What

Kat needed was blood, tasty sweet blood. A player was probably the best choice. She could just ask them directly for a nibble. That's what she'd done after waking up a vampire, but the jerk had played grab-ass with her as she fed on him. Kat wasn't in the mood for getting manhandled tonight, so an NPC was going to have to do. Looking west she saw the sun was half over the horizon. Her debuff was starting to diminish as the light faded. Casually she walked down the street towards the docks. There were plenty of workers and fewer guards hanging around the water. Most of the patrols were concentrated on the gates and inner city. It took her a few minutes of wandering to find the right target. Finally, she picked a young looking man that was moving in and out of a warehouse. Her excitement grew just a little as she watched him. Biting someone wasn't a combat initiating action, though it could be used in battle if you immobilized a target. The danger was if a guard or other NPC saw you. Then you'd better run like hell.

She slid into place about ten feet behind the dockworker. The twenty-year-old hefted a canvas sack of something to his shoulder. Probably grain for brewing the beer everyone drank so much of. The shadows crossed over his body as he walked inside the darkened warehouse, and Kat slowly followed making sure to walk with a light step. Stopping in the door she saw he was moving towards a pile of similar sacks. Her fangs began to grow. They lengthened as if being drawn slowly from the sheaths in her gums. In the dimness of the warehouse, her dark vision took over. She stepped towards the man as he bent. The bag made a dull thumping sound as it landed with the others. As he straightened Kat's arms wrapped around his in a hug. Quickly her lips closed over his pulsing neck, and she relished the moment her needle sharp fangs broke the skin. The man grunted in pain but was paralyzed by the poison she injected into his bloodstream. A second later sweet blood was filling her mouth and she drank. Kat's belly grew hot like she'd downed shots of vodka. Next, her skin started to tingle pleasantly as she gulped. It didn't last long, twenty seconds was enough, and she withdrew her fangs feeling a sensual guilty pleasure in the taking of his essence.

The dockworker slumped as she started to let go of him. Carefully she guided him down, settling the young man against the pile of grain sacks. His eyes were half closed as if drowsing and she patted his smooth skinned face. Standing Kat ran a finger over her lips. It came away mostly clean, and Kat was satisfied she hadn't made a mess of her lipstick. A message appeared in her periphery.

Liam has logged online

"Kat?" He asked in guild chat.

"I'm here." She responded immediately.

"Where?"

"In town, I needed to step out for a bite." She sent and was reminded of the boy. His head was lulling, but he seemed to be regaining his senses slowly. Kat turned and walked from the building.

"Ahh, yes vampire. I forgot about that."

"It's going to be annoying to match our leveling with the sun."

"You could always hang out nearby for the experience," Liam suggested. Kat turned the street corner and walked back up the main drive.

"Efficient but boring watching you have all the fun." She sent before opening the door to the apartments. The sea dog was behind his desk reading or pretending to read a faded old book. He didn't look up as Kat ascended the stairs to the second floor. Their apartment was near the end of the hall. She opened the door to find Liam looking out of the window again. He seemed to like people watching. At her entry, he turned those glowing green eyes on her. She closed the door and walked over to the necromancer.

"Sorry it took me so long getting home. I had to stay late because an inventory bug crept into the system." He said in the usual rock slide of a voice.

"What do you do?" She asked curious of his real life.

"Officially I'm inventory management. It's my job to buy all the materials for the factory. In reality I am more like a jack of all trades there. I end up on crews when their short-handed, and cleaning factory floors when time permits. Sometimes I'm the runner when we absolutely must get something." Liam's tone belied an unhappiness with the work. He'd already told her about the co-workers that had tricked him. Humiliating him for their juvenile enjoyment. And here they were in the twenty-second century.

"Sounds like you're all over the place. Your boss must like you." She said

"It's job security and I get bored sitting at my desk." He admitted coming away from the window. His skeletal hand rose, reaching for her face. Hard finger bones clasped her jaw. His thumb wiped at something next to her lip. It came away red.

"You had some left," He said in that deep rocky voice. Kat found the gesture oddly romantic.

"Thanks," She said turning towards the mirror on the desk. Nothing else appeared to be on her face. Kat would have to remember to buy a pocket mirror next time she was in the market.

"Shall we go?"

"Yes. Have you found anything out about the area?" He asked in return.

"I went into the tavern a couple of hours ago. A party was planning a group dungeon, and they had a map, so I asked them about it. The wizard said he drew it with his scribe skill." Kat said digging through her rabbit purse. The inventory screen came up and she withdrew the parchment.

"He graciously offered to make a copy," Kat said unfurling the map. She was quite sure it wasn't altruism that had driven the wizard to make the offer. The Tramin Continent took up most of the page. Only a note on the corner provided the direction to Aethon Island.

"We're here on the southeastern coast of the continent. The elves have a small port on the western side, with a dwarven colony further north. There's a city in the valley between the three ports that brings everyone together. I'm told it's quite impressive. Supposedly a massive dragon crashed into the ground there making the valley." She said trying to recall everything the wizard had told her. Around Shellbreak Harbor the landmarks were well annotated. The further out from the city the more empty space lay over the page.

"You didn't happen to ask where to find the cemeteries?"

"I thought it best not too." She said and glanced to Liam. He was holding his chin and tapping at one of his tusks.

"It's a shame I don't have the scribe skill." He said after a few seconds. "Let's start there." Liam suggested tapping the spot again then drew a line to an orc camp nearby.

Kat started towards the door, and Liam followed her to the exit before she stopped him with a look. Kat turned and looked at Liam for a long silent second. Liam caught her meaning. He was still hated outside the room, and Kat smiled when he smacked himself in the face with a flat palm.

"Wait for me, I won't be long." She said and slipped out into the night. As she came out the sea air felt pleasantly cool on her skin. Lamps were already trying to banish the encroaching darkness. The street was clear of people or players just then. A few minutes of walking and she was at the town gate. She had to travel a short ways from the guard station to summon the nightmare. While she could walk the streets her horse stirred up the NPC's into a tissy. Kat stuck her fingers between pouting lips and whistled a loud, long note. Moments later blue fire split the air and the sound of hoofs reached her ears. A black head cleared the rift and she smiled again. He was a sexy creature alright. When the [Nightmare] was fully out he gave a consternated nicker at the cold weather. A foot stomped onto the ground in agitation. Reaching up she pet his smoldering neck scratching him with her long fingernails.

"You should have a name," She said looking him in the eye, and the horse seemed expectant.

"Firefoot," she said noticing the scorched grass under his hoofs. The male whinnied again flicking its dark black mane around wildly.

"You like that?" She asked and he whinnied again. He reared up on two feet and came down on the ground blasting Kat with embers of burned vegetation. She supposed that was a yes. Climbing into the saddle, she rode west hoping she would find the clearing again. Liam wanted to start at the graveyard but Kat had basically stumbled upon it. All she'd done yesterday was look for a quiet place away from town. The road turned north but she plunged into the light forest. Even though the night was her home now the landscape looked alien in her dark vision. It took her almost half an hour to locate the place in the dark.

Dismounting she glanced around checking for danger. A few undead were wandering like before. Pulling another party talisman from her inventory she glanced at the design. It was a small stone circle of abstract human shapes holding hands. Raising it above her head she threw the item to the ground, and it shattered releasing a yellow light. Each little person in the ring started to float into the air. An audible hum of magic started next as the figures circled in space. A flash blotted out her dark vision and she turned her head blinking. When she looked back Liam was standing in the spot.

"Where exactly is this graveyard by the way?" He asked.

"Umm, about two miles west of town." She said and Liam took out the map she'd shown him earlier. His green eyes lit up the parchment as he fixed the place in his mind. It must have been how he managed to get around on the previous island. The land masses were not exactly small.

"Before we start, what are your skills?" Kat asked curious about his character.

"[Paralyzing Grasp] which I used a lot when I was low level. Now I try not to get into melee range. [Control Undead], and [Raise Undead] are my primary spells. With both, I can only manage up to my level. When I hit level ten I received [Chill

Aura] which made creatures feel fear." He said.

"Is that what that was?" Kat asked remembering the way she would freeze up when he came close.

"Yes."

"I don't feel anything now," She said standing just a foot away.

"It doesn't effect us. Only the living can feel the cold claw of death." He said then waved at himself. "At twenty it was upgraded to [Deathly Aura] which projects a negative energy field. The living near me take damage and the undead are passively healed.

"Awesome, you're like a walking heal spell for me," Kat said and Liam chuckled.

"Most of my necromancer spells are dots, roots, or slows. I have a couple of wizard spells outside my school of magic. I'm only allowed a limited number, and their never quite as good."

Yes, Kat remembered he'd asked to get scrolls for his spellbook. "I heard wizards could branch out and be more generalized," Kat admitted.

"They can though specialists have better effects and lower mana cost," Liam said reaching into his robes. He extracted a rather hefty tome.

"That's the book from the lich's room?" Kat asked in astonishment.

"The very same," He replied opening the large grimoire. It was covered with blackened leather and cast with brass fittings.

"What about you Kat?" Liam asked as he paged through the book for a bit. Kat turned and scratched at Firefoot's neck.

"Blackguard is just the opposite of a paladin. Instead of 'Lay Hands' I can [Harm Touch] once a day. [Unholy Smite] and my nightmare horse work the same. The class comes with a fear aura as well. I have some evil cleric spells but not many, and my mana is pretty pathetic still."

"I suppose finding a cleric willing to turn vampire might be tough." Liam mused quietly.

"Well, you're the equivalent." Kat reminded him.

"True, but I think evil clerics might be able to project negative energy better," Liam said in a considering tone. He closed the book then slid the ponderous tome into the folds of his robe.

"Anyway, most of my cleric spells are debuffs. Blackguard appears to be all about demoralizing the enemy." Kat said absently. It was a cool class but left her heals underpowered, and most of them involved taking the enemies life force. Turning to her horse she stroked the neck once more.

"Go home," She whispered to Firefoot who dutifully fled back into his fiery rift. Kat wasn't about to ride while her party member walked.

They located the Orc camp after about twenty minutes. A wooden palisade surrounded the settlement on a high hill, and in the night, the orcish bonfires blazed almost hurting her eyes. Kat could see a couple of guards posted on towers and near the gate. Most though seemed to be inside their animal hide tents. Kat knelt in the grass near Liam. He'd brought along three undead all level twenty.

"Normally I'd dismiss these three and go back for another group." He said eying the fortifications above them.

"You still could."

"I'm tempted, just to have a couple in reserve. With how many orcs I see up there we might be here a while." Liam said considering the odds. Kat was used to just grabbing a group and charging out. Liam apparently spent a lot of his time setting up. Almost an hour had already passed since the sun went down. If he went back that would take another hour or more.

"Do you see any other way inside the camp?" He asked turning to Kat.

"It's fully fenced off, and the front entrance is the only way in." She said pointing to the four guard towers. The circular camp had one roughly equal distant from each other, so at least two of the archers would be able to shoot at them if they pulled the gate guards. In the darkness their accuracy would be pathetic.

"Let's just pull the guards down here. That will probably rouse the camp but they won't know where to follow."

Kat with Liam just behind walked about halfway up the hill. She drew her sword and shield which made her costume disappear. Liam admired the way her armor and costume swapped spaces. A costume couldn't be on during combat. Kat lifted her sword touching the blade with her other hand. "Vampiric Edge," she intoned casting one of her better Blackguard spells. A portion of the damage she caused would automatically give her temporary hitpoints. Liam used his bone staff to point at the ground about ten feet before them. His right hand moved at the same time gripping the air three times. Suddenly a field of [Grasping Hands] began to punch up out of the grass. He then pointed with two fingers at the distant orc guards. Again he said nothing yet his hand started to glow green with fire. A second later a burst of energy shot from him striking the right orc in the arm. It staggered the warrior slightly before both roared a warning. Orcs had lowlight vision, so they knew where the magic had come from. Kat took a place before Liam and lifted her shield up. Seconds later arrows started to come down in their proximity. The two guards were running down the hill with weapons in hand. An arrow hit her shield bouncing off.

When the guard was about twenty feet away, Kat pointed her sword at the unwounded orc. "Affliction," she muttered making a stream of yellow icor shoot up the hill. The bolt of weakness gave the creature negatives to strength and agility. Just ten feet more and both warriors plunged into the area of grasping hands. Their legs and ankles were snagged stopping both in their tracks.

"Attack him," Liam ordered and three undead swarmed a guard.

Kat held her sword above her head. She waited for her [Charge Leap] skill to activate. Just as her fingers start to tingle, Kat jumped crossing the ten-foot space and bringing her sword down across his massive chest. As she landed the hands grabbed her ankles as well. He was a tall warrior. The massive orc was eight feet at least and probably outweighed her by four times. Its name was also bright orange which indicated several levels of difference. The green giant slammed down a dark wooden club on her shoulder, which Kat was too slow to block. A frighteningly impressive chunk of health was immediately lost.

"Disease Cloud," Liam said and a mist of yellowish fog rolled past her. Kat was immune to diseases, but the orcs broke out in boils. "Lethargy," He cast next slowing the orcs attack speed. Next, he pointed to his target with two fingers held together. A green bolt of [Negative Energy] slammed into the orc twice in quick succession. Kat shook herself back into the fight. She'd never seen a necromancer fight before. Most of his spells were pain and disease DOTs. Kat focused again on the orc before her. Kat parried an attack then slashed at the orc's extended arm before raising her shield.

"Hold won't last much longer," Liam advised in a thick voice. Seconds later the Orc Guard managed to kick itself free of the bony hands grabbing his legs. Kat waited for the orc to attack, and held her shield at the ready. It attacked, and Kat used her [Shield Bash] skill against the orc's weapon. The wood club clanged off her shield and the creature staggered back. She slashed twice with her blade across each leg. The blood flowed up her weapon sinking into her arm and making her hit points tick back up.

"Pain Spike," Liam said gesturing towards the first orc. A crackling black energy bolt struck the mob in the chest. Dark electricity danced over its skin as the creature fought back. Out of the corner of her eye, Kat noticed the three undead pets were dominating. Liam's biggest challenge seemed to be keeping his minions between himself and the enemy. Another blow landed on her shield absorbing most of the damage. She struck back healing herself with the orc's life force. A lucky arrow hit her in the forearm and she winced. The sudden sharp pain had felt like someone jabbing her with a needle. The first orc died, and the three undead came to her rescue, flanking her enemy. He let out a bestial roar of defiance. It grabbed it's huge club in both hands raising it overhead. It activated a skill making a visible arc in the night. Kat brought her blade in toward her body. She aimed it at the orc's chest praying her ability activated first. Her sword tip flashed, and she lunged forward with a [Piercing Thrust]. Kat buried her sword into the orc's chest. Eyes widening it took a step away then toppled backward.

"It's a shame I can't raise these. They're just a smidgen higher level." Liam said next to her.

"Sorry, I took so much damage," Kat said lifting her arm. The arrow was still sticking out of it making her flesh tingle. She grabbed the pointed end, and yanked, dragging the shaft all the way through her flesh. Black blood dripped from the missile in fat sticky blobs. She dropped it even as her wound started to heal. Her vampire regeneration and Liam's aura was making the recovery supernaturally fast.

"I thought that went well. The question is what to do about the archers still shooting at us. The camp too, has arisen." Liam said pointing to the enclosure. The monstrous green brutes were madly rushing about searching for danger.

"Could you just hit them with a couple of spells? If they're stupid enough to stay up there then they deserve it." Kat suggested turning to look at the necromancer. In her discolored vision, his eyes glowed like miniature suns.

"I'd have to get closer. Even hitting him with my energy bolt from here would be tough."

She had a bow too but she'd barely used it. The thing was underpowered, and she suspected trying to out snipe those orcs wasn't going to happen. "Let me go up and grab the rest that wants to play," Liam said cheerfully gesturing for her to wait. He jogged up the hill before pausing to cast a field of grasping hands along with a large patch of blackthorns. The archers were still blindly firing in their direction. Near the open gate, Kat saw a green bolt shoot out. The large necromancer turned and ran down the hill. He circled wide around the traps and past her, so Kat followed in his wake. Nine orcs appeared at the camp entrance bellowing with rage. One exceptionally large one was in the back of the group. Together they all charged down the hill.

"Don't engage them just yet. Let's see what they do." Liam said to her right. Kat had to remember the orcs couldn't see as well. The orc army blundered straight into Liam's spells. The first three orcs to hit the root field were stuck fast, and six others poured around them. They slowed trying to work through the black thorns. Three others though were smart enough to run around the brambles.

"Perfect," Liam said and turned to the three undead minions. "Go passive," He ordered before pointing his staff at the remaining three orcs. His hand once again moved in a quick three positions. Spreading forth from his extended palm a wave of mist blanketed the area before them.

"Let's move back a ways." He said and Kat followed as they ran. The big bastard of an orc was still chasing after them with his two pals. For a good five minutes, Kat sprinted through the forest. When it looked like the orcs were losing interest Liam would blast them with [Disease Cloud]. Finally, Kat stopped between a group of trees with Liam and his pets. She caught sight of the orc as he came towards them in the darkness. His name was [Chief Cracktooth]. The letters a blazing angry red declaring him at least five levels higher. Kat pointed to boss as he neared. "Affliction," She intoned shooting a yellowish blob towards the orc. Then the three attackers rushed into their party.

Cracktooth slammed into her shield trying to reach Liam. Desperately Kat slashed at his legs and thighs. It was a hectic fight for the first ten seconds. The two lesser orcs tried to squeeze past her but encountered Liam's pets. She stood in the middle blocking the Chief.

"Now is as good a time as any to use my abilities," Kat thought to herself.

"Unholy Smite," Kat shouted bringing her blade down across a huge green thigh. A black and red flame shot between them into the orc. He bellowed in pain from the ferocious damage. He switched targets using a black battle-axe to swing back at her. The weapon was glowing, some kind of fast activating skill. She dodged the first blow instinctively. Kat had no intention of soaking the damage on her shield. The big blade sang through the air missing her and wedging halfway into a tree next to them.

"Lethargy," Liam said from behind her. The orc grunted struggling to pull his axe from the tree. The undead were fighting the two adds. At least they seemed to hold their own against the sentries. Kat struck again and again at the chief trying to cut him down to size. She returned two blows for everyone the chieftain managed to land on her. His weapon though was doing considerably more damage, but at least her [Vampiric Edge] was still giving her some life back. There was a continuous flow of blood up her weapon and into her arm. Her health though was still dropping fast. Something the color of putrid pea soup struck her in the back which felt strangely incredible. For a second she paused from the sensual pleasure that ran up her spine. Unholy gods that felt good, like orgasmic. Her health shot up from halfway to nearly full.

The chief bellowed and brought his axe down in an overhand swing. Kat used the exaggerated move to start a shield bash. His axe hit her shield taking a huge chunk of life from her. The massive orc staggered back a step from the impact. This was her chance. She stepped forward holding her sword sideways. Kat punched the orc in the stomach and yelled, "Harm Touch." Wounds opened up about the orc and his eyes went wild, and he thrashed about before sagging. Even when the orc fell to his knees, the bastard was still taller than her. Kat jammed her sword up into the orc's throat cutting it open. Cracktooth toppled over in a bloody mass of dead flesh. She passed him to help finish off the two remaining sentries. They were so focused on the undead she freely hacked at their sides and backs.

"Nice," Liam said after the last orc was gone. Kat stood from the bloody body of the final sentry feeling so alive. She jumped up and down whooping. That had been exhilarating, and quite possibly one of the best fights she'd had.

"Lost one of the pets, but you should check out the axe the chief dropped," Liam said from behind her. She turned with fierce eyes grinning at her friend. He couldn't smile but she thought his posture looked pleased. That was a totally new way to fight for her. Walking over she bent and touched the orc chief's body. An axe was there along with a clan totem and some coin. Picking up the weapon she inspected it.

[Cracktooth's Obsidian Axe] - One Handed Battleaxe

This jet black axe has long been a symbol of the chief's dominating power over his tribe. It is unclear whether it has spilled more orcish blood than human. Because of this, the weapon will do extra bleed damage to both types of enemies. The long curved blade is shaped obsidian stone. Tales say the femur for the bone handle belonged to Cracktooth's father, the former chief.

Kat equipped it and instantly fell in love with the curve bladed battle-axe. It was most definitely an improvement over the longsword.

"Ready for more?"

"Oh hell yes," Kat replied testing the heft of her new weapon.

CHAPTER TWELVE

Liam - Work

Liam
California
Wednesday, 04:48 am

As the digit within the clock rolled over a small signal was detected, then rerouted. Milliseconds later the alarm began to blare loudly filling the room with a deafening noise. Liam's eyes belatedly cracked open, reluctant to let go of sleep. He licked his lips with a thick, clumsy tongue. Not enough rest, not by a large margin. A hand shot out from under the covers to clasp the square clock, and he managed to get the noise to turn off. For a moment he considered just rolling over and going back to bed. Liam's sense of responsibility wouldn't let him though. One foot left the blanket then the leg as he struggled out of bed with a moan. He stumbled into the bathroom and turned on the water. He first splashed his face with the cold liquid before reaching for his toothbrush. After his morning absolutions, he walked out into the garage.

Closing the rusted door to his car he stuck the key in the ignition. Instead of a chronic cough and whine, all he heard was a soft ticking sound. He tried pumping the accelerator before turning the key again, but there wasn't even a ticking reply.

"Well crap," He thought sourly. Reaching down he pulled the hood latch. He slid from the driver seat and popped open the hood. His alternator cable was completely missing. It must have finally slipped off while coming home yesterday. Liam was already running out of time and he didn't have another belt. He slammed the hood down in annoyance.

"Just great," he thought to himself. He'd have to drive his baby to work.

Fetching the key to the streetcar it quickly started with a loud roar. Gas guzzling sports cars like this were growing rare, if only because gasoline was such an expensive commodity. The garage door opened at the touch of the button and the sports car backed out into the early morning dawn. The roads were empty which let him goose the engine more than usual. The bass music thumped loudly further helping to dispel any exhaustion. As he expected the modified streetcar turned a lot of heads as he parked it. The music shut off as he got out.

He clocked in and went to his desk to start work. His first order of business was to check any overnight emails. There were a few orders for parts from overseas. It wasn't hard to pass the information to the factory floor computers. Liam got up and went into the break room to fetch a cup of coffee. A few hours passed like this with frequent trips for caffeine alertness. Finally, lunch rolled around. He hadn't brought food, so he spent his time looking over Nigmus Forums. Slowly the game was creeping into his blood, and he couldn't get away from it even when logged out.

A heavy form sat down in the chair next to his desk. Seconds later Liam smelled the Old Spice and shit coming his way. He didn't bother looking to see who it was.

"Hey Jelly," a voice said.

"What do you want, Cole?" Liam asked in a bored and weary voice. He'd not forgotten the prank.

"I heard you rolled in with a sweet machine. Who did you have to blow?" Cole asked in a friendly if slightly challenging tone. The asshole, seriously? Liam knew the man made like three times what he did.

"That is my project vehicle. My usual car is down." Liam said casually.

"Give me the keys. I'd like to take it for a test drive." Cole replied. Just like that, not even asking for permission. He just assumed it would happen.

"Hmmm, how about no," Liam said turning to look at the man. Cole was wearing a wife beater with open arms, and he had to be cold with the current temperature.

"Excuse me," Cole said in disbelief.

"In case you misheard me, hell no," Liam replied a little surprised by himself. Maybe this was the effect of playing his character for the last month. Telling so many people to bugger off.

"Why not?" The man asked anger now dripping into his tone.

"Because you totaled your last two cars. Remember that old v8 corvette you were so proud of. No way am I letting you behind the wheel of my classic." Liam said easily. While he spoke the other man's face was turning a shade of red in anger. As he recalled Cole had gotten drunk and plowed into a federal mailbox. He'd destroyed government property and a hundred-year-old muscle car.

"Fuck you, Jellyroll." He barked standing. The chair fell over behind him as the man stormed away.

"It's Liam," Liam muttered after the man. He knew Nigmus was changing him. A month ago he'd have quietly handed over the keys to his baby. All the while praying it came back semi-intact. Cole would treat it like it wasn't his of course. With a sigh, he turned back to his Internet sleuthing.

He suspected some form of retribution would be short in coming. The bully would never let a slight pass him, but nothing appeared to torment Liam for the rest of the day. This was almost as surprising as his ability to stand up to Cole. When the last whistle blew he was ready to head home. He could get in another short nap before the sun went down. Pulling on a light coat he wandered out to the parking lot. At first he didn't see Cole when he walked out of the building, but several people looked away from him as he passed by. His shit-storm senses were starting to edge into full red mode as a small crowd dispersed from the vicinity of his car.

"Well double crapper," he thought to himself. What had that

bastard done? He walked quickly over as people made way. Lines of jagged peeling scratches had been dug deeply into his car. Some were just long streaks across the sides. Lots of badly scrawled words like 'Fatty' and 'Jelly' were written on his hood. The car security system hadn't gone off. Liam had personally reduced its sensitivity annoyed by the alarm, so it would only go off when a window was smashed or the door was opened without the key. There was only one culprit that came to mind. Cole had done it, of course. The bastard had restrained himself from smashing any windows. Finally, Liam saw the man leaning against a vehicle some fifty feet away, a shit-eating grin on his face. Liam stormed over.

"You self-centered little prick," Liam started jabbing the man in the chest. Cole slapped his hand away still smiling.

"Nice paint job, I think it suits you," Cole said grinning. Liam wanted to sock Cole's smiling face. Unlike Nigmus he couldn't attack the bastard.

"Fatty should get into his car and go away," Doug said from nearby. His friends were moving to back Cole up, and the extra eyes meant more witnesses. Liam was suddenly reminded of why he parked his car in that spot. He smiled back at them and turned from the group, then quickly walked into the building. They probably thought Liam was going to complain to the boss, which was true, he would. Cole was still there twenty minutes later when Liam came back out. He approached the group lounging by their cars.

"You should have just let me borrow the keys," Cole said with a belittling smirk.

"Stupid fuck, you forgot about the surveillance cameras," Liam responded holding up a blank check. Finally that smile on Cole's face slipped. It hadn't taken long to save the file to a thumb drive. A short discussion with the boss had followed. He could either cut Liam a check or the cops would get called. Baby Cole would be spending some time in jail for wanton vandalism.

"I think daddy wants to see you," Liam continued in a high singsong voice and got into his car. He was still furious at the man, but it was the company that paid for it. The engine roared to life and he rolled the window down. As Liam cruised slowly by he gave them each the finger.

Liam drove to the auto parts store and bought an alternator cable. Next, he drove his keyed streetcar to a paint shop. The small crew was just as angry as he about the damage to such a classic vehicle. Liam opted for the most expensive repaint available. Some kind of heat changing color scheme that altered depending on the sun and weather. He grinned sliding the check across the table. The darkly tanned Mexican man named Donovan promised it would be done in two weeks. One of the boys drove him home in a courtesy car, and it was dark by the time he walked into his front door. There was no way he was going to get a nap now. Tomorrow he'd deliver a copy of the order form to the boss.

***

Liam - Level 23
Shellbreak Harbor - Apartment

"You're joking?" Kat said when he told her.
"Sadly I'm not."
"That asshole. Just because you wouldn't let him drive your car." She said still in astonishment.
"Probably," Liam said though he knew it was simpler than that. Liam had said no at all to the man, so Cole needed to punish his punching bag or he might lose his favorite toy.
"Tomorrow you should key all their cars," Kat replied adding in the three friends. Liam chuckled at the idea. It might make him feel better but would generate more enemies.
"The stupid man looked so proud of himself until I waved the check in his face," Liam admitted a little smugly. "Daddy wasn't happy either. I'm guessing it's going to come out of Cole's pay.

Anyway, there's another reason I logged in." He said feeling a little sorry.

"Oh?" Kat asked glancing at him.

"I have to beg off tonight. We've been grouping most of the night for a week straight. I'm sorry, but I need to catch up on some sleep." He said hoping she wouldn't be mad. Together they'd managed to get her up to twenty-two.

"That's fair. I knew it would be tough only being able to level at night." Kathrine said from near the window.

"I'm sorry, Kat."

"It's OK. I can try something else for tonight." Kat said easily.

"Are you going to solo?" He asked worried he might get stuck in the apartment.

"No, I will go over to the starter island and meet some guild members. We've got three or four low-level vamps that I wanted to personally welcome. I can help them level a little. They keep asking me if you're the necromancer." She said smiling at Liam. "You could be more active in guild chat." Kat remonstrated him. As a co-leader, he should be a little more friendly. Mostly he didn't say anything because they'd start asking him questions.

"Just tell them I like to be mysterious," Liam said wiggling his fingers.

"You still haven't posted the info on the class?" Kat asked.

"Something tells me to keep it a secret, but maybe I'm selfish. After seeing how powerful and disruptive necromancers can be I don't want to see more running around. Plus I'm not totally one hundred percent sure how it happened." Liam admitted.

"All you did was touch the book as a commoner after the lich was dead," Kat replied.

"You have to be near death as well but I'm not certain," Liam added and climbed onto the bed. He waved a hand lazily towards the petite vampire.

"Tell the boys I hope we can all group soon." He said and activated the menu to log out.

"Sleep is for the weak," Kat said sticking her tongue out. She'd have to spend two hours on the boat to reach Aethon Island.

CHAPTER THIRTEEN

PVP Combat

"He who fights with monsters should be careful lest he thereby become a monster. And if thou gaze long into an abyss, the abyss will also gaze into thee."
— Friedrich Nietzsche

Falken - Level 25
Tramin - Shellbreak Harbor - Kraken's Breath Tavern
8pm

"I'm telling you it was that fucked up looking necromancer." A man shouted loudly from a nearby table.

"Please, it was already dark," the returning voice drolled skeptically. Falken perked up hearing the word necromancer. The paladin was sitting with his dungeon group he'd been with that day. It was a frequent event to spend an hour or two in the tavern after leveling. Setting down the mug he looked over the head of the group cleric.

"Seriously! The bastard, he looked right at me as he went by. I swear he was smiling." The man continued to bellow.

"How can he smile without lips?" Someone at the table asked.

"It was his eyes, I tell you, they did all the smiling for him. He ran by with a full caboose train after him. Thirty bandits were chasing him right through our camp." The large warrior continued. Falken got up from the table and walked over with his mug. He sat down amid the group who turned at his sudden entry.

"Hello," he said looking to the powerful warrior. "I'm interested in hearing about the necromancer."

"See, the man knows what I'm talking about. He's a menace, a terror, and a smelly undead." The warrior said pointing to the paladin.

"When was this?" Falken asked.

"Tonight, ruined our camp so we hoofed it back home." The chain wearing warrior said still loud as an explosion.

"Exactly how long ago and where were you?" The Paladin asked again pointedly.

"I dunno, two or three hours ago." The man replied suddenly cautious. Falken opened his inventory and dropped some gold on the table. The little purse made a clinking sound as it hit.

"Twenty gold for exact info," Falken said and the other man glanced at the purse. It wasn't a fortune but the gold was several days effort at least.

"Up by the old mansion and the bandit castle. You know the one I'm talking about?" The man said and Falken pulled out a scroll. The guild had a good scribe which gave everyone access to the best maps.

"This one?" He asked and the man eyed the map enviously. He tapped a spot about twenty miles to the northwest. After a few seconds, the warrior nodded. Falken rolled the scroll up and left the table. The other man quickly snatched the purse and called for a round of drinks. Folken sat down with his group.

"We have a mission from the boss," Falken said quickly.

"I'm not with those PK bastards." Remus, the cleric, said darkly. Falken secretly agreed with him.

"We're going after the necromancer. I have it on word that he's a free target." Falken said glancing around the table. He hadn't liked the way the guild was going either but this was an opportunity.

"Sorry man, I got work." The cleric said draining the last of his mug.

"How about you four?" Falken asked the rest of the group. They nodded to him and stood. Five melee fighters against one spell caster. This would be a piece of cake. He'd done his research on the undead mage in preparation.

"Head over and get your mounts. I need to stop by the bank to collect some sun stones."

The cleric looked a little sad as he begged out. "Duty calls," He said turning towards the stairs to the second floor. The guild maintained a few rooms for members.

Falken walked out of the tavern with his party. He headed towards the market square bank. Inside a few tellers were sleepily manning the counter. He withdrew a dozen stones for the upcoming battle, and put them in his belt pouch then headed towards the stables. Four fighters were already mounted and ready. Sticking gauntleted fingers into his mouth Falken blew a whistle. A few seconds later a white war stallion appeared amid a flurry of lightning flashes. He quickly climbed into the saddle and turned to the men.

"Tonight we kill a necromancer. I've gotten word he's up by the old mansion and bandit camp. That was two hours ago, so let us not waste any more time." He said equipping a torch to his shield slot. They would need the light in the darkness. Garth and Umber were both half-elves with low-light vision but that didn't help the others.

"Let's kill this scourge!" Garth shouted pulling a sword free. He pointed it towards the road and the party charged. Outside their circle of torchlight, the darkness was all pervasive. This was why most people stayed inside or raided dungeons after dark. It was easy to get turned around. By horse, the manor was about forty minutes away. For the first ten minutes everyone had galloped hard to the crossroads. There they turned west and slowed to a trot.

"Orenthal asked you to do this?" Someone asked. Falken thought it was Umber leading the group from the front. With his eyes, he didn't dare look at the torch light.

"Yes, a personal request," Falken admitted and the other voice was silent.

"I don't like that dick," Umber finally said.

"I prefer you lot," Falken admitted and there were grunts of agreement. With such a large guild there was bound to be people that clashed. Folken was just glad he'd found some like-minded companions.

"We better not get red rings for this," Garth said after another minute of riding.

"Nope, I heard you can kill undead players," Falken replied quickly. He'd read up on that fact wanting to double check the rules. Now he just worried they'd miss the little creep. That doubt was remedied after another twenty minutes of riding. They found the first bandit corpse on the overgrown road.

"NPC bodies disappear after an hour, right?" Falken asked the group. Everyone nodded in unison. Player bodies expired after twenty-four hours. This was good. It meant the caster was still pulling monsters, or at least he had been recently.

There were a few more bodies along the way before the old decrepit manor came into few. Falken stopped his horse and slid from the saddle. Quickly he motioned for everyone to dismount, they'd make less noise. A smattering of bandit corpses lay around the front door. It looked like a slaughter had taken place. At least a dozen were piled up on one side. In the torchlight, everyone checked their gear. Falken made sure he had the sun stones in his belt pouch. Then he dropped the torch to the ground and it died quickly. The others discarded theirs as well. It took a minute for his eyes to adjust to the dim starlight. Everyone was an even gray against the darker black.

"I'll go first," Garth said moving away from the group. The three humans followed with Umber taking up the rear. The door to the mansion opened into a dark foyer. Shapes of more corpses lay scattered around. Old decay clashed with the smell of fresh blood. They crept through the darkness going deeper into the main foyer. As they moved the door about twenty feet away opened suddenly, and in the darkness, a set of flaming green eyes floated. Falken knew exactly who they belonged too, the Necromancer. What's more, they had caught him unprepared. The tall skeletal spell-caster turned and fled from them.

"Charge!" Garth yelled and all five party members leapt after the lich. They chased him for one turn, then two, and a third. In the darkness, they followed the subtle glow of his eyes as they illuminated the space before him. He turned to face them after they cornered him in the last room.

Falken had gotten in front despite being human. He charged the tall necromancer with his silver greatsword held high. His adrenaline filled heart was pumping like a racehorse. It was his first taste of Player vs. Player combat. Despite his aversion to the murders it was exhilarating.

"Smite!" He cried and divine light lance up his arms and into his weapon. It started to glow in the darkness as he brought it down. If he was lucky he could cut the necromancer down to half or more in just one hit.

"Unholy Smite!" A female voice cried immediately after him. A tiny darkly armored figure stepped from behind the doorway. Red crackling energy raced over a black wicked battle axe. Their weapons met in the space between them. The resulting clash of arms caused a thunderclap of energy. Falken was blown backward by the force into the rest of his group. Holy crap, the necromancer wasn't alone. He had help and it was a Blackguard to boot.

"Attack," An impossibly deep voice said as Falken gained his feet. The spell caster had managed to catch the smaller warrior. The explosion of holy and unholy energy had thrown the little blackguard back as well. This left the doorway clear of obstacles. Their advantage, however, disappeared the next second though. His group was suddenly flanked on the left and right. Three undead bandits came out of open doorways short sabre's swinging.

Darkness blossomed around them as the small armored warrior took its place in the door again. The necromancer pointed his staff at them and was using his other hand to macro cast.

"Shit," Garth called as the void enveloped them.

Belatedly Falken realized he'd walked right into this trap. Fear made his stomach clench into knots. He fought the negative emotion down fiercely, he could manage this. Falken stuck his hand into the belt pouch and withdrew a sun stone. Hurling it towards the floor the fractal gemstone shattered apart. The flare of sunlight lit up the corridor briefly, and the bright light canceled out the darkness, but used all it's energy up negating the magic. Now the Necromancer couldn't use his darkness spell. Alternatively, he couldn't waste his remaining stones. The blackguard raised it's shield and axe in invitation. Falken could see some magic working on the edge of the axe blade, it glowed crimson in the dim doorway. Undaunted Falken stepped forward to attack the armored figure. With his strength, he tried rushing past the figure but it was like pressing against a brick wall. Instead, he was the one shoved back into the small cluster of battle before the doorway.

"This is no good, guys. We should bail." Umber said from the back of the group. As if called by those words hands sprang up at their feet. Falken took an axe cut to his arm before swinging back. He knew he could take the evil players. It was five to two with their favor.

"Kill the pets, then attack the blackguard," Falken said continuing to swing his great-sword in the narrow hallway. A wave of foul smelling miasma swept past Falken. He almost gagged from the stench of disease and rot. Trying to ignore this he continued to hack at the armored being before him.

"Shit man, I'm already down to half," Garth called from nearby. Falken shifted the grip on his sword, letting go with one hand. He turned long enough to place a hand on the half-elf's back. Garth was far more lightly armored than the others. He used agility and two weapons to fight but was suffering the consequences now.

"Lay hands," He said and a yellow glow spread over the fighter's body. Falken could see his companion's health almost topping up to full in the group box. The enemy's response was almost by script.

"Harm Touch," A female voice said as pain spread over Falken's chest. He turned back quickly to see a fist retreating from his breastplate. His life was cut by a third. Falken could [Lay Hands] once more, but that would be it. He only had the one extra use.

"We got one pet down," Umber said as they turned to engage another. Folken was suddenly on the defensive as the Blackguard advanced. The short battle-axe was handling much better in the corridor. A swarm of little mosquitoes landed on their bodies and started sucking blood. Falken was glad he was a paladin and resistant to diseases. The same wasn't true for his group. He'd have to cure them after the fight which they were still winning.

The hands below his feet started to break apart but were quickly replaced with black thorny tendrils. They did damage to him every time he tried to move. An axe dug into his arm taking another chunk of life. He watched his own blood work its way down the haft of the axe into the armored arm of the blackguard.

"I need a heal!" Erick called. Falken turned to give the man his last lay hands. As he did a green bolt of energy lanced out striking the wounded fighter. A skull suddenly appeared next to his name as Erick fell dead. He cursed in anger and turned to see another axe swing taking a chunk of life from him.

"You think that's bad?" The female before him asked. The skeletal necromancer chuckled as he raised his staff. The spell caster did something but Falken was too busy defending from the little whirlwind before him.

"What the hell?" Garth called from beside Falken. He risked a glance and saw Erick getting up from the ground. The eyes were gray and lifeless as he turned towards them, then Erick attacked.

"You can freaking raise players?" Umber asked surprised it was possible.

"So long as they're my level or less." Admitted the necromancer in a genuinely amused voice. Just to make sure none of them left more hands sprouted from the carpet. Damn it, he should have called for a retreat when it was possible. Now they were stuck for another minute. Being in the front row was not a good place to manage a fight from. His health was getting dangerously low. Falken had led his group into this. He wouldn't waste his last [Lay Hands] on himself. He turned and used it on another wounded fighter, who instantly rose to full life. That's when an axe cut into his neck and a green bolt slammed into his shoulder. The world went dark as he felt himself falling. He hoped, prayed that some of his group got out.

***

Folken - Level 0 Commoner
New Hearth City - Plaza

The dark didn't last long. Falken was brought back to the main menu of the game. The ghost of his paladin stood in with the selection pad with a one hour cooldown ticking away. Falken had three other empty pads. He could only make a new player, wait for the timer, or exit the game. Anger and resentment bubbled, and the thought of losing two months worth of effort was a burning coal in his breast. He selected the option to make a new character. He'd have to see how things turned out. It didn't take him long to generate a random half-elf male. Next, he skipped the tutorial and jumped into the portal to New Hearth. A female commoner was standing nearby.

"Erick?" He asked and the person turned to him.

"Who are you?" The girl asked irritably.

"Falken," He said with a sigh. He'd spelled it Folken this time just to create the character.

"I'm so mad at you. My ghost is gone, I can't resurrect." The girl said and he looked away in response. His resentment turned to guilt. Folken had led them into that mess.

"The necromancer raised your body to attack us," Folken said.

146

That probably would be enough to keep the man from coming back. He had a right to be spitting angry because that was months worth of playing down the drain. Not to mention the money, items, and magical gear he'd worked so hard for.

"I'm sorry man," He said holding up his hands.

"What happened?" Erick asked.

"That's what I'm going to find out." He said starting to message in the names he knew. None of the other party members responded. It didn't bode well. Another twenty minutes later four commoners stood around the little plaza. Three were eying him angrily. Garth, the last group member, was either running or had rage quit. Finally, he tried to send a message to the guild leader.

"Orenthal, I tried taking the necromancer out." He typed to the man. Falken hoped he was still online.

"Who is this?" The guild leader replied.

"Falken, the Paladin." He sent back.

"Ahh, so you died. Did you at least kill the necromancer?" Orenthal asked.

"No," Falken replied feeling a little annoyed.

"I'm getting messages that you lost four warriors." Came back to his chat box.

"Yes, I'm sorry. They aren't happy with me." Falken typed back. They were still glaring at him and typing in their own chat boxes.

"Neither am I."

"Can I get a guild invite?" Falken asked.

"Ummm no, I don't need people who can't handle a simple task," Orenthal replied quickly.

"I only went after him because you wanted me too." Falken countered feeling his anger rise.

"Now I want you to go away," Orenthal replied back. After that every message Falken sent was either ignored or blocked. The implications were immediately apparent to him. He had twenty-four hours, twenty-three if he was being technical to get a resurrection. Without access to the guild, it would be next to impossible to get one. Fyre had burned too many bridges to seek outside help, do nobody was going to drag his corpse back to town. His paladin was as good as dead.

Falken was furious, he hadn't been interested in PvP. Now he lost his guild, all the stuff in his bank, the friends he'd made, all gone. That unmitigated bastard. Orenthal had sent Falken out like a tool to be used and discarded. He wanted revenge, badly. Not that he'd ever get a chance but he added Orenthal to his enemies list. Falken didn't even bother going to an inn. Instead, he logged out right there in the plaza to start looking up some information. The fact the necromancer had help was completely new. He had to find out more about them.

CHAPTER FOURTEEN

Kat - Chat

Kat - Level 23
Tramin Continent - Mirza Mansion

"That's what you get!" Kat yelled pointing a finger into the corpse's face. The damn player killer had come all the way up there to murder them. Part of her wished she could hack the body up some more with her axe. She kicked the dead fighter in anger, and her monstrous strength caused the corpse to slide across the floor.

"Now now, the humans can't help themselves," Liam said from behind her. That just made her even angrier.

"We didn't go looking for trouble. You and I were just up here by our lonesome grinding bandits." She said pointing at the bodies. Kat stalked over kneeling next to the corpse she kicked. She touched his body and opened her inventory. Well, great goblin banks. The man had over two hundred gold.

"You get used to it," Liam said touching the paladin's body.

"Did you notice some of them are wearing the same guild mantle," Kat said pointing to the corpse Liam was before. Over his chest was a red and orange tabard depicting a stylized flame.

"Fyre," Liam said simply.

"Who?"

"I've seen them creeping around the edge of town. They like to jump people for fun. Most stick to picking on the new players leveling on Aethon Island." Liam said with a shrug.

"A player killer guild." Kat hissed with disdain.

"We are going to have to move now, because they might send even more." Liam said and Kat grimaced. The experience had been fantastic for the last three hours. It was so sad being forced out because of the PK guild.

"You might as well take all the gear on them and portal home. I can't raise anymore for another hour." Liam continued after a few seconds.

"Will you be ok here?"

"I'll wait out on the hill nearby so I can watch the road. When I see any lights coming up the trail I'll take the one minion and leave. If we're lucky we can have two player pets for the rest of the night. Next time I get a bonus feat I am going to upgrade how often I can raise undead." Liam said pointing to the corpse of another fighter.

"That one was just shy of my level. The others were all over I think. Check his pockets for gold or other items but leave his gear on." He said and Kat went over to look. Another money bags who didn't bank his coin. There was over five hundred gold on him. He also had a heavy collection of potions and food. She dragged everything that wasn't weapon or armor to her inventory. It was a good night for her wallet at least. Taking out her portal stone she activated the blue gem. After a few seconds, she vanished amid a magical flash. Back in the apartment, she dumped everything into storage. In the morning she'd start auctioning everything off.

There was one piece of gear she'd taken note of, and pulled the belt of troll's regeneration from the stash. Kat was currently wearing a belt of overburden. It gave two points of strength and came with eight extra inventory slots. She wondered if the troll regeneration from the belt would stack with her vampire ability. She slipped the yellowish wort filled leather around her plated waist. After equipping the accessory she was happy to see the little icon flash in her view. Perfect, now she would have three sources of regen. She paused at the door to type into her guild chat.

"Liam and I just destroyed five player killers. They tried to jump us while we were farming. So much loot." Kat said and smiled. The chat was briefly filled with replies.

"Woohoo!"

"Good job you two!"

"Holy crap, how did you do that?" One asked.

"Brought them in like NPC's. They fell for such an obvious trap." Liam replied in chat. It was too bad they couldn't share screen shots. Kat had taken quite a few of the corpse-laden hallway. Maybe she could pay for a guild website to exchange information.

"I think we just made over two grand in gold after I sell off everything."

"Give us some," Several begged.

"No freebies. My shoulders sure do feel sore from lifting all this gear though. They aren't going to rub themselves." She replied back.

"For that kind of coin I'll rub anything you like." Someone else said and she chuckled. Kat left the apartment and jogged out of town. After a short walk she called her horse forth. It took her forty-five minutes to ride north to the mansion. The closer she got the more slowly she moved. Finally, about two miles from her destination she dropped from the saddle and dismissed FireFoot with a scratch behind his ears.

"Didn't see anyone coming north," she typed into the guild box.

"Good, all clear here," Liam replied and Kat moved up the trail. On foot, it took her another twenty minutes to arrive. She found her party member inside the mansion. He was just raising the second fully equipped pet. The last three bodies were naked except for boxer shorts.

"I could carry a third corpse," Kat offered but Liam shook his head.

"Without gear an NPC usually has more health." He said turning away. Kat followed after giving the paladin a quick extra kick in the side. It was too bad Liam couldn't raise clerics or paladins. They'd make for powerful pets. Unfortunately their souls were protected by the goddess. Together they decided to head southwest towards the elven camps. This was to avoid any humans looking for revenge.

***

Shellbreak Harbor - Apartment
10am

Oh, how she hated the sun. It's big bright nasty debuffing glare annoyed her. Liam was off taking a nap but she didn't feel tired just yet. He lay like the dead on his side of the bed with blank eye sockets. She cracked open the storage chest in their room. Because of the sunlight debuff, she couldn't carry nearly as much, so she was going to have to make four or five trips to the auction house. The weapons were solid grinding equipment which she slid into her inventory. Next, she took all the health potions and gems inside. With her weight allowance at max she walked out of the apartment and down the stairs. On the street she made her way towards the market with the loot. It was early morning and the east coast people would soon be storming the server. Until then the streets were fairly clear but for light foot traffic. Few players were about so only the NPC's wandered to and fro.

Going into the auction house she posted the gear and started back towards the apartment. Kat was walking up the street when she noticed a man's eyes suddenly snap to her. Not quite to her but to something above her head. There was no red halo above her she knew that. This had to be someone who'd listed her as an enemy. As soon as she'd come within range it would have alerted him. She pretended not to notice as she walked past him. Choosing not to go into the apartment she crossed the street into the tavern.

Kat took a seat in the corner of the room so her back was to the wall. It was impossible to be attacked in town but she wasn't taking any chances. The man followed her in after a minute, and walked over. With his gear he had to be and ultra low level rogue or archer from the leather armor he wore. The medium height man stopped before her. Kat flicked a glance to him acknowledging his presence. He was staring at her in return as if trying to memorize her features. Then he sat down at the table opposite her. Kat made casual note of the pointed ears poking out of dark tufted hair. So the man was a half-elf. She continued to ignore him as a waitress approached.

"Elven red cherry," Kat told the girl. She could afford the imported liqueur with the recent influx of gold.

"Beer," The man added as the waitress looked to him. Kat continued to wait. There was no sense in giving away more information. If he didn't leave she could just rent a room then portal back to the apartment. She wasn't about to give away where she lived.

"I was surprised after reading your guild advertisement. That was a nice lie." The half-elf said lightly.

"What part did you think was a lie?" She asked casually.

"The good dead," He said snorting.

"It's the Lawful Dead. We never said anything about being good." Kat replied smoothly. The wine came and she picked up the small copper flute. The man snatched up his beer and started to drain it.

"I suppose stalking me for revenge is helping fill your sense of justice?" She asked after sipping the red tart liquid.

"You led us into a trap," The man said and Kat laughed. He was so stupid.

"Did you think we wouldn't see your torches? They blazed in the night from a mile away. Then you go bumbling around in the dark with plate mail on. Fool, we didn't go looking for trouble... You came to us." She said setting her wine down. After drinking blood for the last month she found the wine unpalatable.

"I was ordered to come find you," He admitted with some annoyance.

"So you did," Kat replied glancing at the low-level male.

"The leader of Fyre wanted the necromancer dead."

"We noticed the guild tabard, yes. Lots of people have tried to kill my friend. Your guild leader will just have to get in line." Kat said in a cold, dry voice.

"This is hard, I'm trying to apologize." The man said making Kat's eyebrow raise. This certainly was an awkward way to say I'm sorry. Kat had seen the dark side of the game and now she was on guard.

"Apology accepted," She replied quickly. If words were all it took to make the man go away, she'd give him a few puffs of pointless air.

"I want to join your guild." He said glancing at her face. Kat stared at the half-elf for a full five seconds then she barked a laugh. That was good, more than good. The joke was funny on so many levels. She managed to stop herself when he didn't join in. The half-elf was serious.

"First you try and PK us, now you hope to join my guild. I most certainly won't let you in." She said standing. The man was insane if he thought she would trust him.

"Wait, I can give you information. I do want to join you. I know the names of most of the PK'ers in Fyre. I saved them all to my enemies list previously. It carried over to my new character."

That might help forewarn them if they were being followed. Still, it relied on trusting the names he gave her. Kat sat once again as she eyed the man. "Why?" She asked.

"I hated them. Fyre when I first joined was a normal guild. We all tried to level up, and help each other. The leader and a few others started player killing. They dragged a bunch of good people down into their circle." He said holding his beer between his hands. He opened his mouth, then closed it. His dark eyes flicked to hers again.

"I can't go back," The man said looking away. Was he admitting he couldn't return to his old guild?

"Which one were you? We left most of the naked bodies. Just pay someone to fetch your corpse, then leave the guild." Kat said without much pity.

"I went up there already. My Paladin is gone, the guild must have moved the body." The man said and Kat again considered him. That was pretty cold to have your guild hide your corpse. That didn't change the fact he'd brought five people to murder Liam.

"Even if you weren't a PK'er you still came looking for us." Kat reminded him.

"I'm sorry, it was a stupid mistake." He muttered staring down into his mug.

"Hmm… send the list over," She said and a plethora of names appeared in her chat box.

"How do I know these are guild members?" She asked before dragging the text into her enemies list. There were almost eighty names there now. If anything she would know if Fyre was following her out of town for the next month.

"Some of them wear guild emblems on their gear, but the PK'ers don't."

"And your name?" She asked.

"Folken," He replied. Kat finished her flute of wine and set the goblet on the table. She selected the name and added it to her enemy list. A little red gem appeared over his head when she did this. Yep, that was how he'd found her on the street. She was almost positive he was trying to worm his way into the guild as a spy. The fact it was such a clumsy attempt was what made her pause.

"You have to be undead to join my guild," Kat said and he nodded quickly.

"I know, I was going to kill myself and start over."

"Why do that?" She asked checking him over. The man was totally and averagely good looking. Black hair, dark smoldering eyes, and a narrow noble chin. He was medium height with a lean build. Folken looked like thousands of other hero's running around.

"Last night I just hit random, and started a new character," Folken said with a sour face.

"So? That's not a very good reason to off yourself." She said staring at the man. "Was he so vain?" She wondered.

"My previous character was a Paladin. I didn't really want to be a Rogue." He said after a minute.

"Maybe you should try it since you're already a half-elf. Besides as a vampire you'll gain even more stat bonuses. Strength, agility, perception, dark-vision." She said ticking off the points on her finger. He nodded to this in consideration. If the man went ahead and turned undead she might accept him. Vampires were few and far between. Kat wouldn't make it easy for him though.

"Right now I'm not impressed. You seem to have an odd sense of right and wrong." Kat said to the former paladin. He looked down into his empty mug.

"I realized too late that I was getting led around," Folken said.

"Don't let revenge make your choices. That is like hooking up with a girl just to piss off someone. You're not going to end up happy." She said and he gave a chagrined grimace.

"Did you find the map?" He asked and Kat looked at him. They had found the massive map on his body. It was an incredibly detailed sketch of the entire world.

"We did," Kat said flatly.

"Good, that's Fyre's official guild map. It contains everything they found so far." Folken said with a grin. He was taking his death a little too casually now. Kat tilted her head considering him.

"Since you're in such a giving mood how about you let me bite you. I could use the blood." Kat said.

"Umm ok," He replied suspiciously but she pointed a pale finger at him.

"I am much stronger than you. Grab anything I don't like and you'll die. It won't be considered combat to carry your ass to the sea. Vampires don't need to breath and I can hold you under the water." She said letting her red eyes bore into the half-elf. It was an empty threat. She couldn't grapple him in town due to the combat restrictions. The man smiled though.

"A better way to go than falling off a building," Folken said with an easy grin. Kat stood and dropped a few coins on the table. He followed her out and around the corner into an alley. Folken managed to keep his hands to himself as she fed. It was probably the only reason she'd give him a measure of trust.

"Will I turn?" he asked touching the wound on his neck.

"No, it's daylight out. You have to spend three days in total darkness. You're a rogue so you should be able to find the vampire during your class quest in Southport." She said and patted his cheek. Kat turned jogging back around the corner, then found a noisy spot in the market place and used her portal stone. With a flash of light she was back in the apartment. Just to satisfy her paranoia she decided to log off for the day. Kat could wait for Liam to get online to sell the rest of their items.

CHAPTER FIFTEEN

Liam - Free Time

"If you prick us, do we not bleed? if you tickle us, do we not laugh? if you poison us, do we not die? and if you wrong us, shall we not revenge?"
— William Shakespeare

California
9am

The cold war had been ongoing for almost two weeks. There were times it felt like the entire factory crew was against him. Liam dared not drive his repainted streetcar to work. He was back to using the old rusty bucket of bolts. That though hadn't stopped someone from keying his car again. The event had prompted him to check the security cameras. Of course, the one he needed was carefully pointed in a new direction. That was all right. He'd backed out from the parking stall directly into Doug's vehicle. As the headlight tinkled to the ground Liam casually drove home. They'd slashed his tires the next day. More than one so he'd have to get a tow, and he'd responded with long tacks under each of their tires. As soon as they backed up it would penetrate the rubber into the tube. None had noticed the damage until the following morning when they tried to get to work. Accusations had been leveled which he denied vehemently. Today Cole hopped into the chair next to Liam's desk with a snide smile on his face. How wonderful.

"You look chipper. Did you rape a monkey on the way into work?" Liam asked Cole.

"Only one getting fucked around here is you," Cole replied still smiling. He obviously knew something was up. Liam continued to type on his inventory report. Still, the jerks presence was annoying him. He flicked a glance at the offending man.

"Boss wants to see you," Cole said after a suitably dramatic pause.

"About what?" Liam asked in reply.

"No idea," Cole said his face splitting into an even bigger grin. Liam sighed and saved the project. He got up wearily turning towards the front of the building.

"It was nice knowing ya," Cole whispered as he sauntered away. Oh goody, how subtle a hint. Liam walked to the front of the factory and into Frank's office. It smelled like old coffee and machine oil. The older man was already sitting behind his desk. The boss was ugly as a bulldog from an old car accident. Liam always thought it gave the man's face character. Unlike his son Liam had a fondness for the boss. He'd always been fair and respectful of Liam. Today his face was set in a suspiciously neutral mask.

"Liam, have a seat," Frank said and gestured to one of the chairs. Liam decided to try and derail the situation. He suspected what was coming but hoped he could make Frank change his mind at the last second.

"Is this about the Carnigan Deal?" Liam said politely. It was the latest major bid they'd managed to acquire for the forth quarter. Sadly he didn't take the bait.

"Liam, I don't know how to put this. I'm sorry but I have to let you go." Frank said with an even stare. Well shoot, Liam had hoped he could distract the man.

"Is there a problem?" Liam asked carefully. He knew full damn well there couldn't be. Unlike most of the employee's Liam had never been absent or even late. He certainly hadn't been the one to start the shit lately.

"You've been a damn fine man to have on the crew," Frank said putting both his hands on the desk. He interlaced his fingers for support.

"Why then?" Liam asked still politely. His anger was starting to rise, and he tried to keep his voice even. Liam put in half a dozen years of his life for Frank and the factory.

"It's our balance. I can't afford to pay you. All I can say is that I have to let several go this week." Frank replied still calm as ever. If he was worried about money why the hell was he keeping his useless son on?

"When is my last day? Who is going to take my place doing inventory?"

"I'm sorry but you leave today. I asked Sandy to take over the purchases for now."

"I see," Liam said seeing all too clearly. The old man had kept Liam on for many years. The boss knew about his mistreatment, everyone did. Only now Liam was fighting back and it was costing the company money. Like the six grand for a kingly paint job. Instead of getting rid of the problem children he was dropping Liam. Removing him from the equation would take away the target. "I see," Liam repeated as Frank stood and reached over the desk extending a hand. Liam seriously considered ignoring the offer and walking out. He didn't like what the boss had settled on but he wouldn't disrespect him. Liam shook firmly giving Frank a hard grip. He wanted to let the man know his displeasure if only fleetingly.

Liam let go and left the office. He didn't even notice the stares and whispers as he made his way to his desk. A cardboard box was already present. It took less than five minutes to clean off his desk. He walked out to his vehicle sliding the box into the passenger seat, and started the old car. Liam drove to the parking lot exit before he stopped. For a full minute he sat there as the traffic went by.

His anger was building, and a little part of Liam reminded him that he never needed the job. He was filthy rich without the trickle of money. All that time he'd just needed anything to do. So he'd sucked in his pride and did the work. Money... money, that gave him a new idea. Liam turned right instead of left towards his house.

He drove to town, specifically to his broker's office. Most of the time they communicated by phone or email. This was only the second time he'd been to the building in person. What he was about to do was probably a mistake. His father had told him never to make decisions while angry. Liam would come to regret not taking that advice. He walked into the office just past ten in the morning. A woman was sitting at the desk who looked up at Liam's entrance.

"Is Tad Johnson in?" Liam asked.

"Do you have an appointment?" She asked and Liam shook his head.

"I came in on the spur of the moment," He admitted. "I have an account here and I wanted to talk to Tad in person," Liam added next. That would be enough to get him in the door, probably.

"Your name?"

"Liam Zeki," He said and the receptionist picked up the phone. She made a brief call.

"He is available to see you; second floor, office six." The woman said. He made his way to the elevator and up a floor. Tad was doing well for himself. He'd moved up a level since Liam had been here last.

He knocked once before trying to door handle. The agent was sitting behind a mahogany desk. Tad was a handsome blond haired forty-year-old.

"How can I help you?" Tad said standing from his chair. The man went so far as come around and shook Liam's hand. He'd maintained a portfolio here since turning eighteen. One that was worth millions in total.

"I need you to look up a stock," Liam replied with an icy smile.

"Which one?" Tad asked moving back to his computer.

"SLTKO," Liam said spelling out one letter at a time. The agent's fingers flew across the keyboard in long practice. Liam already had a few shared in the company through the employee options.

"Hmmm, not trending well. In fact, the stock is down five points since the beginning of the fourth quarter."

"I'd like to buy as much as possible," Liam said taking a seat.

"As your agent, I would advise against it. The market is down, and not many people are investing right now. Why are you interested in this particular company?" The agent asked right.

"I worked there. Though I wasn't in the office so I did hear things. Between you and me I know the business isn't doing well." Liam offered and the man seemed thoughtful.

"In that case wouldn't it make more sense to short the stock?" Tad asked. Shorting a stock was gambling that the price would go down. Liam suspected with the Carnigan deal going through it would go up. It was worth big money.

"Right now I suspect people are selling. I want to buy and hold. His reason was simple. He wanted to make Daddy Slatko send him big fat dividend checks each month. "Sell off everything that is down and buy into SLTKO," Liam said settling back. For about ten minutes his agent typed away on the computer.

Tad finished with a flourish. He turned to Liam still a little skeptically. "You own 20% of the available shares now. It was pretty thinly traded. Since you worked there I wouldn't advice selling for at least a year."

"That's fine. I intended to hold for the long term." Liam admitted standing. Tad leapt to his feet extending a hand. He had a lot of money invested through Tad. It was good for him at least. Liam left the office knowing he would own the company that he had just been fired from. Even if the stock didn't give Liam control it was still a significant chunk. Frank Slatko was going to be paying Liam whether he liked it or not. Liam left the office just past noon. He was in the mood for some lunch.

Liam sat at a little Japanese restaurant. Specifically, he sat on a tall wooden stool before the sushi counter while he waited for the chef to complete his meal. Taking out his phone he activated it with a thumbed code. Flicking through the few phone numbers he found the name of his newest one. He selected it and started a new message.

<Liam> I'm now free to play Nigmus Online more. Just got fired. — He set the phone down and took a sip of sake. If Kat was in the game she wouldn't get the message for some time. To his surprise, the phone beeped a text alert back. It hadn't taken more than thirty seconds.

<Kat> OMG Slatko fired you?

<Liam> Yep. Though I got something for revenge.

<Kat> Did you buy a shotgun?

<Liam> Much worse, I bought the company.

<Kat> WHAT!?

<Liam> I told you I had money.

He replied back with a smile. Kat knew of his ongoing war at work. In retrospect his getting canned was inevitable. A little tray of sushi and wasabi was slid before him. He looked up at the older Japanese man, nodded his thanks, and picked up the chopsticks. His phone didn't just vibrate for a text. It started going off from a call coming in. It had to be Kat. He didn't want to be rude to the chef so he took his plate and phone away. After sitting at a far table he answered.

"Liam," He said and waited. This was the first time he'd spoken to Kat in the flesh.

"You have to tell me everything," A young female voice nearly shouted. It sounded polished with a hint of Texan. It was pretty close to the one used by Kat's character.

"Wow, you sound cute," He said covering the tuna with a sliver of wasabi.

"Don't change the subject," The voice said as he bit into the sushi.

"You know most of the details already." He said around a mouthful of rice. Instantly his tongue and sinuses started to tingle from the green spice.

"Are you eating?" She suddenly asked.

"Sushi," He said after swallowing.

"Oh god, I haven't eaten that in so long," Kat said wistfully. Liam knew she was sick but wow. "Ummm," Liam said awkwardly. Kat must have quickly realized her mistake and spoke. "I didn't just say that."

"So tell," Kat demanded after a second.

"The boss called me in to feed me some line about the company finances," Liam said letting the subject change back to the main topic.

"Is it true?" Kat asked.

"There's a recession, so it's partly true," Liam admitted and stuck the other half of the sushi into the soy sauce. He dipped it twice before nearly swallowing the whole thing

"I was a little irritated at what happened, so I went to town. There was a nice man who was willing to look into making some inquiries. Two hours later I walked out with twenty percent of the company." Liam said after swallowing. His eyes were starting to water from the heat and he reached for the sake.

"That's just..."

"Stupid," He suggested. Liam knew his father would be turning in his grave.

"Amazing," Was the reply and Liam smiled.

"It will take a few days for the realization to settle in." He said picking up another piece of sushi. This one he didn't bother with wasabi.

"Are you sure you are OK?" Kat asked tentatively.

"It probably was a poor choice. I might end up losing quite a bit of money. There's a twisted sort of vindication even so. Instead of a tiny paycheck, I'll get dividend checks for ten times as much. In a way, I feel quite liberated, and I should have quit that shit job years ago." Liam admitted taking the sake cup in hand. He drained it and felt the liquid burn the back of his throat.

"You are so evil, you know that Liam," Kat said and he chuckled darkly. Liam would have broken out into full maniacal laughter if he hadn't been in a public restaurant.

"Do you want to be my hot minion sidekick. I'll buy you a

uniform and everything."

"I'm nobody's sidekick," Kat said in a huff.

"We have dental," Liam continued.

"Yeah, no thanks," Kat said dryly. "Are you going to be home soon? Its almost dark." Kat said changing the subject.

"I've had some alcohol so I have to sit around for a while. I'll be home in an hour or so." He said eating one of the California rolls.

"Ok, I'll see you on Nigmus," Kat said as he chewed.

"See you soon," Liam replied.

"Liam," Kat said and he grunted after swallowing. He reached for some water to clear his throat.

"Yeah?" He asked.

"You have a sexy voice too." She said and hung up.

Liam was left a little speechless and confused by this. He finished eating then took a walk around the block several times. After a while, he made his way home. When he pulled into the garage he turned the old beater's engine off. It was likely the last time he was going anywhere in that car. He got out, locked the door, and slid the keys onto the post. Before heading inside he turned to admire the pearlescent blue and black streetcar. When the sun hit the paint it would start to turn red and orange. Nothing of the scratches could be seen on the old Mazda. They'd done a fantastic job buffing out the damage.

He went inside to shower, use the potty, and eat a few nutrition bars. The sushi was already starting to wear off. The trail snacks would help keep him going while in virtual reality. Moving into his room he set a bottle of water on his night stand. After laying down he slipped the helmet over his head and touched the activation button. Like always there was a soft hum from the machine as it powered up. The world disappeared as he accessed Nigmus Online.

Liam - Level 26
Shellbreak Harbor - Apartment

Kat wasn't in the room as he woke. He saw that she was online though along with nearly a dozen guild members.

"Liam is here," Someone typed seeing his icon pop up.

"I was just telling the troops how evil you are." Kat sent via guild chat.

"Only to those that annoy me." He replied back getting up from the bed. "How is everyone tonight?" Liam asked next. The flood of responses was heartening to see. He wasn't sure what Kat was up too so he brought up her name in chat.

"Where are you at?" He asked Kat in a private message.

"Showing two new recruits around Southport. They let themselves be bitten by players. So, of course, neither knew the city layout or where to hunt at night."

"Since you're on the island I'd like to test some things involving the Necromancer class."

"What's that?" She asked quickly. Liam had a habit of never fully saying what he was doing, so Kat often had to drag it out of him.

"I want to visit all the crypts on the island to examine the books again," Liam said in response.

"Is that what you were doing when you found me?" Kat asked meaning their first encounter. That fateful evening when he discovered a paladin chained to a certain bloody alter.

"Yes, I want to see if the tome respawns after a lengthy amount of time. It's been over two months."

"OK, let me finish up and I'll find a safe place to summon you," Kat said leaving Liam some time to inspect his character. He opened his menu to look at his newest stats.

Name - Liam
Half-Orc/Undead Male
Class - 26 Necromancer
HP - 100 (Con) + 166 (Class Lvl) = 266
Mana - 220 (Int) + 80 (Wis) + 390 (Class Lvl) = 690
7 - Strength
5 - Agility

5 - Perception

6 + 4(Item Bonus) = 10 - Constitution

16 + 6(Item Bonus) = 22 - Intelligence

16 - Wisdom

3 - Charisma

Liam sometimes worried he'd made a mistake putting so many points into intelligence and wisdom. It left his health feeling inadequate. The math too had seemed off by ten points until he added those from his commoner level. His mana, on the other hand, was almost more than he needed. Only the longest of fights caused him to run out of spell juice. The robes, arm wraps, and rings he wore gave him even more from the intelligence bonuses. His last item was a powerful Amulet of Constitution. Liam was going to have to keep an eye out for some resistance items soon. He was immune to disease, dark energy, and poison. He naturally was resistant to lightning and cold, but Fire or Holy did extra damage. Maybe he could have Kat look for some rings of fire resistance on the auction house.

"Ready?" Came up in a message box. Liam stood and picked up his staff.

"Yes," He sent back. A circle of light formed at his feet and he waited for the magic to take hold of him. It was possible to avoid being summoned by simply stepping out of the light. He didn't though and within seconds he was standing on a grassy knoll. In fact, Liam was just outside the undead crypt from before. Kat was in her usual gothic black and white dress.

"How are they?" He asked.

"Good, I sent the two new guys off to kill goblins." She said turning to Liam.

"If they catch up we can all start grouping." Liam offered.

"That's the idea but only if everyone stays relatively close together," Kat replied.

"Thanks for summoning me here." He said gesturing with the white staff towards the crypt door.

"It was pretty close to Southport anyway," Kat admitted and pushed inside. The big stone door creaked open on rusty iron hinges. The same green flames and flickering lights greeted them. Liam wasn't interested in spending much time here so he intended to use one of his wizard spells.

Pointing his staff at Kat he murmured 'Feather Fall,' and a white light hit the petite vampire making her glow slightly. Without waiting for Liam she leapt from the landing into the darkness. As soon as she reached the top of her jumping arc her descent slowed. Kat let out a girlish squeal of delight as she floated down. Liam recast the spell on himself and followed her. Stepping off the ledge he slowly glided down.

"How many other wizard spells do you have?" Kat asked as Liam landed beside her.

"Five, mostly utility spells. One extra spell per five levels. At level thirty I'll be able to memorize teleport. No more having to use party stones." Liam said patting his robes down. They had fluttered about as he dropped below.

"Don't those go to towns?"

"You just have to know the location. Most people purposely hit towns for a safe portal." Liam said. He'd done his research before committing the scroll to his grimoire. It was one of the most popular spells wizards picked up, hence its incredible cost.

Liam pointed to several undead to control them. He didn't expect trouble, but the act was more a force of long habit. As always the three dutifully trotted into place behind him. Kat was moving towards the two double doors with the skull relief. He caught up just as the Blackguard pushed open the portal. Inside the room, Mothau stood from his chair after seeing Liam. He pointed a bony finger and hissed.

"You'll not steal my power, necromancer." Lich Mothau said in a rasping tone. Instantly his two guards started towards Liam. This was a total shock. No undead had ever attacked him. Surprised he back peddled past his three guards.

"Attack," he ordered and his own minions charged.

"What the hell is going on?" Kat asked from beside him.

"I have no idea." He replied before a black void appeared before them. It was the darkness spell the lich liked so much. Not that it had any affect on them being undead. Kat and Liam split apart taking a place on each side of the entryway.

"Is this supposed to happen?"

"Last time I came down here your group had already killed him." Liam said trying to think through this startling situation.

"Maybe we should go," Kat suggested. "You keep saying were not supposed to fight our brothers." She continued but Liam wasn't so sure.

"Did he say anything when you fought him?" Liam asked.

"No, all he did was stand up and start casting spells," Kat replied before a frosted path of icicles shot past the door. It froze Liam's feet to the ground taking off a few points of health.

"That's a wizard spell." He said pointing down. It was an evocation spell called 'Tundra Path.' He'd forgotten the lich had used this attack before. It wasn't in Liam's book as he had plenty of rooting and slowing spells.

"Should I help? I don't want to get a halo."

Liam pointed into the boss room. There was only one combat wizard spell he knew. He'd memorized it for fighting constructs. "Acid Arrow," He incanted and a greenish yellow blob shot from his hand. It struck an undead that was being double teamed by his minions. Within seconds its remaining health dropped. The creature collapsed in a smoking pile of bones and rusted armor.

"It's just like attacking bandits or raiders. We don't get red rings for killing NPC's." He said and Kat nodded. She drew her axe and the costume morphed into her dark armor.

"Target the lich," He suggested looking inside. Another path of cold icicles shot from the weaker boss. It flashed past Liam making his feet stick to the ground again. Raising his bony hand he shot another acid arrow at the second guard. Kat's martial skill quickly cut the spell caster down with a series of solid blows. Liam's undead dispatched the last guard.

"Well..." Liam said in surprise as he stepped into the room.

"That was a first," Kat finished for him.

"I agree. The lich said something about stealing his power." Liam mumbled thoughtfully and walked to the boss on the ground.

"He also called you necromancer," Kat added. So the NPC was aware of his class. He poked the lich and brought up his inventory. There was another bone ring of intelligence. He took it if only for the extra gold from selling it.

Kat was already over by the altar glaring at the edifice. The location of her near murder. Standing he moved to join her but stopped at the lich's grimoire. The tome was blank just like before, this confused Liam even more greatly. It hadn't replenished it's magical power yet the lich had protected it. He touched the papyrus paper with a bony finger and nothing happened. Flipping pages revealed nothing new. He tried picking the book up, and for a brief second, it seemed glued to the stand. Then as if grudgingly it came away in his hands.

"I can pick up the books, but this one is still used up." He said snapping the tome closed. The NPC was protecting his precious grimoire from being stolen. Now Liam had a blank tome in his pocket. Maybe he could find a use for it later.

"So you have what you need now?"

"Probably not. I might need another tome. I think all the lich's might attack me. They likely see me as competition. I'm like a rival spellcaster." He said turning to the still armored Blackguard.

"Let's try going to another crypt. I know there are two more on the Aethon Island that should be easy for both of us."

The next two dungeons were level fifteen and twenty. Paladins and clerics liked to farm them for experience before leaving the island. They left the crypt and jogged quickly northwest. Just like before the undead didn't attack until the boss room. The new lich stood from her throne in a skinny tattered blue robe. The female said the same thing as the last. This time though Kat had gone in first. Before the spell caster had even risen from her chair Kat was cutting into her, and Liam strode in with his three pets to help.

"This book still has writing!" Kat said excitedly after the fight. It was a dark blue skinned tome with silver buckles. Kat touched the pages with a flourishing triumphant finger. Nothing happened, except the magical glyphs continued to writhe. Next she tried picking it up but the tome wouldn't come away from the desk it lay on. When Liam touched the book the words suddenly stilled but didn't glow. He couldn't read the glyphs but they recognized him. The blue spell book easily came away from the table when he picked it up. He pocketed the tome starting his grimoire collection.

It took another two hours to walk to the last dungeon. It lay in the foothills of the northern mountain. Far down within the icy cave, they located the third lich. The battle lasted longer but Kat's presence proved decisive. This book was a whitish gray like dirty snow and had black iron snaps. The script stilled again and he picked it up. Back home in the apartment, he had two tomes and the blank book on the bed.

"What are you going to do with them?" Kat asked from her side. She had one of the tomes open and was thumbing through the pages.

"I'm not sure. The lich seemed very protective of them." Liam said as he tapped his tusk.

"We could make more necromancers," Kat suggested closing the white book. The little black hasp made a clicking sound as it locked.

"That would certainly draw guild members in, but for now I'd like to sit on them. Maybe after we collect a few more we can use them as prizes." Liam said and sat next to Kat. Like many things in the game this was an intriguing mystery.

CHAPTER SIXTEEN

Kat - Magus Symbol

"The greatest treasures were most often guarded by the slyest and cruellest dragons."
— Adam Nevill, House of Small Shadows

Kat
Homespace

Kathrine sat in the living room with her feet up on the coffee table. She had the tablet in hand and was checking on the guild page. The forum was up and they were actively advertising. The benefits of being a vampire were starting to bring more members. Soon they'd have over fifty players. Her phone started to ring and she picked up the device. Well, that was a surprise, Liam was calling her. Accepting the call she raised the virtual mobile to her ear.

"Hey tall, dark, and handsome." She said in a teasing voice. Kat had taken to flirting with him more.

"Good Morning, Kat. How are you?" He asked in his contralto voice. It was deeper than most men's but nothing like the necromancer in the game.

"Lonely," She admitted and Liam chuckled.

"I got something going on. You know that skull symbol I sent you screenshots of?" Liam asked in a cheerful tone. Kat did recall the weird skull with a sunburst of light. That's what she thought it was at least.

"Yes, the one in the empty coffin."

"I just stumbled on a post in the information forum. Someone linked the same symbol carved into stone. They're looking for help."

"How exciting," Kat mused. Personally, she thought it was a developers mark. A way for some artist to sign the work he'd done.

"They insist on meeting in public," Liam said with some annoyance.

"So you called me," Kat said feeling a little disappointed. She had been hoping he'd called just to talk.

"I also like to listen to your voice," he quickly added and she felt somewhat mollified. Kathrine supposed she was interested. Liam had a gift for stumbling onto little stories within the world.

"Where at?"

"She's paranoid. Wants to meet near the guard station in Shellbreak Harbor." He said over the line.

"Probably is afraid of getting ganked," Kat said knowing how the person felt. It was becoming common place for five or six low-level rogues to attack a high-level player. It made entering or leaving a city hazardous.

"You meet her after sunset," Liam said and Kat nodded. A vampire could still be back stabbed and the daylight debuff made them easy targets before dark. They might as well be paranoid on both sides.

"Ok, I'm going to hit the sack for a few hours then," Kat said getting up off the couch.

"Sweet dreams, beautiful," Liam said before hanging up. Dang, she wanted to be the one to tease him last.

***

Kat - Level 25
Shellbreak Harbor - Gatehouse

The lamp posts lights spilled onto the cobblestone roadway. It was an hour past dusk so the darkness was all encroaching. Kat stopped near the door to the guardhouse and casually leaned against the wall. There wasn't anyone obviously waiting nearby. That didn't mean a rogue, or many weren't lurking nearby in stealth. Several groups of players came through the gate for the safety of town. None paid much attention to her as they walked by.

"You're late," an irritated voice said from beside her. Kat glanced over to see a female face only a foot away.

"The sun makes me sleepy, I woke up late." She said in response.

"I suspected you were a vamp when you insisted on meeting after dark." The woman said taking a spot on the wall. Kat turned to her. She was small, Kat's own size. The girl had vibrant blond hair, but a surprisingly small chest. She was covered in a lightweight scale armor, so either a rogue or an agility based fighter. Based on the armor, she was much higher level, probably somewhere in the mid-thirties.

"Follow me," The woman said and turned.

"I don't think so," Kat quickly responded and the girl stopped.

"You want to do this in public where anyone can hear?" The girl asked and Kat pushed from the wall.

"I'm not going to follow you somewhere you control," Kat told the rogue.

"The same goes for me. How about you just tell me where you found your symbol." The blond said and Kat laughed.

"Do you take me for an idiot?" Kat asked surprised at the woman's gall.

"You need our symbol, and you are the one who posted for help." The two girls glared at one another for a few seconds.

The rogue offered a suggestion. "We get on horses and ride out of town. You lead the way for ten minutes then I lead the way for ten more. After twenty minutes we stop and talk."

"What's your name?" Kat asked.

"Emalee Aerohart,"The Rogue said and Kat added her to her

enemies list. A gem appeared over the other person's head. So she was telling the truth.

"KittKat," She replied in kind and saw the rogue glance up briefly. The woman always kept her back to a wall as if she could be attacked while waiting inside a town.

"Pretty paranoid for someone so high level." Kat offered walking back and forth in the shadows. She was glad she still had her costume on. So long as she didn't equip a weapon her armor would remain hidden.

"I've learned that cities are dangerous places to be," Emalee countered as they walked out of the gate and toward the stables. She brought out a gray dappled courier mare, which was one of the most expensive mounts. It was on the small side, but very fast over short distances. They were far enough from the guards that Kat called her companion, and the flaming nightmare trotted through the rift next to her.

"A blackguard," The woman said in annoyance.

"That will make us nearly equal if we go one on one," Kat said climbing into the saddle. Rogues did not make good tanks, but were very good at hiding. If things did go south Kat was confident she'd put up a fight at least. Emalee gestured for her to take the lead. So Kat kicked Firefoot into a gallop and raced south. After about ten minutes she slowed and let the other catch up. The woman was cool as she trotted by and turned her horse west. It wasn't long before they were in among the trees. She didn't stop after ten minutes but kept going, and they came to a hillock in the forest. It was full of blooming flowers and a small tree at the top. Emalee dropped from her horse before tying it to the tree trunk. Kat simply dismissed her mount, she could call it back several times a day now.

"You must be one of the first players in the game," Kat said in consideration.

"I was a day one player, yes," Emalee said in response. The two girls circled eying the other warily. Even though Kat was online constantly she could only level at night. For forty percent of the day she was stuck inside. Whoever this woman was she had to be grinding non-stop.

"So how about it?" Kat asked after a minute had gone by.

"If you try and screw me I'll hunt you down," the rogue said darkly.

"Your sweet words make my heart flutter. I haven't been threatened in at least a week." Kat replied still standing near the tree. The rogue stopped to glare at her.

"Take off your costume," the rogue ordered moving to stand before Kat.

"Because you want to eyeball my armor and see if you have a chance?" Kat asked and waited, but the rogue only continued to glare. There were times this game was truly frustrating. She withdrew her axe and shield, which caused her armor to morph into existence.

"Happy?" Kat drolled from within her enclosed helmet. Emalee inspected her carefully as if taking a catalog of the gear she wore. When the rogue didn't attack Kat put her weapon and shield away. She didn't like standing around in her armor when she didn't have too.

"Maybe I should look into getting a costume." The woman said after a pause. From a satchel on her side she withdrew a scroll. It was a blown up view of all the continents. She stepped closer to show Kat what she found. Emalee pointed to a spot on an entirely new continent.

"That continent is over level forty isn't it?" Kat asked in surprise.

"It is," Emalee said simply.

"How high are you?" She asked next and the rogue eyed her.

"Forty-four," Emalee said and Kat whistled. Maybe it wouldn't be such a close fight. The woman was almost twice Kat's level at twenty-five.

"You?"

"Twenty-eight," She hedged a little. The extra three levels she lied about wouldn't help her much.

"Where did you find the symbol?" The rogue asked impatiently.

"Near here actually," Kat said and pointed to a spot a smidgen west of town.

"I knew this was a waste of time." The Rogue said in annoyance. She rolled her scroll up quickly and shoved it in her satchel.

"I'm not the one who found it," Kat said as the girl started towards her horse. "He's waiting there if you're interested in seeing it," she continued but the rogue was already up on her saddle. Her horse sidestepped the tree then started down the hill.

"Apparently it was carved into the wood on the inside of a coffin," Kat yelled after her. The horse stopped and the rogue looked back at her.

"You might be thinking it's a trap," Kat said as the rogue continued to stare. "We can go there and you can stealth." She suggested and moved north. Kat had memorized where the girl had pointed, so if she didn't follow that was fine.

They traveled north for about half an hour through the forest, and eventually came out into a new clearing. About sixty gravestones were littered around in four rows. Liam waited in the middle of the small graveyard. He must have taken the time to send the weaker undead away. The giant necromancer was patiently standing next to an open grave.

"How did it go?"

"She's a forty'ish rogue and might be behind me. I know she stopped following me a few minutes ago." Kat replied and sat down on one of the grave markers. She glanced around but didn't see signs of movement.

"The girl is even more paranoid you thought," Kat continued in annoyance.

"Where was the other sign?" Liam asked pulling his scroll out. Kat leaned over and pointed to a place on the new continent.

"Level forty crypt," He said reading the small script. It was undead which seemed promising.

"What do you think?" Kat asked peering over his shoulder.

"It is odd. Even if you drew a line between the points, it is an only ocean in between."

"Maybe there's an island somewhere," Kat suggested. She watched Liam turn the scroll around several times, then started tapping his tusks in thought.

"You won't find it because there's a third symbol I never mentioned," a voice said from behind them. Kat turned to see the thief standing nearby her hands resting on daggers.

"Funny that you were the one threatening me about getting screwed over," Kat said to Emalee darkly. The rogue ignored the comment and walked around the graveyard.

"I am surprised and suspicious," Emalee mused looking between Kat and Liam.

"Paranoid is a better word for it," Kat added helpfully.

"So where is it?" Emalee asked still ignoring Kat. Liam pointed down at their feet. The rogue started to come forward then backed up quickly out of range.

"Ahh, my aura. I forgot about that. Don't spend a lot of time around the living." He confessed in a deep voice. Liam took up his staff and walked away from the gravestone. Kat didn't though. Her blackguard aura just caused fear in humans. The rogue eyed her as she came forward and knelt. She brought out a small glowing red stone. On her hands and knee's Emalee stuck her head into the broken coffin.

"I see," Emalee said.

"This must be where he was first buried." Emalee muttered to herself, stood, and patted her leggings free of dirt.

"Who?" Liam asked from twenty paces away.

"Eremite the Dark Magus," Emalee said intoning a famous character.

"You would have eventually found his symbols after going to the next continent. They are quite prominent in two locations. I also tried to draw a line between those sites and found nothing." Emalee said turning to the necromancer.

"Will you share the third site then?"

"The third symbol is in a crypt. An extensive and ancient

undead city called the Necropolis. It makes the other undead dungeons look like theme parks in comparison. The monsters range up to fiftieth level." She said taking out her scroll again. Emalee showed Kat roughly where to find the dungeon.

"Three points is usually what it takes to find a place."

"Even if you drew a line in between them that would still lead out in the ocean." The Rogue eyed her scroll for almost a minute in silence.

"Maybe that's the point. Who would look for something under the water?" Liam asked. Emalee turned and started walking around the grave with her scroll in hand.

"We could travel there together," Liam said after a few seconds.

"I don't play well with others," Emalee said.

"What do you plan on doing?" Liam asked her from his place several yards away.

"I'll go there, of course."

"Don't we deserve some of the exploration bonuses too," Kat said in irritation.

"If the pattern holds then both of you are seriously under leveled. The location is likely level fifty or more." Emalee replied without looking at her.

"So are you if you're just forty-four," Kat said glaring at the woman. She did not like the annoying rogue.

"I doubt you could hold your breathe for that long," Liam said and Kat smiled. Undead don't need to breathe under water. No wonder the place was in the ocean.

"Water breathing potions are easy to get," Emalee said dismissively.

"An expensive solution and they only last ten minutes," Kat said with a smile. Potions like that were hard to make because the ingredients were rare. If the girl were that determined, she'd end up spending a fortune.

"Fine, we work together long enough to at least see this place. You only need to show up to get the one-time experience bonus." The rogue said tucking her scroll away.

"Is that how you got so high level?" Kat asked stepping

towards her mount.

"Yes. Trailblazing is much more enjoyable and faster than grinding out levels." Emalee said and turned from them. "Meet me at the harbor. There's a boat that goes to the next continent. We can ride it most of the way there." She said and walked from the graveyard.

"I'll wait in the apartment," Liam said and took out his portal stone. The town was close enough that she called her horse and rode to the gates.

***

Kat had never been on this boat before. The large galleon traveled a long circuit between Edoku'kor, Shellbreak Harbor, and the Hinthal Forests. They had been sailing for about three hours now, and for all that time, the rogue hadn't said a word to her... not one. She hadn't even glanced in Kat's direction. Instead, Emalee stared down at her map while she held a compass and tried to mark the miles off. The woman must have been a scout, which made sense considering her obsession with exploring.

"I don't like you," Kat suddenly said to the rogue. Emalee didn't bother looking up from her page.

"The feeling is mutual," was the tired reply. Kat turned away and started pacing around the foredeck.

After another ten minutes Emalee flipped the compass closed, shoved it into her bag roughly, then rolled up her scroll. Lastly, she withdrew a pale blue potion, and drank it with a slight grimace. The next second the rogue was leaping from the ship, and Kat raced to jump in after her. The water was freezing cold as she hit. Kat came up in her clinging dress. In the bitter silence, Kat followed the paddling woman for roughly thirty minutes. Finally, they stopped, and the scout paused looking around at the open sea. They were at the location, or close to it. Kat pulled the party stone from her belt pouch. She needed to get Liam here before the rogue tried anything. She was faced with a small problem though. There was no solid ground to smash the item against. Emalee was looking away and Kat had an idea. She slapped the stone circle hard against the other woman's back. The rogue instantly turned and drew two daggers.

"I needed something hard and dense," Kat explained as the circle of light appeared. The rogue continued to glare at her. Liam splashed into the cold drink a few seconds later.

"Why the hell do skeletons feel cold?" He yelled after swimming to the surface. Emalee remained stonily silent. "I assume we're over the site?" Liam asked next looking to Emalee. The woman didn't respond but dove into the water.

"What's up with her?" Liam wondered aloud.

"It's her time of the month," Kat suggested and dove as well. Thanks to their dark vision Kat could see quite well under water. Liam was just behind her as they swam, but the rogue was already ten paces ahead and kicking downward. Twice the human had to stop and drink her blue potion. Eventually they did reach the bottom. Kat was astonished. She'd expected to find some sunken pirate ship full of gold. She was wrong and glad of it. Out of the murky gloom a tower became visible. As they neared it Kat suddenly leveled up. Holy crap that was a lot of experience. They continued to swim down through the freezing water. The building was tall at almost a hundred feet. It narrowed at the top with a base that sank into the ground. The black tower was made of obsidian stone. Emalee was still swimming hard in front. Didn't she see the undead mobs walking the perimeter? The barnacle ridden corpses were ridiculously red to Kat. She needed to point out the danger to the human. Kat tried to stop Emalee by grabbing a leg. The rogue kicked her in the face and swam down hard. What the hell?

Fine… if she wanted to suicide by mob that was OK with her. Emalee made for what looked like a front entrance, and tried to swim by two undead sentries. They attacked her blocking the way inside. Kat touched down on the silt-laden steps but wasn't about to help. They grabbed the rogue attacking by biting and punching her. Liam landed next to Kat and watched the scene.

He made no move to help either. Suddenly the rogue teleported backward about twenty feet and disappeared. That was a new trick. So a rogue was good at escaping combat. The two undead immediately started looking around for the tasty snack that got away.

Liam tapped Kat on the shoulder then pointed at the door. She nodded back at him in acknowledgment. Moving past the sentries Kat dragged the rusty steel construction open. As soon as she swam inside her level jumped twice. Now she was twenty-eight and close to another. No wonder that rogue had wanted to be first. Kat just dinged almost three levels in a couple of hours. That would have taken days worth of grinding. Liam came in next. Kat saw him clap his hands, he must have gotten a level as well. They left the door open until a figure appeared out of the murk. The annoyance as Kat was coming to think of Emalee closed the exit.

"What now?" Kat typed into a private message to the rogue.

"We leave. The bonuses are for first discovery, first entry, and first boss kill." Emalee typed back with a glare. That was why the rogue had been so eager to get inside first.

"Thanks for letting us know," she typed back angrily. At least Liam knew where this place was, so they could come back here in the future. The rogue pulled a portal stone free of her pouch and held it up. A few seconds later she was gone.

"Why did she leave?"

"The only other bonus experience is from killing the boss. We couldn't handle that." Kat said.

"You're right. I suspect a level fifty lich is at the top of the tower." Liam typed back before he took out his portal stone. Kat followed suit and quickly appeared in their apartment. Saltwater dripped from her as her clothes clung to her small frame.

"That heinous experience stealing mortal," Kat said as soon as she finished appearing.

"What do you mean?"

"She wanted all the experience for herself." Kat explained about each bonus.

"I see, each new person gets half as much experience," Liam said thoughtfully.

"I hit twenty-eight," She admitted.

"At least we are the same level now," Liam offered and pulled out his scroll. Kat was still fuming at the greed of the rogue. No wonder she explored solo, because anyone who spent more than an hour in Emalee's presence would stick a knife in her back. Kat wouldn't forget the kick to her face.

CHAPTER SEVENTEEN

Murder

"Killing is not so easy as the innocent believe."
— J.K. Rowling, Harry Potter and the Half-Blood Prince

California
Late night

A figure knelt in the darkness before the house porch. It was bitterly cold but California had been spared any snowfall yet. A plume of white vapor escaped the man's lips as he searched. There it was, a stone that vaguely took the shape of a frog. Underneath the glint of an old key twinkled. A gloved hand picked up the key and rubbed away the years of dirt. Slowly he rose moving towards the front door. There he stood quietly for almost five minutes. In the darkness he waited ensuring all was silent. Carefully, gingerly... he slid the key into the lock, and prayed he was lucky. It had been such a long time since coming here and the locks could have been changed. There were two loud plonks as the door unlocked. Placing the key in his pocket he wiped his gloves free of dirt, then turned the door handle, and slowly stepped inside. He smiled to himself at the completion of this first step. From out of his waistband he withdrew an ancient relic. The handgun was old and sprinkled with flecks of rust. A stainless steel example of the venerated 1911. He lifted the heavy weapon into sight. The few lights in the room made the steel shimmer like a faceted diamond.

His old sneakers lightly stepped across the carpet. He was careful to remain near the walls where the floor would creak less. The front room was clear and he poked his head into the kitchen. The remains of several pizza boxes lay stacked next to the trash can. Two-liter diet soda bottles filled the recycle bin. The .45 caliber weapon changed hands as he crept down the hall. Everything was silent except the creaking of the house. This far out of town you couldn't even hear the sound of highway traffic. He opened each door slowly as he came to them. First, the bathroom which was dark and empty. The scent of soap and water vapor still hung in the air. He let the door close, almost but not all the way, not enough to make a sound. The next room too was dark, filled with brick-a-brack. A desk sat in one corner heaped with hobby parts, model kits, and remote control car pieces. On the other side a paint easel was set up with a partially completed picture. He stepped back out into the hallway.

It was the next door that had light escaping under the crack. Still with the weapon in his off hand, he stopped before it. There was silence here too. He waited heart pounding for any sound within. Keeping the barrel pointed into the room he slowly turned the knob. With a click he pushed the door open ready with the gun. Licking his lips he stepped inside the room.

The fat bastard was on his bed with hands clasped over a bulging stomach. He wore pajama bottoms and a stretched undershirt. At first he thought the slob was asleep but that didn't explain the light in the room. Then he noticed the plastic helmet, and with a smile, admitted he was getting lucky this evening. The fat fuck was online — probably in some perverted sex dungeon — and wouldn't be aware of anything he did. Moving closer to the bed he stood over the obese tub of lard. The gun moved as he pointed the barrel directly at a double chinned face. Under closed lids the eyes were moving slightly as if in REM sleep.

The trigger started to squeeze tighter and tighter. The anticipation of the recoil was a delicious sensation, but the bang didn't come as the trigger stopped. Confusion wracked him until he realized the problem. He'd forgotten to chamber a round into the gun.

Lifting the 1911 he grabbed the slide and racked it. There was the satisfying sound of a bullet being loaded. Looking upon the rounded face of his victim his plans suddenly changed. Another grin split his handsome features. Leaning down he took one of the meaty hands of the fatty. Carefully he slid the gun into his palm. The weapon was free of other prints, he'd made sure to wear gloves the entire time. The 1911, the fat hand, and arm moved. Now the barrel was pressed against a thick blubbery chest. It dug in just to the right of center, an awkward angle. He managed it though. His own gloved hand joined the one on the gun. Slowly his finger pressed on the one within the trigger well. He spoke for the first time since entering the home. His words were mere whispers in the quiet room.

"This little piggy went to market," He sang slowly making the trigger creep.

"This little piggy stayed home," Further it inched.

"And this little piggy went wee, wee, BANG!" He said as the gun snapped. The sound was explosively loud in the small room, and for a few seconds, there was nothing but a neat dark hole in the shirt. Then the crimson red of blood started to flow. He let go of the gun stepping back quickly. Licking his lips again he turning to go as fear filled him along with a dose of joy and glee. At the door he stopped though. Looking back he spied the helmet. The VR Dive gear was worth a fortune. He wanted it, even if it did stink of greasy hair. This time he tentatively stepped over. Almost afraid the man would wake for some final death throw. The gun was still clutched limply in a fat hand.

The chest had stopped moving and he bent down. The eyes too were still and he let out a breath of relief. The bullet must have gotten him right in the heart. The man stood there for a few more minutes to make sure Liam was dead. He liked the look on the chubby's face he decided. It was a mixture of subtle pain and confusion. Reaching up he grasped the plastic helmet dragging it

free of damp hair. Cables snaked from the device into a large box
on the night stand. While he was unplugging the box from the
wall a cellphone began to bleep madly for attention.

"Sorry, he's unavailable." The man said to the gyrating mobile.
Next he piled helmet and cables onto the machine. He took
everything including the online magazines sitting next to it.
Clumsily he backed out of the room and toed the door closed.
Going out to his vehicle he stowed his loot before returning to the
front door. With the key he locked up, and replaced it under the
frog rock. His hands were trembling as he started the engine. For
a few minutes he drove recklessly away from the suburban house.

An hour later he sat in his truck outside his own home. A laugh
started to overtake him. It began weakly like a morbid bubbling
chuckle. Quickly it morphed into full bellied howls of mirth. His
fist thumped down on the steering wheel in abject joy. After
several minutes he subsided. In the dark cab he glanced over at
the VR helmet sitting on his passenger side. Not only had he
gotten his final revenge on that fat fuck but he had something
new. For a long while he pondered what to do with it. Should he
pawn it, or keep it as a memento? Unable to decide he took the
machine inside. He stowed it away in his bedroom before sitting
down with a beer. He could figure out what to do with it after his
nerves settled down. It took eight bottles to get him into a fit
enough state to sleep.

***

Orenthal - Level 42
Dragonfall - Griffin Wing Tavern

Orenthal threw the copper mug at the annoying little assassin,
but the agile man barely moved to dodge as the cup sailed by his
head. He raised a gloved hand to pat his mouth in boredom.
There was a long sigh from the smaller man.

"What do you mean you want more money?!" Orenthal hissed and the rogue lowered his hand.

"Exactly that, the job is more complicated." The man said coolly.

"One stupid girl!" Orenthal continued to spit angrily. He stood from his chair to glare at the man across from him.

"If you're so set on her death then why don't you dirty your own hands." The assassin said remaining disturbingly calm. Orenthal raged inside, the gall of the petty killer. "That 'stupid little girl' is now a guild leader. The necromancer is always with her." The man said casually. Orenthal's eyebrows rose in surprise. He'd known of the association, but he hadn't known they were together.

"That's impossible," He said slowly. The Necromancer couldn't group with a living player.

"She's turned vamp. That is why I had such a hard time finding her. Only goes out hunting at night." The assassin said in his infuriatingly drool voice. Finally, he recalled word of a companion traveling with the necromancer. A small blackguard. So the lich had been invited to a guild. He was so close to beginning the campaign. Before Orenthal could say anything else the assassin turned to the door. His perception check was obviously better as he heard something. There was a light knock before it opened to reveal a buxom human serving girl. She padded to the discarded cup and bent daintily to pick it up. The human wench turned to them and bowed slightly.

"Shall I get you anything?" The girl asked politely.

"No, get out." Orenthal barked sitting back down, and waited for the NPC to leave. The human girl smiled at them both in disregard to his tone. She bowed again and exited the door with the cup.

"Kill them both," Orenthal said after a few more seconds thought.

"A tall order," The man said smiling. "It might require a paladin and four fighters." The assassin said dry humor coloring his words. The guild leader bared his teeth at the smaller man.

"Do it," Orenthal ordered baring his teeth at the murderer.

"I'll pass, there are plenty of other targets." The smaller man said sighing again as if bored of the conversation. Before Orenthal could say more the man went invisible. Soon the door to the private room opened and closed leaving him alone. Orenthal rubbed the back of his neck and considered his options. He was tempted to kick the player from his guild, but the assassin was right. Many more players needed to die, and most had learned quickly. His PK groups were having a harder time coming up with kills. Maybe he aught to spend the gold on attracting new recruits. Fyre needed to bolster its ranks before the campaign began.

***

Liam - Level 30
Tramin Continent

Dirt and gravel were in his mouth. He spluttered spitting rocks out as he sat up slowly. Reaching up he pulled several wet leaves from between his teeth, and tried to remember what he'd been doing. Slowly he looked about. Liam was half sitting half laying between several bushes. When he turned around he saw the figure of Kat sprawled across the ground. Her eyes were closed and she wasn't breathing. Dead? No, probably just logged out. Now he recalled what happened. The plan was to head into one of the many cave systems for grinding. They'd been heading north-west into the dwarven controlled area. Then, what happened? There was a blank in the events. Had there been a server restart, or maybe he'd experienced a burp in his Internet connection. He was still looking at Kat when she suddenly sat up. So she wasn't dead, just offline as he guessed. She grabbed the front of his robe in her tiny fists.

"What the hell happened to you?" She asked angrily shaking him.

"I don't remember," Liam admitted.

"You collapsed all of a sudden. I had to drag you off the trail before a dwarven patrol saw us." She said with irritation. Kat let go with one fist and punched his chest, and his health dropped a few minuscule ticks.

"How long was I out?" He asked and she pushed away from him.

"Two or three minutes before I logged out. I've been calling your phone constantly." She said in angry annoyance.

"I don't remember anything," He said again a little lamely. It was odd. The VR headset was supposed to dump him out if he lost connection. Maybe he'd had a seizure? That was a dark and disturbing thought. He stood following Kat as she climbed to her feet. After dusting off her dress she turned to glare at him again.

"I was worried."

"We've been playing a lot. I've probably put in eighty hours in the last week." Liam said bending to retrieve his staff.

"Maybe you should rest then, take a night off." She said in a more normal voice. It was still early. They hadn't been leveling for more than a few hours.

"I feel fine now but your probably right," he admitted and reached into the folds of his robe to access his inventory. Kat copied him as he drew out the portal stone. He concentrated on the item and the magic activated. Within seconds he was teleported back home in a flash of blue and gold.

The apartment suite was new. Instead of a bedroom, he stood in a small living room. The walls were a pure white stucco and the floors covered in carpet. Large bay windows let in a splash of moonlight. Kat appeared next to him. She glanced to Liam worry still coloring her red eyes.

"Don't be like that." He said as she moved past.

"Get some sleep, Liam." She said going to the fireplace. The embers had died down and she poked at it to start the flames again. He watched her fill a pot with some water and set it over the pit. Liam sighed. He wasn't tired and he did feel fine. Still, Kat wouldn't be satisfied until he'd logged out for the evening. Maybe in the morning he'd go for a long walk. He needed to get out of the house for a few hours anyway. Liam had been slowly becoming a recluse. Feeding his body just enough to log back into the game. Kat straightened from the fireplace and walked into the kitchen area. Unlike him Kat never seemed to suffer the same problem. She did log off briefly, usually during the day. Though most often she was found in game helping out new players.

Instead of going to his bedroom Liam sat in the easy chair facing the fire. He watched Kat as she made tea. She used a hot pad to pull the pot from the fire. After pouring the boiling liquid into a cup she added some green herbal leaves. Next she withdrew a red vial from the rabbit purse. It was human blood which she added to her tea. Kat often said it was better than honey or sugar. Finishing she moved to sit opposite him and lifted the steaming cup to her lips. She blew on it twice before taking a sip.

"I'm going to log off then." He said with a wave. Liam had his own bedroom now, but the entire suite was private. He was in no danger logging out in the living room.

"Give me a call in the morning." She said after taking another sip. Liam looked up with his eyes and touched the menu. He frowned in confusion when half of the usual icons were missing. More importantly, his logout button was gone. The only selections visible were his inventory, character screen, skills, and social. Liam paused his hand hovering in the air.

"Forget something?" Kat asked from her seat.

"It's not there," He said slowly in deep confusion.

"What's not?" Kat asked.

"The button," Liam said stupidly. The few character icons continued to hang in the air before him. Kat was looking at him over her tea cup. He tried the character menu and it brought up his stats. Closing it he tried opening the system menu again, but was confronted with the same limited choices.

"The logout button, it's gone." He said lowering his hand.

"A bug?" She asked and he slowly nodded. The thought had occurred to him as well. Maybe it had something to do with his earlier blackout.

"Mine is still there," Kat said raising a hand into the air. She set her cup down and touched something before her. Immediately her body relaxed into the chair. Red eyes closed as her arm fell into her lap. Less than a minute later she was back. Her eyes opened to regard Liam.

"Can you call a GM, my button is missing," Liam said sitting back. For whatever reason he wasn't panicking yet. He was feeling confused but quite calm, unnaturally so.

"It's late, I don't think were going to get a response," Kat said but began touching the air before her. She appeared to be sending in a ticket. Kat was right of course as the hours passed. Liam waited as Kat grew increasingly agitated. He instead dragged over a stool and kicked his feet up making himself comfortable.

CHAPTER EIGHTEEN

Dead or undead

Detective Rick Tracy
California
4am

The car rolled to a quiet stop in front of a North California suburban house. Already surrounding the drive was a marked patrol car, an ambulance, and a hybrid BMW. Rick turned the engine off and picked up the coffee mug. He took a much-needed sip from the thick brew. Not only was it strong, but he liked to lace it with a little Irish whiskey. A vice he couldn't kick. He picked up the multi-tablet aiming it at the house.

[Liam Zeki - Delta St, Redding, CA 96003 - Responding Officer requests a detective presence. Examiner on-site.]

Rick was a senior detective—at fifty-five years of age—one nearing retirement. He hated these new fangled gadgets, which was why he tossed the multi-tablet back on the passenger seat. Rick awkwardly exited the car, a bad knee that was acting up in the cold weather. He didn't quite slam the car door, but it did rattle. Rick sighed, it was way to early to be up. Rick walked towards the California ranch house. He recognized the medical examiner's car. Odd that he'd gotten here first. No, he lived nearby, if Rick recalled correctly.

Police tape was up already. The front door was ajar, the glass broken in. He lifted the tape up and ducked inside. A man was just inside waiting, a boy really, he couldn't have been more than twenty.

"Officer Daniels," Rick said quickly reading the officers name tag. While Rick didn't know the man personally he'd give the young deputy the professional courtesy. The young man smiled a little to eagerly.

"How are you this morning, Detective?" Daniels asked.

"It's too early," Rick complained and the officer smiled. "What's the story so far?" He asked.

"A neighbor heard a gunshot sometime around midnight. She called it in. I was detached from late patrol to check it out. The house was dark when I knocked. I tried again more loudly, rang the doorbell, knocked again."

"You broke the door?" The detective asked glancing back.

"Yes, I walked around the side of the house and looked in the windows. One of them still had a light on. I saw a man covered in blood laying in bed, so broke the lock to get inside." The deputy explained.

"I called it in then cleared the house checking the doors, and windows. Everything was locked up."

"Lead the way," Rick said gesturing for the officer to proceed him. He glanced around at the large living room. Leather couches were placed in front of a massive flat-screen. It had to be a hundred inch television at least. The kind of set a super-bowl party was thrown around. The kitchen was something of a mess as he passed it.

The third bedroom was open. The kid stopped at the door way letting Rick pass. Medical Examiner Pratchet was already in the room. Next to the older man, a bag of equipment sat on the floor. He was just pulling on a pair of purple latex gloves. Sam must have just arrived before him. He smiled at Rick seeing who had responded.

"How are you doing, Rick?" The man asked.

"Could be worse... could be better. How are you?" He asked in response.

"Better than our dear friend here," Samuel said turning to look at the body. He was a large man, some would say obese. His nightshirt was stained dark red with blood. An old rusty pistol was still clutched in his hand.

Samuel handed Rick his multi-tablet. It was a combination high definition camera and intelligence gathering device. The thing was already recording audio for the file. Rick took it and started snapping pictures. The body, the bloody chest, and the weapon in his hand.

"Judging from the skin coloration, and the 'not quite' stiff fingers I'd say he died between four and five hours ago," Sam said lifting the man's hand. The arm still moved relatively easily. He uncurled the finger from the trigger well. Then he picked up the gun and turned it over to expose the serial number. Rick snapped a picture so the multi-tablet could start it's magic. It automatically detected the weapon serial and send a query to the national firearms database. It beeped after only a second.

Ruger 1911 [R2778692], made in 2042 and last sold in Ohio state. It was purchased by one John Platono [Deceased] in 2080. Rick did the math in his head. Twenty-Four years ago, quite a lot of time. You didn't have to register firearms, only the sale, and transfer of a gun. At some point it had crossed state lines into California. Most likely when the person moved here. Not uncommon especially for older guns made last century. It might have changed hands a dozen times in those years. Sam bagged the pistol and a single casing on the floor.

"The wound?" Rick asked next.

"A single gunshot to the chest that appears self-inflicted. Managed to knick himself in the heart, and bled out quite fast, which is why there's so much blood." Sam said pulling out a bottle. He swabbed the man's finger which turned a shade of blue. "Gun powder residue on the hand. If you look closely you can see burn residue around the entry hole. The weapon was pressed quite hard into the chest before it fired." Sam said putting the bottle away. Rick took a few more pictures. "No other wounds are visible, nor a sign of struggle," Sam added looking around the room.

A mobile phone was sitting on the night desk. Rick used didn't touch it but waved the multi-tablet over the device. It automatically skimmed the phone's contact list and recent calls. A number listed as Kathrine had called the phone at 11:23 pm last night.

A voice spoke from down the hall, "I found another gun." Rick followed the voice into a kind of craft room. The closet was open and the kid was standing next to the door. He pulled out an old shotgun and a half a box of shells. Rick took another picture of the serial number.

[Mossberg 500 [MS-2845] Made 1979 - Last registered purchase Clark Zeki [Deceased] 2023. So the man had a hand me down from his grandpa. He appeared to have some guns, enough for self-defense but he wasn't a collector.

"Any pistol rounds?" Rick asked the young officer. He shook his head. Only the shotgun and a few old shells. No bullets for the pistol though, which was odd. They had the weapon, and it was bagged for evidence.

Sam poked his head through the door. "Glad he used the pistol, the shotgun would have made a terrible mess." He said coming forward. "There is a security system but no cameras. It was turned off at the time except for the alarm on the garage."

Rick considered the evidence. They had the weapon, no forced entry, and no sign of struggle. Was there reason to kill himself. Did the victim have the motive to commit suicide?

"Did you find a note?" He asked the officer. The deputy was putting the shotgun back where he'd found it.

"No sir, I didn't find a suicide note." He said.

"Not uncommon, people sometimes kill themselves on the spur of the moment. He hadn't seen any alcohol bottles or other drugs." Rick thought. He wanted to double check so he walked into the bathroom, which was surprisingly clean. He opened the medicine cabinet by the edge. An Aspirin bottle, some cough medicine, and a half-full container of codeine. The label said the pills had expired two years ago, not that it would stop most pill poppers.

There wasn't any sign of feminine habitation. Only one toothbrush and a single bottle of shampoo in the shower. "Lived alone, no close family," Rick thought to himself. He checked the multi-tablet calling up additional information on Liam Zeki. His closest relative was a cousin in Florida. The man was fired from his long standing job just two months ago. That might be considered motive enough to kill themselves. The man hadn't tried to get unemployment, didn't look for a job either.

"Looks like this guy got canned and just gave up," Rick muttered leaving the bathroom. He walked into the kitchen again, it was a mess. Ten or twelve pizza boxes were stacked next to the trash bin. Plates and glasses filled one-half of the sink. Everything indicated he hadn't left the house in a week possibly two.

"Rick, I'm letting the ambulance crew take the body away," Sam said holding out a hand. Rick gave him back the multi-tablet. All the information was centrally held on the data-center anyway. Rick could call up the information with his own tablet later.

It was so weird. The guy apparently had money, a lot if he could afford a place like this. It wasn't a mansion but I was a million dollar home in the California suburbs. He never could understand why the rich killed themselves. Wasn't money happiness?

"What do think?" Sam asked. There wasn't any question about it. The only niggling fact to him was the appearance of the gun. It wasn't listed as being bought by Zeki or any relatives. The house was locked up tight though, no sign of struggle. The man just laid down and shot himself.

"Suicide," Rick said turning to the medical examiner who was just finishing his report.

"I'll write it up after I get to the station," Rick said. He followed after the body as the ambulance people took it away. Outside the cold air was hard on his lungs. It was just past five in the morning. Not even close to sunrise. Walking to his car he got into it and started the engine. The coffee was cold, but the whiskey helped warm him.

***

Kat shoved open the door to the living room and rushed in. A glowing godly being floated in after her. The creature was a very abstract looking rabbit. Like a tiny angel had grown bunny ears and little rabbit feet. Surrounding its body was an aura of power, and waves pulsed from its feet as it floated inside.

"Here he is," Kat said gesturing to Liam. The creature stopped next to Kat and turned golden eyes on Liam. For his part he rose from the chair.

"Are you sure?" The rabbit angel said in a melodious male voice.

"I've been in the same room with him the whole time," Kat said in exasperation.

"It's just hard to believe," The GM said cautiously.

"I was with him when he collapsed on the road. He came back ten minutes later, and we portalled back here. We've been together all night." Kat said coming closer to Liam.

"I'm more inclined to think this is a trick." The angel said slowly. Almost as if he didn't want to call the girl a liar.

"Walter, I know it's him," Kat said coming to stand before Liam. She put her fists on her hips as she looked up at his bony visage.

"When did we first meet?" She asked hotly.

"I recall a young paladin chained to an alter. She was about to get a dagger plunged into her chest."

"What?" The angel said with anger. "That is illegal to imprison someone, even virtually." It said but Kat turned to face the creature.

"Liam saved me and the culprits died," Kat said gesturing to Liam. She was looking at the godly rabbit as she continued sharply. "Walter, it's him and he can't log out." Walter continued to float a few feet off the ground. Liam had seen GM's work before. He thought the eyes seemed distant as the man worked. Finally, the rabbit made a grunting sound.

"I am confused, deeply. You're not connected to the server." He said refocusing his eyes.

"What do you mean, obviously he is," Kat said stomping a foot.

"I mean just that. There is no net data concerning his character." Walter said looking back to Liam. The rabbit remained where he was but seemed to be examining him.

"Can't you just force him out?" Kat said after a full minute.

"That was the first thing I tried," The rabbit said with widening golden eyes. "You haven't been logged in since 11:10 pm last night. At least as far as the system is concerned." He continued moving forward. The angel floated closer then circled Liam slowly. The rabbit seemed to be wrestling with his doubts.

"What VR machine do you have?" Walter asked.

"T250-D Dive Helmet," Liam answered immediately.

"That is an unrestricted developer set, how did you get that?" The rabbit asked next.

"I had money and I just bought the most expensive dive helmet I could find," Liam said shrugging his shoulders. The rabbit grunted non-committally.

"Try using the console," Walter responded.

"How?" Liam asked. He'd never heard of that option before.

"Just think 'Console,' and a drop box will appear in your vision," Walter said and Liam did but nothing happened.

"Console," Liam said after another second. Nothing occurred and the GM continued to circle him.

"I could delete your data, that should force you out," Walter said but Liam shot a hand out. His fingers curled around the neck of the rabbit. Instantly the angel froze in place with a face wrought with surprise. Within seconds the small floating angel vanished and reappeared several feet away.

"How did you do that?" The angel rasped angrily as the waves of power began to turn red. Cracks started to appear in the floor beneath the rabbit. A god was becoming angry. Liam faced the

GM summoning his staff to hand. The dark wood was shot through with green veins. The head of the staff carried an eldritch flame as if clutched by wooden fingers. He wasn't sure but being deleted sounded very final. Kat though got between them her arms extended.

"Stop it, both of you." She shouted turning a baleful glare on each.

"Walter, will you please help?" Kat asked after another few seconds. He relented.

"Of course I will, there are legal repercussions to this." The rabbit said his voice cooler. The aura of red violence shaded back into clear waves of power. The cracks in the wood floor began to fade. With a small pop of air the angelic rabbit was gone. Liam felt the tension leave his skeletal body. It hadn't been fear exactly, but he still held the urge to live, to exist. He sat again in the easy chair as Kat turned to glare at him.

"What was that?" Kat asked in irritation. "Walter was only here to help."

"He was quite blasé with his experiments. Will you do me a favor Kathrine? Can you find the number for the police in my area. Ask them to go to my house." Liam said keeping his unblinking gaze on his friend.

"You think something has gone that wrong?" Kat asked unable to hide the worry in her voice.

"The police have the jurisdiction to kick open my door and turn off the VR helmet." He replied reaching up and touching the side of his head. There was an emergency button on the device that could force a user to logout. Liam then gave her his address. She repeated it several times in order to remember it correctly. Instead of just leaving Kat took the time to go into her bedroom. The door closed and locked with finality.

CHAPTER NINETEEN

Kat - Muder/Hotline

Kat
Homespace

Kathrine was afraid, scared of the answer that would come with calling, but she picked up the phone and dialed.

"Nine-One-One please state the nature of the emergency." A professional female voice said.

"Possible medical emergency. The address is Delta St, Redding, CA, Liam Zeki." She said into the line.

There was long pause, but the woman came back. "Thank you, I'm going to transfer you to another line.

"Lieutenant Tracy," A male voice said.

"My name is Kathrine Ines. I'd like for someone to go to Address to check on a friend of mine." She said quickly. Her heart—though she didn't have one—felt like someone was squeezing it with a vice.

"When was the last time you talked to Mr. Zeki?"

"Last night, we were online together. Is he alright?" She asked. Her voice was trembling, she couldn't help it. Why couldn't she just cry to get rid of some of this tension? That would be helpful right now.

"I'm sorry to tell you he is dead. When did you see him again, please be specific?" The detective asked again. That was impossible, Liam was alive. She'd just talked to him a few minutes ago. Who had logged in, who had been sitting with her in the apartment?

"Just after 11 pm maybe close to midnight." She said after a few moments, and the detective made a grunting sound.

"11:23 pm," he said.

"Yes."

"Did you have an argument?"

"Argument? No, we were playing a game together and he suddenly disconnected." She said in a heated voice. Her confusion was mounting.

"Did he seem sad, or despondent?" Detective Tracy asked next.

"No we were just talking. He didn't seem any different than normal." Kat said quickly. Why was he asking if he was depressed?

"What happened to him, officer?"

"I'm afraid the case is still under investigation, so I cannot say."

"Where were you last night?" He asked next. Despite his consoling tone the words came out challenging. That pissed her off.

"At home obviously. I was online, logged into a virtual game with him."

"Where is that exactly?"

She decided to give him the address to the research lab. Let him visit her. Wouldn't that be a conversation? She'd welcome the look on him when they met face to brain tank. Kat knew she was getting angry, the cop was infuriating her.

"Did you know the victim recently lost his job recently?"

"I did, he told me that he was fired. It was bullshit what they did to him." She said still feeling annoyed. Why did he keep going on about the shit that went on with Liam's life? It was almost like… She didn't want to finish that thought.

"The victim didn't try and find new employment." The detective said.

"Of course not, he didn't need one. An hour after he was fired he owned the company he was fired from. At least twenty percent of it." Kat said in a scoffing tone.

"Did he have any enemies?" The detective asked. Kat laughed

bitterly before speaking, "Almost everyone at work. They treated him like shit." There was a slight pause in the conversation. The detective must have been taking notes. "I see. Is there anything else you can tell me?" He asked.

"Are you saying Liam committed suicide?"

"I can't say, ma'am."

"How could he hurt himself if he had a fucking dive helmet on? He would have been immobilized."

This time there was a much longer pause. Finally the detective spoke, "We found no virtual Dive Helmet."

"He had one, how else would he be playing with me?" Kat said getting angry for real now. The thick-headed detective was getting it through his skull. Something was fishy.

"Ma'am, I will continue to investigate this case. Thank you for calling, it has shed light on what is going on. Do you happen to know what kind of helmet it was?"

"I don't know," she said honestly before letting out an angry pent up breath. It was stupid getting so worked up at the guy.

"Let me give you my number. Are you calling from home?" He asked and she told him it was. The detective gave his number, which Kat jotted down. "If you have any more questions or information please call me." There was a pause. "I'm sorry for your loss." He added and Kat hung up numbly.

She sat there staring at the wall, eyes unfocused. Was that it? She couldn't believe the conversation had been so short. Kat almost dreaded logging back in. Liam was dead, gone, so who was logged in?

***

Sleep did not come to Liam, instead he got up and walked to the window of the living room. The apartment was high up in the city so it had cost them dearly for a month's lease. This though gave Liam a beautiful view of the city and the dragon bones. White marble buildings were festooned with brilliant banners.

Many of the facades were painted in garishly bright colors. As if the inhabitants refused to be overshadowed. It was the titanic set of rib bones that drew the eye. They say it was a dragon, but if it was, the creature was larger than a mountain. The story went that one of the gods had gone hunting. He'd chased the dragon across the sky for many years before he managed to wound the colossal creature. It had fallen so hard the valley had been created. The god had taken the head as a trophy leaving the body to decay. Over millennia the creature's flesh fell away until only a giant rib cage remained. It was morning still so the shadows across the city were long. A thick mist hung over the streets. The long bone shadows moved ever so slowly. A living city within a dead corpse and here he was, an undead man within.

Liam couldn't log out. He might very well be stuck in this world. Well, that wasn't so bad he reflected. In fact, he spent most of his waking hours online anyway. How long would that last though? Kat found him standing by the large bay windows. She'd come out of her private quarters without him noticing. Her face was still shocked.

"Who are you?" She asked from the bedroom doorway.

"Liam Zeki," He replied without looking back.

"That man is dead."

"How unfortunate, I'd feared the worst," Liam said in a tired voice.

"Who are you?" Kat asked more forcefully.

"I am Liam Zeki. Didn't you ask me earlier how we met?"

"This isn't possible."

"Dead?" Liam said aloud searching the sky outside the windows. The clouds were perfect, picturesque in their movement across the horizon.

"How?" He asked.

"They wouldn't tell me, but I got the impression from the questions the cop asked he thought it was suicide." Kat said her voice cold and distant.

"That is odd. What did you say to them exactly?" Liam asked after a few more moments. He turned finally to look at the petite woman. She continued to stare at him in response. After a time Kat spoke.

"I told them I was worried about you, and gave them your address. Asked me a lot of questions. Things like where I was last night. When did I talk to you? They wanted to know if you seemed depressed or sad lately. I told them I didn't know if you had any guns or not." She said trying to remember the long conversation with the detective.

"I can't remember all the details now. He was pretty intense." She said still staring at him. Suicide? Liam felt oddly detached about his death. Though, he'd expected them to find him stone cold from heart failure.

"Kathrine, I assure you. I did not kill myself. My life has been more fulfilling in the last few months than I can ever remember." He said in deep measured tones. The hardness in Kat's red eyes softened at his words. "Something doesn't make sense though. Why did they assume suicide?" Liam continued to ponder.

"I couldn't get anything out of the cop. I got the impression they were still investigating. He patently refused to say anything useful. It took him forever before he asked about the Dive Helmet and something clicked." Kat said moving closer to him. She wondered about that.

"That's right!" Kat said snapping her fingers. "Anyone with a pair of eyes would have seen the helmet you were wearing. You couldn't have done anything if you were logged into the game." She said thinking through the problem. That should mean whoever killed Liam took the Dive Helmet.

"You were murdered! Whoever did it took your helmet." Kat nearly screamed.

"Probably," He said in reply.

"Why are you taking this so calmly?" She asked suddenly.

"Should I beat and flail at the injustice? Honestly, I feel liberated now. If anything it's annoyance and confusion." He said searching his emotions.

"I'm not letting this go," Kat said and Liam approached her.

"Not asking you too."

Liam didn't think that was going to change anything. They might keep the case open while waiting for the dive helmet to turn up at a pawn shop. Liam suspected it was a drug addict that had snuck into his home. Walter appeared again in a flash of angelic light. He too seemed at a loss.

"Your character logged out close to midnight, and the account hasn't been accessed in that time." He said shaking his head, bunny ears flopping. None of them added much to the conversation. For about two hours they talked in circles edging around the idea of souls. None willing to speculate on the nature of Liam's new condition. Was he alive, or dead, or a ghost in the system? A phantom left over from his mortal shell. For his part he remained mostly silent as Kat and Walter talked. He didn't feel like some empty shell. Liam remembered things, many things. His sixth birthday party, which had been a disaster. Highschool, trips to the convenience store, even those shitty days at work. Walter's duties took the high-level GM away. Though he promised to keep looking into the mystery. Kat moved about the front room. She made herself busy by brewing another cup of her blood tea. Liam was content just to watch her.

"What will you do?" Kat asked taking a seat nearby. They sat across from each other as the night before. He smiled remembering Kat had asked that same question on another continent.

"The same thing I always do." He replied still grinning a deaths head.

"What's that?" Kat asked over her tea.

"Try and take over the world," Liam said with a dark gallows chuckle.

"I mean… you know," Kat said dryly waving her hand towards the apartment.

"Level," Liam said as if it were obvious. It was the only real option left to him.

"You could die," Kat said a little more sharply than she intended.

"I have already died Kat, but I understand your meaning. I

could be killed again." Liam glanced over Kat's shoulder at two squares of bright light that poured in from the bay windows. The late morning sun was high over the valley walls. A shadow though was present among the two splashes of light. A rib as large as a castle tower was casting a shadow partly on the apartment.

"I will go stir crazy in this room," Liam admitted looking around the suite.

"I can relate to that," Kat said in all seriousness. Liam let out a cleansing breath. Without lungs the effect was more mental than physical. It gave him a few precious seconds to think.

"If I don't level… if I hide someone will find me. I'll be weak, and easy to kill when that happens. There is danger in leveling as well. So I have a choice between certain death later and possible death now. I'm not afraid, Kat. I think that's been taken from me." Liam said standing.

"You could be safe in town," Kat said as if urging him to remain.

"Am I?" Liam asked gesturing towards the door. If he so much as stepped outside the guards would attack him without mercy. Going out to level was hazardous too. The PVP attack of some weeks ago was still fresh in his memory. They'd brought five people to kill what they thought was one man. Not very sporting.

"You're right the risk is high. Maybe it's time to help level the guild up. Besides you kept telling me I should be more active with our members." Liam said before reaching up and touching his menu. The social window appeared before him. He was glad to see he was still part of the guild. His name was even listed as online. Liam would forever be so now.

"Wow, I didn't know we had over fifty members already." He said after a few seconds.

"You would if you'd talk to them," Kat said in an annoyed huff.

"I am suitably chastised." He replied in a more humorous tone. Liam was still scrolling through the list of members. About ten of them were just over level twenty, so he and Kat were nine levels higher. Most of the guild was sitting in the mid to upper teens.

Only a handful of names were online. As a whole, they would start logging in as dusk approached. People would get off work, eat dinner, then get online to play.

CHAPTER TWENTY

Questions and Answers

Walter Nowel
Communal Social Space
5pm

Walter was wearing his human avatar for once. He hadn't broken out the model in so long it lacked many of the features his main avatar had. His facial expressions were limited and it was missing a few add-ons he'd grown accustomed too. Sadly it was necessary for meeting in this realm. They didn't allow non-standard avatars within the Chinese netspace. This was a long distance connection anyway. The lag was quite noticeable. The small rickshaw stopped before the oriental restaurant. He climbed down clumsily and waved at the smaller oriental NPC. The Chinese driver tipped his wide straw hat and pulled back into traffic. For a moment he watched the footman disappear. This world was like many social realms, which reflected a point in history. Specifically the Yang Dynasty in 13th century China.

Walter was here to get some answers. Only after he'd started digging had he encountered the rumors of ghosts. The word 'Gui,' had been repeated frequently. He'd been hampered by the language barrier. That was why he needed to meet an old acquaintance. When working on the game characters he'd become friends with the Chinese programmer. He knew the man was still on the Asian programming board. This was why he'd contacted his associate and asked to have dinner with the man, virtually.

Liam the poor soul had been online for three days straight. To every appearance the necromancer was a permanent entity within the world. There was one all-important question Walter wanted to ask. What happened when the servers went down? Would Liam vanish? There was a scheduled patch coming in a few days. It wasn't large but there was no way to stop it. That's what had spurned this meeting. Walter turned and walked up the stone steps. At his approach the double doors were opened by two kimono wearing girls. They spoke in the local historically correct Chinese dialect. The words automatically translated for him.

"Good Evening Lord. Welcome to the Golden Dragon," Both girls said in unison.

"I'm here to see Mr. Chisan," Walter said to the girls. A new NPC employee appeared from a nearby door, and bowed as deeply as her formal white kimono would allow.

"I can show you to our private booths." The girl said pointing with a slim hand down the hall. Walter followed walking past several closed rice paper doors. He could see the shadows of people inside. Their words though were thoroughly muffled inside. The thin privacy screens were more than just for show. The woman stopped about halfway down and the girl slid the door open. Ji Chisan was already waiting but stood as the door opened.

"Walter, its been forever." He said in nearly perfect English.

"I agree. We both have been very busy though." Walter said entering the private booth.

"I've already taken the liberty of ordering for us, I hope you don't mind," Ji said coming around the table. He held out a hand which Walter warmly took.

"Not at all, you always had good taste," Walter admitted. Ji's avatar was very close to how it had looked long ago. His facial features were young but round showing his ancestry. Dark hair was carefully combed back with a clean shaven face. The one thing that set Ji apart from others was an eyebrow piercing. It was something of a family tradition for the man.

"You haven't changed at all," Ji said moving back around the table. He sat easily within the redwood oriental chair.

"Not my usual avatar," Walter said coming forward. He pulled a chair free from the table.

"The white rabbit and the rabbit hole?" Ji asked with amusement.

"I always did like Alice in Wonderland," Walter admitted taking a seat. "How is the family?" He asked.

"Wei is in art college and doing part time work for Fuko Animations. Chun is married to an accountant and already on her second baby." Ji admitted, pride color his words.

"That is good to hear. I remember Wei's sketches even in middle school were good." Walter said with a pleasant grin. He did, in fact, recall the young boy's art. Walter still had a few of his pictures saved to a hard drive somewhere.

"Have you gotten married yet?" Ji asked.

"Sadly not, I always spend too much time at work. Not enough hours left for chasing girls." Walter said and Ji nodded as if he knew the answer. Walter did spend much of his time working inside the game world. It was becoming faster and easier to do everything virtually.

"You should, its a shame you don't have children," Ji said and Walter nodded. Maybe he would look into it but he had more pressing problems. The food arrived before he could ask his questions. Three girls swept into the private booth with several plates. His mouth began to water from the smell of the spicy food. Taking up the small red lacquered chopsticks, Walter brought the first bite of food to his lips. It was a flavor explosion. Heat stung his tongue and sinuses from the Chinese chili peppers. His impression was solidified from several more bites.

"Damn." He said lowering the chopsticks. Ji looked at him over his food.

"I'm going to have this on the brain until I order it for real." He said and the other man grinned around a mouthful of rice. The meal continued pleasantly though Walter had to reach for the water several times.

"How do you like being a GM. I had not thought you would

part from the coding circle."

"It is very fulfilling. In a way, it is like watching a baby grow. At first my children groped and flailed during the first week. They struggled because everything was so new. I caught a lot of heat for not telling people how they should play the game. Soon, soon they began to crawl, and even walk. Now it is keeping me very busy watching as they start to run."

"I see, maybe this game is your family," Ji said carefully.

"This is also part of the reason I wanted to talk to you," Walter said watching Ji over his chopsticks.

"One of my children has a problem." He admitted and Ji's face seemed curious. Walter didn't have a good way of asking so he just let it out. "Have you heard of players who cannot log out?" He asked in a casual tone. The other man laughed and shook his head.

"You are joking with me now?" Ji asked but something in his tone was different. It sounded measured maybe even a little distant.

"Ji, I'm not joking. I've heard company scuttlebutt the Chinese officials have been snooping around Shanghai branch. Why is the government interested in what were doing?" Walter asked and saw a further closure from his friend. If anything he suddenly seemed nervous. He set his chopsticks down carefully and lifted a napkin to his lips.

"I'm sorry, Walter I can't stay," Ji said apologetically and stood. He'd been so friendly up until that question. Walter suspected he was on the right track.

"So its true?" Walter asked quickly. Ji friend stood, but he reached for him and grabbed a wrist.

"Is that why suicides are skyrocketing in China?" Walter asked desperately. Ji pulled his wrist free and walked out of the door and down the hall. He was left alone with the remains of the meal. Walter sat back down in his chair in surprise. Ji had all but run away from him in his haste. After a few seconds he realized he hadn't even asked the question he came here for. The update was just days away. He had no idea if Liam would disappear when the servers went down. He felt suddenly sick, and pushed the plate of food away from himself. Maybe he wouldn't get any Chinese for himself tonight.

CHAPTER TWENTY-ONE

Lich Born

Kat - Level 29
Tramin Continent - Mirza Mansion

In the dark foyer Kat held a party stone aloft, and smiled at the other vampires gathered around her. After a few seconds she hurled the small artifact to the carpet. Quickly it broke apart into a large glowing circle. The large room was filled briefly with blinding magical light. Then five more vampires stood in the group.

"Come along children, the others await," Kat said brightly beckoning everyone deeper into the old mansion. Tonight was a gathering of the host. All that was online was meeting for a friendly talk. A short raven-haired female trotted up next to Kat and eyed her gothic dress.

"That's such a cute dress." The girl said eying Kat's outfit jealously. Today it was a red and black corset with matching skirt. The fabric parted to show off a bare leg that ended in black high heels. Her arms were covered in a see-through lace.

"Thank you. It's a game store costume, which cost about ten shards." Kat said smiling at the tiny girl. Ten shards were about how much all the full outfits cost. Smaller items like hats and accessories cost between one the three shards each. The girl though made a pouting face.

"I can't afford much more than the monthly subscription." The young vampire admitted.

"It is a good investment. Keeps people from telling what class you are at a glance." Kat said still leading the way. Her heels clicked loudly on the old wooden floorboards.

"That could be useful," Someone in the crowd said. They reached the dining room and Kat pushed open the double doors. More players were waiting inside, forty vampires all in the same location. It made Kat's undead heart flutter at the sight. Typically she only ever saw two or three in a group. Most were seated, others talked in small groups by the tall stain glass windows. It was a cloudy night and the large moon fought for space in the sky. It made for a particularly dark evening.

"Where is the necromancer?" A raspy voice asked from the shadows. Slowly a player became visible, and Kat recognized the half-elven rogue. She still wasn't sure she trusted the man but he'd made the effort to join. Apparently, the question had occurred to more than a few because quite a few people were keenly watching her.

"Folken, it's nice to see you made it. He'll be here shortly," Kat said politely. None had ever lain eyes on the mysterious co-leader, except Folken in his previous incarnation. As if the demon himself had been called the door at the far end opened. The creaking hinges squealed in protest as it did. All eyes turned at the sound.

A tall purple robed mage stepped into the dining room. The malformed skeleton carried with him an eldritch flaming staff. It made the white marble crown of his skull turn a shade of neon green in the light. Trailing the necromancer were four undead bandits from the ruined castle nearby. He'd recently hit level thirty and gained a new pet slot. Each carried a pair of short cutlasses and mismatched leather armor. Without pausing he strode forward into the room. Kat moved to him with a bounce and took his bony hand.

"Everyone, may I introduce Liam." She said loudly. It wasn't like they didn't know his name.

"The only necromancer on the server." A man within the group whispered.

"I'm glad to see you all," Liam said in a deep voice. He walked with Kat to the table and pulled the chair out for her. She graciously smiled at him and took the seat at the head of the table. Liam moved a second chair to sit at her right side.

"So how did you do it?" Someone finally asked as they all seated themselves.

"That question is exactly why Liam has remained mostly silent in guild chat," Kat said before Liam could answer. "However that is part of the reason I called this meeting." She said loudly enough to reach all ears. In response Liam withdrew two tomes, both identical as he set one on the table.

"One of these grimoires is Liam's tome. The other is a blank. In order to change class you must find a lich's spellbook. Then you bond with it. Just like when a wizard earns their spellbook from the guild." Kat said as Liam pushed the blank tome down the table. That was it. The secret wasn't so impressive once you figured it out. Hands turned and flipped the grimoire's empty pages.

"When a necromancer is made that lich's spellbook no longer functions. The one you see before you is from the crypt south of New Hearth." Kat said pointing at the grimoire in question. It was still making its way down the table slowly.

"You mean he's the only one?" Folken asked down the table.

"For now, I called us here so that we can get another," Kat said and silence descended.

"We can make more? Be the only guild with necromancers." The girl from earlier said with avarice glee. Kat smiled at the tiny vampire.

"That is our hope. There is still much about the class that is cloaked in mystery." Liam said cutting in for the first time. His deep voice was a sonorous boom in the dining hall.

"The trouble is the local lich is surrounded by monsters. He's carved himself a home within an old mineshaft. Most of the caves are filled with dwarven claim jumpers and their automata's. It is roughly level twenty to thirty, so it will be no walk in the park. We're going to make it a raid and leveling night. We only have one cleric who's going to be stretched very thin keeping us all undead and beautiful." Kat said gesturing to the under leveled human down the table. He was so new he was still garbed in his white priest robes. The holy symbols had been burned off, scoured away by fire. His cleric class had been changed to something called a heretic. The man was going to be popular as the guild's sole healer.

"I'd like everyone to group up roughly by level. I'll start a raid and invite the leaders into it." Kat said and waited. For a few minutes there was a flurry of talking. Excited people were locating others of their level range. While waiting Kat sent an invitation to Liam. He accepted and she saw his icon appear on her window. She let out a quiet sigh of relief. It was the first time they'd grouped since the event. She'd been secretly fearful he couldn't join them. Next, she withdrew a half dozen party talismans and passed those down the table. They were for the leaders which they'd summon after getting to the mine.

"How long will this take?" Someone asked and Kat nodded at the question.

"It won't take long to assemble but the mine is old and extensive. We don't have maps of the tunnels themselves. So it could take all night. Anyone who needs to leave during the event can just portal home. We are bringing more than we need as overkill. I want everyone to have fun and be safe." Kat said and stood from her chair. Others joined her as she rose. Kat was worried for Liam. The enemy lich was reportedly level thirty which matched Liam's power. Kat had told him in no uncertain terms to let the guild do all the grunt work. The blank grimoire finally made its way around the dining table. Liam scooped it up and back into his robe. They could always get more later.

"Before I head out I'd like to offer a recruitment bonus. We're a growing family and I like that. Whenever you bring in a child of the night the guild will give you a hundred gold." Liam said before stepping back from the table. Kat thought this was an excellent idea. One of the nice things about the guild bank was that it taxed its members. A tiny ghost tariff was added to anything they bought or sold. People could also buy equipment directly from the guild bank. The rarest equipment Kat and Liam found always went to their members. It was good business to keep the market close at hand.

"What if we bite them too?" A large green and brown half-orc vampire said. His voice was nearly as deep as Liam's.

"That seems like the easiest method for gaining new members. How about this. Each month the person with the highest recruitment will earn an additional thousand gold." Kat cut in. With how fast the bank grew it wouldn't hurt to add the extra incentive. If anything Kat could now afford the expense.

Liam took out his staff again. As a necromancer his newly acquired teleport spell could only affect himself. A conjurer using the spell would spend half the mana and be able to take an entire group with him. Liam's staff was held before him base touching the ground. A large bony hand shot past the hefty dark wood in a series of gestures. Circles of energy formed around the necromancer as a hum filled the dining room. A long ten seconds later he was gone.

"He's nicer than I expected." A girl said in a bubbly voice.

"Liam saved my life once when I was mortal," Kat told them. It didn't take long to teleport everyone from the mansion to the mine entrance. Soon they were delving inside.

Kat didn't much like being underground. She wouldn't admit it to anyone but she was mildly claustrophobic. Maybe it stemmed from so much time in her little hospital room. She did her best to fight down the emotion. The eight groups of vampires were well adapted to hunting in the dark. Dwarves too never bothered with torches. It was one of the reasons people liked playing the stout little race. Not to mention the cool steampunk technology they got to play with. Kat was standing near Liam and watching the action. Two groups of newbies were tackling a level twenty-five drilling bot. Another smaller group was killing the two dwarven claim jumpers. So far she hadn't done much. She and Liam would jump in to help if things turned hectic. Thankfully the guild members were sticking together. The raid system partially divided any experience gained from each monster. Over half still went to the most damaging group. That was why the lowest level groups were doing the lion's share of the work.

"This isn't bad," Liam commented next to her. Kat nodded and glanced at the scout group coming back. They were dragging along a dwarven foreman and a sentry bot.

"Bastard has a water cannon," Folken said running past them.

A hairy faced dwarf wearing loose coveralls had a large metal backpack on. It was chugging madly as belts and gears whirred. The little dwarf was as fat around the middle as he was tall. Still, he ran towards the raid flesh jiggling. A plume of steam announced the activation of the water canon. The dwarf foreman skidded to a stop aiming the nozzle at the retreating rogues. A jet of hot water shot from the end striking a vampire square in the back. The blow sent the scout bouncing across the ground. Kat hoped the cleric was already moving to heal the man. The attack had taken a massive HP chunk from the lower level player.

Next came a strange piece of equipment. This was the first time Kat had seen the technology. The sentry bot was all gears and steaming valves. The metal contraption stalked quickly forward on six legs like a spider. One arm ended in a spinning saw blade while the other wielded a large heater shield. It raced past the dwarven foreman towards the raid. Kat waited with Liam trusting everyone to work together. Her guild members did their jobs well. The primary blocking force moved in past the scouts. Unable to target the first attackers the sentry bot switched to the new group.

While they did this the dwarven foreman was moving forward. His backpack was chugging away again trying to reload the pressure chamber. Liam made no move, not even to send in the few undead dwarves he'd raised. Finally she couldn't resist, Kat stepped towards the foreman. She came towards it with shield raised. Its water shot became ready with a loud hiss just as Kat got before it. The squat dwarf was grinning maniacally as it aimed at her. The force of the impact on her shield shoved her backward. Even with the protection her health dropped by a good fifteen percent. That water gun was slow firing but it packed a punch. The raid was already mopping up the sentry bot. Four groups converged on the hapless foreman. Kat was happy to make way for them. With so many attackers the dwarf was brought down before he could reload again.

They hadn't lost any guild members so far. Only a couple of close calls from the lowest level vampires. Kat joined the scouts as they moved further down the cave. Soon they pulling and killing again. The raid groups cycled forward and back after each fight. This let others rest while the fresh troops fought.

It took a while to find the entrance to the lich's labyrinth. By 2 am half of the raid had gone home for the night. Day jobs and responsibilities took their toll on their numbers. Kat had three groups left. They'd found the entrance by first locating the heavy dwarven defenses. Layers of sentries were set up with low rubble walls. A killing maze of paths the mindless undead couldn't navigate.

Finally, they discovered the dungeon entrance. There was a clear separation from the caves they'd been dug from. Magically cut stones were fit together to form arched hallways and rooms. Age had taken much of the beauty away. Cave moss and dirt covered most of the fine stone work. The undead were captured dwarven miners forced into undead servitude. At least the raid could simply walk past the monsters. Traps though were still an annoying danger. Arrow and pit traps were unusually prevalent as they went deeper. The rogues proved their worth here along with Liam's endless supply of pets. He often ordered them to blunder into a trap to activate it.

At last they came to a large room, more of a pit really. Almost a hundred undead shambled back and forth. A sea of decaying flesh and dead-eyed stares. An elevated circular floor floated above the mass by some central pillar. On the far side, a open doorway could be seen. Something lit the space showing the distant skeleton sitting on a throne. Kat had no doubt the floor was meant to drop the unwary into those waiting claws. The raid group stood before the platform, none quite willing to get onto it. Liam had his minions though. He pointed out into the center of the floor.

"Move there," He said and four pets shuffled past. Almost immediately the floor began to descend. The weight of the dwarves caused the large trap to tilt. Soon it was angled so much the pets fell into the pit. As they slid free the floor started to reset itself. Everyone looked down into the mass. Liam's undead and the zombies were bumping into each other but not attacking.

"Let us go down," Liam said to Kat.

"What?" Kat asked in confusion.

"What about the floor?" Someone else asked just as confused as she.

"Maybe it's a logic puzzle," Kat admitted already thinking of the weight allowances. She'd come up with the idea of sending one person across at a time.

"It's a trick, think about it. All this time he's used annoying traps, making people fight to get across. By now everyone wants this dungeon finished." Liam said pointing across the way.

"Too much weight and it tips. So we just cross one at a time." Folken said from the shadows nearby. "Let me try," He went on. Nobody protested the idea of him triggering the trap. Kat stepped aside as the scout approached.

"You could die," She said to the former Paladin.

"Meh," Was the reply. As soon as the rogue stepped out onto the floor it started to descend slowly. The large circle was perfectly balanced and any extra weight made it tilt. The half-elf moved away quickly reaching the center of the large disk. Soon the floor began to reset itself now that the thief was in the middle. A dagger became visible as Folken threw it. The missile sailed across the forty feet and struck something bouncing off. The distance though was too great to see any detail, especially with dark vision. He turned and ran back. The floor descended again from the extra weight.

"Make room!" Folken shouted as he sprinted forward. The raid members quickly backed away for the man. The floor was at least ten feet down but the agile little vampire made the jump. He hit the edge and climbed quickly.

"You were right, its an illusion. I couldn't see past the floor but I'll bet two testies there's an even bigger drop on the other side." Folken said not even panting. The remaining raid members looked to one another intrigued. The game did not set up puzzles for players to pass. It worked hard to kill the players like they were supposed too.

"That's quite a dirty trick if you think about it. Some group starts charging over one at a time." Liam said in appreciation. Each adventurer came to you and mostly injured at that. "I think I like this lich." He said after another second. Kat wondered how many parties had made it past this point so far. Without notice Liam stepped onto the floor edge. Taken by surprise Kat followed. Several others followed suit and the floor quickly hit the ground twenty feet below. Broken and crushed bodies lay nearby as each stepped off. Being undead they weren't attacked. Faces looked down at them from above.

"One group at a time, try not to kill us coming down," Kat said before turning to look for Liam. The necromancer seemed to be circling the far wall. In small clusters the entire force came down.

"This way!" Liam shouted from further away. The zombie horde turned to face the noise. Kat followed after her friend. Halfway across the room they found a railing. It was a barrier to keep the mass of zombies from falling into the pit on the other side.

"Oh you cheeky bastard," Liam said pointing to a gate and stairs just on the other side. From here she could see the far wall was a polished silver metal. It was angled so anything hitting it would fall into the pit.

Kat went down the stairs first. She opened the simple latch and followed the stairs down the inner side of the pit. It descended forty feet almost directly in front of the lich. A pool of still water on the ground cast a mirror image of the boss. This is what was reflected above. A pile of bones lay before the throne to indicate previous victims of the trap. A set of heavily armored skeleton surrounded Kat on each side. Kat stepped off the stairs to let others go by. When the first group came down she pointed to the throne.

"Go over there by the lich. Attack him when he starts to move." She said to the leader. The half-orc nodded to her and moved to flank the throne. Another came down so she gestured towards the nearest guard. Liam was halfway down the stairs when the Lich stood.

"Necromancer," It hissed in a sibilant wheezing tone. "You'll not steal my power." It said next as the guards moved in.

"Attack!" Kat yelled before turning to the nearest undead. Drawing her weapon caused the armor to morph around her body. She hacked at the undead warrior with her obsidian battle axe. Spells were already flying back and forth above her.

"Acid Arrow," Liam boomed from above. Yellow magic flashed past to strike the lich.

The last group rushed past her as the raid came down the stairs. Liam remained above though as he fired at the lich from his height. She was glad he was taking his safety seriously. The large undead attacked again brutally. Her battlefield had narrowed to the high level skeleton trying to kill her. She shield bashed at the magical weapon as it came down. The skeleton staggered back. This gave her time to circle the creature's other side. Her axe flashed yellow letting her know she'd activated the flanking skill correctly. As the undead came in for another attack she blocked. Sparks flew from her heater shield as it absorbed the weapon's attack. She was losing the battle one on one. It attacked again using a warrior's triple strike skill. Kat's health dropped again before the raid began attacking her target. Above her, Liam was shooting his eldritch bolts down onto friendly vampires. Liam could provide incredibly good targeted heals. The absent cleric was much better at party sized spells. With more than twenty on her side the fight didn't last long. Kat ducked a sword swipe from the undead and she killed it with a blow to its exposed leg. Liam hopped the last few stairs to land beside her.

"Holy Crap!" A deep orcish voice said.

"We just got a first boss kill bonus." Another said excitedly. It was the higher level group she'd sent over to flank the undead mage.

"Got two levels killing that lich." The orc added which answered a previous question. Nobody had quite made it this far to kill the boss.

"Were we supposed to do that?" The fighter asked sheepishly.

"A necessary evil," Liam said walking past the raid group. Kat followed moving by the throne. It was intricately carved with white polished stone. Trap symbols were lit up all over the arms of the chair. Was that to let the lich know who was coming? What an odd wizard. The lich seemed less about turning undead than putting them back together. Rows of half completed bodies were set up like grotesque mannequins. As if the necromancer was assembling them from the pieces of left over adventurers.

A strange thing happened then. As Liam got near the spellbook stand the air started to hum. He stopped in surprise. This was new, the book was shaking visibly where it sat. Its pages flipped back and forth as if in anticipation.

"Is that supposed to happen?" One of the vampires said from behind them.

"It's new to us," Kat admitted but Liam took another step forward.

With each foot he traveled closer the noise became louder. The hum turned into murmuring voices. Like a thousand souls whispering over one another. As Liam's bony hand touched its pages a wave of eldritch power swept past Kat. She shielded her eyes briefly from the green flash of light. When she looked again two new books floated in the air before the necromancer. A blue tome and a light gray one with black iron clasps. Slowly the three books started to circle Liam, their pages flapping back and forth wildly. Circles of greenish fire formed around him. Liam's spell book appeared next. It came free of his inventory on its own. Slowly it opened until the spine was revealed. From inside an orange magically chained mote of light came forth. Green and black glyphs stretched from the pages to bind the ball of energy. Liam slowly lifted from the ground to hang in the air. His arms forced out away from his body.

The whole group was spellbound by the sight. The three extra books started to add their own chains of symbols to the orange ball. Green and black tendrils were snaking out to encircle Liam's soul. Faster and faster the books flew around Liam. With each rotation, the ball of power grew larger. Soon it was melon sized and pulsating with power. Instead of going back into the spell book the soul moved towards Liam. He cried out as the ball sank into his chest. As it did the three circling books crumbled into dust, just like a scroll after it's been used. Another booming wave of eldritch power ended the spell. Liam landed heavily on his feet and he staggered back. His grimoire was clutched tightly in his hands. Kat rushed towards him but stopped as she caught sight of his visage. He was different. The flames that had once been in his eyes now encased his whole head. The green aura licked back and forth around his deformed skull. As if his powers were so great they couldn't be contained any longer. The lower half of his jaw was missing. Instead, his head floated between his shoulders by a non-existent spine.

"Are you Ok?" Kat asked tremulously.

"That hurt like a bitch," Liam said in a voice that too was changed. The deepness was still there but now it thrummed and echoed with power. She approached him and took his hand. That at least was the same.

"What was that?" Folken said from the group.

"I think he just classed up. He was level thirty, remember." A female in the group said.

"Oh," Liam said simply. He raised a hand in the empty air to check his character. "I've ranked up to Lich," Liam said still touching open air. "I can make more grimoire too, but it costs a lot of experience." He said in a power echoing voice.

"It destroyed three of our books." Kat reminded him.

"Now I can make as many as we need," Liam said and Kat grinned at him after a few seconds.

"That is a pretty good trade in the long run," she admitted. The raid didn't have much to do after killing the boss. All that was left was to divide up the remaining loot and portal home. The guild said its goodbye's via chat and started to log off.

CHAPTER TWENTY-TWO

Patch Day

Liam - Level 30
Apartment Suite - Dragonfall City
02:45am

He had a dilemma for sure, though not exactly life threatening. Sure he looked cool, even a few of the vampires had backed away from Liam. The flaming head was wickedly impressive. His voice too seemed to project from him instead of coming from a voice box. His problem was more subtle. It was the fact he had no lower jaw. Certainly the effect was visually appealing but it came with one major drawback. He had nowhere to put his hand when he wanted to relax. Gone was the time he could rest his chin on his palm. The best he could manage was fingers pressing on his temple and two knuckles tucked under his cheekbone. Unfortunately this blocked half his vision and forced him into a strange sitting posture. The long tusks he finally grown accustomed too were missing as well. He could no longer tap at them in thought. It was a small but somewhat vexing problem.

The second problem was technically more concerning. Walter had come back with a short reply. He couldn't say if Liam were going to survive the coming game patch. He couldn't or wouldn't admit that Liam soon would cease to exist. There was no way to delay the scheduled update. The patch had been planned weeks in advance and today was its launch. The announcements had started several hours ago warning players to find a safe location to log out. Liam wasn't exactly worried, the fear of death was suspiciously absent in his emotions. All he felt was annoyance at being unable to take any action for his own safety. His existence was out of his hands, so he sat quietly waiting. Sat awkwardly because of his first problem. Kat though seemed to be doing the worrying in spades. Her diminutive form paced back and forth in the living room. Her quick short treading was wearing a path in the carpet. Liam tried to calm her.

"I think it was good to get the children together," Liam said casually in his deep, measured voice. He'd meant the guild members of course. Kat affectionately called them her children of the night. She stopped mid step to look at him. His statement had thrown a wrench into her grinding gears. Kat said nothing for a few seconds as she replayed his words in her mind.

"Yes, I agree. Now they know they're not alone." Kat replied after some consideration. "It was a productive raid, and almost everyone leveled up." She continued turning from her place. She came closer to Liam unafraid of his new appearance.

"How close are you to thirty?" He asked.

"A few hours of grinding," Kat said dismissively. She wasn't to be put off the worry train so easily. As if to rattle her further a system announcement popped up. It appeared right in Liam's face so that he couldn't ignore it.

[System Announcement]
[The server will be going down in 15 minutes.]

Liam touched the translucent square to dismiss it. Kat slapped hard at the air before her face. Her dainty fingers sliced through her own window like a steel blade.

"You should log off Kat. I can tell you from personal experience a forced logout is unpleasant." Liam said and Kat scowled.

"I'm staying with you to the end." She replied throwing herself next to him on the large couch. The fireplace was going, a forgotten pot of water boiling away. Kat clutched at the sleeve of his robe. She needed a distraction badly so she played with the fabric of his dark purple robe. Liam suspected she got that habit from one of her parents.

"Tell me about yourself, Kathrine." He said shifting to look at her. In response, Kat took one of his bony hands and dragged it into her lap. It was so she could inspect it more carefully. Her fingers traced over his thick hand bones. She stared at it as if she could divine something by reading his fleshless palm.

"Not much to say really. I was well… disturbingly normal. At fifteen all I liked was boys and pretty clothes." She said running cold smooth fingers over his knuckle bones. Kat still wasn't looking at him but remained deeply interested in her inspection.

"Around that time I started to have painful flashes on my left side. They thought it might be the warning signs of a stroke. Soon though the sensation spread to both my legs. In a short time I lost most of my mobility. They took me from doctor to doctor, and all had their ideas. Within two years I was paralyzed from the neck down. I couldn't talk or even turn my head." She said haltingly. The memories made her voice shake with emotion. Kat's strong little hands started pulling at his skeletal index finger. As if she could pull off one. They refused to come away farther than a half millimeter.

"I'm dead," Kat said in a small voice.

"Like me?" Liam asked.

"No," Came the whisper barely audible. "They cut out my brain and put it in their VR machine. I don't even have a body. Just a lump of gray floating in a glass jar." She said suddenly regretful she'd ever signed on for the procedure. All the time she spent in game made sense to him now.

"Is that why you don't like tight places?" Liam asked and she finally looked up at him. Her red eyes lacked any tears but looked as if she was about the burst a dam.

"How did you know?"

"You kept checking the exit like you were reminding yourself there was a way out," Liam said looking down at his small companion.

"Ahh, yes I guess so. I think it is also from my time at the hospital. Three years stuck in a tiny little room." She said pushing his hand away finally. There was another announcement indicating they had ten minutes left. Kat growled and slapped the air. Their last moments together were being timed down to the second.

"What about you?" Kat asked.

"Overweight since middle school. Didn't have a sliver of self-esteem for years. Not until I started playing Nigmus where the rules were different. I didn't have to listen to anyone I didn't want too. My blocked list is two thousand names deep."

"You're kidding." She said with a stifled laugh.

"Nope. Once an entire guild started spamming the word 'Die,' over and over. Two hundred names went on the block list in minutes." He said remembering fondly as the inane chat dialog trickled to peaceful silence. Kat seemed to remember the pot on the fireplace and pulled it free of the pit. She didn't try making herself any tea though. Instead, she came back directly to sit next to him. The conversation took a hiatus. Kat refused to look at him as she played with the folds of her dress. A five-minute warning came and Liam dismissed it immediately.

"I like you, Liam." She said not looking his way. Black hair was down covering the side of her face hiding her profile from him.

"I was falling for you too." He admitted.

"Not now?" She asked glancing towards him. Did he like Kat? He searched himself, looking within what counted for his heart. His emotions danced around his mental fingers. Despite not being able to grasp them firmly he did feel.

"I do," He said making Kat look at him with those big red eyes. Kat reached over and clutched at his robe again. "I enjoy your presence." He admitted and she continued to search his face. Time seemed to slip away so quickly. For minutes she stared at him, memorizing its every detail. The final announcement came. The system was being shut down. At the last second, Kat lunged towards Liam. Her arms wrapped around his shoulders as she kissed him. Soft lifeless lips pressed against his sharp teeth.

Then it all ended, but not like an explosion. The world did not end with a bang but with a whimper. Everything slowed like an old tape deck being stopped. Characters and objects slithered into a frozen state. The last half millisecond of life seemed to drag on an age as the world dissolved. Sensations began to blur. The smell of Kat's body mixed sensuously with the touch of her lips. The feel of the couch under him and sound of the crackling fireplace smeared together. Then there was nothing. Liam was not aware but time did pass. Almost three hours went missing for him. Real mortal technicians ignorant of Liam's plight applied the scheduled patch. Engineers rushed to match the deadline for launch. Patch checks were made and the server was green lit. Finally, the Chief Server Tech brought the stable build up without going live.

Even before the world loaded he was conscious. Liam saw the living room created like a light switch being thrown about him. After a few seconds the body of Kat appeared atop him. Her eyes were closed but her lips were still pressed against him. Kat's head lulled as gravity took hold of her body. Liam caught her and lowered Kat like a rag doll to the couch. He had time now to look at her face. Her pale skin and dark hair were at peace like a child resting. He brushed at the tangles of hair moving her locks back behind her pointed ears. His emotions were still in turmoil. Walter appeared before he could try and sort them out. With a comical little pop a glowing rabbit body arrived in the living room. Liam turned and saw the high-level GM as he came over.

"I'm glad you are OK," Walter said relief written on his small cherubic face.

"Me too," Liam admitted.

"How was it?" Walter asked curiously.

"I didn't feel a thing," Liam said after a short pause. He was searching for any memories in between the sudden kiss and now. There was a blankness, like a clock missing time. After a second he dismissed the vague feeling with a shake of the head.

"The servers aren't live yet. The technicians are checking

stability now." Walter said in a matter of fact tone.

"I see."

"It will be another twenty minutes before any players can log in," Walter said next and Liam stood from the couch. Liam felt restless and he wanted a moment away from Kat's body. She was still distracting him.

"You said this is happening in China?" Liam asked moving towards the window. He had the urge to see the city streets without players filling them.

"I can't say for sure. I've heard rumors of suicides skyrocketing in Russia and China. Of course, I can't seem to find anything credible." Walter said floating around the little apartment.

"Thought it might be something to do with the necromancer class," Liam said still looking out over the city. It was no longer early morning now. The sun was up over the horizon and casting long shadows from the dragon bones. He still couldn't decide if he liked the garishly painted buildings.

"Coincidence; listen, I have to go but I'll keep looking into this," Walter said.

"Thank you," Liam called before another little pop sounded in the room. He was left alone again with his thoughts. Time enough to come to a decision about his life. He'd told Kat he wouldn't hide in this room. Cowering in safety wasn't his style. In fact what he'd said then was just as true now. He knew with certainty he'd be around. At least as long as he survived and the servers continued to run. Ten years? Twenty? He needed to carve out a place, a home.

CHAPTER TWENTY-THREE

Kat - Rankup

KittKat - Level 30
Tramin Continent - Fungus Dungeon
Just before dawn

Kat prepared her axe. She held it behind her out of sight as the fungus warrior battered her shield. It was a purple and green mushroom-shaped blob of stinky spores. The monster slapped at her barrier again followed by a third heavy blow. She brought the axe around slashing the extended tentacle. A visible trail of light followed her weapon as it struck. The fungoid squealed in pain as it rocked backward off balance. It was too bad that these mobs didn't bleed like mortal men. She couldn't use her favorite axe buffs. Folken appeared behind the creature and struck out with twin burning daggers. They sank into green molding flesh with a crackling sizzle. Its health nearly vanished from the brutal backstab. Kat lunged forward planting her weapon squarely in the thick midsection. Its arms flailed one last time, lashing out before it died. Slowly as if deflating the fungoid warrior sagged in on itself. A cloud of spores expelled from its corpse. She backed away from it. A mortal human could catch quite a nasty disease by inhaling the spore. Being undead she was immune to such things, but it left a stink that lasted for hours.

Folken stood slowly from where he'd leapt backward. The level twenty-two thief had come a long way since joining the guild. He was the lowest member of the party but he was holding his own. He spent most of his time in stealth. Only when the monster was low health did he strike with a devastating attack from the shadows.

"Still want to be a paladin?" Kat asked the young thief.

"Not anymore, I think you were right. I let others decide what I wanted. Besides, I don't feel very righteous now. I have a new goal." Folken said flicking the knife around in his palm.

"What's that?"

"Orenthal sent me out to be an assassin. So I'm going to be one. I'm going to bury this dagger in his chest so I can watch the light go out of his eyes." Folken said lifting his right blade up to eye level. He twisted the flaming blade so that its light danced.

"Simple goals are always the best," Kat said with a sly smile. Nearby Liam, Sarge, and Astrid were finishing their fungoid warrior off. The dungeon cave had been serving them well for the last few hours. Kat had leveled and was already nearing her next. They came over to join Kat and Folken.

"Phew," Kat said waving a hand at Sarge. He stank of mold spores and rotting fish. The tall half-orc was a dappled camo skinned male. After level thirty he'd classed up from fighter into a Defender. That was happening a lot lately. New classes were being discovered left and right. Sarge wore plate and carried a large tower shield on his right side. He shook a rare one-handed war hammer quickly. Fungoid flesh and spores flew off slapping noisily to the ground.

"You didn't jump back fast enough." Kat accused the Defender. To this the large vampire shrugged with a devilish smile.

"I got caught by one earlier so I'm not bothering." He replied. "Speaking of reeking I should probably shower before bed. All the adrenaline from fighting makes me sweat something fierce."

"Are we done for tonight?" Liam asked the fighter.

"I'm good for another hour or two," Folken said from the shadows.

"How about we fight our way up to the entrance before Sarge

ports home for the evening." Kat offered.

Everyone agreed this was an acceptable plan. They had only made it about half way down because of the fast spawning monsters. With all five together it became short work to ascend upward. The cave system circled its way around a large underground waterfall. The spraying water kept the dungeon filled with a humid mist. Tiny clouds hung in the air over the large hole in the middle. The path wound its way back and forth past jutting ledges. The night sky was clear as they came out of the cave entrance. Bright stars glittered like jewels in the clear winter air. Almost immediately the temperature dropped thirty degrees to freezing. Around them snow still clung to the ground from a previous flurry. It was calm as lake water, not even a small breeze rustled the nearby trees. That was why Kat was so surprised by what happened next.

A crack in the ground began a few feet away from her. Red and green hellfire spewed upwards as the fissure expanded. It circled the dungeon entrance preventing them from moving away. The whole group drew weapons and prepared for a fight. More and more the hole grew until it looked as though one could fall all the way to hell.

"Retreat?" Sarge asked looking back towards the Fungoid dungeon. They could still run into the entrance and portal home.

"Wait," Liam suggested. From within the crack three demons appeared. Two of them floated up through the flames on massive wings. A third crawled slug like up the wall and onto land. The demons arranged themselves before Kat. All three stared at her with their evil piercing gazes. Finally, things began to make sense when a popup window appeared before her face.

[Rank up]
[Chaos Knight]
[You have attracted the attention of one or more Demon Lords.

Pledge your allegiance to one of them in order to gain their domain power. Kneel before the demon you wish to serve. Alternatively, you may choose to give your favor to none. You may walk away to class up to Black Knight. Demons are fickle beings, and they shall not make the offer a second time.]

"It says I have to pick one or walk away," Kat said to the group. They visibly relaxed at this. Now she knew why they hadn't appeared in the dungeon. It had waited until she was in the Overworld.

"Which one should I choose?" She asked growing excited. Many people around her had been ranking up which had left her feeling a little jealous. This was pretty sweet. She mused on each one for a time. The game did not give her any indication as to who these demons were, nor what they could do for her. Folken was the one that seemed to have some knowledge on the subject. The rogue appeared beside her.

"I went to a boys camp for our church. They had a big thing about the major demons." He said pointing to the first one on the right.

"That nasty looking bastard right there is Nergal, the Lord of Pestilence," Folken said as he gestured to the demon. Its body was like a huge, corpulent maggot. It stood about fourteen feet tall if standing was what it was doing. Large pustules pulsed on its body with sickening regularity. "Picking him will probably grant bonuses to your disease spells." He amended and Kat shook her head. She was not about to walk around with flies buzzing around her. Nor did she think worts would be a good look.

"The small one is Lilith, Queen of the Succubi and the Demon of Lust." He said pointing to the middle figure. The red skinned demon was only about six feet tall. She was nearly naked wearing only a thin scaled halter top and a tight bikini thong. The demon was every man's wet dream. Big eyes, big lips, tits to match and hips that could knock out a rhino. Folken paused as he considered the beautiful figure. "Not to be sexist but she probably just showed up because you're a girl. I have no idea what she could do for you in battle. Maybe you'll get a hard-on aura." He suggested after a few seconds.

"That one?" Kat asked already moving on. She was not about to be anyone's playmate. The last figure was a typical demon. Red skinned, scaled, and standing a little taller than Nergal. It was about sixteen feet if you included the horns on its head. Smoke seemed to roll off the creature like it was always afire.

"I'm going to say its Asmodeus. Demon of Wrath, banished by Raphael in the Book of Tobit. Sometimes he's called the Lord of Blood." Folken said guessing at this point. Her mind was already made up. She was not about to kneel before a slug, and she didn't plan on skipping around in bikini armor. Kat walked forward towards the third demon. It loomed over her as she knelt before it.

"You pledge yourself to Asmodeus?" It asked in a booming voice. The smell of fresh tangy strawberry blood hit her in the face as it spoke. A popup appeared before her and she reached up with a gauntleted finger hitting yes.

Fire blossomed around all the demons as the popup vanished. The first two descended back into the depths but Asmodeus remained. He bent towards her. Smoke billowed from his mouth and surrounded her body. It began to seep into the cracks of her armor and quickly became attached to her like a second skin. Her black aura had the subtle smell of wood smoke and blood. Almost like cooking meat. While she was admiring her new character page the demon turned towards the rift. It disappeared into the gap floating down into hell once again. Shortly the wound in the earth healed over leaving only fresh earth.

Silence followed.

"Well that was a whole lot cooler than when I became a Defender. All I got was a bunch of NPC's clapping and cheering." Sarge said in annoyance.

"If it makes you feel any better I think I peed myself a little," Kat said to the large warrior. He huffed in response and took out his portal stone.

"I'm out for tonight." He said next and was quickly gone in a flash of light.

Kat turned towards Folken. He was still standing nearby looking vaguely distant. She was reminded of his previous character. The paladin she'd killed a few weeks ago. It was probably because of that PVP kill that she managed to rank up.

"You ok?" She asked and he shook himself.

"Yeah, I think I should log too. Might as well get some extra sleep." Folken said before disappearing to his own residence. Astrid left next, so she and Liam followed suit.

Kat appeared in the Dragonfall City Apartment next to Liam. She walked towards her bedroom, Liam followed. At the inner door he opened it and held it for her. Kat went in and over to the standing mirror. Her full plate armor was black with highlights in red. Kat had possessed an aura of fear for months, but now it was visible to the eye after her rank up. Tendrils of inky smoke wafted between cracks in her plate. Especially the back of her neck and under her arms. As she stood it started to form a shifting cloak. As if blood and violence were ever wrapped around her shoulders. The effect would have been scarier had she been a seven-foot tall male. Right at five feet, she seemed a bit like a child playing dress up.

Liam came into her room after her and into the bathroom. She heard the water turn on. Kat removed her helmet and shook her hair out. Her raven black locks spilled down over her armor. At least she didn't look silly, more cute or childishly adorable. That had led several players to mistake her for weak. With a sigh she tossed her helmet onto the bed. She unequipped her gauntlets then sat on the thick mattress. Then her boots and leg plates came off. Finally, she dropped her breastplate to the floor and stood. Kat could have put everything in her inventory but it was easier just to drop it. The sound of water stopped and Liam pushed open the door.

"Your bath is ready, M'Lady." He said in an officious tone. Kat moved towards him in her underwear. As she approached Liam's eyes raked over her body. He wasn't entirely immune to her charms. That was nice to see.

"Scrub my back?" She asked as she neared him.

"I'd love too." He replied following her inside. Kat paused before the large porcelain tub. The water steamed and a few black lotus flower petals floated atop. The candles nearby were just bright enough to keep her dark vision from activating. It was the little things like that she loved. She slipped from the bra and panties laying them on the small end table. Liam already had a hand held out for her. Clasping it she stepped onto the little ladder then into the tub. The water was just right. Hot enough to leave her skin feeling warm again.

She sank back against the tub letting the heat relax her muscles. Liam took a bottle and poured it into the water. Immediately it began to foam up. His large bony hands started to run over her skin. Yes, it was the little things she liked about Liam. They couldn't make love, which was truly unfortunate. Still, he'd found ways like this to be intimate. Kat let her head rest against the lip of the tub. Hands stroked over her upper chest.

"I enjoyed tonight, and the guild is getting better too," Liam said from above her and Kat grunted in agreement. Five out of six was almost a full group at least.

"We're up to sixty-five members or so, but the numbers can be a bit misleading. A few haven't logged in for some time. People can't get over not grouping with the living part." Kat said after a few luxurious seconds. She was nudged forward. Large hands started to massage her neck and shoulders. Liam switched topics rather abruptly.

"Do you trust him, the rogue?" He asked a little too casually.

"Folken?" She mused before cracking an eye. Liam's skull floated above her awash in eldritch fire. In another time the sight might have scared her half to death.

"He had the opportunity to back-stab us. Only five in the group and we spent several hours in that dungeon. Could have called in

239

his old allies to ambush us. When they came he could have attacked you to keep you from portaling out. Maybe tonight was something of a test for him." Kat said with a shrug of her shoulders.

Liam's fingers dug into her hair massaging the soap into it. She closed her eyes again letting herself sink back into the hot water. "I don't fully trust him, not with my children. He's on probation for a while longer." Kat said after a short while.

"We needed people." Liam offered.

"Exactly, we aren't in a position to turn anyone away." She admitted before letting out a long sensual groan. The bath continued but thankfully talk subsided. She allowed herself to be prodded, pinched, massaged and scrubbed down. By the end she was ready for a nap. After being toweled off she donned her underwear again. Liam led her to the bed where he pulled the covers back. He climbed in beside her and wrapped big boned arms around her waist.

"Good night, Kat," Liam said near her ear.

"Try to get some sleep." She said sleepily. Tonight had been quite exciting with her rank up. She was ready for a few winks herself. It was a tall order for Liam. Considering she couldn't sleep while the game was punching sights and smells into her noggin.

"I will," He lied smoothly. Kat knew better; he'd lay next to her all night. She reached up with a hand and accessed the system menu. A few seconds later her world faded to black.

CHAPTER TWENTY-FOUR

Walter - Interview

Walter Nowel
California
8pm

Walter pulled into the small garage of his California condo.
He'd had a long but productive day. The Server had held a
special event to commemorate the first level sixty player. The Orc
warrior was just as surprised as everyone else. Though as the
leader of a boss killing expeditionary guild it wasn't one to
Walter. The bonuses they received for first kills were worth the
danger. There were others that would follow soon. Quite a few
empires had players on the cusp of greatness. It wasn't the max
level in the game though; there was a soft cap at sixty.

The elevator dinged as he thought all this. The doors opened
and he stepped aboard the lift. Once at his floor, he unlocked his
apartment and went inside. He immediately removed the tie.
This he tossed onto the couch as he went into the kitchen. The
refrigerator was empty when he opened it. Thankfully he'd eaten
on the way home. So he pulled out a Mexican import beer. Drink
in hand he went to sit on the couch.

"TV On, News." He said to the apartment. The plasma screen
on the wall flicked to life and automatically switched channels. It
was a CNN report. Probably something recorded earlier that day
and replayed. He cracked open the beer before settling back to
watch.

A set of high definition cameras went live as the interview started. A handsome man of about forty sat easily. He wore a crisp dark suit without the requisite tie. Fashions had changed and men were beginning to discard the accessory as old. Instead, a gold pin was placed on the collar of his throat. His dark brown hair was carefully oiled and styled. A matching goatee framed the features of his face. He smiled at the female reporter opposite him. She was blond and uncommonly beautiful even for Big Apple standards. Held in her lap out of sight of the camera was her datapad of notes.

"Thank you for coming Mr. Olson." The reporter said politely.

"It's a pleasure, Gwen." He said omitting her last name.

"You are the chief of relations at VRTek?" Gwen asked.

"That's right. I'm the CR at the company."

"Please tell us about VRTek for anyone not familiar with your business." She continued still smiling politely.

"It's an honor to be apart of something so amazing. Over the last twenty years, we've been researching a neglected technology. Using a device to directly signal the brain. Instead of a monitor you perceive the information as if it were all around you. No speakers necessary as your audio center is signaled directly. We can even match the feeling of hot and cold weather. The smell of baked bread and freshly mown grass." Olson said expansively opening his arms to take in the whole of the idea. Gwen didn't reply to this statement so he continued.

"Hundreds of games have already been made for the system. Everything from educational historical simulations to combat arenas. You can fly above the clouds as a bird or experience a Shakespeare's play as actor or audience. Imagination is the only limit." He said in a voice still ringing with pride.

"That sounds incredible." Gwen offered.

"It is. Imagine experiencing your favorite movie from the inside. You could interact with the protagonist directly. With our technology you don't just watch someone else be the hero. You could struggle and help the main character. You could learn to fly a real plane with virtual lessons. Get musical tips from Beethoven himself." Olsen said expansively. He carefully didn't mention smut clubs and the popularity of sex dungeons. Those were by far the most played games. Followed by death matches and shooters.

"Many of our viewers have expressed concerns over a growing trend," Gwen said neutrally switching topics.

"Concerns?" He asked in response.

"The technology is quite dangerous," Gwen said as if a fact.

"No more dangerous than browsing the Internet." He said with a long smile. Olson continued before she could say anything to his quip. "Computing technology and our understanding of the human body have grown considerably. Especially that of the mind. We began with full immersion pods for industry users. Those early prototypes greatly increased worker productivity. Like the computers of old the technology began to show up in homes."

Gwen had on a face that looked only slightly puckered. As if she were tasting something vaguely sour. "You're saying its perfectly safe?" Gwen said with a slight edge to her voice.

"There are at least five safeguards on every system. Heart and brain wave monitors hard-coded in the machines automatically eject users. Then there are several proprietary measures." Olson said in a long practiced way. A question he'd come prepared for.

"What about the people that have died?" Gwen said.

"People die, its a sad but realistic fact. Our collated data shows only thirty incidents in the past five years." He replied lifting his arms in a carefully measure shrug. "That matches death rates on golfing and is three times safer than swimming." He added afterward.

"I'd like to invite you to the office to try it." Olson offered.

"I couldn't possibly," Gwen replied immediately.

"You're a brave reporter. Surely you'd be willing to see both sides of an argument." He said still smiling. Olson had obviously caught her off guard with that comment.

"We'll see if I'm available," Gwen said her own smile now brittle. She reached up playing with a lock of her hair. Really she was pressing the ear bud a little further in to listen to instruction.

"I'm afraid that is all the time we have for today," Gwen said and turned to the camera directly.

"Thank you for watching and now a message from our sponsors." She said before the image changed to a diet drink commercial.

"TV off," Walter said relaxing back. Public opinion of virtual machines was slowly shifting. This wasn't the first time he'd seen someone attacking the technology. The rumors in China hadn't helped matters either. Lifting the bottle of beer to his lips he took a long drink.

Walter's cellphone began to go off and he pulled it free of his pocket. The number was unlisted and he considered ignoring it. It rang again as he stared at the screen. The bottle of beer he'd been drinking had gone to his head. There was no way he was going to be driving tonight. Still... It could be work, likely it was. He accepted the call and brought the mobile to his ear.

"Walter Nowel," he said.

"Ahh, I apologize for calling you so late Mr. Nowel." The other person said. The voice was vaguely familiar with a decidedly Chinese accent. Walter took another sip of beer and switched the phone from one ear to the other.

"I'm sorry, who is this?" He asked in a slightly regretful tone.

"I am Ji Chisan, we talked about a month ago." The other said and warning bells went off in Walter's mind. The other man filled the silence that followed. "I wanted to apologize for my behavior last time we met. It was incredibly rude of me." The last time they had talked Ji had run out of the restaurant like Walter had the plague, but now he was randomly called at home. To say he was without words was not an exaggeration.

Ji spoke again, "I am in California for the VR Conference."

"Oh, I'd forgotten that was this month," Walter replied trying to mentally catch up.

"Would it be possible to meet?" Ji asked.

"Was it in connection to their last conversation?" Walter wondered to himself. For whatever reason the man seemed willing to talk face to face. At least he might get some more answers. "How about tomorrow at lunch?" He replied.

"Thank you, yes. That would be fine." Ji said rather formally.

"Tomorrow then," Walter said and Ji agreed before hanging up.

***

The man looked nothing like his avatar. Or he did with some significant weight gain and a corresponding hair loss. Ji Chisan was about five foot four and easily sixty pounds overweight. Walter saw this after getting out of his car. The Asian man bowed again rather formally before extending a hand.

"Thank you, Mr. Nowel for seeing me. I want to apologize for my behavior." He said as a greeting.

"Think nothing of it," Walter said opening the door to the restaurant. They had decided on Mexican. Walter followed Ji inside and waited for the staff to seat them. He liked this place enough that he came here at least once a week. The waitress came and he ordered for both of them.

"My son was quite excited to be remembered by you," Ji said before pulling a book free of his satchel. "Wei gave me one of his sketchbooks to convey to you." He added and handed over the thin book. Walter accepted this and opened the artist's diary. The fantasy drawings were done in a dark gritty style. It was quite different than the adolescent anime he remembered. They were good, actually quite incredible, matching anything he'd seen done at Dreamshard.

"These are amazing," He admitted.

"For a time Wei considered working as a concept artist, but he is more comfortable where he's at," Ji said fatherly pride coloring his tone. Walter continued to flip through the book. About half of the pictures were concept art for locations.

"So Ji, are you going to the VR Conference?" He asked hoping to steer the conversation.

"I am. There is a talk on data compression styles that I am interested in." The other man admitted. Well, he was at a loss now. He'd hoped he could get Ji to admit to something. Walter remained silent for a time as he flipped through the sketchbook.

"It is directly related to what we talked about," Ji said a little conspiratorially.

"It is?" Walter asked in surprise.

"Yes, I am working directly with the Gui. To understand them." Ji said. This was progress Walter knew. He'd been struggling with how to direct the conversation.

"The Ghosts, what are they?" He asked quickly. Walter had seen Liam's character dump. It was densely packed data, mostly just encoded gibberish to his system. Certainly larger and more complex than most items in the game. Liam by his nature seemed closer to some of the highest level bosses.

"They are memories, no more. Though we all are just a collection of our experiences." Ji said and asked a question of his own. "If I mention the word 'grass' what happens?"

"I think of the smell of it, maybe remember an old game of soccer as a child," Walter admitted. He could almost hear the excited playful cries of his old friends. The green stains on his knees and elbows.

"Yes exactly," Ji said excitedly. "We don't remember every detail of our lives. We have archives of stored sensations and experiences that link together." He said and reached for a salt shaker. He poured a little out onto the table. After this he pushed groups together into piles. Next he linked them together with lines of black pepper like a matrix.

"I see. How did it happen?" Walter asked but was interrupted. The food arrived and the waitress eyed them for the messy table. Walter swept the salt into his hand and onto a plate. He and Ji ate for a time.

"Like most discoveries it was an accident. Three college students wanted to play Nigmus. Being poor and at an engineering school they came up with a plan. They bought six broken virtual pods from a cafe. Three of them they successfully fixed. One had a faulty heart rate monitor. It would kick the player out if it registered any rate over zero. So they just bypassed it. Unfortunately, the one who ended up with the machine had an unknown heart condition. During a particularly long fight the man died. His friends saved his character though thinking he'd been logged out. Ten minutes later the friend was back and they had a laugh about it." Ji said once he'd finished his enchilada. Walter remembered the story of Liam. How he'd been unconscious for a few minutes before waking. Ji scooped a chip full of salsa and ate it.

"The friends logged out that night and went to bed. They didn't find his corpse until morning. The police were called and the body taken away. A few days later they logged back into the game to find an irate ghost. This surprised all of them of course. A GM was alerted and it finally came to our attention." Ji said then reached for another salsa chip.

"Why didn't you tell us?" Walter asked.

"For the same reason you didn't." Ji accused with a smile. "You didn't want the company to over react and shut the servers down. It's why the Chinese government has quietly placed people in locations to take over. In case word comes down that America is reacting. Though Russia wasn't so quiet about it. They've already nationalized the game."

"Impossible," Walter said and Ji smiled crookedly.

"The same people might be sending emails but government admins repair the servers. Armed soldiers guard the buildings. They see this as something profoundly new." Ji said picking up his glass of water taking a sip. He moved the rice and beans around his plate absently.

"The suicides?" Walter asked and Ji put his fork down with a sigh.

"Those stupid boys again. They couldn't keep their mouths shut. Soon people approached them for how they'd accomplished the feat. The government stepped in with an interest as well. Within a month people were streaming over the digital border on cobbled together machines. Without information people were trying everything. They killed themselves in their eagerness. VR Cafe's closed down because bodies were found every night. Of course, none of those people made it across. The machines did their jobs." Ji said pushing the plate of food away from himself. Talk of death was making him nauseous.

"Those weren't the only fools. People tried becoming immortal in combat arenas, adult clubs, and strangely kids games. Only Nigmus it seemed had the right combination of object coding and net data."

"It's still happening?" He asked.

"Yes, but thankfully people know now. In both Russia and China very rich moguls are paying millions for high-level characters. It is particularly bad in Russia. They are donating lots of money to certain people to get legendary level items." Ji said with a puckered look on his face.

"That ruins the game. The common people get sick of the pay gap and stop playing." Walter said feeling disgust. He'd always hated pay to win games. They never lasted very long.

"Ahh, they at least came up with an interesting scheme. The rich immigrants are given a piece of land in game. Some mansion or manor some place away from town. Within that territory the players are gods. The items though are tied to that place. Once they step outside they're back to normal. In some cases even worse off than regular players.

"What about death?"

"Yes," Ji said simply and let out a long weary sigh.

"Even those below level five don't come back. A Gui that dies is summoned to the graveyard and falls down. They have lost something in the transfer. The spark of life apparently happens just once. If lost that is it, there is no coming back." Ji said before drinking more water.

"That, however, is a small blessing in disguise," Ji said.

"How?" Walter asked.

"I've been approached by some very unsavory characters. They wanted to make living dolls. Non-player characters that could be programmed to perform in-game actions, like sex for example." Ji said and Walter swallowed hard. He finally pushed his plate away. He thought of Kat in her predicament. How easily someone could take advantage of that. Still, he wondered if it were possible to make a lifelike AI. Such a thing would be years in the future though.

"I have another reason for talking to you," Ji said turning even more serious. Walter got a sinking feeling in his stomach. Of course Ji had wanted something. He wasn't going to risk giving away this information without something in return.

"We have been making strides but were stuck. I only get the compiled code and patches from North America. Walter, I need the source code." Ji said looking directly into Walter's eyes.

"That's corporate espionage. I could go to prison for a long time." Walter said with a suddenly dry mouth.

"The Chinese government is willing to grant you asylum," Ji said taking another piece of paper from his case. He didn't give it to Walter but showed it to him. It was a citizenship transfer form, already filled out.

"I'm just a GM now. I'm not in the coding circle anymore." Walter admitted.

"You're 'The' Game Master. If you need to see the code I'm sure they'll let you check your old work." Ji said with some confidence. This was way to much to take in. Ji continued as if he'd practiced his speech. "You are a bachelor, nothing to tie you down. You don't own any property. Lastly you're talented, someone we would like to have on our side." Ji said and Walter watched the other man warily. He'd done his homework alright.

"I need time to consider," Walter said after a pause. Ji slid a piece of paper across the table toward Walter. It was an anonymous email account he could contact. The conversation took a turn for lighter roads. The topic moved to the VR Conference for a time. A way to ease out of the serious talk, idle banter before the check came. Ji insisted on paying.

CHAPTER TWENTY-FIVE

Liam - Skirmish

Liam - Level 38
Tramin - Dragonfall City

They'd had the apartment suite for two months. The year was almost over and they were into late winter now. The world had just passed the longest night of the year. The hunting had been good as usual. Soon though they would have to move on to another continent. Tramin seemed to cap out at around level forty. A few high-level enemies could be found in deep caves or dungeon ruins, but not enough to consistently level with. Liam was currently waiting in the living room. He didn't use his bedroom much. Mostly because he didn't sleep. At best he could manage a vegetative doze. So a lore book was open on his lap, but he wasn't reading it. He was contemplating his transference to this world. No further information had come about his apparent 'suicide.' Liam wasn't bitter, quite the opposite. Now he never had to log out for bathroom breaks, or food, or sleep. Well… he did miss sleep a little. It got quite boring sitting around all day long. Liam turned in the chair to look out the window. The sun was still up overhead, would be for several hours. Some of the east coast members might be getting on soon.

Dusk would arrive and all the vampires would start waking up. Kat too would be among them. She was in her bedroom offline. Probably doing some guild page management or advertising on the forum. Guild chat became visible in the corner of his vision. The name of the guild member was Vlad the Destroyer.

"Is there an event going on in Shellbreak Castle?" Vlad asked. Liam could safely ignore the question. He had no idea about such a thing. The GM's were constantly running events around the world. It added extra spice to the usual goings on.

"No, why?" Someone else asked.

"I had a rogue quest to deliver some goods to the bandits there," Vlad said in response. That explained why he was online so early. Fetch quests were easy enough to accomplish even with the sunlight debuff. "There's a bunch of players sitting around the castle." He added after a few seconds. Liam knew Shellbreak Castle well. He and Kat had farmed those bandits for several days. It lay next to a lake that overlooked the town. A small stream led into the lake from the hills. The river cascaded down a couple of falls before disgorging fresh water into the harbor. This was where the large sea crabs mixed with the river shrimp. The little pocket of water was home to some strangely shelled crabs. Hence the name of the harbor.

"I haven't heard anything in town." The previous vampire said.

"How many people?" Liam asked after a minute of silence.

"Holy shit, the boss," Vlad said in reply.

"The boss is offline playing with the website. How many are there?" He asked again. Even though he was Co-leader, he generally deferred to Kat.

"I dunno, lots. Fifty or sixty just on the walls." Vlad said after another pause then added. "I'm currently in stealth near the road. I'm headed back to town now." It could have been a guild meeting. Kat had used the nearby mansion for their event. The walls would give them a measure of protection while everyone was talking as well. He wondered which clan it was. There were quite a few large guilds in the game. Liam closed the book in his lap and set it aside. This was starting to sound interesting, but he was forced to wait for some time.

"After asking around town I found out they've been up there for three days now. A couple of rogues went up to turn in the same quest as me. They got turned back by Fyre." Vlad said after about twenty more minutes. Now Liam's attention was focused. He smelled an opportunity when it approached. That bloody Player Killer guild had tried to whack him, and he was ready for a little payback.

"Is the guy sure its Fyre?" he asked eagerly.

"Yes, they told him Fyre was holding a week long meeting. Then they shot at him for good measure. Chased him off." Vlad said after another pause. That sounded strange indeed. Keeping players in one spot day after day. Though that did explain why they had guards on the walls. Many many people wanted a piece of Fyre.

"Vlad," Liam typed.

"Vlad," He repeated making it clear he wanted the man's attention. "I'm wondering what kind of guild meeting Fyre has going on. Sneak around up there. Count heads on the wall and more importantly what level they are." He typed before pacing towards the window to look outside.

"I can do that," was the reply.

The window faced south so the yellow sun was visible as it hung over the valley. An hour or possibly two and the sun would set. Last night the moon had been a sliver of its usual self. Hopefully tonight it would be just as dark. An idea began to percolate. Tonight, Fyre was going to know what it felt like to be hunted.

***

Almost three hours later. Roughly fifty vampires and a single lich were huddled in the forest near Shellbreak Castle. It was everyone in the guild that was above level fifteen. Across the small lake the wall was lit by several torches. A group of bored looking characters sat on crates playing cards.

"So are you going to tell us what you're planning, Liam," Kat said a little dryly. As usual, he had refused to discuss his ideas until more intel had been available. He was also on the fence about the rogue Folken. The thief was here and could have already ruined their plans if he wanted.

"Vlad here has already been inside the castle once. I'll let him describe what he saw." Liam said and gestured to the twentieth level rogue. All eyes turned to him and he smiled in pride. The rogue liked the sudden attention.

"Well, I remembered there was a sewer outlet that fed into the lake," Vlad said excitedly and several people made faces.

"They shit in the same lake water they drank from?" A young vampire asked voice dripping with disgust.

"Apparently," Vlad said without missing a beat. "The passage is underwater. It leads directly into the keep of the castle. There are two restrooms on the ground floor. The barracks is partially collapsed with a storage room near the kitchens." Vlad said as he drew a crude drawing in the dirt. It was a square with a line going from left to right.

"Oh god, I'm going to gag." The small vampire said.

"How many players did you see?" Kat asked trying to steer the conversation.

"I didn't go up inside the castle to check. The boss said to remain hidden." Vlad said deflating a little.

"You did well." Liam offered and patted the vampire on the shoulder. He didn't look at Folken as he spoke. "The plan is quite simple. The rank and file of Fyre might not all be PK's. The higher ups though are sanctioning the actions of a few. So we are going to go in through the sewer entrance and attack the meeting in progress." He said waving a bony hand at the distant castle walls.

"After that?" Kat asked and Liam shrugged.

"We take it as it comes. Most likely we retreat after doing some damage." Liam said after a short pause. Even at night there was at least forty enemy players standing the walls. Three groups stood roadside defense. Two parties each manned the flanking sides. A single sorry looking group was watching the lake. The shape of the castle was a basic square with three of the walls in disrepair. Holes large enough to drive a semi through riddled the defenses. The only fully standing wall was the fourth. The one side directly abutting the lake.

"Are we going to become PK's if we kill someone?" A voice asked.

"No, we are undead. We can kill the living without consequence." Kat assured them quickly. "We don't Player-Kill indiscriminately, but Fyre brought this on themselves."

"Vlad, Folken. You two lead the way inside." Liam said and the two thieves nodded in unison. Turning they walked directly into the lake. The water splashed slightly but the noise was minimal. Everyone else formed a loose rank and followed after. The cold lake water began to soak Liam's robes as he submerged himself. Water crest and lake plants spread along the shore front. Soon their passage was disturbing the sleeping lake fish. It took minutes to cross the body of water to the outer castle wall. Liam stopped just outside the sewer passage. It was some twenty feet under water. The castle base was made of cement and river stone. Light from the player torches was just visible from above. Kat went in first and he followed. The passage was shaped like an elongated hexagon. A roughly flat bottom with two sloping sides. He had to crouch quite far to keep from going to his hands and knees. About forty feet in Folken stood waiting in a pillar of light. The first restroom was directly above them.

"No talking once inside." Kat reminded everyone.

Liam climbed upwards. Several rusting rungs had been set into the cement long ago. Likely to make it easier to clean the passage in case of backup. He exited the water a few feet up. Slowly he climbed until a hand came into view. He grabbed the offered hand and ascended out of the hole. Liam straightened trying to clean his hands on his robes. The toilet had been smashed long ago. What remained was the hole down into the sewer water. Kat was already waiting with a disgusted look on her face. Folken came up next followed quickly by Sarge and Astrid. The half-orc had a grin on his face as he came out. He was obviously enjoying himself greatly. The restroom led into a side corridor for the keep.

Doors to the right opened into the kitchens and storerooms. Indistinct voices came from the end of the hall. The thick door muffled the sounds coming from the Hall.

Vlad went past them and towards the door shifting to stealth as he neared the end. By now half of the raiding party was crowding the bathroom and hall. Everyone was dripping water and looking a little ill from the experience. The door cracked open a tiny fraction.

"Twenty players visible, most red to me. So at least level twenty-seven or over." He typed in guild chat. That could mean they were level thirty, forty, or higher still. His troops were mostly mid-twenties. Only the top officers were the high thirties. That made it a twenty versus fifty fight with weaker players.

"Entries?" Liam typed.

"Just the main doors out into the foyer and us," Vlad replied which made Liam very happy. Everyone was checking their gear at this point. Potions and salves were being put into quickslot pouches. Kat withdrew her axe and shield changing into combat mode.

"The heavy hitters will get into a group. Our biggest challenge will be keeping reinforcements out." Liam said after some consideration.

"Rogues group together. Your job will be to kill clerics when the fight starts. Everyone else is in mixed groups by levels. You all know who you group with usually." Liam typed next. He pointed towards Kat and her group. "We will make for the main doors then hold against a counter attack. The rest of you will form a blob around this door. Push in and kill everyone inside." Liam typed next and gestured to the hallway exit. The cleric was a problem. They only had the one still and he was too valuable to lose.

"Our resident cleric will play medic here. Anyone wounded should break contact and come through the door. Everyone that isn't level twenty yet will stay here as reinforcements." He said and stood before Kat poked him in the chest. She began to type angrily in the air.

"You're not going in either," Appeared in the chat window.

"We need heals," He typed back coolly. It would be a slaughter if they didn't get some directed healing. Kat continued to glare at him.

"You're not going in first." She said before pointing at their Defender Half-Orc. "Sarge, stay with Liam."

"That will weaken the blocking force," Liam argued.

"I can hold the door," She typed before turning away from the conversation. Well, that was that. He could continue to argue but it was likely pointless, so he and Sarge formed a mini-group.

"Rogues go in first, then in twenty seconds Kat's group charges. Then we move in mass." Liam typed.

"Good luck children and happy hunting." Kat typed quickly. It was evident she wanted to do this too but was worried for Liam.

They were noticed right away. A fighter relaxing near the door turned as it was pushed partially open. He looked at the ajar portal with a queer expression. It had just opened itself. Had he been just a little faster on his feet he could have lived. Well, lived a little longer. Behind him Fyre was still shooting the shit, trying to pass the time. He approached the door reaching out, but it flew open as he neared. It crashed against the wall as he was shoved backward. A tiny darkly armored body slamming into him. He was knocked off his feet and skidded to a stop. Five more players charged past him without a pause. He hadn't even noticed the red eyes. Not until a mass of fighters and warriors poured from the side hallway.

"It's an attack!" A voice bellowed from behind him. He started to draw his weapon but little too late. The luckless and now nameless warrior was cut down before his steel could even clear the scabbard. The Fyre members had been lounging around in small groups. Liam's rogues struck before they could begin to organize themselves. They'd already selected their targets. Four thieves plunged their daggers into a high-level cleric. His friends leapt up and began to attack. The cleric though rolled over, already dead from the multiple critical hits. To their credit, Fyre put up a fight. The remaining members quickly clumped together and fought back. Liam would later realize it was all that PvP combat that helped them. They'd learned to expect sudden attacks. It didn't scare them like it would have another guild.

Liam strode into the Grand Hall after the battle had been going on for a minute or two. Sarge was beside him as he walked into the large room. His guild had formed a bulging line going from the servant's door to the main entrance. A large male warrior was sitting on the throne near the back of the hall. A Spellsword possibly if the light armor and spell book hanging from his waist was any indication. He was bellowing orders and trying to get reinforcements.

"Fighters form a line, and archers take out their mages." The man yelled. An arrow almost immediately struck out for Liam. Sarge sidestepped and brought his shield up. The other commander must have realized both their forces lacked healing. It was all down to pure damage. Another sad fact was that Liam had no pets. He couldn't have brought them up through the secret tunnel. He began casting spells. His fingers danced as he started a simple spell macro. A void of darkness appeared around himself and his guard. It expanded slightly to encompass part of the fighting. The medium sized sphere would help the undead on his side. Next, he selected a low healthed name from the raid list. A rogue caught behind the fighting. He pointed his fingers sideways at the guild member. The magic built before a green bolt of energy flashed out. It struck the thief in the side and dragged his HP back into the yellow.

The next spell needed two targets. Since he was standing in darkness he didn't need the Defender's protection as much. He pointed at Sarge holding position before him.

"Casket Swap," He intoned and a white marble coffin erupted from the ground. It engulfed the large half-orc before disappearing into the stonework. Liam pointed to the thief. Thirty feet away another marbled coffin consumed the rogue. The high-level Defender immediately replaced wounded player. In the time it had taken to cast the spell the rogue had already lost a significant chunk of life. Folken looked quickly around before settling on Liam.

"Thanks," He said with only a hint of chagrin.

"You're welcome, go back to the cleric for healing," Liam said before turning his attention back to the battle. There were more names going into orange. Despite the fact his troops outnumbered Fyre he wasn't winning quickly. The enemy was doing the same thing he was. They specifically targeted the weaker members of his force. Most of the time they totally ignored the fighters. By now the guards outside were starting to push in. Kat was standing just inside one of the double doors. She hacked and shield bashed anyone that dared try to get past her. Another warrior was swinging a two-handed maul in the second entry.

"Get in here!" A voice boomed from the throne. It was the human commander trying to get his troops inside.

"Mid-armored troops back up. Force the enemy to fight our warriors." Liam yelled loudly. His deep voice cut over the tumult of battle. The shouting of skills being used and the clanging of steel made it hard to hear anything. He was being forced to heal dangerously low people far too often. They weren't backing out of combat fast enough. Arrows had been slinging past him much of this time. A half-elven mage phase shifted past him. The young vampire cast a chain lightning spell into the fighting crowd before dodging to the side. The wizard narrowly avoided the hail of return fire.

The enemy had been doing well, very well. Even without heals a few of his own people lay on the ground. It came to a head though, like the pressure on a pipe going critical. The right side of the enemy force fell. The Defender he'd sent over there had been hacking away all this time. Fyre was compelled to retreat. Less than half remained, those that did were centered around the throne. Liam turned his attention to the hallway doors. Kat was a beast as usual. Her health fluctuated between yellow and orange as she slashed. The other warrior was doing badly though. He didn't have the armor for a stand-up engagement. Liam pointed to the floor just beyond the doors. A field of grasping hands punched through the stones grabbing feet and ankles. The warrior gratefully backed away to fetch a potion.

"Mages, concentrate on 'AOE' past the hall doors," Liam ordered before returning his attention to the throne. The commander was finally doing something different. He held a portal stone in hand and its magic was encircling his body. Liam pointed at the man as his magic built. A green flash of eldritch energy zipped past the fighting. The glowing yellow and blue light of teleportation magic encompassed the human in its halo. His bolt struck true in a flash of multi-colored magic. It was times like these he wished he could grin. As the light vanished the human remained, his expression furious.

"A captain should go down with his troops." Liam remonstrated loudly. "Reinforcements enter now, go to the front doors." He added after pausing to fire off another spell.

The Spellsword stood from the throne finally drawing his weapon. With a snarl he phased directly past the line of warriors. The commander sprinted quickly for Liam. The sword flashed and Liam barely got his staff in for the parry. The commander pushed an empty hand towards him. "Greater Flame Touch." He said as fire blossomed over Liam. He was instantly grateful to Kat. The two rings of flame resistance completely nullified his weakness to fire. It even gave him a moderate resistance to the damage. Still, this was an uncomfortable fight.

"Suffocation," He said in reply pushing his own hand out. All he needed was to touch the target. A black snake wove its way up the human's chest. It tightened down brutally around the mortals throat. The damage over time spell immediately silenced the Spellsword. He tried to cast another spell but found himself muted. The battle was waning around the throne. The high-level Fyre members were being cleaned up, but the forces outside were trying to push inside. A bulge had formed where they batted to get in.

A sword slashed across Liam's face at his distraction. The

commander quickly followed Liam backward as he reeled. The Spellsword was much better at melee combat. Liam could barely keep his blocks up. There was enough going on around them that their personal duel wasn't noticed. Again and again the commander slashed at Liam. After almost a minute the black snake vanished from the neck of the warrior. He cleared his throat, then grinned. So far Liam hadn't been able to get off more than a few bolts of negative energy. Each time he was damaged it destroyed the spell he was casting.

"Did you think you were special necromancer?" The man said in a sneering voice. Again the sword slashed and Liam was forced back.

"You're nothing but a dressed up conjurer." He continued as he slashed again. Liam was taking a serious beating as he was forced back against the wall. His troops had finished up on the throne. Liam's guild mates were moving to help him. The rest of the guild was busy fighting around the door.

"I eat mages like you for breakfast." The Spellsword spat in defiance. The commander likely knew he was going to die but just wanted to take one person down with him. Liam though had his own surprises. Defiantly he stepped forward towards the commander. With a massive hand he grabbed the Spellsword. Immediately the human was paralyzed. His very first ability still occasionally came in handy.

"I'm glad to hear that, I could use a pet like you." He replied as his guild mates attacked. They began hacking at the commander's back and sides. "I haven't had a player pet in a while, you should feel lucky," Liam added with a dark laugh. The human glared at him with all the hatred it could muster. Then as his health dropped to zero his eyes went out of focus. They rolled up into his head as he sagged in death. Liam didn't let go though. He poked the Spellsword with his staff.

"Raise Dead," He muttered a little too smugly. The creature's eyes opened again but this time its pupils were milky white. It was as if the enemies outside knew their boss was dead. He'd just gotten his pet up when the doors to the hall cleared. Outside Fyre members were running far enough away to portal home. The cheer went up, and a chanting cry. The sound of their voices followed the Fyre members as they fled.

"Lawful Dead, Lawful Dead, Lawful Dead." Many voices cried in unison.

CHAPTER TWENTY-SIX

Kat - Occupy

KittKat - Level 38
Tramin Continent - Shellbreak Castle
Just before midnight.

Kat turned around as soon as the front doors were clear of enemies. She scanned the room quickly looking for Liam. He stood with a pet near a group of guild members. She let out a held breath. Part of her had wanted to call all of this off. Fyre had this coming, but Liam shouldn't have put himself at risk like that.

"What do we do now?" A voice asked her. She turned to see BoneScrapper looking at her with fierce eyes. He was still coming down from his barbarian rage. His exposed skin was steaming from the sweat of battle.

"Close the doors for now and keep two groups nearby." She said reaching for one side of the entry. Grasping the massive wooden portal she easily swung it shut.

"We're not going after them?" Bone asked looking out into the night.

"Can't risk getting split up. Besides, we did what we came here to do." She said already turning away. Liam was moving towards the throne. There was a conversation going on she was missing. Sheathing her axe and shield, she morphed back into her usual dress. Liam stopped next to the body of a fallen guild member. He knelt by the corpse. Willow, that was unfortunate. She was low level at around twenty-one, always bubbly, and a fun person to have around. Again Kat regretted that they couldn't raise the dead yet. She walked over joining the others next to the fallen guild member.

"How many did we lose?" Kat asked stopping next to Liam. She could have just checked the guild page herself.

"Five," Sarge said dropping another body next to Willow's. The guild would take them with as they left the castle. There was little hope they could bring them back in time before the body decayed.

"It's too bad our cleric doesn't have the goddess's blessing now. As a heretic he can't use the 'resurrection' spell. Maybe after level thirty he'll be able to if that's possible." Liam said with a sad sigh. The goddess hated the undead, wouldn't touch even a vampire with a ten-foot pole. It was possible the 'Raise Dead,' spell was restricted to the living though. Sarge crossed himself then moved away to collect another corpse.

"Five dead, for twenty higher level officers and another fifteen or twenty that tried to get through the door. Just under forty enemies in total." Liam said after a long pause. Kat nodded in solemn agreement. True it was a win, but they'd lost ten percent of their force doing it. Other members were coming up and paying respects. Kat followed the lich as he moved towards the throne.

"That was odd," He said after looking down at the empty seat.

"What was?" Kat asked.

"That commander just kept sitting there most of the battle. He only got up when he knew he was going to die." Liam responded pacing back and forth.

"Maybe he thought his troops could handle it?" Kat offered.

"Even when they lost more than half he still just sat there. Eventually, he tried fleeing by using a portal stone. That makes me wonder." Liam said tapping his upper teeth. "What were they doing up here for three days?" He asked as he circled the throne. He swept the chair free of dust then turned to Kat. She took the hand he held out for her then sat princess like on the throne.

"Anything?" He asked.

"It's still warm from the human," She said relaxing back.

"Anyone want to take a guess what Fyre was doing?" Liam typed to the guild. Many of the members were looting the dead. The Fyre members had dropped some superb gear. That in itself was almost worth the losses.

"Guild meeting like they said?" Someone tried.

"Lets try that. I'm calling a guild meeting for the next seventy-two hours. All of you have to stay here." Liam said loudly, this was followed by a chorus of groans. "People have better things to do than sitting around playing cards." He added after a few muttered curses. There was a long silence.

"They were doing... something here." Kat said after Liam let the silence linger.

"So that's why Orenthal was killing people," Folken said appearing nearby and most of the guild looked to him. "I was in Fyre before dying." He added as explanation the people assembled. The rogue poked at Liam's new Pet. The Spellsword commander that had been sitting on the throne.

"He must know there's something important related to the castle. This wasn't all of them, only about a hundred guild members. Orenthal probably has his ass parked in the throne at King's Landing. The man had a habit of going up there." Folken said still prodding the Spellsword.

"You're saying its possible to claim this castle?" Liam asked but Falken shrugged. "Only thing that makes sense." He said after a second.

"We could have a base?" Several guild members asked.

"No," Kat interrupted. She purposely stood up from the throne before addressing them all. "We are sixty members strong with our losses. There is no way we can hold this castle. It's way too close to town and there are guilds out there that put Fyre to shame. As soon as everyone figures it out they'll come directly here." She said looking to Liam. His eyes were flaming, it was obvious he wanted this. "We just aren't strong enough," Kat said before pointing at the Lich.

"Wait a second. Didn't those lich's all have thrones?" Kat said her voice rising in excitement.

"You're right, that lich in the dwarven mines had that fancy stone chair," Sarge said from nearby.

Liam snapped his finger bones together. "The necropolis, the one that human scout told us about. Its on the next continent over. We could take that, the undead won't attack us." He said his excitement building at the realization.

"Unless there is another lich in that throne room," Kat remarked.

"Easy enough to deal with," Liam said dismissively.

"So that's it?" Sarge asked into the silence. "We're just going to leave the castle?"

"No, that wouldn't be any fun. Besides Fyre is probably already putting together a counter attack. I'll tell the other mortal guilds to come here. Then we let them fight over it." Kat said with a wide ear-splitting grin.

"In the mean time I can raise some more of these humans as pets," Liam added. That would at least deny Fyre the ability to resurrect them later.

"Good idea, that will help bolster our strength," Kat added before clapping her hands loudly. All heads that hadn't already been listening turned.

"I need any extra gear you have dropped here. We need to re-equip our pets for them to be at full strength. Then we wait." Kat said impishly.

"What about when the sun comes up. We also have work." Several people asked.

"I'm going to log off and look for a mercenary company to hire. Maybe one of the other empires, elf or dwarf maybe. We need to hold on for a few hours to a day." Kat said after some thought. She paused though after looking at the dead vampires. "I also need to contact our fallen. Maybe we can scoop them back into the fold." She added. Kat sat on the throne again and reached up for the logout button. Liam was already moving around looking for the next strongest corpse to raise.

Kat found herself sitting in bed. The tablet was already on the mattress nearby. After powering it up she started a search crawler.

Nigmus+Mercenary+Guild+Dwarf Lots of hits, one of which was called Copperbeard's Mercenary Company. That sounded like something right up her alley. She sent him an email explaining what she wanted. Next, she logged into the guild page. Several people had already posted asking what happened during the fight.

"I am sorry you died. We did however kill over forty Fyre members. Please consider joining again with a new character. We believe Fyre was up to something as well. Our attack has screwed that 'Player Killer' guild." She typed into a new thread. Next she sent all five messages pointing them to the thread. A new email came in as she was doing this.

"You have a job?" Copperbeard said simply.

"Yes," She typed then explained a second time what was going on.

"I want to meet face to face." Was the reply.

"That's fine, we can meet right now if you like." Kat offered and waited. It was almost a minute before a curt email was sent back. "Good." It said simply. Well not very personable she thought. Finally, Kat did one more thing. She went to the official Nigmus Forum and created a post.

KittKat [Guild Leader - Lawful Dead]
"Fellow players I bring you an idea; a theory if you will. We all know that the land has fallen into barbarism. The empires of old crumbled leaving the people in a dark age. I ask you all. What if? What if we are the ones to make a kingdom? What if we are the ones that will bring light to the land? You doubt me. You suspect this is just another rambling rant. I think someone agrees with my theory. The leader of Fyre knows. Go to King's Landing and ask him why his guild is sitting there. When you believe, come to Shellbreak Castle. The Lawful Dead holds the keep. For you to have your own land, claim a throne. Remain seated for an

unspecified amount of time. I suspect your patience will be rewarded." She typed before closing the browser.

With a smile she dropped the tablet and launched the game again. It was near midnight though. She doubted anyone would see the post for some hours. By daybreak, the news would spread and things would begin happening.

As she sat up in the throne there was a chaotic bustle around her. The guild was organizing the bodies by their highest level. Discarded loot piles littered the ground. Liam was over inspecting a second pet. The new undead was tall and equipped with shield and sword. A fighter to back up the Spellsword Liam had. In an hour he'd be able to raise another two pets. Kat stood seeing that she wasn't immediately needed. She decided to wander up to the keep roof. The night was still young technically with a moon that barely cast any light. Meeting a few mercenaries was something she could do by herself. She sent the dwarven leader instructions on where to go. They'd have to talk outside of the castle. Liam's undead pets would attack them otherwise.

"We'll be there in an hour." He replied back. Kat walked down directly into the lake. It took about five minutes to get to the spot, there she waited. As she did she watched guild chat as they talked excitedly. Her children were enjoying themselves this evening. So there she stood, waiting for over two hours. She sent the dwarf several more messages.

Her shoulder rested against the tree. A foot tapping impatiently on the ground. If the dwarf didn't show she'd have to log off again and look for someone else. They needed help guarding the walls until Lawful Dead was ready to leave. Her first warning of combat was a chunk of health disappearing from her bar. Her head was knocked sideways as a lead ball smashed into it.

CHAPTER TWENTY-SEVEN

Liam - LandGrab

Liam - Level 38
Shellbreak Castle
Midnight

"Where is Kat?" Liam asked looking around. He'd just finished raising an archer and equipping the pet.

"I saw her go upstairs, think she's exploring," Sarge said from nearby. The large half-orc was exceedingly good at organizing the equipment for the undead. Each corpse had a small pile of loot already laid out before it. That would make it easy for Liam to hand over. Liam walked up to the Keep roof unable to find Kat. He wasn't worried, she could take care of herself. It wasn't like she needed a minder. Still, he made his way down into the throne room again. At last, he sent a group request to several high-level vampires.

"What's up?" Sarge asked accepting the invitation.

"We have some time before I can raise another pet. Might as well do a walk around the castle." He said taking control of his pets. He pointed at the three then said, "Follow." They dutifully kept pace behind them.

It wasn't until they were out in the forest that they discovered something wrong. There was a flash in the distance and a popping sound. As one they moved towards the commotion. It happened again and then again. An explosion went off some two hundred yards further. When they finally caught up, they found

Kat fighting. She was surrounded and getting murdered by dwarves. One was already laying on the ground dead. Kat's life though was deep in the red, and Liam immediately turned to Sarge.

"Casket Swap," he said and gestured towards Kat. An explosion just in front of the wounded vampire picked her up off her feet. As she flew Sarge disappeared into the soil. White marble burst from the ground under the guild leader. It closed over her like a giant mouth. A second later another coffin appeared next to Liam. Kat's armored form spilled out of it. She lay there dazed with barely a handful of hit points left.

"You should have told us you were going out." Liam barked at her. She smiled up at him still in a fog.

"It's nice to see you too, Liam." She said dreamily. He held out a hand then dragged her to her feet. When she let go he jabbed her in the stomach and sent an eldritch bolt into her. She shuddered feeling the magic work on her health.

"Attack," Liam ordered pointing towards the dwarves. They were already starting to flee. He wasn't watching though as he took Kat's hand again. He pulled her further away from the fighting. When he stopped, Kat leapt up kissing him on the cheek. He wasn't so easily mollified.

"What were you thinking?" He asked angrily.

"I was still a little giddy from the fight at the keep." She explained lamely.

"They're mercenaries, of course they are going to backstab you if they can." He said as if it was obvious. "We need to get back to the keep. There are already people showing up at the gate." Liam said swiftly moving away.

"That was fast, I just posted a thread on the forum," Kat said in amazement. She was nearly full health now as they walked quickly away.

"Well, it is just a few right now. That's going to change as dawn comes." Liam said moving quickly.

It did, oh by the dark lords did things change quickly. Much of the guild had logged by morning. It was down to just two groups.

Guild members that were interested in how things turned out. They all stood on the keep roof looking down on the growing numbers. Two thousand players had to be in sight. They stood in large clan-sized groups just outside the castle walls eying each other darkly. Fyre was there as well. The 'Player Killer' guild was holding the gatehouse and broken walls. They were trying to keep the other players from getting inside. He was grateful he'd raised so many pets. Now Fyre wouldn't be able to recover and resurrect them. At least none of the highest level corpses. Fourteen were down below in the keep. Two groups formed a blob just inside the main doors. Two extra were standing over the shitter guarding the secret way in. Fyre had already tried poking their heads inside once. Now they'd have to deal with the undead before taking the castle. Liam had only saved two pets. During the night he'd pushed them out into the middle of the lake.

"You were right," Liam said disappointment coloring his tone. There was no way they could hold the castle against such numbers. It was only a matter of time before the battle started.

"We'll find a home soon," Kat said reassuringly and patted his arm for emphasis.

"Funny, Fyre thought they could capture the whole eastern continent by themselves." Liam thought to himself.

"Why didn't they take some of the castles on the forty plus continent?" He asked instead. There had to be bigger and better on the next land. Shellbreak Castle was little better than a fort with some extra walls.

"Logistics," Sarge said leaning out over the parapet. He spit, hocking a loogie towards the battle lines.

"I don't follow," Kat said in a confused tone. To this Sarge took out a handful of gold coins and held them up.

"Think of the players as a resource, just like gold. If they hope to make an empire he's going to need a steady supply of fresh meat. The starter island can't be taken by anyone. Players can get up to level twenty without worrying about allegiance. So Fyre hoped to make a safe place to level people from twenty to forty." Sarge said moving gold from one hand to another.

"That cheeky bastard," Folken said from nearby. "That's why he was killing guild leaders for the last two months. He's been getting rid of the competition."

"Smart in away if he wasn't discovered. He's spread himself too thin though. Fyre only has about five hundred people. Half of them are down below trying to look tough." Sarge said pointing downward. "As soon as he tries to take the keep the others will attack him from behind. He'll be sandwiched between us and the other guilds.

"The guilds might fight each other too," Kat added.

"Probably will, it's a straight up turf war now," Sarge said spitting once more.

It happened quickly after that. Some of the crowd began inching towards the castle. Like a parasite thin arms began reaching outward from the mass. After a pause a surge of people rushed towards the walls. It looked as though Fyre would fight. They cast Area of Effect spells ahead of them as a barrier. Then some broke, running for open ground. The rest quickly pressed together and fled out one of the breaches. Over a thousand players crowded into the castle walls. Fighting broke out, messy and chaotic. The doors below crashed open. The few undead pets Liam had raised were pushed aside. They barely slowed the zerg rush of players.

"Time to leave," Kat said taking a portal stone out, Liam followed her example. Below the fighting took on a fevered pitch. Blood and bodies were hitting the hall floor with sickening speed. Later Liam was going to have to come back to collect the Spellsword and Fighter he'd hidden in the lake. Those character pets would come in useful. Besides he liked the thought of hanging onto that arrogant pricks corpse for a while longer. Liam activated his portal stone and was gone in a flash of light.

***

It was some hours later when another guild meeting was held.

Kat had taken the boat over to the next continent. Most of the guild was on and currently present for the discussion. The Fyre map Liam possessed was pinned to the tent they were standing next too. He pointed to it with a long stick.

"This is Edoku'kor," Liam said poking the continent in question. It was almost directly north of Aethon island.

"Does that translate to 'hot ass desert,' in elvish?" Someone shouted followed by a series of laughs and cat calls. Liam paused to look around at the landscape. It certainly was an apt description of the place. They were surrounded on three sides by sand dunes. The ocean could be seen from the wayside camp the guild occupied. They'd landed in the northern part of the continent. Most of the area was a sandy wasteland.

"It just might," He said after the group calmed. Liam pointed with the stick to the lower section of the continent. "The land here is what soaks up water from ocean storms. Not much is left after it passes over the jungle and mountain. The only way into the area is via a narrow strait located here." He said pointing to the tiny sliver of land. "On the map it shows a fort or castle nearby. That should make it easy to defend from invasion later. The necropolis itself is deep within the jungle. The southern coast is a mess of high cliffs and dangerous waters. There are a number of wrecks littering the reef." Liam said while using the stick to point out those locations. A hand was raised within the group.

"What level are we looking at?" A new voice asked.

Kat jumped in, she moved forward and touched the map roughly where they were located. "It fluctuates quite a lot. Around here its level thirty-five to forty. Near the eastern mountains there are some high-level monsters. Strangely enough, the closer we get to the necropolis the weaker the creatures get. Most of the undead in the city are mid-forties to fifty." Kat said filling in the information. She'd been offline studying the forums about the new continent.

"Thanks to the Fyre raid most of you are around thirty now. Still, this is a high-level continent. We'll move with the weakest members in back and strongest in front. I'd like to get to the city as fast as possible, but it's going to take us about two hours by foot. I suspect it'll take longer the more we stop to fight." Liam said dropping the stick.

"What if the undead attack?" Another person asked.

"We run like crazy. No way can we take on an entire city." Kat said quickly and turned to the sixty vampires. They sat or stood in the sand forming a rough semi-circle. "I've been in contact with the five who died during our raid. They've all agreed to become vampires again, so take a minute to greet them." She said and sent five names to everyone. They wouldn't be able to join the guild for at least three days. The time it took to turn a living creature. "I remind everyone to stay safe. We move in a group." Kat said clapping her hands together. She shifted from her goth costume into her armor. Liam removed the map from its place and rolled it up.

Kat and the other high-level fighters made a wedge. The rogues within the guild went into stealth and fanned out. The rest of the members formed a mass within the middle. Liam got into place within the mob. He stood three rows back behind Kat. He hoped they would run into some monsters he could raise. Liam had been forced once again to leave his pets behind. Maybe another day he'd go back for them. They traveled for about an hour with some ease. All they had to do was follow the coast south over the dunes. A sandstorm started to kick up as the night wore on. It got bad enough that even dark vision became useless to them. Visibility was only about five feet.

"Sand Giant on the right!" Someone shouted. Liam turned to look but could barely see a huge shape. It was a dark mass within the whipping sand.

"It's noticed us!" The same voice called. A few shapes raced past the group towards the figure. Kat's icon along with Sarge was moving with them.

"Mages and archers hold attack!" Liam boomed. They didn't need to attract its attention. This wasn't the first Giant they had seen, only the first they'd been forced to fight. The giant bellowed something in its native tongue. There was a loud smashing sound and a metal body flew into view. It rolled to a stop within the sand. Sarge got to his feet with an ear-splitting grin on his face. He was minus a large chunk of health. The cleric nearby cast a heal spell on the fighter.

"It hits like a truck alright," The half-orc admitted.

"I have its attention!" Kat shouted. Her voice was pitched high to reach over the sound of the storm.

"Mages try cold spells first," Liam yelled and moved forward. The giant's backside resolved itself as he neared. Liam stood with most of the guild just fifteen feet from its hairy ass. He wasn't sure if he could rely on his disease spells. The wind was so fierce it would probably just blow the effect away.

"Acid Arrow," He said pointing at the giant's right leg. A yellow blob shot from his hand striking the creature. His attack joined a half dozen frost waves and frozen needles peppering the giant. It bellowed staggering backward but it's feet slipped on the frozen sand. Everyone raced to get out of its path as it crashed to the ground. Kat appeared climbing onto the giant's chest. She began hacking at the Sand Giant from above. Liam aimed at the head of the creature. Its massive shape was almost impossible to miss from this close. Many arrows and crossbow bolts were already stuck in its neck and head. He fired several green eldritch bolts. The Sand Giant died as it tried to stand. Those massive knee's buckled once again as it fell back to earth.

"Anyone need healing?" The cleric called. The only one that had been hurt seriously had been Sarge during the first few seconds of the fight. Kat appeared as the group formed up again. They still had a long ways to go tonight. Now though they were going even slower than before.

CHAPTER TWENTY-EIGHT

Necropolis

The trip was a harrowing one. Thankfully, the sandstorm abated after another twenty minutes. The scouts ensured they went around any more monsters. They found griffins, large sand worms, and of course more giants. As the guild passed the strait, the desert began to morph. It changed into scrub hills then quickly into a jungle. The wildlife also shifted from high forties to mid-thirties. The air grew humid and moist. Instead of sand, it became insects and birds. Visibility once again dropped as the guild plunged into the forest. Tree's and vegetation blocked sight lines in all direction.

When they finally stumbled upon the city a gasp rose from the group. One second they'd been pushing through vines and bushes. Then a rock wall loomed before them. About a hundred feet ahead a large arched entrance stood open. Giants had been carved from the stone to either side. The figures were skeletal warriors in plate armor.

"Cool statues," Sarge said.

"Those aren't statues," Kat replied smiling. Liam looked again at the large forms. Kat picked up a stone and threw it towards them. As it landed nearby both undead giants turned their heads to stare at the sound.

"Holy shit!" Several people exclaimed. Liam had joined them in expressing that.

"So who wants to get near them first?" Sarge asked and nobody moved. The birds sang, and a few insects chirped nearby. "For bloody sake," Liam said in impatience.

"No Liam," Kat said moving to stop him.

"If they are undead, they are our brothers." He said not stopping. The undead giants turned to look at him as he approached. Kat yanked him to a stop though well before them.

"Let me go first at least." She said after getting Liam halted.

"Fine," He said and Kat turned. She looked at the two giant skeletons only sixty feet away. As if psyching herself up she jumped up and down several times and clapped her hands to her face. Then she ran towards the guards. The guild pulled in close watching as she neared the Giants. Forty feet, then twenty, well within aggro range of the monsters. Kat was screaming as she dashed passed them into the city. The guild members followed but refrained from yelling as they ran past.

The city was a splendor of white marble even under the vines and mold. Tree's grew out of old fountains and some buildings had collapsed. Kat was bent over on one side looking like she was going to throw up. She ran to Liam and hugged him.

"That was scary," She said and the guild members laughed. Finally the guild noticed they weren't the only undead. Zombies and skeletons wandered slowly around town.

"Stay together," Kat warned. The first level of the city was a business district. Broken shops, plaza's, and a large market took up most of the space. The city rose upward as they went deeper. Each level gave a good view of the one below. Waterways long dried up were instead filled with rubble. The streets littered with trash and broken buildings. The guild came to another wall within the city. The beginning of a castle fortification. This one was unlike many others. The keep and walls were located deep within the town. Most other defenses on Nigmus were located some distance from the city. Not so here.

A gate once again stood before them along with two additional giant statues. The group passed cautiously inside. More waterways wound their way through a dead maze-like garden. On the far side of the space a large white marble palace stood. The structure was huge, much bigger than the keep at Shellbreak

Castle.

"This place must have been something back in the day," Liam commented. One of the front doors was broken. Its heavy wooden construction sagging on bent hinges. Inside the dead went on with their old jobs. Cooks did little more than stand beside cold fires. Undead servants pushed broken brooms and scrubbed at missing glass. Everyone was staring around in awe. They found their way into the Grand Hall at the back of the building. There was a problem in the final room, a skeleton sat within the seat. Thankfully it wasn't a lich but an undead monarch. Its red name was simply Skeletal King. Kat and the group approached. It remained sitting but tapped its bony hand on the armrest of his throne. It was as if he impatiently waited for court to start.

"What do we do now?" Kat asked and Liam shrugged at a loss. He'd half expected the undead king to attack them first but that didn't happen.

"The bandit king sat on his throne too. So someone had to kill him." A thief in the group said. Unlike the simple keep from before, there were many doors leading to this hall. It would be impossible to keep reinforcements from joining the battle. Liam only hoped the king wouldn't call in help.

"Everyone over there," Kat said pulling her axe and shield free. Sarge followed her lead along with Folken and Astrid. She gave Liam a dark look as he stepped in to join them though she said nothing. The Skeletal King was higher level than any of them.

"Drink your potions now if you have them," Kat added and pulled an orange vial from her quick pouch. She downed it and her body blurred slightly; a potion of haste. Then she drank a second and third colored vial. Liam withdrew a tincture of enlightenment. It would increase his mana regeneration for an hour. Then he too drank a potion of haste.

"Sarge you're up first." She said gesturing with her axe. The half-orc stepped up to the undead king. His skin was reflective in the dim light after drinking a potion of Iron Skin. The guild shouted their encouragement but moved further away. Sarge banged his war hammer against his shield activating his defensive buff. For every enemy attacking him it would increase his armor.

"You dare attack me!" The king said as Sarge struck with his warhammer. A kinetic wave slammed into the group. Everyone was knocked away from the throne. Liam shook his head as he regained his feet. Where a simple tattered king had sat a new monster stood. The Skeleton King wore high-level scale armor and wielded a bright red blade. The weapon was large, almost a two handed sword. "Oh snap." Liam thought bitterly. It was a Blade Master, of course.

The King attacked Sarge as the defender stood. Kat and Astrid ran forward flanking the monster. Liam was at a serious disadvantage in this fight. Most of his spells had no effect on the undead so he first sent his few pets to attack. With his friends so close together he couldn't use his rooting spells either. He attacked with an acid arrow hoping to damage the King's armor. Kat slammed her axe into the monster's back. It turned parrying a thrust by Astrid next, quick as lightning it slashed at the vampire in riposte. The King twirled again catching Sarge's hammer in a weapon lock. As the fight wore on Liam pointed to Sarge. He struck the tank with a negative bolt healing the undead fighter. This had the immediate effect of attracting the King's ire.

"Bloody ball sacks," Sarge cursed as he chased after the King. It had somehow gotten past them trying to cut Liam down. He was grateful for the haste potion he'd drunk earlier. Liam fell back dodging around a marbled pillar.

"Soul Edge," The king intoned as he chased after Liam. The single skill cut Liam down to almost seventy-five percent.

"Liam!" Kat cried running forward. He, in turn, sprinted toward the group as they closed on the King. He pointed at the space just behind him and cast 'Grasping Hands.' A field of skeletal fingers grabbed at the Blade Master. This gave Liam enough time to dodge away. Kat ran forward jumping into the rooting area. She used every one of her daily abilities in quick succession. Finally, she culminated in her black shroud of blades. The king was a blur as it tried to parry at all the weapons attacking it. For every attack the King reposted the aura of wrath struck right back. It was like a black tornado and a red hurricane had collided in a violent orgy.

Kathrine's health was dropping fast but so was the undead king's. Sarge and Astrid were both attacking the flanks. Liam's pets were trying to squeeze into melee as well. Their effects though were a mere sideshow. The DPS was coming almost entirely from Kat. They remained locked in a duel to the death like two ancient martial artists. Liam healed Kat by pointing into the dark hurricane. A green flash lit the black blur. The Blade Master suddenly turned looking for Liam. He tried getting past the guild leader by ducking low. With a triumphant roar Kat brought her axe down on the king's neck. The last sliver of health vanished as his head rolled free. A pop-up appeared before Liam along with the sound of a level up.

[You have successfully killed the Skeletal King for the first time.]

This was followed by the sound of another level. He'd just gone from 38 to 40 from the massive EXP boost. The guild cheered and ran forward. Everyone in the group was wounded but alive. That had been a harrowing fight. Kat knelt next to the King and touched his body. The King's Crimson Blade appeared in her right hand and she smiled standing. The sword was an obvious and massive upgrade for her. Kat had been using her obsidian axe since level twenty. Liam moved to the throne.

"Go ahead and sit," Kat said joining him.

"No, I think it should be you," Liam said turning to the diminutive guild leader.

"You wanted a home," Kat said sheathing her new weapon which now hung on her back.

"I was thinking about that tower we came across before. The Dark Magus Tower. Since I'm a mage that would make for a fitting home." Liam said and took Kat's hand guiding her to the throne.

"You're sure," She said looking up at him.

"I am," He replied turning the Chaos Knight around. Kat sat slowly, lowering herself onto the throne.

CHAPTER TWENTY-NINE

GM Meeting

Walter Nowel
GM Station - Orbiting Nigmus
6am

Walter hopped into the room on small rabbit feet. A couple of
hundred Game Masters were present but not all were visible. The
room itself was about thirty feet long, so only level four GM's and
above were present in avatar form. They were like a strange
collection of cos-players at a science fiction convention. A
muscled war god sat next to an ancient clunky robot. A few were
barely recognizable as avatars. Within the admin section most of
the GM powers were shut off. Too many deities in one room
could lead to very strange effects.

"Good morning everyone," Walter said leaping into a raised
chair. He planted his furry little butt down and set an old
briefcase onto the table. "I'm sure everyone already knows this
but let's just state the obvious. As of 10 pm, last night King's
Landing was officially claimed." He said and many of the GM's
looked to one another. The war god was smiling, this was one of
his projects after all.

"That is three months ahead of schedule," Aphrodite said after
checking a virtual datapad. The beautiful goddess was the event
coordinator. This would halt most of her planned scenario's, at
least for the next few months.

"It appears our calculations were off. We only predicted

roughly when someone would discover the secret." Another GM said defensively. His servos whirred as he turned to look at the goddess.

"I am surprised by this but not entirely displeased," Walter admitted moving the conversation forward. Next he activated the halo display in the center console. A world appeared between the Game Masters. Using the controls on the table Walter began to zoom in. The view dove through the clouds zeroing in on a coastal harbor. It came to rest just above a small castle, Shellbreak Castle to be exact. Red dots of corpses filled the screen along with a large group of yellow ones.

"This is the site of a current battle ongoing. After the system announcement last night three guilds fought for control of the throne. That though was exactly as predicted." Walter said before entering a few more commands. The view shifted to another fort some distance away. Only a few red dots littered the area. It shifted again to another broken tower along the coast. "People are going to be fighting and dying. Emotions will be high." Walter said in a clear loud voice. He stopped the view just above a battle between two guilds. Fireballs and steel were being traded with quick and deadly regularity. It was easy to see the anger on their faces.

"Game Masters, I want you to remain vigilant against abuse. Verbal, chat, and physical abuse will not be tolerated. I will be granting level two GM's the power to temporarily ban players. This will be a twenty-four hour timeout. It will automatically transport the player to a nearby city jail and log them out. You may watch the fighting but we are here to help the players." Walter said shifting the view again. This time it was centered on a Dwarven Hold. A mass of yellow dots was grouped around an inner throne room.

"During the next few days we're all going to be busy," Walter said shifting the display back to an overview of the world.

"What about the undead faction? That wasn't supposed to happen for almost a year." Aphrodite said interrupting.

"Again, a pleasant surprise. They will capture the Necropolis in a few days. I suppose that will make getting reinforcements even more difficult. Most people that die choose to create a character in another faction." Walter said. The goddess was looking at her datapad with a decidedly puckered look on her face.

"It was the undead faction that alerted the people to the ability to claim land," Aphrodite said before adding. "A forum post, that has since been locked and deleted."

"I believe she indicated Fyre as being the originators. Considering they also hold the first castle I would suspect them first. If were looking for any malfeasance maybe we should examine this guild more closely." The robotic GM said in a dry synthesized voice. Walter knocked on the table loudly with a pawed fist. All eyes turned to him.

"At the moment I don't suspect any insider information. If this had happened a month ago maybe. For now let us focus on keeping the game civil. Level Four GM's, please coordinate with the server techs. If we see a surge in player movement we may have to move cloud servers on the fly." Walter said before glancing at each Avatar.

"Level Two and Three GM's will have the job of keeping the peace. Level Ones will continue to work through the help tickets." Walter said looking partially up into the air. He was directing these words to the hundreds of unseen watchers. After a second he glanced down again at the world. Red blobs of the recently dead continued to ping across the globe.

"Any questions?" He asked and nobody said anything. Walter liked to keep the meetings short and focused. "Very well, get to work." He said hopping down from the chair. Many of the GM's vanished as they teleported directly into the game world.

***

Orenthal - Level 46
King's Landing

4pm

After logging in Orenthal sat fuming on his golden throne. Damn it, things weren't supposed to go like this. He should have possessed half of Tramin continent by now. He raised his fist and smashed it down onto the padded arm of the throne several times. Work had been agony. Only the fact he'd banned dozens of players had allowed him to survive the tedium.

"Lawful Dead," He muttered darkly. They were the ones that had raided Shellbreak Castle several days ago. Then that woman, the vampire had fucked things up for him. He could have taken the castle back with relative ease but she'd gone and told the world what was going on.

Orenthal stood and stalked angrily into the next room. The central table was waist high and contained a massive magic map of the world. It was currently centered on King's Landing. The castle, city and surrounding land glowed yellow. This signified his possession of the area. This was the seat of power for the former empire. It sat atop a cliff bluff accessible by two drawbridges, both destroyed at the moment. The only other way inside was a tiny path curling around the bluff face. In short, he possessed a nearly impregnable castle now. Though the accomplishment was now pointless. King's Landing was a poor province in reality. The city was missing its docks and few people stayed in town. By the time anyone reached the area they were ready to move to the next continent. The only useful material he possessed was the gold and silver mines.

"Damn you," He hissed going to stand next to the map.

He put his hands onto the relief and pushed. The landscape slid forward under his fingers. Shellbreak Harbor came into view and he stopped. That was what he needed. The port was home to thousands of players. All of those people buying and selling goods. The taxes it generated would be ten or twenty times what he would make. Not only that they had access to shipping. That would ensure the city became the trading center for the human empire. [Insomnia] currently held the castle. The guild possessed the largest player base of all the clans. They even surpassed his own by almost a thousand. Had he gotten the castle first he could have negotiated, but not now. All they had to do was sit on the fortification long enough to rebuild the walls. By then it would be far to costly to retake.

The door to the map room opened and a half-orc entered. It was his third lieutenant. After Raff had died at Shellbreak Castle that had bumped up this player.

"The rooms have been divided out. I think most people are moving out to start leveling again," The barbarian said coming into the room. He walked to the map looking down at the castle. "King's Landing is a long way from the hunting grounds. I think most guild members are going to remain bound to either Shellbreak Harbor or Dragonfall." He said with a sad expression.

"Just great, another reason this castle was now pointless." Orenthal thought bitterly.

"You should have held," Orenthal said pointing down at the map to Shellbreak Castle.

"The players aren't soldiers. They won't throw their lives away." The man said looking to Orenthal. Only to himself he thought, "You are not that good a leader."

Orenthal considered his options. The lieutenant was right, most of the guild would be unruly for days. They wanted to level, have fun, not sit around a castle wasting time. He put his hands onto the map again and moved it north. He shifted the view to a mining town in the west. A small fort, not even a castle was its only protection.

"Take this," He said to the man.

"The fort?"

"Yes, with the fort we will possess nearly all the mines on the east coast of Tramin." Orenthal said looking up from the map. He'd control seventy percent of the ore industry at least. All he had to do then was set the tariff to a steep ten percent.

"People will just go west of Dragonfall. There are loads of old mines in that direction." The man said and Orenthal grinned.

"Humans are about to find the west side of Tramin a very

dangerous place. The dwarves are going to be a bit possessive of that area." The guild leader said with a delightful sneer.

"So they're taking land as well?" The man asked in an amused voice. Of course they would be. All the factions were racing to claim land.

"Go quickly, offer gold to anyone willing to help you," Orenthal said pointing past the man to the door. Other guilds were already out searching for places to call their own. Forts and towers all over Tramin were currently scenes of mayhem. Everyone was scouting madly for unoccupied land to take. The lieutenant left the room. Good, that would keep the man busy. He'd feel special being in command of the small fort.

Orenthal zoomed out from viewing the mining town. Ever since he'd first seen the world he'd loved it. That only hardened when he'd been told just how deep the game was. He did not just want to watch others play, no. Orenthal wanted to possess it all, to own everything. He wasn't supposed too, he'd signed the agreement not to participate in the game. So he'd been forced to go to great lengths to make his accounts. His hands rested on the edge of the table as he leaned over the map. The fighting would last a couple of months. Everyone would grow tired of killing their own kind. The red rings people wore now marked them for death. Yes, about three months. The power struggle would die down as guilds found their places. In time they'd start looking at the other empires. The orcs and elves were natural enemies. They both lived on a stringy set of continents to the southwest. There was a single settlement for each race on Tramin. That ensured all the factions got a chance to fight over this continent. Orenthal suspected it was the dwarves he'd be battling soon. Either that or those cursed undead.

Anger filled him at the thought of them. He should have tried harder to kill the lich and vampire off. Now it would be even harder to take the next continent. Finally, he left the map room and walked to his private quarters. It was ransacked but he laid down on the bed and logged out. He had things he needed to do out of game.

CHAPTER THIRTY

New Faction

KittKat - Level 40
Edoku'kor Continent - Necropolis Palace
3am

Kat sat up in the throne as the world changed. A massive dialog box appeared before her person.

[System Announcement]
The [Lawful Dead] has successfully claimed the Necropolis. The empire of undead has begun. Immortal and fearless; the revenant dead are spreading from Edoku'kor Continent. This new race may now be selected during character creation. They receive a number of benefits. Dark vision, immunity to dark energy, disease, and poison. Be warned though Undead take extra fire and holy damage. Undead may not be Clerics or Paladins of the Goddess though they may be corrupted priests.

"Congratulations Kat," Liam said from beside her. He had waited with her for the entire week it took to claim the castle. Five whole days, five bloody long boring days. Even Kat's virtual ass was tired from sitting.

"Thank you," She replied before a new dialog appeared. Necropolis Castle has been claimed. You are now the leader of this fortification and the surrounding city. This affords many new options. Would you like a tutorial?

Kat reached up hitting [Yes].

The castle is considered your guild's property. You have
complete control over its access. You can exclude individuals,
guilds, and of course other races. The city and surrounding land
are considered a part of your domain. You may not change access
to these. However, you can alter the tax and tariff on the land.
More on this soon. The palace is now the seat of power for your
empire. To make changes you must sit on the throne to access the
empire menu. Please do so now, which Kat was already doing.
She looked up and selected the menu. A new icon was visible in
the form of a castle. She selected this and a pop up appeared.
    "Good job. Select Taxes and Tariffs." It said, and she did so.
    "Any transaction made in town will result in a small tax added
to the price. It will include inn rooms, auction sales, merchant
stalls, and private property sold. This coin is automatically sent to
the palace treasury. You may select a tax rate between one and
ninety-nine percent. By default the rate is three percent. It's also
possible to alter tax rates for specific guilds. A resource tariff is
another form of tax. You may also change this rate to anything
you desire. By default the guild will receive three percent of any
goods gathered. This includes but is not limited to wood cut, ore
mined, or fish caught. The resources will be transferred to your
castle stores."
    "The next tab is the Build tab. There are many items that can be
repaired or built. Here you can upgrade roads, fix walls, or even
create useful buildings. The first thing you may wish to do is fly
your guild's flag. From the list of items select Replace Banners."
Kat eagerly pressed the lit characters because it was a free
upgrade. Around the room tattered and decayed cloth vanished.
New banners unfurled with the Lawful Dead guild image. A
white fanged skull with a halo over its head floated on a black
background. Liam next to her smiled glancing at the change.
    Finally, there is the Diplomacy, and War tab. The tutorial was
interrupted. Right around then a guild member burst into the

hall.

"Zombie players are already showing up in the city," Astrid exclaimed and Kat stood. The dialog box vanished as she did so. Kat would play with the empire settings later. She jogged after the guild member. Liam got into step beside her. As Kat left the palace she noticed a lot more had changed than she expected. The undead had previously been mindless. Zombies and skeletons had pushed broken items absently, now the NPC's stood alertly. The sentries straightened to attention as she approached, arms clanging against rusty breastplates in salute. The city was still a run down mess but it was alive once again. On the bottom level Kat passed a bank and auction house that wasn't there before. Player characters were already walking around the area. Kat and the guild stopped inside the market. In the middle of the square a tall obelisk stood. Undead flowed out of the portal in a steady stream. They were filling the large area quickly.

"I guess everyone wants to see what the new race is like," Liam said in amusement. Most of the players looked like freshly dead corpses. All were scarred by wounds, some were missing patches of skin or body parts. The injuries covered the lot of them like badges of honor. A few came towards them.

"You are human," One accused.

"We are vampire, we are the Lawful Dead," Kat said in reply. The undead man had a massive gash across his face. It stretched from his temple to his chin. He looked around at the ruined marble buildings.

"What do we do?"

"Same thing you do in other starting areas. Find some quest givers and learn the city." Sarge offered in a gruff sardonic voice.

"That sounds like a novel experience," Liam said turning to Kat. "I'm going to go explore, look for a few crafting skills maybe." He said to her. Kat bounced up and kissed him on the cheek before he left. As the lich made his way through the market the mass of newblets turned to gape. It was impossible to miss the flaming skeleton in the crowd. Kat might be the guild's chief leader but Liam was its mascot.

"I'll keep him company," Sarge said moving past her.

"He's perfectly safe, you don't have too." She said quickly.

"Someone has to keep an eye on the man." He offered starting to jog away. Sarge had a way of seeing what was important. He hadn't ever asked but seemed to grasp that Liam meant a great deal to Kat.

"Thank you," She called to the half-orc. Kat had been seriously frightened by the fight with the Skeletal King. Liam had taken massive damage from the high-level boss. She was sure if he hadn't caught the Sword Master in his root he would be dead now.

The market was still filling as players created characters. Most of these people wouldn't stay for long. It was just like Liam had said. These Players were testing out the undead race to see if they liked it or not. Kat checked her inventory and noticed another new item. It was a costume piece and she grinned seeing the object. Selecting it she moved it to the costume slot of her character. A crown fit for a queen appeared on her head. It was a gold braid with a single piece of onyx in the middle.

She turned to wander away from the stalls. Her guild had quickly dispersed to follow Liam's example. They were exploring and finding out where everything was in the town. Kat liked this, she owned this city. That tree over there was hers. That shop selling armor was at her behest.

"I could get used to this." She mused to herself as she sauntered along. Kat spotted a familiar figure in an alchemist's store. She turned pushing into the run down shop. Folken was sitting at the crafting table with a mortar and pestle. He wore a mishmash of dark gray and black leather armor.

"What are you up too, Folken." She asked with interest. Kat hadn't seen the rogue for a few days now. The assassin turned to look at her. His red eyes rose to the crown on her head. She smiled at him pleasantly.

"I'm practicing my potion crafting. Assassins get a bonus to the trade skill, at least for poisons. So anything I make is more efficient when I hit thirty and rank up." He said before turning back to the burner. He poured the contents of the mortar into a boiling bowl. This he began to stir absently. Kat watched the rogue for a while in silence. The man had a melancholy aura about him, yet he was well liked by everyone in the guild. He'd been working hard to level his thief.

"Tell me the truth Folken. Do you like your character?" She asked bluntly. He didn't look at her as he continued to work. Kat moved to lean against the wall next to the crafting table. Folken slowly stirred the powder until it was fully dissolved.

"I liked my paladin a lot. My friends, we had fun running dungeons. I was ignorant but happy. I've had a big dose of ice water thrown on my parade." He said before taking the pot off the flame. Purple smoke had started to waft up from the liquid. He tilted the pot into a large vial. A green and purple oil dripped down into the glass container.

"I'm not angry with you or Liam, not for some time. That's like being angry at a flame. Orenthal was the one that tossed me at the bonfire hoping to put you out." Folken said sadness dripping from his words.

"Learned my first day this game has a dark side," Kat said to the man. Folken was pushing a cork into the vial now that he was finished with his concoction.

"I would like to make you an officer," Kat said next. Folken spun towards her dropping the vial, which broke apart over the ground. Almost immediately the wooden floor boards began to blacken. "You don't have to be so surprised," She said chuckling at the look on his face. "It's not like I want to keep you from your vengeance. If Fyre's guild leader were in sight I'd happily toss you at that bonfire. A man needs more than hate to keep going though. The guild is growing which is good. Unfortunately, it's large enough that I can't personally help everyone. I need officers that can help our new recruits. Sarge has agreed to work with our warriors." She said and paused to glance at the storekeeper. He'd moved from behind the counter and was wiping up the floor with a dirty mop.

"You trust me?" He asked.

"I do, Folken. Please don't betray it." She said in reply. Glancing up she touched the system menu and accessed the guild page. She selected the thief's name and promoted him. He became a new officer in the guild.

"Is Spy Master acceptable?" Kat asked the still stunned half-elf.

"Yes," He said awkwardly. "What does that mean? I don't know much about being an officer." He asked after checking his new title out.

"Well, Liam and I are the founders. If some misfortune befalls both of us then Sarge becomes guild leader. You would be fourth in line of succession." Kat said pushing away from the wall. "Your first duty is to figure out where the thief trainer is. I need someone who can help new recruits find out where to go. Your secondary duty will be as the Spy Master. I may on occasion send you out to practice your rogue skills on a mortal." Kat said moving away.

"Thank you," Folken said with feeling.

"Have fun, that's why were all here," Kat said leaving the store.

CHAPTER THIRTY-ONE

Folken - Shadows

Folken - Level 28
Edoku'Kor - Necropolis Underground

Every city had a sewer, and every sewer its rats. Folken
remained in stealth but stepped over another one. The diseased
and skeletal vermin were all over. He outclassed them but the
creatures attacked without regard. The suicidal little beasts could
be annoying in large packs. He however was still floating on his
new promotion.

"Spy Master," He mused to himself. The parents would freak if
they found out he was a vampire. It was a good thing neither had
a clue about the mysterious little helmet. The virtual dive gear his
grandfather had bought him was another toy. Folken was sixteen
and yes he had been duped. He felt stupid, incredibly so for
getting suckered by Orenthal. He'd joined the Lawful Dead out
of sheer spite. Now though he felt like he was doing something.
Liam and KittKat were fighting for a place to exist, he could
appreciate that.

He paused in the sewer corridor. Ahead was a pack of ten or so
plague rats. In his dark-vision the animals were a mass of black
and white shapes. Folken decided to wait. If a thieves guild was
down here, it had to be accessible to a level zero character. The
rats chittered to one another. Finally, as one pack they darted
down a side passage and into a small den. Once it was clear he
advanced to the intersection. The left the sewer tunnel continued

into the dark. The rat-pack had gone that way, so he turned right instead and walked along the stone pipe. That was one nice thing about being in a dead city. Nobody had used the facilities in centuries.

After about a hundred feet the pipe opened onto a flat reservoir. The square room dipped into a culvert. Pillars stuck up out of the ground with bridges spanning between them. Nearby a set of stairs led up to a landing above. Carved into the wall next to the stairs was the symbol of the thieves guild. So he was on the right track. He climbed up and then crossed several rickety bridges. The next room looked almost exactly like the one on Aethon Island, except for the zombies. Several undead men were playing dice on a wood crate. Further inside a small female was throwing dirks at a target. In the back of the chamber, a figure sat in shadow. The zombie leader eyed Folken as he approached. His name was shown as Master Thief Triskin.

"Guild member, can I help you?" Triskin asked in a broken voice. It sounded like the man had his throat cut open then poorly repaired. At least the NPC recognized Folken as a thief already.

"Any jobs?" Folken asked. It was a standard question to most non-player-characters.

"None you'd be interested in. If you are looking for work, I suggest Armless Annie." The guild leader replied. "That would not be fun," Folken thought, being undead and armless for eternity. He tried to imagine how you'd go about backstabbing someone.

"Where can I find Annie?" He asked hoping the quest giver was close.

"Deeper in the sewers, she's gone a bit loopy. Sorry, I can't tell you where exactly, Annie wanders about. Says she's looking for the darkness within the shadows." The man said lifting a hand to his temple and made a little circle with his finger.

"Thanks," Folken replied and turned away. The girl with the throwing knives stopped as he approached. He noticed several dirks were sticking out of her chest. Like she couldn't be bothered to properly sheath them. So she'd just pushed her spare knives into her flesh.

"What can I do for you cutie?" She asked leaning against a barrel.

"Goods for sale?" He asked.

"I've got knives of course. Lock-picks and some leather armor, take a look." She said and a merchant window appeared before him. This too was similar to Aethon Island. The low-level items didn't interest him but it was good to know. He closed the window and canceled the trade. "Another time, maybe." She said pulling a dirk from her stomach. As he left she turned and threw it at the small target nearby. The two zombies playing dice would probably be quest givers. Though he was too high level now to take any.

Folken entered stealth before leaving the guild hall. Like usual he spent most of his time in this mode. It was good practice, or maybe it was just habit. Walking across the bridge, he descended the stairs into the sewer again. It was certainly harder to become a thief here. A new player would have to get past several low-level rats and that pack. Kat had been right to send him down here. He paused at the entryway to the reservoir. The sound of chittering grew louder. Quickly he backed against the wall as the pack from earlier ran towards him. Folken held his breath, he always did even though undead didn't need too. They passed him and ran down into the pit.

Well that would make going deeper easier now. He walked up the tunnel to the three-way intersection and continued straight. The further he traveled the higher level the sewer creatures became. Slime molds began to appear as he approached the middle-class area of the city. These were between level four and ten. Lizard creatures appeared close to the city palace. He spent about an hour looking for the quest giver. There were a couple of miles of sewer tunnel to explore. Occasionally long vertical pipes connected the passage to a man-hole above.

In the darkness he found her, not by sight though. That was why it had taken so long. Folken heard a female voice muttering, talking to herself. Footprints in the dust moved along the passage wall. He reached out grabbing the invisible thief. As his fingers closed over a shoulder she became visible. An undead girl turned to face him with pale white eyes.

"Yes, what is it?" She asked impatiently and Folken glanced down. Annie was definitely armless, and it was quite the disturbing sight. Her left arm was gone at the shoulder while her right ended in a few inches of stump.

"I heard you have a quest." He said to the woman. Despite himself, he felt guilty looking at her disfigurement.

"Annie want arm back. Was looking for something, found beast instead. Took my arm… gobbled it up. Cut the mean lizard open and fetch it." She said wiggling her stump at Folken. He saw now there were strips of flesh dangling from the end.

"Ok," He said glancing up. Annie was only a couple of levels lower than him. Whatever took her arm would be hard to kill. Slowly, as if dawning to him what she had said registered. She'd been looking for something. The guild leader too had said she was searching for darkness, whatever that was.

"What were you looking for?" He asked and Annie squinted at Folken. For a few seconds she eyed him up and down as if measuring his worth.

"Annie looks for the dark. It's there, there, there…" She said pointing to several places nearby. The sewer pipe held nothing of interest. So the girl had gone loopy. "Listen, feel, hear the silence in the dark," Annie whispered moving her head back and forth. Her eyes rolled crazily searching the ceiling and floor. She crouched suddenly and began to dig her ragged stump into a trash heap. Folken backed away from the crazy NPC. He had his quest, not that he was going to attempt it anytime soon. He started back hoping he could find his way out. If Folken planned to spend time down here he'd better start mapping it out.

Folken stopped, pausing to listen. "No, way." He thought.

He'd just passed by a section of sewer that seemed unnaturally silent. His footsteps had softened as he passed by. Moving closer to the wall he touched it with extended fingers. Nothing happened and he tapped the stone with his knuckles. The sound was muted, distant. He started searching the brickwork until he found a loose one. He pushed it in revealing a black space. Where the hole was a shadow seemed to spill out. It began to fill the cracks in the stones until a rough black door took shape. Folken stared, inside the space his dark vision couldn't penetrate.

Slowly he entered and was consumed by the dark. Folken couldn't hear the sound of his level going up. He'd just gotten awarded an exploration bonus. His right hand touched a wall. The stone was completely smooth and featureless. He bent exploring with his fingers. The shape of the corridor was different than the sewer. It was older in some indefinable way. He walked forward with fingers touching the wall. Slowly the tunnel descended before turning right, left, right, then right again. Five minutes he tread until he had no idea where he was. He couldn't say if he was below the palace still or not. The wall disappeared from under his fingers. He stopped frozen in a moment of panic. Moving backward he reached out to touch the wall again, only it wasn't there. The silence was all pervasive. It came with a sense of pressure and heaviness to the air.

Folken considered just portalling out. He took out the stone from his inventory. It was so dark he couldn't even see his hands. There was a sibilant whisper like a snake moving through grass. It took him a second to realize it was speech.

"So you walk in the dark?" It asked he remained still as a statue. Though Folken was undead his real teenage heart was pounding.

"Are you afraid?" It continued in a voice like the sound of blades scraping together. As if speaking through miles of foam he could just barely make out his own shaking voice.

"Who are you?" He asked tremulously.

"Who am I?" It pondered aloud in a voice that was almost too quiet to hear. The bass tones even deeper than Liam's. "I predate names before the world was born, I was. Before the stars fought for space in the sky, I was. Other creatures stalk the shadows. They proudly call themselves 'the things that go bump in the night.' I am that night; I am the dark." It continued slowly. Folken was left feeling very small indeed. Still he didn't portal out.

"You walk in the shadows thief. Do you seek me?" It asked. He sensed something new here. Was he in the presence of a god? A primordial being? Was this something like what Liam experienced becoming a necromancer? Or Kat when she saw those demons. He was afraid, so scared he probably was peeing himself.

"Yes," He said failing to keep his voice from cracking.

"Step forward into the dark," It replied. Folken gulped feeling his stomach begin to revolt. His booted foot slid a few inches across the smooth stone. One more step, then another, followed by a tentative third. Ten short shuffles forward and he was having second thoughts about this. Suddenly he felt nothing but air under his foot. He paused arms flailing about for balance. He fell backward onto the ground. Folken cussed, which would have really made his parents mad. With his boot, he felt the edge of a pit. The smooth stone just dropped without warning. He tried reaching down and seeing if he could feel a ledge below. Nothing, his hands touched nothing but black space.

"Step into the dark," The being said once more. Now its voice was a purring woman, sensuous and alluring. Was he about to do something stupid? Despite what the god said he continued to search. He found the hole was about ten meters in diameter and perfectly circular. Folken tried holding a torch, then a small glowing gemstone for light. Nothing in his inventory could pierce this darkness so he had no way of knowing how far down it went. It might be a two-foot drop or two thousand. Folken could turn away from this. Kat and Liam had made him an officer. Slowly he'd found a new family. Friends that greeted him when he logged in. He wet his dry lips. Folken lifted one foot into space. With all his will he forced his body to tilt forward.

His stomach flipped as he fell.

CHAPTER THIRTY-TWO

Liam - Council

Liam - Level 40
Edoku'kor Continent - Necropolis Defiled Temple

At first he'd been surprised to hear there was a Church of the Goddess in the city. The Deity hated the undead with a passion. Now though he understood. The windows of the temple were smashed out. The giant statue of the goddess was a disfigured parody of its former glory. The head, arms, and legs of the statue were gone. The torso hung suspended by rusting chains above a sinister alter. The godly robes had been carefully chiseled away. Two swollen breasts were leaking a black oily milk. The belly of the god had been cut away into the shape of a leering mouth.

The cleric of their guild had finally ranked up. His title was an apt one considering the location. A Defiler, yes apt indeed. Liam was here to witness the guild's very first resurrection. It wasn't called that according to the cleric. The goddess could resurrect, the undead defiler had the ability to reanimate, which was an interesting distinction. Just below the floating statue, a black and bloody altar had been constructed. The corpse of a mage lay atop the evil edifice. The body of a guild member that really should have known better than to solo.

"Ready yet, Josh?" Liam asked watching the cleric move about. The defiler turned finally noticing he had an audience. The guild member had the rather annoying name of xXHeals4HugsXx, which was why everybody called him Josh instead. The heretic had grown used to it.

"All that's left is to toss the coin into the sacrificial fire and start the spell," Josh said moving to the altar. The cleric accidentally kicked the step stumbling. He cursed loudly as his knee hit the hard stone. Josh wasn't the sharpest tool in the shed, but he liked the game. Despite his lack of IQ, he was a surprisingly good healer. The defiler withdrew a huge sack of gold from his inventory. One thousand coins made for an expensive reanimation. He tossed the bag onto the green fire. It flared consuming the sack making the money spill out. He lifted his hands up to the defiled torso in benediction.

"Orum Entu Corpu Animata." He intoned before the corpse. Green fire burst from the sacrificial sconce. It spread around the altar in a circle. Soon the fire made glyphs over the floor. Slowly particles of light began to float together above the corpse. They merged growing larger and larger until a yellow soul was visible. Again the pit flared with green fire. Little black and green chains began to circle the light. Within seconds it was dragged forcibly into the body. As it did, the corpse jerked and spasmed for a second then went still.

"I suppose someone will have to message the guy and tell him to log in," Josh said looking a little pleased with himself. Josh would likely become very popular. He was the only person capable of raising the dead in the undead faction. The defiler tried to move the corpse but couldn't. Now that the body was owned again the town restrictions were in effect. Nobody could force his character from the spot. Josh sighed dropping the arm before speaking. "He should be able to select his character again though I don't think he'll be happy about losing a level."

"Better than starting over completely," Liam said coming closer to the alter. The marble torso hung grotesquely above the corpse. He was glad his power over death came from arcane knowledge and not a dark god. The developers needed a bad guy, an evil to fight. Still, Liam had a severe distaste for the foul deity.

"True," the cleric replied.

"What's the cooldown on the spell?" Liam asked prodding the

player. Even Liam couldn't shift the body despite his strange nature. The Defiler in response took a black tome from his inventory.

"One hour except when I'm at a temple altar. Then there is a fifteen-minute reset timer." Josh said examining his prayer book. That was roughly the same as Liam's ability to raise pets. He supposed that was to be expected. The developers wouldn't want one person to be able to raise an entire field of fallen players. They'd have to bring the corpse back to town to bring them back to life. Even with the reduced cool-down [Lawful Dead] would need to be selective who got raised. Josh was usually active for five or six hours a day which also limited their numbers. Liam suspected more clerics would take on the class soon. That though would be two months down the road.

Of course this didn't personally help Liam at all. Walter had already contacted Kat and told them the sad news. He as a ghost had just one chance, no resurrections. He could only hope that changed in the future.

"Liam, we are having an informal guild meeting at the palace." Kat sent to him in a private message.

"I'll be there shortly," He replied turning to leave the vandalized church.

It had been two days since the undead faction became official. The population of zombies had leveled out to about five thousand. He passed by freshly risen corpses in armor and robes. The young group was banding together to brave the level five slime sewers. A new mage paused mid-sentence to look at him as he passed. Liam ignored the jealous glare as he mounted the city stairs. He passed by the two giant guardians into the palace gardens. It was still a dead wasteland as he approached the castle though it was nice to see the guild banners flapping about.

Liam found everyone in the map room. Among all the things he'd seen so far it was this room that fascinated him the most. A circular table took up more than half the space. Within the table sand had been poured to form the map. Kat had chairs brought in and eight of the twelve seats were taken.

"Good, this is everyone who's online. I sent Folken a message, but it's still early." Kat said as he approached. Liam took a seat at her right side.

"Our guild has become quite important in the last few days." She said gesturing to the map. White sand rose to form the mountains and jungle of southern Edoku'Kor. Around the Necropolis black sand colored the terrain. This indicated their area of influence. Kat pushed her fingers into the sandy map. It changed, the sand shifted as it zoomed in on the city. Black-colored sand flowed from below to mimic the buildings, tree's, and even people walking around.

"I called this meeting to ask a simple question. Can we take the strait?" Kat asked moving the map further. It shifted northwest across the jungle. A castle came into view above a modest town. The six-sided fortification looked impressive, or it would if one of the walls hadn't been completely knocked over. Inside the courtyard, Sand Giants walked about on patrol. They had taken the castle for themselves.

"The one we killed before was level 39 right?" Sarge asked from his place. He leaned forward sticking a finger into the moving sand giant. The little figure collapsed cut in half by Sarge. The map quickly reformed the model on its perimeter rounds.

"It was. We can expect them to be between forty and fifty. Intel on the forums says that the Sand King has two guards always nearby. A third giant sometimes approaches with food." Kat said zooming the map even closer. The castle grew larger so that its remaining walls were two feet high now. The giants were about half as tall. They had kicked apart the front of the keep to get inside.

Liam checked their guild members via the social tab. Only twelve people had made it to thirty-five so far. Any battle would be a pointless fight and a waste of energy. The same conclusion occurred to everyone else. Even ten extra members wouldn't help. Not against a level fifty chief and two guards.

"Even with our low-level members we'd lose most of the attack group," Sarge said sitting back in the chair.

"So that's a no then," Kat said after a pregnant pause. It would have been nice to solidify their position here in the southern jungle.

"I have a suggestion," Liam said shifting the chair. He slid a hand into his robe opening his inventory, then selected a grimoire. "Yesterday I made this, it's a copy of my spell book. We can now make another necromancer. I was hesitant to spend my experience because of a recent spell I acquired. Thankfully at level forty it only took about half a level." Liam said sliding the tome over to Kat.

"This is great," She said flipping the book open. Black glyphs moved about the page. They shifted snaking around and in on themselves.

"Yes, but there's a problem. In the item description is says this grimoire copy is of inferior quality. I believe that means its suitable for turning a person into a necromancer. However, it will likely lack the ability to make a full lich." Liam said gesturing to the book. Kat checked its description and frowned.

"So you are the only one?" Astrid asked.

"Remember we found other NPC books. I think for now we should focus on acquiring as many of these as possible. You are partly correct though, there will be a limited number. Fifteen lich tomes are unaccounted for based on the Fyre map." Liam said glad he'd purchased the scribe skill. When he ranked up he might be able to edit the map later. Having access to a city had allowed him to buy quite a few hobby skills.

"It takes three tomes to rank up, so that would be five upgraded necromancers in total," Sarge said from his place.

"New continents might bring more books." Liam offered.

"Still, that will help us level as well. We'll have something to focus on while our members grow." Astrid said more enthusiastically. Liam nodded to this in agreement.

As he was turning away a shadow across the room moved. His eye immediately noticed the strange phenomena. It began to bulge pushing out from the wall. Just barely it took on a humanoid shape. It had thin arms and no legs. The lower torso blended together into a wispy set of smoke like tendrils. He almost attacked it. The sight was so strange that it set off alarm bells. Only the [Lawful Dead] guild tag floating above its head prevented him from doing so. This mechanic made sure people didn't attack each other in large battles. Not every ally was in the same group or raid. It was only because of this Liam waited. His attention on the figure made everyone turn. The others didn't react so well. Most of the guild members leapt to their feet drawing weapons. The black shadow laughed.

"Who the hell are you?"

"What are you?"

"How did you get in here?"

The questions were asked by several people at once. Each talking over themselves in a rush. The shadow laughed even more. "You are the one that told me to come to the meeting." The shade said to Kat.

"Folken?" She asked in a strained voice.

"The same," Folken admitted stretching his long arms out.

"What the hell happened to you?" She asked more calmly.

"Ahh, funny that. I went down into the sewer to find the thieves guild. That done I was exploring. Under the Necropolis there's something primordial. So I got the chance to upgrade." He said in an amused tone.

"How did you do it?" Sarge asked putting away his weapons. The shadow's face grinned widely at the Defender.

"Maybe I shouldn't say, keep it a secret like Liam," Folken said coming closer to the table. Instead of moving the chair he simply slid into the dark space, then rested his thin elbows on the table.

"To be honest I don't know. All I can say was that it involved a test of courage." Folken said shrugging shadowy shoulders.

"What are you?" Liam asked.

"An undead shade. It is both my race and my class now. My twenty-nine thief levels were converted into shade ones. I gained True Sight, which is even better than dark vision." Folken said pointing back to the shadows. "I don't need doors anymore. As a shade I can move between shadows. So long as the room isn't locked I can move inside it. Instead of entering stealth mode I just jump into the darkness." He said with a smile.

"How does that work?" Astrid asked from her place at the table.

"It's like swimming under a frozen lake. I just push myself into a shadow then jump from place to place." He admitted.

"That is fucking awesome," Sarge said a little jealously.

"There are some big drawbacks, two of them actually." He said holding up a finger. "The first is this body is incorporeal so I can't wear any items. I'm naked, completely." He admitted gesturing towards his chest.

"Your AC must suck balls," Sarge said laughing. As a tank he lived and breathed by his armor stat.

"Zero armor rating, actually," Folken said scratching at his chest. His hand slid into the body of his shadow. "Mundane weapons can't touch me. I'm highly resistant to most elements except fire and holy. Those do double damage and blessed weapons can hurt me as well." Folken said accessing his character info. He seemed to be checking the numbers.

"How do you kill someone?" Sarge asked.

"Well I do have one item, a shadow dagger." He replied and magically drew a blade into his hand. It was black, the same as him but didn't shift or move in the light. The knife was about a foot long and curved slightly as if to dig under the ribcage.

"The second bad thing is sunlight. If you thought the vampire debuff was bad, this is worse. I take constant damage from standing directly in daylight. Enough that within minutes I'd fry like a piece of bacon on a hot tin roof." Folken said putting the dagger back. He sheathed it near his waist though Liam couldn't tell where. "I'm sorry I can't tell you the prerequisites for getting this class. I stumbled upon the location. When I tried to go back to look for it again I couldn't. The doorway had moved or refused to open." Folken said a little more apologetically.

"That's fine. I didn't know how I became a necromancer until weeks after it happened." Liam said forestalling any more questions. He'd respect the man's wish to keep the secret if he wanted.

"What were you talking about before the excitement?" Folken said not quite hiding the humor in his tone.

"We had decided to go looking for more Lich books. I think it might be wise to try and recruit some more vampires as well. Our sixty or so children are highly outnumbered by the zombie players." Kat said taking charge once again.

"A sensible plan," Folken admitted.

"Let's get started then," Liam said standing.

CHAPTER THIRTY-THREE

Kat - Gold Merchants

KittKat - Level 41
Edoku'Kor - Necropolis - Queen's Suite

Kathrine didn't log in right away. She stood on the selection pad for a moment admiring her character, her only one. It was interesting seeing the avatar of her persona from the outside. KittKat stood in black plate mail armor. The red eyes of the vampire followed her as Kat walked around the pad. They matched the crimson longsword sheathed on her back. She'd come a long way. Level forty-one and leader of an empire. Five months of gameplay. It seemed so long ago that she'd stumbled into New Hearth city.

After making several rounds of the selection pad she stopped before her character. Reaching out a hand she touched its chest. Her view shifted, diving into that of the avatars. The area went dark as the server logged her in.

Kat opened her eyes. She lay on her side within the silken sheets of her bed. An arm encircled her chest pulling her closer. Teeth bit at her ear and she smiled. Liam liked to sleep in her bed, and logging into this was very, very nice.

"You are finally on," He said and Kat's smile froze. It wasn't Liam's voice. She turned sharply to see a handsome elven face. His eyes were a bright, brilliant green. Kat screamed leaping from bed. As she cleared the sheets, Kat withdrew her weapon and shield. All of her armor was still in her inventory though. So it meant she was fighting in nothing but underwear.

Thankfully, the intruder was unarmored too. Not just in underwear either. He was naked, full on, man bits out naked.

"Who the fuck are you?" She asked angrily.

"I was hoping to surprise you," The elf said. That he did alright. Kat saw Liam was in the room and unconscious. He was sitting in a chair within the shadows. His skull was drooped low to the chest like he had fallen asleep. Instinctively she put herself between the attacker and Liam.

"I don't know how you managed to get into this room." She hissed loudly. The strange elf would die if he didn't immediately portal out.

"I've frightened you, I'm sorry Kat." The elf replied sadly. The tall exotically handsome creature swung its legs to the ground and stood. As he approached Kat put her shield before her. Her crimson blade held behind ready to strike.

She whispered, "Greater Vampiric Edge." The blade glowed now even more brightly with the weapon buff.

"I see, I've made a terrible mistake." It said, at the same time its eyes rolled up into his head. The elf fell backward collapsing onto the stone floor. Green fire began to flare from its mouth and eyes. A face like a skull became briefly visible in the flames.

"I'm sorry, Kat," Liam said from behind her. Kat whirled to see Liam looking up at her.

"What the hell?" She cursed.

"I wanted to surprise you," He said and Kat let out a pent up breath.

"Next time you want to surprise me, don't." She said anger still filling her voice. Kat then let out another cleansing sigh. "Our lives are already filled with enough danger. Surprises are almost never good." She said a little more calmly.

"Please forgive me," Liam begged. He even went so far as to slide from the chair to his knees before her. He grasped her hands in his large bony ones. Well shoot, she couldn't stay angry with him now.

"What was that?" She asked.

"It's called Soul Vessel. I got it when I leveled to forty. It lets me control a corpse like a puppet." He said and Kat instantly felt better. Kat pulled on him forcing him to stand.

"You don't have to leave the palace to level?" She asked hoping that it would enable him to remain safely tucked away behind these walls.

"Sadly no, I cannot use any skills or spells while in the body. Not even the skills the corpse previously possessed. All I can do is walk around and interact with the environment. I think the developers put it in so a Lich could finally enter town. At level forty they can have access to a bank and start a guild."

"Also the body is one-time use," Liam said pointing past Kat. She turned to see the last vestiges of the elf crumbling into ash. Well, not as impressive as she first hoped. "On the bright side we can now go into other factions looking for more lich books. Maybe we could recruit some dwarves or elves at the same time." He said moving back to the chair. Kat glanced back to the little pile of ash on the carpet. This too was already starting to fade.

"Of course, the dirty minded boy wanted to fool around. Not that they wouldn't but that was later." Kat thought to herself.

"We have things to do actually," She said trying to change the subject.

"You're not mad?" He asked turning towards her.

"I'm…" She paused considering her words. "I was just rattled. Surprise me with chocolates next time." She said giving Liam the look. The one all girlfriends eventually learned. It was calculated to say drop it, or you are in trouble. Liam coughed doing exactly that.

"I was contacted by someone who wants to meet in Shellbreak Harbor," Kat said opening her inventory. She started to equip her armor one piece at a time. Finally, she shifted into her costume. The black armor morphed into her vampire dress.

"What for?" Liam asked.

"He wanted to talk about switching factions," Kat admitted sitting down at the vanity. A bone brush was there and she started to use this on her hair. She attacked any tangles quickly.

"All he had to do was get bitten by a vamp," Liam said in a suspicious voice.

"That is what I'm going to see. It's in town so there is no PvP." She said dropping the brush. Kat stood and turned to Liam.

"Help me teleport over there?" She asked and Liam nodded. Thanks to him she wouldn't have to waste several hours on a boat trip.

***

It was called the Drowned Sailor. Not a bar she'd frequented while living in Shellbreak Harbor. It was a barge that was tied to the docks. So technically it qualified as a boat. She walked in and noticed only a dozen or so players. Most had to be commoners working on their sailor rank up. They sat drinking and talking about nothing important.

Several stopped to look in her direction as Kat entered. She moved past the bar towards the back of the tavern. A big man was standing next to a door labeled private. The NPC didn't seem impressed with her though it did eye her cleavage.

"Money Talks," The man said holding out a hand. Kat selected the amount she'd been told to give him. Forty-six silver and eleven copper were in a small purse. She dropped this into his big palm and waited. The tough knocked on the door and it opened. Now everyone in the inn was looking at her as she walked past the man. Most of the Players had never seen anyone go inside that door.

It was a short hallway that turned once to block the view from inside the common room. The door was already open. At first she thought he was an NPC. The man was fat, like mountainously large. His hair was a bright flaming red with a heavy smattering of freckles on his face. It was his eyes that she looked too. They weren't the unintelligent dull of an AI controlled character. His twinkled behind a pair of spectacles. A second player was leaning against a nearby wall.

"My name is Amas Mooney." He said standing and extending a hand. Kat moved into the room and approached the table. It was filled with wine bottles and plates of candied fruit.

"Everyone calls me Kat." She replied shaking his hand. He didn't seem put off by her fear aura. Maybe he was just that good at hiding the effects.

"Thank you for seeing me. I apologize for the subterfuge. Since all this business with empires starting up everyone has grown a tad edgy." The man admitted waving for her to seat herself. Kat pulled a chair out from the table. She wished Liam could join them for this but he'd have to leave his real body dangerously exposed. The man smiled and held up a many-ringed hand. "That must be nice." Kat thought to herself. A merchant apparently had additional ring slots. "Before we begin, please let my friend do his magic." He said gesturing to a nearby rogue.

A man wearing leathers stepped away from the wall. He pulled an object from his quickslot pouch and tossed it towards the center of the room. Kat looked away from the small flash and pop.

"Two rogues; one is in the corner, the other is under the table." The unknown thief said in a bored voice. Kat realized the man must be a Trickster. It was the ranked up form of thief. The class was good at laying traps and detecting other rogues. The large man still had a smile on his face when he turned back. "Are they yours?" he asked Kat. So a trickster could see Folken even within the darkness. That was frankly worth the trip to find out.

"Yes," She said feeling the urge to get up and leave. The rogues were her extra protection in case anything went wrong.

"I only wanted to verify we are the only listeners, Gerald?" He said turning again to the thief. The man set a small toy on the table and started it spinning. There was a nearly inaudible but annoying buzzing that accompanied the object's motion. The thief then left the room.

"That will prevent sound from traveling very far." The man said gesturing to the toy.

"Guild member?" Kat asked.

"No, he's an acquaintance I've used for business dealings before. I pay him well for a few minutes of his time." He replied.

"This is quite a lot of cloak and dagger," Kat said a little sourly.

"Ah hahaha." The man laughed loudly setting his belly rolling. "You'd be surprised how cut throat the marketplace can be." He continued still in good humor.

"I've never spent much time considering it," Kat admitted. To her, the auction house was just a place to dump loot.

"You know what I like best about this game?" He asked and she glanced at his corpulent form. He had double chins bordering on a third. His belly was so large Kat could easily fit inside it. Not for the first time she wondered about his mental state. Why make himself like that on purpose?

"It's quite beautiful," Kat offered.

"True, but I like it for another reason. It has so many interlocking components. They aren't obvious at first glance, or to the average adventurer." The man said taking a cigarette out of his pocket. He stuck it between his lips and lit it. The thin cigar smoke was sweet. He withdrew the stick and pointed it at her.

"Everyone in the game has a purpose. You adventurers go out into the world getting experience. In reality, you are the ones that make money. Gold drops only from humanoid creatures, and boss fights. Resource gatherers collect items from the world. Fish, wood, and ore, everything that we use as components. Crafters make most of the items that adventurers use. Rare equipment does drop on bosses true but all potions are made. Arrows need to be fletched, scrolls created, weapons enchanted. The little things in the game are all player created. This is where I and others like me come into the picture. A merchant. We few, we greedy few bring all these pieces together. Not only do we add to the game but we make gold doing it." He said finishing his monologue. Apparently, he'd put some thought into the topic.

"Is that why you made your avatar look like that?" Kat asked and Amas laughed again slapping his massive belly.

"I tried a fighter at first and was immediately bored. As I looked about I saw how many pretty people there were. Sure joke characters are running around but so few. I'll admit I was in a fit of pique when I made this avatar. I wanted to create someone I could relax with. I've found that it helped me stay focused on what I enjoy most. Once as an experiment I put on some cheap armor. It was so funny I just couldn't stop laughing." He admitted chuckling.

"If you're not interested in fighting why would you want to be a vampire?" Kat asked still confused by the man.

"Ahh, now we circle back to the meat of this conversation." He said smiling. "I am probably the third richest man in the human kingdom." Amas continued a little smugly.

"How can you tell?" Kat asked.

"I am a Merchant by trade. You have combat skills that I could never possess. I, however, have information skills. More specifically I can tell who is buying what at the auction house. For example, I know that your guild was buying sun-stones for months. It was smart in a way, keeping such dangerous toys out of the hands of your enemies. We merchants let it be because it drove up the price. I made quite a lot of gold from that." He said and Kat felt annoyed by this but the man continued unconcerned. "So when you play the market for long enough you get a feeling for how much money each merchant has." He said as explanation.

Kat wasn't stupid, she could see the implications. "So you want to jump into a new empire with all your gold."

"Exactly so," He admitted.

"I've been considering moving to a different faction for some time. Since your empire is so new it was a delicious opportunity." He said smiling.

"You know it takes three days," Kat replied.

"I do. Which is why I set up this meeting. If the other merchants found out they'd obviously alter their buying and selling habits." He said wiggling his many ringed fingers in the air.

The game catered to many different people. Not everyone was into the hack and slash side of Nigmus. She was coming to understand an empire needed an economy. She sat for more than a minute looking at the merchant. Did he want to become undead just to corner most of the market? He'd be in a position to rake in the gold, and she'd love to make use of his talents.

"Why don't you join my guild?" She asked the man finally.

"I planned on starting a merchant guild." He admitted with an apologetic face.

"Alright," Kat said standing, she went to his side. Drinking from his neck seemed a little too icky. So she picked up his arm and bit into his wrist. He waited patiently as his hitpoints started to drain. After only twenty seconds the man was at half health.

"Won't they get suspicious when you log out for several days?" She asked after letting his arm go. He examined the wound with some interest.

"I can access the auction house anywhere via a pet," Amas said producing a small green imp from his pocket. It looked like a miniature goblin about the size of his palm.

"It's so ugly its cute," Kat said admiring the hideous little creature. It leered up at her with big yellow eyes.

"I'll set it up so all my bids will close out before I turn. That way I can shift locations easily." The man said standing.

"Why don't you bring the resources with you? The bank has lots of space." Kat asked the man. Her own bank was barely half full. She could access it from any town she went too, even across factions.

"I deal with tons of material. Unfortunately, far too much to fit into my bank. I'd need to ship the items to the new continent. That would entail finding a boat captain and locating a port." Amas said digging a potion from his inventory. Quickly he pulled the stopper and drank the elixir.

"There's no docks at the Necropolis. Very high cliffs." Kat said moving towards the door. Their meeting was almost over anyway.

"Ahh, how sad but I figured as much." The man replied standing as well. Instead of following her he withdrew a portal stone.

"Hope to see you around," Kat said as the man activated his

item. He was gone quickly and Kat turned to leave. They had some Lich books to find.

CHAPTER THIRTY-FOUR

Folken - Spies

"Trust, but verify."
— Roland Regan

Folken - Level 31
Edoku'Kor
Two weeks later, Early Spring.

The meeting spot was deep within the jungle far from the Necropolis. Though it was an hour until dawn it was bright as day. Almost a hundred sun-stones had been tossed about. This cast a maze of crisscrossing shadows because of the jungle trees. Folken stepped into the glade. Actually, a corpse was doing the walking. He was slipping along in the shadow of Liam's vessel. The dead man was medium height with dark brown hair. On his hips, he wore a pair of impressive daggers. Moderately leveled leather armor covered his body. In most ways he looked exactly as Folken once did. All except the eyes, Liam couldn't hide his bright green pupils.

A willowy man stood in the center of the glade. An old acquaintance by the name of Hermes. Folken was glad he'd remained below the vessel, in its shadow. Hermes surreptitiously glanced above the vessels head. He was checking for the red gem of someone on an enemy list. The man would see his gem floating over the corpse's head. A neat little trick.

"What a waste of good gold," Folken said ignoring the glance. He waved at the sunlit glade.

"Can't be too careful nowadays," The man said with a shrug.

"I was under the impression you wanted to catch up on old times. You said you wanted to meet someplace away from the city." Folken said shifting. He moved a little further from the light of the sun-stones into a deeper shadow.

"I do, Folken. You were in on the attack at Shellbreak Castle?" The man asked.

"I was; just business," He said, and it was Folken's turn to shrug.

"Could have warned us," Hermes said in a tired tone.

"Would have ruined the big surprise though. Fyre hadn't done me any favors." He said with an equally tired voice. It was like watching an overly acted drama being played out. Each actor exaggerating their lines way out of proportion.

"A lot of good people died," Hermes replied without much feeling.

"Please, let's not pretend Fyre hasn't murdered its fair share of 'good' people," Folken said raising his fingers in little air quotes.

"I am surprised you made officer in the very guild you attacked," Hermes replied a little more caustically. Finally he seemed to be showing a little emotion.

"Ah, you heard about that," Folken said with a smile. That told him there was at least one spy in the guild.

"I'm just disappointed," Hermes said shaking his head. The other people in his party were shifting in the forest. They moved about, searching for anyone unwanted.

"Disappointed? I'd think you'd be happy I was moving up in the world." Folken replied genuinely surprised.

"They trust you?"

"The guild leader does, some others not so much. They understand it wasn't personal." Folken said and paused. He took a second to lean against a nearby tree. The other people were tossing more sun-stones around. Liam wanted to make sure he was standing within darkness. He continued in a droll tone. "You know, I'm starting to feel like you didn't just come to chat about old times."

"We have an offer for you," Hermes said with a generous smile.

"What's that?" Folken asked. He'd known something like this was coming.

"You can join us again."

"Hate to point out the obvious, but I am a vampire. There is no cure from turning undead that I'm aware of." Folken replied.

"You know what I mean. We can give you gold, power level you and give you a place in Fyre again." Hermes said walking closer. He too took up a position on a nearby tree. His shadow just happened to fall over Liam's, how fortunate.

"That's a generous offer. What would I have to do for this?" He asked.

"You're an officer in the guild now, fourth in line. We set an ambush for everyone above you. When you become the leader pass on the mantle to my alt." Hermes said with a conspiratorial smile. This was why officers needed to be trusted. It was too easy for an 'accident' to happen.

"If I'm the leader why would I pass the mantle?" Folken asked then added, "I'd be in a position to own the Necropolis."

"That's fine with me, so long as you come back into the fold. The officers you select are alts from our guild." Hermes said and Folken smiled. What a convenient way to kill him off. After all, the same ploy could be used to pass the mantle to someone they trusted. Folken pretended to consider the offer.

"I'm afraid I'll have to pass old friend." He said and Hermes sighed regretfully.

"I am not surprised but very disappointed," Hermes replied touching a hand to his tunic collar. A flaming arrow struck the vessel in the leg. The fire spell doing considerable damage to the corpse. The vessel stumbled back hobbled.

"Hermes, I thought we were friends," Folken said with a pained expression.

"Think of this as just business," Hermes said before a nearby mage cast a flaming hand. The spell took the shape of a massive fist. It grabbed the corpse in its grasp and slammed it into the ground. Hermes came forward drawing a glowing sword. They'd made sure Liam wouldn't escape. With the flames doing constant damage he couldn't stealth.

"Don't think badly of me for this, Folken." He said taking several swipes at the vessel. Quickly it's health disappeared from the blows. None of them noticed the eldritch flames within their fire spell. A green face lifted from the corpse and raced away. Folken moved then, he detached from the shadow of Liam's vessel sliding under Hermes. He rose wrapping one thin arm around the fighter. His other hand held a Shadow Dagger, a blade crafted from pure darkness. He plunged this into Hermes back between his mail tunic and pants. The poison on the blade immediately paralyzing the man.

"Capture Victim," He whispered dragging the mortal down into the shadows. Ten meters away they fell out of the shade of a tree. Folken continued to stab the man underneath the chinks in his back plates.

"I'm the one who's disappointed, Hermes." He said slipping the blade into a kidney. His friends were rushing to help. A Lancer shot forward closing the distance in the blink of an eye. He plunged his iron weapon into Folken's shadowy form ineffectually. He was now totally immune to mundane weapons. Even the electrical enchantment on the lance did little.

"I only came here to see if you had a spy within our officers. Now I know you have no one important in a position to hurt us." Folken rasped as he struck again. The fighter was almost dead but the fast acting paralytic poison was wearing off. Hermes started to struggle flailing with his glowing sword. Folken shifted grabbing the man by the shoulder. Reaching up he plunged the dagger into the side of his neck. He dragged it across Hermes's throat as hard as he could. This final backstab was all it took to finish him off. As the man screamed in bloody anger Folken used a new level thirty ability.

"Shadow Clone," He hissed sibilantly. Darkness poured out of Hermes like ants escaping a host. The clone had the same abilities and stats as Folken. A carbon copy of his character. The shadow turned to Folken looking for instruction.

"Attack nearest," Folken said to the pet. The shade screamed jubilantly and launched himself at the Lancer attacking Folken. The man yelled rolling away from the pet. Four adventurers were still converging on the fight. He, however, slid back into the shadows. Folken shifted moving some twenty feet away to another tree. It didn't take long for them to kill his pet. The creature broke apart, dissolving like smoke on the wind.

"Shit! Hermes died." The Lancer cursed coming toward his fallen comrade.

"It doesn't matter, we killed an officer tonight. Hermes, we can resurrect when we get back." An Arcane Archer said coming into view. Folken grinned from his place under the tree. They were wrong about that. The shadow clone spell consumed the soul of the targeted creature. He might look fine on the outside but there wasn't anything left. They'd discover soon enough he couldn't be resurrected.

"At least there's one less undead. Orenthal wanted to weaken them from the inside. We can always try again with the alts. Then we'll have an easier time of it when we take the northern desert." The man said sheathing his lance.

The small group converged on the body. The Lancer bent, dragging Hermes's corpse over his shoulder. None seemed to notice the vessel they killed was gone, destroyed by eldritch fire. Folken shifted shadows again as the small party took out portal stones. He moved slipping under the space next to a robe wearing man. They activated their items and soon became enveloped in the blue yellow magic. Folken reached out grabbing the ankle of the high-level mage. Folken drove his blade into the hamstring of the wizard. The man cried out falling over in a tangle of red robes. His friends though were too late to cancel their magic. They teleported away in a flash. Falken quickly lept upon the man.

"Phase door," the mage almost said. Folken though pushed a hand over the man's mouth.

"Void Silence," He quickly said and everything went eerily quiet. Within three meters complete and total silence reigned. Only he could talk in this spell. "Shhhh," Folken whispered sliding the knife in between the mage's ribs. The man couldn't do any complicated spell macros with Folken on him. The mage pushed a hand into Folken's face blasting him with fire. It felt like someone was spraying him with a blow drier set on overdrive. His weakness to fire doubled the damage of the spell.

"Go out like a gentlemen," He said thrusting again. The thin young man was scrabbling, trying to wrench the shadow hand from his mouth. The thief's strength though was much higher than the wizard's. He used the opportunity to attack the man's side several times. "There now," Folken said as the man died. His eyes rolled back into his head as he relaxed in death. It had been a good evening. They had discovered several interesting facts. One was that several spies were in their ranks, not unexpected. In fact, it would have been strange had there not been. At least the spy or spies were simple members, no one in a position of power. The second fact was that Fyre was looking to expand again. That wasn't so surprising either. Quite a few human groups were roaming around up North. Folken stood and looked to the east. The sun was rising over the horizon. A tiny sliver was visible over the jungle canopy. Its deadly rays were already starting to damage him.

"Time to go," Folken thought.

Bending he picked the wizard up over his shoulder. Folken awkwardly took his bind stone out and portalled home himself. He appeared within a windowless room in the palace. Folken liked this bedroom for two reasons. First it was dark, obviously useful. The second was the secret sewer entrance just down the hall. Folken liked getting in and out of the palace unnoticed. It had helped his reputation within the guild. He dropped the corpse to the stones. As he bent to inspect its inventory someone knocked on his door.

"It's open." He said still kneeling. The mage sadly had been a miser. No coin aside for a few hundred silver. He'd banked everything except for a dozen potions and some food.

"I'm glad you are alive," Liam said stepping into the room.

"I appreciate that."

"What happened?" Liam asked next. He'd been there for most of the conversation. Liam had been the one controlling the vessel. It was he who'd been talking all along.

"Killed Hermes after he took out your vessel. Sent a clone to distract them as I pulled back. When they started to portal out I picked off one more." He said gesturing to the wizard.

"Are you going to use him?" Liam asked and Folken shook his shadowy head.

"I already used the clone ability. The corpse will be gone before the cooldown resets." Folken admitted before turning to Liam. His ability was a daily one. It would take twenty-four hours before he could cast Shadow Clone again. The corpse would decay at roughly the same time.

"Do you want it?" Folken asked.

"What kind of mage is he?" Liam asked.

"He used a lot of flame spells so an Evoker in all likelihood."

"That could be useful," Liam admitted stepping closer. He pointed his staff at the body and moved his hand in a three pattern macro. Green fire spread around the body as it began to reanimate. The corpse started to rise, standing up to his full height. It looked to Liam for orders.

"I want to apologize, Folken. It took me longer than it needed to trust you." He said after a finishing his spell.

"No need, there was reason to distrust me," Folken replied moving towards a bed.

"Still, I'm sorry," Liam said apologizing again.

"Thanks, well... I'm going to log. As it stands I have class in three hours." Folken said and started to tap at his menu screen. He clicked the exit icon.

"Have a good day," Liam said before Folken's game logged out.

CHAPTER THIRTY-FIVE

Walter - Suicides

Orenthal - Level 47
Tramin - Kings Landing

Inside he fumed. Orenthal had given explicit instruction to offer the former paladin anything. Anything, instead they'd botched the meeting completely. It was a good thing Hermes was dead. That saved him the trouble of kicking the fool from the guild. Now they'd have to do it the hard way. All of these thoughts went on in his head, but he smiled. A neutral uncaring smile.

"Don't worry about it." He said pleasantly. The group of players before him visibly relaxed.

"They weren't able to resurrect Hermes," West0n said a little sourly.

"Of course not fools." Orenthal thought to himself. They hadn't recognized a shade when they saw one. He did admit the undead were becoming an annoyance to deal with. Ember had died while the party had been portaling away. That was an even more serious loss in his opinion.

"It's some undead necromancer trick." He lied smoothly. "If Hermes contacts us offer him some power leveling." He suggested, at least he'd be useful as cheap cannon fodder. "Give him his items and gold as well," Orenthal said next. It had taken some convincing but everyone was now depositing their money into the guild bank. This meant when people died their items and gold didn't vanish. It also meant Orenthal had much more wealth to play with.

"Thank you for the report. I appreciate you coming here personally." He said to the assembled players. They nodded turning to go, most looked relieved to still have a place in the guild. Orenthal was a leader known for his temper.

Once again he wondered why he was surrounded by failures. They shouldn't have killed the vampire. That would just tip the undead guild off that something was happening. At the very least they would have kept the enemy rogue as a contact. Possibly turn him later, not now though. He drummed his fingers on the armrest of the throne. Nearby the hearth crackled, embers flying into the air. Orenthal relaxed back in the throne. Guild tapestries and banners hung along the main hall. The castle was looking splendid now that he'd invested the money into its renovation. NPC servants were sweeping and cleaning the white tiled floor.

A circle of light formed near the end of the hall. The blue lines grew in intensity before a flash lit the space. A half-elven conjurer appeared. She was tall with robes like the morning set. Orange on bottom slowly darkening into a dark purple.

"Welcome back," Orenthal said.

"Thanks," She said moving forward into the hall.

"How did it go?" He asked. Freya drew in a long breath. "[Legion] patently refused to come. [Insomnia] and [RageQuit] are willing to meet on neutral ground." She said, and he nodded in response. It had been expected Legion wouldn't show. Orenthal had killed two of their leaders before the war started.

"Did they give you trouble?"

"I'm glad I met them in town." She admitted going to a side table. Bottles and meats were set there, and she filled a wine flute.

Orenthal sighed, things weren't as bad as they seemed. The mines he held were needed for item crafting. The rare gems essential for jewelry and enchanting. This didn't endear him with the merchants, but that couldn't be avoided. He needed money, running an empire cost a lot of gold. The guild had grown of course. Fyre finally had a thousand members, but everyone was recruiting with a fervor. The smaller guilds were being consumed or vassalized by the stronger ones. Of the ten largest Fyre was right in the middle.

It was this fact that was so troubling. He saw no further way to improve his standing. The council meeting tomorrow was for a joined push into Edoku'Kor. Orenthal suspected the other guilds would demand territory for their help. Orenthal needed an edge, he was going to have to do something drastic.

"Freya," Orenthal said and the conjurer turned. 'Hmm,' the elf said still eating.

"I'm going to be late getting back from work tomorrow." He said to the half-elf.

"Should we push back the meeting time?"

"No, if I don't show up start without me." He said turning away. First, he needed sleep then some time to consider what he was about to do. It was something he'd been planning for weeks now. Going up the stairs to his suite he closed the door and laid down.

"Drastic times requires drastic measures," Orenthal said to himself as he exited the game.

***

Walter was surprised to see the ambulance in front of the building. Several police cars blocked off the parking spots nearest the entrance. The sight of the emergency vehicles sent a cold chill down his spine. He pulled into an available parking space and got out. As he neared the entrance a gurney was wheeled out of the glass doors. A white sheet covered the body from view. Ice water filled his veins at the sight. The two medics loaded the person into the ambulance as he watched. Neither attempted resuscitation on the corpse.

Stunned, he swiped his employee card and went inside the glass front doors. About forty employees were standing around the lobby. They clustered around the windows and doors.

Unconsciously needing to be near the exit. Walter spotted a familiar face in the group and walked over.

"Alice," He said to the woman who turned with tear-filled eyes. Her mascara was running from crying.

"Walter, isn't it awful?" She asked.

"What's going on?" He asked. Alice sniffed and brought a tissue to her nose. She blew noisily before answering.

"Someone committed suicide last night, the janitors found the body." She said, and he rocked backward. Walter didn't believe in coincidences. Already his suspicions were growing.

"Who was it?"

"I'm sorry I don't know his name, never talked to him personally. All I remember about him was his stupidly long GM name." She said sniffling again. "Is that bad of me?" Alice asked.

"I don't know everyone either," Walter admitted already dreading the board meeting that would come from this.

"It was religious, something to do with kings," Alice said after another second.

"Nebuchadnezzar," He said feeling another chill. "Thou, O king, art a king of kings: for the God of heaven hath given thee a kingdom, power, and strength, and glory." He said under his breath.

"Yeah that's the one," Alice said.

"His name was Daniel," Walter replied wondering if he was going to get an ulcer. His stomach felt like someone had poured battery acid in it. Walter's phone rang, and he picked it up.

"This is Hithrow at corporate, what is going on?" A man asked without preamble.

"I wish I knew. Just came in through the door. Nobody saw fit to call me." He said feeling more annoyance at being caught with his pants down.

"There's a meeting in two hours. You will have answers by then." The man said before hanging up.

"God damn board members." He thought hanging up as well. The bastards were a bunch of tight wads that almost ruined the game before. He hated that the studio needed the financial backing. Soon he found himself in the company of a detective. The man was short with balding front hair.

"My name is Detective Rick Tracy. Can you answer a few questions?" The balding man asked. Walter nodded his head not trusting his voice just yet. He took a swig of coffee to try and wet his dry throat.

"Did you know the victim?" The detective asked.

"If it was suicide why call him the victim?" Walter asked curiously.

"I've learned recently that suicides aren't always the case. We can't rule out anything at this point. Please answer the question." Detective Tracy said dryly.

"I didn't know him personally. He was a low-level employee. From what I understand he didn't interact with the other GM's." Walter said shifting in the coffee lounge chair.

"GM?" The detective asked.

"Game Masters, it's just a fancy word for administrators." He said taking a sip of coffee. Despite the fact it was adding to his upset stomach he continued to nurse it.

"Did Mr. Webb show any signs of stress lately?" The detective asked next.

"The game has entered a critical stage. We've all be working long hours. To be frank I'd be surprised if anyone would have recognized the signs." Walter said. The detective made several notes on his pad.

"What kind of employee was he?"

"Quiet, rather reserved. His work log said the man always went home right after shift ended. He rarely volunteered for overtime. I can't imagine this endeared him to the other employees in his section." Walter said sipping his coffee again. It was no wonder nobody knew the man.

"I see."

"I'm sorry I couldn't be of further help. Detective, I have a meeting with the board in an hour. Is there anything you can tell me?" Walter asked the man. The detective pulled a heavily chewed pen from his mouth.

"Daniel Webb was found this morning by your janitorial staff. A bottle of prescription pills was found on the table next to the victim. Toxicology will take samples but it'll be a week before we get the results." The Detective said finally. Walter did not ask if the pod had been tampered with. He was quite sure it had been. That would lead the officer to question his motive for asking.

"Thank you," He said and left the officer to his work. Walter needed to make sure nobody used that machine. It was dangerous now with whatever modifications Daniel had made to them. Going down into IT Department he asked one of the techs to move the pod. "Just shove it in the corner and put a do not use note on it." He told the men. After this he ran up to his office. He needed to log into the system to make sure of his suspicions.

Walter checked the game log from his office computer. The man had logged in early yesterday and put in the required hours. First a morning shift, then a lunch break, followed by four more hours. That's when things changed from his regular schedule. Instead of leaving like usual the Game Master had logged in again. Twenty-five minutes later the net data disconnected. Not logged out, it just vanished.

/teleport WalterRabbit X_4.59114 Y_-56.38026 Z_1.01

This was the last known location of the Game Master. Walter silently popped into existence above a mountaintop on Tramin Continent. What he expected to find was a body. The avatar of the Game Master should have been laying on the ground invisible to all but another GM. Only it wasn't there. After logging in the man had come here around 5 pm. Walter turned west looking out over the mountains. It would have been a glorious view for watching the sunset. A nice place for ending one's life.

For once Walter wished the game recorded sight and sound in a location. He wanted to be able to go back in time and see the man in person, to know what he was thinking.

"Console," He thought and a drop box appeared in his vision.

/Search_Avatar Nebuchadnezzar

[No Avatar Found] - Was the only response.

The character that had been Nebuchadnezzar was no longer listed as an avatar in the world. This meant he couldn't find the man, not unexpected. Liam as a Ghost was an object, a permanent thing in the world. One among trillions of items.

At least he knew for certain now. A Game Master had become a ghost. This was a troubling turn of events. A person with such power could cause a lot of damage in the game. The only thing Walter could be grateful for was the fact the man was only level two. This limited the powers he could use. If the ghost still retained those abilities, for now he would assume he did. All he could do was teleport around and alter character information. Thank heavens he wasn't level three. Then he could create, delete, and edit objects in the world.

The meeting with the board would start soon. Walter was going to have to leave, but he needed to recruit some help. He needed to see KittKat and warn her. Walter didn't want to send a message because the system logged them. He teleported directly into her private quarters. A black haired vampire was sitting at the vanity brushing a comb through her hair.

"Kathrine," He said making her scream. She spun throwing the hairbrush at him. Walter slid to the side dodging the flying object.

"Why does everyone like to scare me?" She said angrily.

"You have an amazingly cute squeal," Walter replied but continued before she could argue. "I don't have much time. Something happened at work today. I have reason to suspect a game master has become a ghost."

"Like Liam?" She asked shifting moods immediately.

"Yes, which is why I can't locate him. I have to be careful how I move right now. So I need help, I need another pair of eyes. If you or Liam find someone suspicious please contact me." He said and Kat looked worried.

"Is it that bad?" She asked.

"An admin loose on Nigmus. I can't imagine what he could be doing. Quite frankly I don't see this thing turning out well." Walter said already thinking of possibilities. A hard reset of the system would be his first move if he were the board. That would likely delete Liam and this new ghost. An alarm buzzed getting his attention. "I have to go," He said teleporting up to the admin station. Walter spent several minutes preparing himself for the board meeting. It was going to be a shitty day.

CHAPTER THIRTY-SIX

Liam - Lab Experiments

Liam - Level 43
Tramin Continent - Wiyach's Laboratory
9pm

Liam loved being a lich. The extra bodies around him seemed more like a miniature army than a troop of dim-witted pets. He inspected them casually as they waited to regenerate from the last battle.

A level 38 Spellsword affectionately dubbed Mr. Mouth for all the arrogant talking he did. Liam had finally managed to retrieve the enemy commander. Next was the same level Defender obtained at the same time. Pyro was his level 42 fire mage Folken had acquired for him. Liam especially liked the "Emblazoned Hand," the Evoker often cast. It was too bad he had no control over its attack pattern. All he could do was point the undead at a target and hope for the best. The final pet was a pickup mob. A level 37 mutated corpse with a broken pitchfork.

The rest of the party consisted of the usual suspects. Astrid and Sarge up close and personal. Folken was hiding in the shadows. Kat stood next to Liam casually protecting him from harm. She'd switched to debuffing with her cleric spells. Only after the battle was ongoing, did she jump in with the extra DPS.

"What do you see?" Sarge asked in a hushed whisper. A

shadow was moving slowly back and forth near the boss room.

"The lich is bent over a huge pot, he keeps adding things and stirring the mixture," Folken replied from under the door. That ability to hide within the shadows was proving to be a serious boon. The thief seemed far more involved recently. He was more chatty and laughed more often. Liam thought it because he'd found a unique class, one many were envious of. The rogue though had kept his lips shut about the requirements. He seemed inclined to keep it a secret for just a little longer.

"Just the boss?" Liam asked with interest. It was a mild surprise. Up until now all the lich's had at least one bodyguard.

"I don't see any of his mutant experiments," Folken replied. The lich had taken up residence in the ruined manor. Surrounding this was a small farming village, one that had fallen victim to the undead mage. Cattle, dogs, and especially people had all been used as test subjects. Experiments on fusing the dead together. The last room was filled with men wearing the heads of cattle. The most disturbing thing about the fight had been the mooing.

"So we proceed like usual. Liam waits out of sight until we're in position. Then we focus on the lich." Sarge said moving towards the door. Astrid was just behind him with Kat in the rear. Liam left his pets at the entrance but walked down the hallway.

"Ready?" Sarge asked and everyone nodded.

As they opened the door Liam heard the lich speak. He was surprisingly loud even from around the hallway corner. "Ah, guests. I needed someone to test my newest experiment on." It said with a decidedly British accent.

"Foment Abomination," The lich said next and all hell broke loose. A massive creature began to crawl out of the cauldron. It was as if three separate bodies were merged at the cellular level. The abomination had five arms and two heads. No three heads, the last was sticking out of its back like a demonic monkey.

"Sarge take the abomination, everyone else on the lich!" Kat called from the doorway. Liam knew things were already well past controlled. He ran down the hallway to join the fight. The pink and purple abomination towered over Sarge. Its legs had double knee joints so that it moved awkwardly. Sarge approached smashing his shield with the side of his hammer. The two heads swiveled to face the Guardian. Kat and Astrid ran towards the lich who had retreated to the back of the lab.

"Bone Wall," The lich incanted pointing at the place before himself. Out of the stones, a six-foot-tall structure sprang. It was composed of thousands of bones layered atop each other. That was not a spell Liam possessed though the lich was two levels higher. Liam mused on that fact briefly. He couldn't do anything about the wall so he focused on the unexpected monster. Liam pointed to the undead abomination.

"Attack," He said sending his four pets into the fray. The Spellsword, fighter, and trash pet walked forward to enter melee. His mage started to slowly weave a spell. While that happened a wave of miasma spread into the room. This was cast by the lich hiding behind his makeshift fort. Kat and Astrid attacked the wall trying to destroy the spell. The undead monster swung at Sarge and his pets at the same time. It seemed fully capable of attacking with all his limbs. The extra head on his back meant nothing could flank him. Liam spent the first few minutes raining [Acid Arrow] spells upon the large undead.

Liam's pet mage 'Pyro' finished incanting its fire spell. "Scorching Beam," The undead said focusing on the abomination. A spot on the ceiling began to glow. It went from red to orange, then something broke through. It was as if the heavens themselves opened up on the abomination. For a few seconds the only thing visible was a white and orange beam of light. Liam's two other pets had taken considerable damage being within its range. The abomination's health though had been cut almost in half. Sarge had wisely backed away shielding his eyes from the light. After the spell was finished he came back in swinging.

Kat and Astrid were finally breaking through the wall of bone, though not fast enough. The lich was busy casting something big. It had to be for how long he'd been muttering back there.

"Undead Fusion," It said sending a beam of eldritch energy out from its body. The lich pointed to the abomination in the room. The creatures legs and arms began to merge into its body. Bones shifted as the lich flew towards the abomination. They collided in the middle of the room.

"Fuck me!" Sarge cursed backing away from the spell area.

The pet Guardian and pickup monster were pulled inside. Sucked in as if the thing possessed an intense gravitational pull. "Follow me," Liam said quickly as two of his pets sank into the mass of flesh. Thankfully his Spellsword phase shifted out of danger just in time.

"Everyone out!" Kat called running for the door. It was time to bail on this fiasco. Liam agreed, the better part of valor was survival. He turned sprinting for the open door. The undead mass in the room was pulsating. Legs and arms shot out then sank back into the creature. Heads rose from the gray flesh screaming in pain. The blob was rearranging itself trying to find the right form.

Legs sprouted from its lower torso like a spider. Though it was still changing the head of the necromancer floated just above the body.

"An interesting development," The lich said with that British brogue. It turned chasing after the group as they ran from the manor. The thing was as fast as a horse with all those legs. As they ran outside the creature got stuck in the foyer.

"What do we do?" Sarge said as they neared the horses. Liam climbed atop his skeletal mare before looking back. The massive abomination was tearing apart the front door to get outside. They were not going to be able to take on this thing by themselves.

"You're vampires, there's a town nearby, let's kite it into that," Liam suggested.

"That's so evil," Astrid said but lead the group away. All galloped away from the manor with the abomination hot on their heels. For about twenty minutes they raced down the dirt road. Liam as undead, couldn't enter the protection of the town. So he'd slowly moved away from the racing group.

Moving his skeletal horse into a copse of trees he finally

stopped. The town was within view so he got a good look at the battle that unfolded. The players and guards that were coming out of the small town weren't prepared at all. Astrid and Sarge ran their horses directly to the gate before running inside. Kat had to sprint the last two hundred feet to the safety of town. It was about then the humans saw the twenty-foot tall monster headed their way. A stampede of mid-level players ran for the gate. The massive abomination slammed into the herd. Bodies went flying as the town guards took action. It was a sight to behold.

Alone the lich had been level forty-five or so. As a merged monster its name was a blazing red. It may have been over level fifty from all the absorbed corpses. Held within its many hands was a tower shield and sword. Other hands grasped the broken pitchfork like a throwing speer. It struck out with all its hands attacking players and guards alike.

Liam lost sight of his party members in the brawl. Their icons though were still active on the list so they'd managed to get inside. The town rallied. Archers and mages climbed the short city wall to shoot at the abomination from above. A town guard fell, certainly no mean feet. The lich immediately cast raise dead on the NPC. It rose up slowly and turned to attack the city.

When players died the abomination would snatch a weapon from the ground. Within minutes it was fully armed with three shields and six weapons. All the while the lich continued to spread a dark miasma over the battlefield. The abomination pushed its way inside the city gate. For a level forty-five lich to cause so much damage. It made Liam's virtual heart sing. This demonstrated just how powerful he might become. He could do without the extra heads though. The lich was making himself a little army of undead followers. Another body rose from the pile of corpses before attacking player. A third joined the fight, then a forth.

It took close to twenty minutes for the fight to end. Players had rallied near the town square to kill the lich. They boxed it in then hit it with a dozen root spells. Next they hurled oil canisters while the mages cast fireballs at it. As the monster died the massive abomination exploded. The magic that held its pieces together violently backfired. Arms and legs flew off in all directions. Black blood and gray flesh rained down in the city street. Smoke rose from the square. Thirty or forty bodies lay along the road in a path of destruction. Many of them would be resurrected. They were high enough level to pay the price. Still, it was a sight to see.

"Everyone OK?" Liam typed into party chat. He could see their HP bars so at least all were alive.

"Yes, it appears so. That was a hell of a fight." Kat replied and Liam agreed.

"Let's head back to the manor before that lich respawns. Now that it's dead we can get the grimoire." Liam typed quickly. He turned his horse away from the gruesome battlefield. He trotted toward the road and started down it. Sarge rode up first looking around.

"Where's Folken, I thought he was with you," Sarge asked.

"I'm here," The thief said from near the ground.

"How are you keeping up?" The defender asked with surprise.

"I haven't moved at all, Liam is doing it for me." He replied pushing a black hand out of the shadow. He wiggled his fingers as the horses continued to trot. The others found them as they neared the manor. The front of the foyer was in ruins, this was a good sign. It meant nothing had been reset. The grimoire when they finally uncovered it in the lab was a disgusting thing to behold. The tome was the color of bruised flesh. Purple and blue skin was held together by black iron. A clasp made of teeth held it closed.

"You are not using that spell," Kat said to him.

"Don't fret, I am already strange enough. No need to add any more arms and legs to prove that. I have never seen such a thing. It makes me wonder if it was unique to that lich." Liam admitted putting the ugly tome into his robes. The group looked worn out from the experience. Liam though was happy to have another grimoire. This brought their total to five now. Another and they'd be able to rank up two necromancers.

"There's another lich further north. Its level forty-eight though." Liam suggested and everyone made a face. Even Kat seemed disinclined to try again. They quickly agreed that one was enough for this evening. Liam pulled his portal stone out and activated it.

"You look happy," Kat said once they were back in their palace suite.

"I am, from now on I think the liches we encounter will be very powerful. That is good to see. When our members level up we are going to be a force to reckon with." He said clasping his bony hands together. Kat moved past him towards the side kitchen.

"That spell the lich used might be tied to the location. There was a throne near the laboratory as well. I've heard other wizards have gained special spells after taking certain towers." He added following her.

"You still want that Dark Magus Tower?" Kat asked and he nodded.

"I keep thinking about it. Wondering why the lich went to such trouble to hide that tower of his." Liam said and Kat shrugged. She thought the developers just put things in hard to reach places for fun. He believed that nothing in this world was there by accident. It had to mean something. Liam wanted to find out.

CHAPTER THIRTY-SEVEN

Walter - Source Code

Walter Nowel
California - Dreamshard Studio Offices

He was considerably more nervous than he thought he would be. Walter had never considered himself a bad person, but this was definitely illegal. He was convinced of his reasons though. The events of the last month had crystallized his contempt for the financing coalition. Dreamshard might own the source code technically, but it was the board that managed everything. More and more they seemed to be reaching their grubby fingers into every aspect of the company. Anytime something even minor happened there was a meeting. Like after the death of the GM. Things had been getting worse steadily since that event. People had been let go with seemingly no reason. No, Dreamshard was under new management.

That was not good for the souls like Liam and Kat. Thousands of Chinese and Russian citizens were charging into Nigmus without a clue. Little did they know how tenuous their situation was. A single word from the right board member would be all it took. Just one call would shut the servers down and wipe the world clean.

He kept telling himself the reasons, but that didn't help his stomach. It was churning like burning lava in his gut. Walter reached for the box of antacids he'd brought into the office. He popped two of them and began to chew.

His first task was to get access. Everything hinged on being able to get to the servers. So he opened the email program and began his message. For twenty minutes he typed. At the end of each attempted email he would delete the words. He knew he was rambling; the stress was getting to him. At last he forced himself to say what he wanted as tersely as possible.

"It has come to my attention that some strange effects have been reported with certain high-level spells. I need access to my old work to check on its stability." There; it wasn't perfect, but it gave him a plausible reason to get into the data center. He sent this email to the studio director. Walter rocked back in the chair feeling somewhat relieved to have sent it. He would almost welcome the rejection. At least he would have tried, made the attempt. His stomach was already starting to settle, so he considered some lunch. He'd left the apartment having not eaten a thing this morning.

Walter rolled the chair back and stood. He stretched then grabbed his empty coffee mug. Just as he was about to exit his office the computer chirped. It hadn't even been two minutes since he'd sent the email. He stopped at the door staring back at the desktop monitor. The worry was back, even worse now. Walking back to his chair he sat and stared at the response.

"Sure Walter, I sent HR a heads up."

That was it, just eight words. He let out a small laugh but the knot in his stomach didn't go away this time. Lunch would have to wait he supposed. It was best to get this done now before he lost his nerve. Getting up he again went to the door. This time though he walked down stairs to administration. He knocked lightly and opened the door to access control. A bored looking woman was sitting at the desk.

"I need access to the Datacenter," Walter said taking his keycard from around his neck. He dropped it onto the desk.

"Going down to the dungeon, eh?" The girl said and he smiled. That was the unofficial nickname for the programmer's offices.

"Yeah," He said in reply. She took his card and slid it into the reader. Turning back to the computer she pressed a combination of buttons then took out his card. She extended it to him with a bored and weary smile.

"Don't let them bite you, the infection could spread." She said and he took the keycard.

"I have blood offerings already prepared," He admitted.

"Wise man," She said turning back to her interrupted solitaire game.

The entire building was made of glass but it was something of a fortress. Keycards allowed employees access only to certain areas. Companies learned some hard lessons about corporate espionage, which was why he had to go through all these hoops to get the code.

There was a break room, a kind of large kitchen with four huge refrigerators in the corner. He made a pit stop here for ten or so cups of coffee. The girl hadn't been joking about the programmers. It was a tough job and they could be a bit snappish. With snacks and drinks in hand he walked to the back of the building. He slid his keycard through the reader and the elevator door opened. Going inside he awkwardly reached for the down button. Someone had covered the 'B' with white-out then drawn a skull on it.

The elevator smoothly descended into the basement. He stepped out into a long hallway containing a desk and a guard. The man was local security. Walter came forward and set the drinks down. The guard was sitting not quite stiff-backed in the chair. He watched as Walter again pressed the card to the reader on the desk. Turning the man glanced at the monitor then nodded.

"Any electronic devices?" The man asked and Walter nodded. This he knew would happen. Walter took out his mobile phone and dropped it into a plastic tray. The guard placed this in a cubby hole behind the desk. This was to prevent information leakage. It was meant to keep the programmers focused. Without phones or outside Internet people tended to get more work done.

The next room was a server bay. It was noticeably colder as his breath came out in puffs. This wasn't the data center but a relic of the past. The first test world had been created on these machines. It was still used for rolling out beta patches and testing stability. The actual game though was designed to work on a web of cloud servers. Finally, he entered the airlock. Most called it the cell phone destroyer. Powerful magnets created an EM field scrubbing any device clean of data. It was responsible for no less than a hundred destroyed mobiles.

"Holy shit! The old man is back!" A voice said as soon as he came through the next door. Heads began to poke out of offices and cubicles as he let the door close.

"I've come bearing gifts." He said holding up the items.

"Sweet lord and savior," Several called stampeding over.

"Are you coming back to us. Do these moldy walls call to you?" Evan asked taking one of the drinks.

"I just came in to check on some things. Some artifact bugs in my old code."

"Whats wrong?" Evans asked curiously.

"Nothing serious," Walter said quickly. He'd forgotten the younger man had taken on his side of the program.

"Just some visual glitches I'd like to look at. You don't mind?" He asked the man.

Evans shrugged taking one of the donuts. "Is there a computer not being used?" Walter asked and another man gestured to a far cubicle. Walter would have preferred one of the offices. He'd hoped someone was out today, now he would have to work out in the open.

He nodded taking a donut himself and bit into it. The jelly insides quickly filled his mouth. More people were moving to the snacks sensing the feast underway. He made his way to the indicated computer and sat down. For the first twenty minutes he didn't do anything. All he did was scroll through the spell scripts. Most of them had undergone some changes since he'd left. Evans was a thorough coder with a habit of commenting on everything. On one hand, it was nice to see the young man took his job so seriously. Unfortunately, it was going to make his job harder.

He stopped at a divination spell and started scrolling through it. Casually he crossed legs bringing his right shoe to rest on his leg. There was a plug in his sole, pulling on it revealed a tiny metal lined compartment. He had spent some hours with a Dremel and an old pair of sneakers. From out of this, he withdrew a microdrive. Here he paused stretching to look around. With the device in hand he slid it into the keyboard. As soon as the computer recognized the microdrive the program on the disk activated. It started to copy the primary source code. Most of the game was content. Objects, textures, sensation files for all five senses, and countless other items in the game. They made up the tetra bytes of data the world was made of. However the core programming was relatively small. In just a minute the files had been transferred.

"So what's wrong?" Evan said coming up behind Walter. He started at the voice and turned looking at the man. For a second he froze, his brain too stunned to answer. Walter coughed forcing himself to say something, anything.

"The scrying spells. There some visual artifacts when looking at sneaking characters." He said pointing to the screen.

"I know, that's on purpose," Evans said and Walter lifted an eyebrow.

"If it's in stealth then nothing should see them short of a tricksters abilities," Walter responded.

"I just added a new hint that something was there. This lets Diviners work as makeshift detectors, but it's not perfect." Evan said pushing his glasses up his nose.

"I see what you're saying, I didn't know you had done that," Walter admitted feeling annoyed. This was something that should have been brought up at one of the meetings. Especially before it had gone live.

"I put it in the change log," Evans said defensively.

"At least now I know whats going on. I was afraid it had been something left over from the original spell." Walter said before Evans turned even more defensive.

"Hey we work hard down here to get things rolled out

quickly." Evans barked making more heads appear. It wasn't unusual for spats between programmers. Walter smiled disengagingly lifting his hands in surrender.

"You're right, I'm sorry Evans. My fault, I could have saved myself the trip by simply emailing you." He said making the other man frown. He'd been working up a head of steam, happy for a target. The man stalked away to his office and slammed the door.

Walter sat again then withdrew the microdrive from the computer. Palming it he crossed his right leg over his other. The drive slid snuggly into his shoe before he replaced the small rubber plug. Just like James Bond, only with thinning gray hair and some stomach pudge. He was anxious to leave, but he forced himself to visit each of the coders in person. They'd all worked together for quite some time. It would seem not only rude but out of character if he didn't. Finally about an hour later he stepped into the airlock. There was a buzzing sound from the magnets working. He prayed his makeshift cage protected the drive. Walter was sweating now. Even with the cold server room his armpits felt sticky. The guard glanced at him as he passed. All he wanted to do was get to the elevator and safely back to his office.

"Hey," The guard said sharply. Walter froze again in a moment of panic. Had they caught onto him already, seen his activity log? He turned slowly to see the rather large man approaching him.

"Yes?" Walter managed in a dry voice.

"You forgot your phone." The man said holding out a mobile. Walter almost fainted with relief but calmly took his phone.

"Are you alright?" The guard asked looking at his face. "You look kind of pale," He added stepping closer.

"Stomach bug, I left my Tums upstairs," Walter said praying his excuse worked.

"I heard that's going around." The guard replied immediately backing away.

That was it. Walter got into the elevator and went up to his office. Instead of doing any work he sent out a few emails saying he wasn't feeling well. He walked out of the building into a spring rain. Walter managed to get to his car before throwing up.

"I'm way too old for this." He muttered wiping the vomit from his mouth. His manufactured excuse was quickly becoming reality. Walter drove home and sank ungracefully to his couch. All he had to do now was contact the email address he'd gotten from Ji. He was way too deep to back out. Walter knew they'd find out about the leak eventually.

CHAPTER THIRTY-EIGHT

Folken - Blind Test

"Sometimes darkness is a good thing. When it's light, you can't see into a place that's dark. But when it's dark, you can see what's around you much better."
— Sam Fisher - Splinter Cell

Folken - Level 36
Edoku'Kor - Necropolis Sewers

With his true vision he could see the thieves slowly moving up the sewer culvert. It was one of the perks of being a shade. Nothing could hide from him in the shadows. He watched them as gray outlines against the brighter sewer backdrop. Unlike dark vision, he could see in color. Of the ten that had started out only seven remained. A pack of saurian lizards had crossed into their path a few minutes ago. Instead of waiting to catch up they'd risked it. The three had bungled into the man-sized lizards and lost their stealth. The low-level players hadn't lasted more than a few seconds. Folken had watched not bothering to help, having warned them they were on their own. This was just another part of the test. The guild needed careful patient thieves. Anyone stupid enough to bump into a mob three times their level didn't deserve to be a shade.

"How far is it?" One of the thieves asked.

"We're taking the scenic route," Folken lied moving further along. In reality he was looking for the entrance. The door to the Well of Darkness moved randomly about the sewer. The opening never appeared in the same place twice. It was one of the reasons he'd kept this secret. He continued to search for another ten minutes before finding it. The audible sounds within the sewer dropped into a dull background noise. Today It was on the floor next to a rusted grate. He slid forward before the others arrived. Reaching out a hand he pushed on the stone to activate the door. The metal grate fell away into the darkness as it expanded. The seven thieves neared making a circle around him.

"This is it?" The same boy asked.

"Yes," Folken said before putting a hand out to stop the thief.

"You get one chance. Take your potty breaks if you need them." He warned, and they looked to one another. None logged off though, probably thinking this was another test. Folken went in first sliding into the darkness like he was entering a fire warmed home. The void was where he'd been born after all. The thieves fell in one at a time, some landing more gracefully than others. They were all startled by the darkness, he hadn't warned them about this.

"What's going on?" The boy mouthed in the darkness. His voice was muted like all the other sounds. They groped blindly around the space.

The other applicants were silently voicing their concerns. Folken turned moving deeper down. He wasn't interested in watching them crawl along like he'd done. Instead, he would wait at the Well of Darkness. That would give him time to reminisce.

"He'd had a very eventful day." He thought to himself.

Earlier he'd gotten home from school at the usual time. Today though he'd taken his homework with him into Nigmus. One of the things he wanted to keep any eye on was enemy movement. The mortals had already tipped their hand they wanted the continent. So he was relaxing and doing his Math and English work in the shadows.

It was just after four when a group of mortals entered the strait.

Folken perked up seeing the riders. Setting aside his work he started to type into chat. The private message he sent to Liam first. The man was always online.

"Humans are attacking the strait, twenty so far." Folken sent to the guild leader.

"We're on the way," Liam replied almost immediately. Folken closed the chat box and focused on the group again. He was surprised by how many clerics there were. More than half rode along with blunt maces bouncing on their hips. He supposed they were coming down to deal the undead. Paladins and Clerics were the best defense.

He slid from the shadow of the rock formation and waited. As they passed him he jumped into the mixed group. The raid group continued south passed the town. They were headed almost directly for the Necropolis. Folken doubted they were intent on assaulting the city. It was more likely they hoped to catch some low-level characters leveling.

"Should he alert the zone?" He wondered. There was a zone chat, it was often used to warn others of an attack. Folken though worried there might be spies. If he said anything this mortal might turn itself around. That wouldn't be any fun at all.

"Where are they now?" Liam said to him.

"Heading south, five minutes north by northeast of the necropolis," Folken replied. He hoped the guild leaders were gathering a reprisal party.

The mortals found a level seven undead fighter. He was grinding out some experience on some jungle monkeys. Poor guy didn't stand a chance. The twenty humans came out of the trees almost right on top of him.

"Cleanse the Abominations!" A cleric shouted raising a mace. He brought it down on the head of the fighter as he went past. A holy charge raced over the undead like white lightning. The necromancer arrived first. He came out of the opposite tree line on his skeletal horse. Right beside him Kat's Nightmare was setting vegetation ablaze. She held her sword above her already charged with unholy energy. More undead were sprinting out of the forest.

He unsheathed his shadow blade. Folken's knife was good at backstabbing mortals and slicing open arteries. He struck at the horse's leg. It whinnied throwing the cleric from his saddle. The man tumbled passed Folken who struck out slicing into the back of a fighter. He leapt from the shadow of a tree towards the man.

"Shit it's the shade," The man called just before Folken drove the knife in again. A paladin turned his horse in his direction. "Holy Smite," The man said charging towards the shade.

"No thank you," Folken said dodging away. He used his shadow ability to slide out of striking range. The sword slashed cutting into the ground were Folken had been.

This allowed the cleric to stand and draw out his hammer. "Bless," The man said causing holy light to surround the mortals. A nasty tingling sensation settled over Folken like ants crawling on his skin. One person was thinking at least.

The rest of the raid group was clashing with the undead. Liam and Kat both charged into the mortals like a storm. The tall lich aimed his staff at the ground. His hand moved in a spell macro as the magic activated. Black briar thorns sprouted in a thick patch. Horses and men tripped falling over themselves. Anytime someone moved within the area it would scratch them with plagued thorns. Folken slid into the space next to the cleric. He accepted the HP loss but was able to start attacking again. His knife slashed out at a healer cutting the girl across the face. The female ignored his attack as she continued to cast a spell. Kat turned clashing with a Paladin with her enchanted longsword. Folken sidestepped the cleric and drove his blade in. The backstab thankfully halted whatever magic the healer was using. The mortal went down quickly after that. It wasn't even a battle after that. Several players still on horseback turned to flee.

The paladin ducked instead of dodging. Kat shoved her blade deep into his stomach using that fencer's thrust. Kat kicked the corpse off the end of her sword. It sailed a dozen feet before skidding to a stop against a rubble pile.

"Thanks for keeping a watch out," Liam said coming forward.

"It went almost exactly like you said it would," Folken admitted circling the bodies. The guild leader had suspected an attack like this would happen, so they'd taken turns watching the strait. Folken smiled at the memory. He was coming to enjoy being a spy master.

Something snatched his attention back to the present. The figure of a thief came into view partly up the tunnel. A female was slowly walking along with her bow in hand. She held it like a walking cane before her. The end of it tapped the smooth stone floor as she moved. Her eyes were closed and her face slack. Folken was immediately impressed, more than a little. It had taken him forty minutes to get this far down. The girl had done it in less than ten.

As soon as she came out into the chamber the hallway vanished. A new one appeared some distance away if any other recruits came down. The girl though stopped feeling the difference in the air. Her head tilted to the side as she tapped with her bow. Folken could see her frown as she tried to find the entrance.

Below him a dark foggy cloud shape-shifted within the well. Folken liked to think of it as Father Darkness. The creature had no body, no physical form that was discernible. It was like a cloud with tendrils and feelers. Every now and then a mouth or eye would rise to the top. One such mouth spoke filling the space with an impossibly deep baritone.

"Do you walk in the shadows thief?" A deep voice asked. The female rogue froze for a second at the sudden sound. She cocked her head in the direction of the well.

"Every day of my life," She said after a few more seconds. So she was blind, Folken had suspected that from the way she moved.

"Are you afraid?" It asked next. Folken remembered these questions from when he'd come down here. The thief slowly came forward with her makeshift cane.

"Of the dark, no; of you, very much." She admitted. Below an eye formed and rose from the cloud. It peered at the thief for a few seconds. The girl was very low level, not even fifth yet.

"Step into the dark," It said finally. This time its voice was a hissing snake. A tongue flicked out between fangs. Folken was glad it had accepted the girl. He'd feared there was a level requirement to becoming a shade.

"Are you stupid? I am in the dark." The girl said hotly. Folken chuckled under his breath. Oh he liked her, she had some sass. Below Father Darkness continued to churn and shift. It said nothing as the girl came forward. Her cane touched the lip of the well and she stopped. Folken moved out of the way as she slowly walked in a circle.

"Step into the dark," Father Darkness said in a female voice. Again the girl tested the well holding her cane as far she could. Then she dropped the bow cocking her head to listen. The weapon fell into the cloud in total silence.

"I shouldn't have done that." She admitted to herself. He took pity on the thief.

"It was a good idea," Folken said finally making the girl turn directly towards him.

"You're here?" She asked with some surprise. Her words were thin and distant within the space.

"I've been watching." He admitted moving closer to the girl. The woman had an interesting set of features on her. Like she wasn't quite sure what beautiful was supposed to look like. Her nose was short and rounded with high cheekbones. Her lips were full and her eyebrows were like caterpillars.

"You're doing better than I did," He continued halting a few feet away.

"How far down does it go?" She asked and Folken split a grin.

"You'll find out if you jump," He replied.

"Jerk," The girl muttered under her breath. For a second she paused there at the lip, but she screwed up her courage and lifted a foot up. As she stepped from the edge she started screaming. Even in the muted void the sound echoed off the walls. It was the kind of scream that came from true fear. The kind that came from falling and falling in the darkness. Tumbling in the black waiting to hit bottom with bone breaking force.

As she slid into the roiling cloud her voice cut off abruptly. Purple and dark green flashes lit the area within the chamber. It was Father Darkness working his magic on the thief. Inside she would be floating as if held within a gentle palm. Then he would squeeze her, pressing his darkness into her body. Her hit points would slowly drop until she had just one remaining.

The change completed, with so few levels it hadn't taken long. The shape of a shade came into view. A dark appendage dropped the female within the chamber. Her legs were gone replaced with smoky tendrils. Still, she sank to the floor feeling the hard ground. As if to reassure herself she was no longer falling. Folken went to her and put a long-fingered hand on her shoulder. A dark face looked up at him. The transformation into shade caused her features to blend together.

"Welcome to the club. We have Taco Tuesday's and a secret handshake." He said giving her another squeeze.

"Really?" She asked still a little dazed.

"No, but we could. Come on let us go see what became of the other recruits." He said bending down. Folken took her hand which was cold and long fingered like his. She allowed herself to be pulled along.

"What's your name?" Folken asked.

"Edith," The female replied. Folken lifted an eyebrow at her. It wasn't her character name he knew that at a glance. She must be rattled enough to give her real one.

"I'm Francis," Folken said and the girl snorted. His last name was Alken which was how he'd named his first character. In the darkness she looked up at the name floating over his head. With the murder earlier today he was still sporting the red halo.

"Who names their kid Francis?" She asked.

"The same kind of people that name their child, Edith." He said tugging her forward. They slid along for a short way in silence. He, however, was wondering about something. "You're blind in real life?" Folken asked casually, maybe a little too casually. It was something that few in America had to deal with. Medicine had advanced enough that all but the lowest of incomes could afford ocular implants.

"You heard that," The girl replied in a careful voice. It became suddenly guarded.

"What's it like?" He asked with interest. For a few seconds, she didn't reply as if weighing his earnestness.

"I was more afraid of seeing than I thought I would be. Watching as something came towards me." The girl said.

"Since I became a shade I find myself closing my eyes more often. I tried walking down the street without looking. A car almost hit me as I stepped off the sidewalk." He said and the girl laughed.

"I'm sorry, that isn't funny." She said trying to contain herself.

There was a grisly scene at the top of the hallway. Several bodies lay together in a clump. Someone had panicked and started hacking with a dagger. The culprit lay nearby with a bloody weapon. The boy had been forcibly ejected from the system. Probably from his heart rate going too high. Above the rogue's head a red halo floated along with his name. Edith gasped looking at the carnage. She covered her mouth with a long-fingered hand.

"Couldn't see what was attacking them. So they fought back blindly. Since they couldn't hear each other talking they didn't realize the others were friendly." Folken said pulling his shadow blade out.

"What are you doing?" Edith asked.

"The guild does not need people that panic. He failed the test, and he'll demand a retry. It'll be easier just to kill him." He said sliding the knife across the boy's throat. Cold black blood oozed out of the wound.

"That's mean," Edith said from behind him.

"Welcome to the Lawful Dead. We aren't evil but neither are we good." Folken said cutting into the boy again and killing him. He stood sheathing his knife.

CHAPTER THIRTY-NINE

Mortal Advance

Walter
California - Cafe

Walter walked into the small coffeehouse and inhaled deeply. The smell of expensive java filled his nose making his mouth water. He moved to the drinks counter and ordered. After collecting his beverage and danish he walked to a far table. It was here he set down his laptop. He took a sip of latte and a bite of his breakfast before opening the computer.

He'd bought the device specifically for today. It was used, purchased from a pawn shop thirty miles away. Walter had paid cash and walked out with the old machine. The screen blinked to life with a fresh operating system installed. Next he powered up an encrypted TOR browser. He connected to the open wireless Internet from the coffee house. The websites were slow from the many proxy servers his signal was bouncing between.

Walter was here to do a simple task, one that required he be anonymous. Withdrawing the scrap of paper Ji had given him at their last meeting, he carefully he typed in the address into the email program, and composed a new message. For a few minutes he struggled with what to say.

"The trip you mentioned sounds nice. I've made my arrangements and packed everything I need." He typed before hitting send. The two simple sentences flew around the world several times before settling into a tiny mailbox in the Philippines.

Walter waited and drank his coffee.

Over the last couple of days he'd been moving some of his money into offshore accounts. It hadn't been very hard with so little investments. He didn't have a house, just an apartment near the offices. The only investment he had was the company portfolio. Walter supposed he was going to lose that soon, but it was a small price to pay, especially if he saw this through. The world was changing and America was no longer leading the way. If anything politicians seemed to be digging in their heels when it came to virtual technology. Many a senator had been brandishing pitchfork and torch lately. An email came back with a simple message, "Send the package."

Walter frowned, growing suspicious. No, he had something very important. Right in his hot little pocket was something that would land him in prison. If he sent them the data, and they reneged on the deal, he was screwed.

"Will bring the gifts with me, just need the tickets." He typed back feeling a sense of foreboding. Walter hadn't made any secondary plans. He had no idea how he'd get out of the country on his own. This time he sat in the corner of the shop for almost an hour. The coffee on the table grew cold as he continued to wait. He was about to close down the laptop when another email came in.

"We'll see about alternative routes. Planes are all booked up." Was sent back finally. Planes are all booked, what did that mean? He'd recently gotten his passport, was Walter already on a watch list? If he tried to leave the country would they arrest him? He could almost feel the net closing in. No wonder the Chinese wanted him to send the data first.

The only thing he could do was wait, and continue to go to work. He'd have to pretend everything was normal until he could leave the country. He drank his cold latte and closed the laptop. The events of the past hour had left an awful taste in his mouth. Things were moving far too fast.

***

Orenthal
Tramin - Free city of Dragonfall
Meeting Hall

Dragonfall City was neutral ground. It sat on the edge of human and dwarven territory. There was no way to claim the city which made it useful for today. Fifty of the most powerful human men and women sat around the table. Not just high level but those in control of largest guilds. Even [Legion] who'd initially refused to join was present. They'd heard of the unclaimed land that was at the table, and dried their salty tears enough to come to the meeting because they wanted a piece of the pie.

It was a bright spring day. The sun had come out early and chased the clouds off. The daylight painted the city a sparkling myriad of iridescent colors. Huge windows were thrown open to let in the breeze. Two attractive human girls were slowly circling the table. A blond NPC stopped next to Orenthal and set a mug of ale down. He casually slid a couple of silver into the girl's smock as a tip. She smiled at him in thanks. The drinks were free though he wasn't above tipping. Especially when it gave him a chance to run his hand over her hip to her backside. He gave her plump cheek a squeeze before she moved on.

Reaching for the mug he took a sip, savoring the brew. It was dwarven ale, good hearty beer. Alcohol was something he was growing increasingly fond of. Orenthal set the mug down and glanced around. There was a lot of power sitting in this room.

Most everyone was relaxed within their chairs attempting to effect boredom at being here. Even in a game as exciting as Nigmus it had its annoyances. Meetings were like taxes and death, inescapable. Not everyone was relaxed, one person was standing. His massive fist pounded the table, splintering the wood. Cups nearby bounced as his attacks continued. The human barbarian was Lector—leader of RageQuit—and he had a lot to be angry about.

"Twenty members, and not a single one I can raise!" Lector spat sinking a fist into the wood again. He raised a hand pointing a thick finger at the leader of Fyre.

"You said it would be easy," He angrily spat. Lector had gone to Edoku'Kor with a raiding party. He'd come back with less than five members. He should be thankful to be alive, the fool.

"I only told you about the undead patrol. It was the right time to attack, but I never said it would be easy." The man said picking up a drink. He lifted the beer to his mouth and drained the delicious amber liquid.

"How did they do it?" He angrily asked. Everyone was curious about that fact too. How had the undead kept corpses from being resurrected? It was troublesome news.

"How should I know? The undead have some ability to prevent resurrection." Orenthal replied.

"You seem to have all the answers lately, what's your game?" Someone asked suspiciously.

"I assure you this is not a game to me," Orenthal replied again with a pleasant smile. "Besides I've lost guild members to them as well, so it's a mystery to me." He lied smoothly.

"While I was losing people you were off checking out the eastern desert," Lector said still frothing at the mouth. The leader of Fyre shrugged and crossed his arms before his chest.

"Insomnia wanted the port city. You demanded the citadel and the jungle that it sat above. The rest of us had to content ourselves with forts and a few small cities." Orenthal said casually. The other council members glanced to one another muttering. It was true. The largest guilds had demanded the best cities. Insomnia— after taking the next castle—would control two ports. That alone would make them incredibly rich.

"Just attack them during the day. Most of their high-level members are vampires still." A girl down the table suggested.

"And lose even more members? My players fight because they trust a resurrection is coming." Lector said scoffing. Orenthal sat forward sensing an opportunity.

"Fyre is willing to take the Citadel. Not only will I take it but I won't lose a single person." He said making everyone laugh. That was a tall boast, especially after the barbarians failure.

"Do what you want, you murdering PK'er," Lector said finally sitting down.

"There are no objections then?" Orenthal asked looking to the other faces. Nobody seemed inclined to help take the castle, which was fine with him. Like most meetings it began to drag on. Each person intent on getting their say in. Finally though it ended about two hours later and Orenthal left the room. The figure of his second in command got into step beside him.

"How did it go?" Freya asked.

"We are going to attack the Citadel," Orenthal said with a smile.

"Why did you need their permission?" She asked.

"They need to think we're apart of their little council. Everything is falling into place." Orenthal said and Freya frowned next to him. She didn't quite grasp his reasons. Orenthal smirked at her before explaining.

"While Insomnia is sitting on all the ports, Fyre controls all the ore mines. Once the undead are out of the picture we'll be in a position to take over. I was happy to point everyone at the empty unclaimed land to give the dwarves time to gather their defenses and level. Everyone will need our crafting materials if they hope to compete." He said while moving down the corridor.

"The longer the fighting goes on the better off we'll be." Orenthal continued.

"I see," Freya said then chuckled. "We're becoming the arms dealer for the human empire. Did you know [RageQuit] was going to lose to the Lawful Dead?" Freya asked next.

"No, I thought they'd deal some damage to the undead. The attack was unannounced, it should have been a surprise. RageQuit failed quite miserably. I will hand it to the Undead, they sure are a tenacious bunch." He admitted pushing open the door to the hall. He held it for her, who smiled, and walked out first.

The city was a hive of activity. Members of every race could be found under the gigantic dragon bones. The one city where everyone could congregate. This made it an ideal place for caravan merchants. Orenthal and his second in command quickly were swallowed by the crowd. They turned moving towards the 'Human' quarter of town. It gave Orenthal time to consider the future.

He'd done it, killed himself to become a ghost. Now he had all the time in the world or as long as the servers kept running. This meant he could play the long game. All of his previous losses seemed so insignificant now.

Freya walked beside him, hips swaying back and forth. Her lithe beauty was a trick. A man rode inside, one with a deeply cunning mind. It was one of the reasons he'd picked her as his second. Although that meant he had to keep an eye on her plots.

"This will be it. The last serious hurdle we have to get over. After the castle is ours the undead won't be able to level. Their faction will decline into insignificance. Then the war with the dwarves will start. Fyre will simply sit back and watch the fun after that." He said.

"When will we attack?" Freya asked.

"We have a few preparations to make. A day or two, but before Lawful Dead can level any more soldiers." Orenthal said after a few seconds consideration.

"Because of your secret weapon?" Freya asked and Orenthal smiled. He pulled back the hood of his robe and looked to his second in command. His eyes were filled with the blue light of his admin status.

"Nothing will stop me now," He said with a feral grin.

CHAPTER FORTY

Kat - Titanwall

KittKat - Level 47
Edoku'Kor - Necropolis - Map Room

"I'd hoped the mortals would give us more time," Kat said
starting the discussion. The sand map before them was centered
on a port and castle. Little people were moving around the walls
and courtyard.

"Right now the Northern Port of Edoku'Kor is being taken by
the humans. In three days [Insomnia] will claim the throne. After
they secure that location the entire continent will be open to all.
The mortals will be able to capture any unclaimed land. The
smart guilds will likely head south immediately. They'll move to
block our expansion by taking the castle on the strait." She said
moving the map. It zoomed in on the area around the strait. It
wasn't hard to imagine what would happen next. The humans
would be able to raid the necropolis at will, and leveling would
be next to impossible outside the city walls. Players would leave
the faction for something easier.

"You said we weren't ready."

"We've all gained five or six levels since last we took the
necropolis. I'm not going to lie, it'll be a tough fight." Kat
admitted. She paused long enough to emphasize the next point.
"Because of that Liam will be remaining behind," she added
looking to the tall lich. "If we fail the line of succession needs to

remain intact." She continued. It was a lie, or partially a lie. Kat wasn't about to let him get close to this fight. She was under no illusion, some would die tonight, possibly many. It was necessary though or the undead faction was in danger of being snuffed out early.

"We have nearly eighty mid-level players. With the combined arms we can do it. Tonight at sunset we move on the castle. The announcement goes out in four hours. That will give us enough time to assemble." She said standing up. Kat didn't mention the spies in the lower ranks would leak the information, which was why Lawful Dead was going to wait until the last second to assemble.

The other guild officers stood to head out to their own preparations. Kat left the map room and walked down to the palace treasury. Four sentries stood at attention next to the guild bank. Inside, gold coins were stacked in large piles. A few boxes had been the only attempt to contain the horde of wealth. Kat marched to the rear of the room and accessed her personal chest. It had made sense to store everything in the guild bank. Especially if she were about to die. She started pulling potions and disposable items into her inventory. Liam was right behind her, looming with his large presence. Kat pretended not to notice.

"You're not going," She said finally.

"We've had this argument before," Liam said in an irritated voice.

"That's because you keep trying to butt in." She replied her anger rising.

"You know you will need me," Liam said moving to stand beside her. He continued to argue his points. "The cleric is only thirty-five. As soon as he casts a heal they'll stomp him to death."

"Better him than you," Kat retorted shortly.

"He's our only method of resurrecting guild members."

"Don't fight me on this, Liam." She said true irritation slipping into her tone. He sighed in response. She'd won the argument but it had probably cost her. Liam hated being babied, hated it with a passion. "I love you," she said and he let out an annoyed huff. The man saw right through her maneuver, though he allowed it. Kat stepped closer to him and was pulled into his embrace. "I love you too." He replied wrapping his arms around her. Liam's chest was hard bone under the robe. Still, the deathly aura of his made her skin tingle. She sighed feeling all the hairs on her body stand up at attention.

"We have four hours until dusk," Liam suggested.

"Hmmm," She mused.

"Our first fight, we should commemorate." He continued to coax running a hand down her spine. She pulled back poking him in the chest.

"You are incorrigible," She said in a silky voice.

"I noticed you didn't say no," He added and she moved away from him. Kat sauntered to the door to the treasury and closed it. Then she locked the permissions so only the leaders could open it, and turned back with a smile.

"Show me what you can do with those big hands of yours." She said stripping out of her costume.

***

Four hours later Kat stood before the assembled guild. Her armor was exposed for once black plate-mail wrapped tightly around her body. Only her helmet was off so everyone could see her face. Kat stood with her crimson sword point touching the ground. Both of her hands rested on the pommel for dramatic effect. She was mildly surprised to see so many show up. Two hundred members stood before the palace gardens, some not even level ten.

"Many of you are new to the guild. Thank you for coming to the summons. I'm sure most of you suspect what is going to happen this evening. We are moving on the strait citadel." Kat said in a commanding voice. The assembled guild members smiled to one another. Many obviously pleased they'd guessed correctly.

"We will form two raids. The first will take the castle, the second will remain near town as reinforcements." She said and nodded to her officers. They started sending out blocks of party invitations.

"While I welcome any help, I'd suggest those level twenty and below remain home." She added after several came forward to volunteer. "Instead of joining in the fighting I'd like to bring everyone to the castle once we clear it. It takes five days to secure the keep. We're going to need eyes and ears around the castle." She said moving towards the officers.

Sarge got on top of a dry planter and bellowed. "Let's move out of the city. Stay with your raid group." It was nice having a reservist in the guild. He was surprisingly good at organizing people. Kat joined the main group. Sarge, Astrid, Folken, Josh, and a new mage called Krilon made up the party. It felt wrong not seeing Liam's name under hers. He'd been a constant companion for so many months now. It had to be this way, though Liam was right, they were going to need him.

They began the hour-long march through the jungle. With so many people the monsters would barely slow them. The forest was dark this evening. The moon was thankfully absent from the sky though it might make an appearance later. She jogged along with the rest of her group. Sarge was leading the raid with a marching song. Something from the army and definitely not politically correct. A solid shadow started to slip along next to her.

"Folken how goes it?" She asked the shade.

"Haven't heard anything from the scouts. They should be watching the northern port. Anyone tries marching south and we'll have two hours of warning." He said in his usual rasp.

"How did you manage that?" She asked a little surprised. Getting players to sit and watch a keep for any length of time was near impossible. It just wasn't fun being on a stake out.

"I promised to show the new batch where I became a shade." He admitted and Kat whistled.

That was quite a prize for only watching sentry. Folken had

already disqualified about twenty people in the guild. "You're going to keep doing it?" She asked making the shadow laugh in response.

"I only promised to show them the door. I never said I was going to hold their hand. It's up to them if they pass the test." Folken replied in a suspiciously sly tone.

"Is it that scary?" She asked.

"Have you ever played tag in a dark room?" Folken asked in reply.

"No, not something I ever tried."

"You'll just have to trust me then. It's your mind's imagination that you have to worry about. Your psyche summons all sorts of phantoms to haunt you." Folken said and Kat nodded to this. She'd lain in her hospital room long enough to develop some serious demons of her own.

The town they passed was dead, literally smashed into smithereens. The houses had been knocked over. Oddly, most of the fields were intact with signs of obvious use. The giants it seemed harvested off the land at least. About a mile out of town the hilly farmland spiked into a mountain cliff. Visible on the bluff were the outer walls of the castle fortress, fires were lit around the upper crenelations. A cleft at the base of the cliff led upward.

Kat looked back over her shoulder. The guild was a mass of two forces. About a hundred and twenty would attack the castle. The remaining eighty or so would follow behind at a respectable distance. Normally she'd say something about staying safe and having fun. That wasn't an option, instead she lifted her crimson blade aloft. Two hundred weapons raised in response.

"For the Lawful Dead!" She shouted and a chorus started. They repeated the words several times as shields were smashed. The first group started up the bluff at a jog. The first sentry was halfway up the mountain trail. He was a sorry looking runt. Only sixteen feet tall with a bare chest and poorly made trousers. In his hands he held a broken two-handed sword like a dagger.

"Tanks form a line across the trail," Sarge bellowed. Kat and twenty other players got their shields out. They stood eight players abreast and two deep. "Mages slow and root, archers fire at will!" He ordered next and Kat pointed to the sand giant.

"Torpid Weakness," Kat said and an oily ball of sludge formed before her hand. It shot away to strike the creature in the side. Arrows quickly followed her attack as it turned in their direction. The giant roared raising its bit of steel in defiance. Wooden brambles, frost paths, and conjured walls of pets appeared on the trail. The giant slammed into these and stuck fast. It tried to kick but the combined roots trapped it's legs.

"Switch to targeted spells," Sarge said as more arrows sank into the giant. It bellowed in impotent rage as it thrashed. Fireballs, acid shots and lightning crackled from the rear line. Finally, it got through the first wall and ran straight into the tanks. It took all of their combined strength to keep the giant from getting past. Someone would be knocked away leaving a hole. Another tank stepped into the path of the mob. Kat could do little other than hacking at the piece of leg before her. The giant's chest was a pincushion of arrows as it fell to its knees. It had taken several minutes to combat just one sand giant. One that would prove to be the weakest of the bunch.

Folken didn't appear fully. Kat felt a hand grab her leg and looked down at a shadowy face. "A force just started south with over a thousand players," He said making Kat swear. It would take the humans two hours to reach the strait. She could only hope they turned away for one of the many unclaimed forts in the desert.

"Tell them to keep an eye on where they go," Kat said and the shadow slipped back into the darkness.

As they cleared the mountain trail the castle came into full view. The Citadel looked like a squat hexagon sitting at the edge of the cliff. It had taken thirty minutes to kill six more giants along the way. One poor fighter had been knocked from the mountain into the mists. Already she was loosing people, and Kat couldn't stop to look for the corpses, not yet. Not with that army marching south. If they survived the Sand King then maybe.

The wall before them was down. Giants had pushed it over to get inside the castle. On each side of the opening a guard stood. Both level forty-two giants wielded a huge wooden timber. Stone blocks were crudely tied to the end.

"Groups five through ten take the right side," Kat said over raid chat. This was the first time they'd been forced to fight more than one at a time. She rushed with the main force toward the second giant. The creature didn't passively sit there. It bellowed and started towards them. The grip on its makeshift mace changed as it swung down at them like a golf club. Kat dodged out of the way as rocks and stones were torn up from the ground. She looked back to see an archer flying off the cliff. The giant was among them stomping down on them with its bare feat.

They killed it though not cleanly. Another two people were smashed to death by the giant. One of them a precious tank. Looking to the other group she saw they too had taken casualties. Josh was bent over a fighter, with a bag of coins, and was preparing a raise dead spell. She grabbed the cleric and turned him away from the bodies. "Raise them later. We need to get inside." Kat said then gripped his shoulder reassuringly. She had been a little harsher than necessary. She continued in a more friendly tone. "Heal the wounded, instead." The Defiler nodded and moved towards the second raid. Things were taking too long, she could feel it like a building pressure on her back.

Inside the castle stones and wood littered the ground. The second floor had been completely knocked down. This left enough room for the giants to move around inside. A path had been made through the rubble deeper into the structure. They stumbled into another giant. This one came out of the kitchen with a wooden pallet of food. A giant roasted boar lay on the square of wood. Around the pig sat dozens of apples, corn cobs, tomatoes, and heads of lettuce. They charged the server while his hands were full. This one wasn't a fighter at least. His health pool wasn't nearly as large as they easily cut him down.

"Second raid group come up the bluff. We've cleared the main walls." She said into chat. Kat had left some eighty or so people at the mountain base. They needed to move up before the giants started to respawn. Things weren't going as quickly as she hoped. The guild had already spent an hour trying to get inside the castle.

"Where are the humans?" She asked the shadow at her feet.

"Still riding south. They'll be at the strait in forty minutes or so. A couple of groups have split off from the mass. Smaller guilds are breaking away to pre-claim land. There's still hundreds coming though." Folken said from below her. During the chaos of battle she hadn't seen Folken fight. Though his form was hard to find in all the spell flashes.

The remaining one hundred guild members pushed inside. There really wasn't a choice in retreating. If they didn't do this the faction would die.

CHAPTER FORTY-ONE

Kat - Sand King

The Sand King was level fifty. Kat knew it the instant she entered the main hall. He sat on a crude throne of cobbled together rubble. Two guards stood on either side of him, which thankfully were only level forty. The three Giants were idly chatting, so none had noticed the raid enter the room. This gave them time to drink potions and plan, so the party leaders knelt in a huddle.

"We could split them up and concentrate on one at a time," Sarge suggested.

"I think we should do the opposite. Tank them together and use AOE to damage them at the same time." Kat offered instead. They had quite a few Evokers left and the Archers could volley arrows. Doing it one at a time would take longer, though it would be much safer.

"With the boss, we'll need to cycle tanks out. Everyone is going to have to rely on potions more than heals." Kat said. Sarge chewed his lip for a few seconds before nodding to the plan. Josh nervously stood behind everyone near the entrance. He'd have to play rear medic again. Anyone close to death would have to duck out of battle to run back for heals. Kat had already lost ten people in combat, and if more died, Josh wouldn't be able to raise them. This was going to be a bad one. Kat could taste it like a poorly made stew, so she started digging around in her quick-pouch, pulling out every potion she had. Some were useless mana regeneration potions, still she chugged them. At this point everything was being used or lost. Finally, she drank a vial of elven blood to top off her vampire regeneration.

The raid assembled into a horse shoe formation. She stood in the bell curve with the other high-level members. The fighters with shields would make sure the two guards didn't get around them. Like before archers and rogues made up the second line with the mages at the rear. Everyone looked ready, buzzing with magical auras. Sarge and the three other defenders entered aggro range of the massive Sand King. As the giant stood from his throne he pointed.

"Little insects, you dare enter my domain." It bellowed at them, and from behind the throne, it drew a massive weapon. Unlike the other giants, his weapon was a colossal forged sword. It was easily ten feet long, and he stood holding the blade in one hand like it weighed nothing. The tanks immediately smashed their shields with an assortment of weapons. Sarge waited, holding his skill until he was closer. The hundred guild members advanced quickly not giving the mobs a chance to run at them.

The three giants slammed their weapons down into the formation. Kat jumped sideways to avoid the giant sword. Sarge though took it. The weapons struck sparks off the tall tower shield before cracking the stone floor. He bashed his shield as he taunted the boss for emphasis.

"Ye enormous turd, I bet your mother was an ogre." He yelled as the giants attacked again.

"AOE attacks now!" Kat shouted moving in towards the boss. Chain lightning and fireballs began to rain down. The archers launched four or five arrows at once not even trying for precision. They just fired at the direction of the monsters.

"Affliction," Kat said pointing her sword at the Sand King. She was going to have to let the other groups concentrate on the smaller monsters. The boss swung again in a wide arc, and Kat was knocked backward along with six or seven fighters. She rolled to a stop amid the second line. Quickly she got to her feet and ran forward again. No matter what Kat needed to keep the Sand King away from the mages.

She reached out with a palm intoning, "Harm touch." Small cuts opened up about the monster's body, but the giant didn't even seem to notice. The damage she'd caused was almost insignificant. She quickly cast her vampiric edge buff on her sword and started hacking. The giant swung again with a horizontal strike. The massive blade caught her on the side, and she was sent back five or ten feet but managed to stay upright. After regaining her balance she glanced at her health. Almost half gone with just two attacks. It didn't bode well that she was already this hurt. Kat pulled a health potion out and drank it. She tossed the bottle down and ran forward. The boss was moving into the gap of empty fighters.

Sarge, Astrid, and the others were having the same luck as her. That giant's strength must be truly massive. It was like they were being toyed with. A blizzard formed over the heads of the mobs. Large ice crystals rained down on the three creatures. More lightning arced between the enemy giants. All the while a continuous flurry of arrows whizzed past. At least one of the guards was looking close to death. He was trying to get past the block of fighters. Guild members hung from his legs as they attacked his lower body. The giant went down screaming, crushing a rogue under its body as it fell.

Kat returned her focus on the Sand King. The giant lifted his sword touching the ceiling with the point. She watched the blade looking for the moment to dodge away. As she waited a massive foot slammed into her body. Not even her shield had been in the way to block. Kat struck the ceiling of the grand hall and bounced off. Next, she hit the ground so hard she left an impression.

She lay stunned for a minute looking upward. Her health blinked red in the corner of her vision. Above her the mortar and loose stone started cracking, and the section of ceiling fell on her. Massive stone blocks pinned her body to the ground. Kat didn't feel the pain, except as excruciating failure. Her health dropped to zero and her vision went dark. Kat died, killed trying to take the castle. She hadn't even had time to use the rest of her abilities. All she could do was wait and hope the guild succeeded.

She expected to see the white selection pad when one logged in. Instead torches began to flare in the darkness. Slowly the red light illuminated the ceiling of a black bricked temple. She was still laying on the ground looking upward. Kat couldn't move her body in the slightest. Immediately she recalled her years of paralysis, and her brain recoiled. A face came into view above her. It was red, large, and had the horns of a demon.

"So you died," Asmodeus said in a dry tone. At least she had an idea what was going on now.

"I did," Kat agreed sourly. She supposed she wasn't that surprised to see the demon.

"Normally I'd just claim your soul and move on. You however have done well enough to get a second chance." He said still looking down at her. He continued when she didn't answer. "I'm pleased with the souls you've send to the afterlife. None of my other champions have so many kills." There had to be a catch. Demons didn't do anything out of kindness.

"What do you want?" She asked.

"We understand each other. You're right, there is always a price." He said touching his fingertips together. "Souls, the only currency worth a damn here. I don't mean monsters or the trash you find in the wilderness. I want adventurers." He said with a decidedly evil grin. The demon meant players of course.

Kat didn't have to accept his offer. If the guild succeeded then they'd just reanimate her from the dead. Her chat box was absent and she couldn't move to type. Anything could be happening back at the citadel. It was the paralysis that swayed her, making the worry claw at her stomach. She feared the guild was getting destroyed by that boss.

"Yes, I'll do it." She said and the demon smiled at her. Reaching down it picked up her left wrist. He pushed one of his long talons into the palm of her hand. Slowly he drew a symbol. Her flesh began to tingle like crazy as the smell of burning meat reached her nose. Lastly he pulled a tooth out of his mouth and forced it into the skin of her hand.

"There now," He said admiring his work. Asmodeus let go of

her arm and stood. "Don't die again little one. I'd hate to see my investment go to waste." He said moving to her side. He began to chant over her as hellfire circled her body. Smoke and magical fire filled her vision before everything went blank.

She knew she was back when she heard the roar of a giant and the sound of battle. The chat was spamming with dialog and her health bar was quickly growing. Kat's entire body felt like she was on a sugar high, and she punched out with a fist sending a massive stone away from her. The pile shifted and she jumped free. Her aura of smoke rolled off her like a bonfire as she surveyed the action.

The second guard was dead, killed sometime after she'd been taken out. The Sand King's health was at about half but he was destroying her guild. Twenty bodies lay around the main hall including Sarge and Astrid. Only a handful of fighters were left trying desperately to keep the boss from the rest of the raid. In the corner of her vision a buff was flashing with a sixty-second timer. [+30 Lvl] was all it said but she could guess what it meant. It was as if she were temporarily level seventy-five.

Kat didn't run, she crouched on the rubble and aimed at the distant boss. Molten lava was flowing in her veins. The muscles of her legs corded up like steel cables as Kat gathered herself. Rocks and dust blew away from her as she lept at the Sand King. She struck him in the back making the giant stagger. With her crimson sword she slashed out across his neck. As she landed the monster turned towards her with his ten-foot bloody sword. He tried to bring it down on her, but the giant's movement seemed slow like moving through molasses. She ducked under the blade and immediately noticed his foot again. The bastard was going to try and kick her a second time. She rolled under his massive hairy foot. As she came up she slashed backward slicing through his heel.

Her entrance into the fight made her guild pause. They stared at her as she attacked the giant's second leg. The boss bellowed in pain rocking backward off balance before falling onto his ass. Everyone rallied then. Whatever mana was left they used in a final spell. Fire fists and magical bolts slammed into its chest knocking the giant all the way over. Kat once again leapt, and in mid air spun so that her feet landed on the ceiling. Again stones cracked as she hurled herself down at the Sand King.

"Unholy Smite!" Kat yelled as her sword erupted into flame. Hellfire flared as she aimed her blade at the boss's chest. When she landed the sword sank to the hilt, and stinking black smoke filled the air around the wound. She twisted the blade, yanking the sword free, and blood erupted from the wound like a fountain.

[Congratulations on being the first to kill the Sand King.]

Her level rose twice as she stood a top the corpse. Everyone cheered lifting their weapons. "Lawful Dead," The guild shouted coming forward. They'd managed to take the citadel, now they just had to keep it.

"How did you come back?" Folken said from near the Sand King. He'd been attacking from the shadows all the while.

"There are perks to being in bed with a demon, Hell wouldn't take me," Kat said to the thief. The buff that had come along with the resurrection faded. She felt suddenly weak, and she staggered off the body. The Cleric came forward with a relieved look on his face. The man was now level thirty-nine from being in her group. He'd gained four levels during the raid.

"Raise Sarge first, we need him right away." She said to the cleric. Josh pulled a bag of gold coins free of his inventory then knelt next to the slain Defender. The spell didn't take long. The green fire spread around the body in a circular sygil as the money melted away. Sarge must have been waiting at the character selection screen because he sat up as soon as the spell was complete.

"So we won?" He asked and Kat nodded.

"How did you get raised?" Sarge also asked. Normally the reanimate spell took an hour to cool down.

"Asmodeous the demon gave me a second chance. Though

now I have to send him the souls of players as payment." She admitted. Under her gauntlet, she could feel something circular embedded in the flesh of her palm.

"You'll get that chance soon enough." Folken piped in nearby. "They just reached the strait. The army will be here in ten minutes." He added.

"How many?" She asked fearing the worst.

"You can see for yourself. The strait is visible from the citadel walls." He replied.

"Sarge go and sit on the throne, let's start to claim this castle at least," Kat said to the Defender, he made a sour face.

"You are going to need me in the fight," He replied. They'd lost almost all of their melee fighters. She had mages and archers in abundance. A smattering of light DPS rogues but virtually no tanks. Kat did need Sarge up front.

"I don't want the Sand King re-spawning. I won't throw a low-level member on the seat just to keep it warm, that might give them ideas. No, you have to do it." She said. The half-orc nodded slowly and turned to the rubble throne. Kat left the hall and walked outside. The courtyard was clear so she climbed the nearest set of stairs.

Folken had been right, that was a large number of players headed her way. She wasn't good at counting groups. It looked like more than five hundred, but less than a thousand. The mortals were already riding past the edge of town. In ten minutes they'd reach the cleft up the mountain. Her guild was going to have to fight for it's life one more time.

CHAPTER FORTY-TWO

Kat - Defense

It was a nice night to die at least. The moon was only a sliver of its usual size making it eerily twilight. The stars were a vast carpet of sparkling lights in the heavens. Only a few high clouds were visible lazily drifting along. Most of the night would be black as pitch, which would help against the humans. Below in the gray scale of dark vision the army approached. Kat could hear the thundering mounts of so many. All too soon they would swing around the village then come up the cleft. She had little time to prepare a defense.

If they fought them at the wall, the humans would probably rush her troops. They'd simply zerg through her people into the castle. She needed to stall and weaken the enemy. Kat shouted for everyone to mount the walls except her remaining fighters. She took a scant forty tanks down the cleft. Slightly more than halfway down she stopped. Above her, eighty wizards and archers could fire down on the mortals with relative impunity. The only problem would be in trying to hold off hundreds of players with so few.

"They are going to push us," Kat said to her assembled fighters. They stood only three deep stretched across the small trail. "Keep a slow retreat going, walk backward while defending," Kat added turning to face the enemy. They had stopped near the base and dismounted. In about ten minutes a block of soldiers started up, and sun-stones broke along the path. The human fighters were throwing them forward of their advance like flares. Kat swore under her breath. There went the advantage of fighting at night. In minutes hundreds of stones filled the lower trail.

Above her mages chanted as arrows were launched down at the approaching mortals. More sun-stones flew forward breaking apart and lighting the way. The trail was a litany of bright yellows, pinks, blues, and greens.

"Remember, slow retreat. Make them pay for every foot!" Kat shouted above the noise. It was becoming increasingly loud as the enemy neared. Finally, the humans came around the corner at last. Most were only level thirty, so she had ten to fifteen levels on most of them. A sun-stone was lobbed far forward of the approaching men. It landed amid her troops, then broke apart flaring bright and dispelled the darkness. The humans stopped seeing Kat and her blocking force. The circle of light cause the vampires nearest to back away as the daylight debuff weakened them. More stones were cast into her midst like fire bombs.

"Kick them over the side," someone shouted. Seconds later the flares were sailing out into the night. Darkness again took hold around Kat and her men. A large blizzard form directly above the lead human. Ice shards and arrows rained down among the mortals. Ice began to cover the small trail. Several elemental pets started to harass both sides from the air. For a few seconds the advancing fighters slowed to a stop. The humans paused unsure what to do, but a man stepped forward pointing with a long sword, then they yelled, charging forward. Kat lifted her shield into the ready position with her blade held at her side. In the darkness the humans blindly ran forward.

"Greater Vampiric Edge," She intoned making her blade glow with red light. Beside her, other fighters were whispering their skills into activation. This was likely going to be a long fight so she saved the rest of her mana for later. The first man hit her barrier hard and she thrust out with her sword. It caught him on the side and she slashed again before he recovered. The human had plate on, superb armor actually, and he must have paid quite handsomely for the set. His weapon lashed at her awkwardly. Kat met his attack with a shield bash knocking him off balance.

After fighting the Sand King this young whelp felt like a joke. A sun-stone flared to life just inside the enemy formation.

"First line back!" Kat yelled stepping out of the pool of radiance. She backed all the way past the second row of fighters. As she passed them they closed ranks, and Kat took her place in the rear of the three deep defense. Her dark-vision kept going in and out because of the constant spells raining down. Fireballs and lightning briefly blossomed among the humans. Kat took out another potion of blood, and topped up her natural regeneration. More sun-stones broke inside her formation. The enemy was getting greedy by throwing stones further than they should. The humans would have to learn quickly as the expensive artifacts went over the edge.

"Second rank retreat," Kat said watching her raid numbers carefully. They were dipping into the yellow and orange. A couple fighters moved past grateful for the break. They chugged health potions waiting their turn again. The humans too were rotating people but several bodies lay motionless on the trail.

"Rogues trying to sneak past near the cliff edge," a voice shouted next to her ear. The dark shape of Folken was already slipping back into the shadows. Kat stepped out of line for a few seconds. She ran toward the edge and slashed at the air. Two leather wearing rogues appeared as their stealth dropped. Lifting a foot Kat kicked sending the first thief into the air and over the edge. The other immediately vanished reappearing twenty feet down the trail. He turned fleeing into the crowd.

"How many got past?" Kat asked moving back into her formation. "Two," Folken said from further away. The sun-stones were quite deadly to the shade. "Hunt them down. They might be able to party summon people within the castle." Kat said moving into the front row.

"On it," Folken said disappearing into the shadows. That true sight ability really was overpowered. It was her turn again to take on the humans. She didn't try anything fancy this time. Instead, she held the shield up and kept thrusting out with her weapon. The enemy player was pushing her back, or trying too. They were no longer content with a few feet at a time, someone in command had urged them forward.

"First Line," Kat called and her forces again slid back. Instead of following Kat allowed the humans to get on her sides. "Asmodeous's Wrath," She said activating her black blades. Her wispy aura of smoke solidified into dozens of weapons. They circled her cutting and parrying the enemy attacks. Even with the sunlight debuff, her aura slashed into the enemy hit pool. It kept the army halted for forty seconds before she was forced back.

As Kat moved to the rear she got a good view of the battlefield. Heaps of bodies lay along the trail as her troops continued to fire down. The enemy looked like an ant column moving up from the bottom as hundreds of fresh troops waited for their crack at the castle. She hadn't lost anyone yet but she'd given up ground, too much for her taste. Already she was nearing the top of the cleft. Her forces would have to retreat to the collapsed wall soon. That would be a tricky feat to pull off.

Kat gasped noticing a new force appear from the forest. How had the mortals gotten reinforcements so close to town? She wondered if they'd been waiting nearby all along. It was easily a thousand troops. They moved like a wild mass towards the bottom of the hill.

The enemy faltered then, which surprised her. Wounded fighters before her still fought but she felt something shift in the air. The pressure of combat wasn't as intense as before, and lots of faces were turning to look down. Kat saw him in the mass. A tall skeleton with a flaming skull was running along in the middle. Despite herself she smiled. Liam to the rescue, just like last time.

It happened in slow motion. Like two ant colonies mixing in the distance. Later it would be called a tactical move of sheer genius, but Kat at the moment, was sure this was folly. Liam had collected every available body logged into the server. It had to be with so many people slamming into the humans rear. There might be a thousand undead down there but Kat knew they were level ten or less. Spell flashes lit the distant forces as they collided. Human mages were doing a good job killing two or three undead at a time. The newbies pounced on the spell casters and clerics they found. Seven or eight undead attacked a single target.

Slowly the mortal army started to change direction. They were reorganizing to meet this new threat. It would be a massacre in a short while. She had to keep the pressure on the enemy.

"Everyone off the walls!" Kat ordered over raid chat then she added. "We attack, push them back." Slowly the spells from above dwindled. For a few minutes the fighters bore the brunt of a fresh assault. "Second line forward," Kat called loudly. A big fighter stepped past her with a two-handed axe. She didn't have time to see what was happening below. All of her concentration was focused on keeping her force moving forward. Her army stepped into the glare of the sun stones. Even though it weakened her troops the momentum was on her side. Seconds later the stones sailed into the night.

It took her twenty minutes to near the bottom. At least the trail was now dark, and empty of annoying flares. The mortal army wasn't pinned between their two forces. That would have been too much to ask for. Instead, they leaked out the side towards town. Near the village they were quickly reforming. The undead at the cleft base came into sight. Liam was near the front with four undead pets. Young players surrounded the lich like a vanguard. He sauntered forward with an annoying proud gait. Bodies lay everywhere, some human, many the corpses of undead. In comparison Kat had lost only eight even though she'd been fighting much longer. He stopped before her thumping the end of his staff into the bloodied ground.

"Do you know how angry I am?" She asked.

"I heard the score, you were set to lose the castle." He said in his infuriatingly logical voice. "If you lose, we all do." He added making her frown deepen.

"You were supposed to stay far away from this," She said.

Liam pointed towards the destroyed town. "The mortals are moving again," He stated ignoring her statement. Kat turned and saw them marching forward. Sun-stones were being cast as before.

"We are going to discuss this later," Kat said stomping away.

She moved towards the base of the cleft. Most of the raid guild was assembled next to it. The battle for the castle sadly hadn't ended. Now they had a thousand or so extra bodies. Liam moved up and stood next to her.

"We are still short on tanks. When the humans arrive we're going to be pushed hard. They've taken losses and will want revenge." Kat said and paused turning to the necromancer. Liam," Kat said saying the name with more bite that she intended.

"Yes?" He said ignoring her tone.

"Can you go up to the keep and organize the ranged characters on the walls. Even the low-level players will add to the damage output."

"Don't try and keep me out of the fight this time." He said walking up the trail with his pets. Kat sighed, she had lost something with Liam.

"Suggestions?" Kat asked turning to her remaining officers. She wished Sarge was here, his experience in the army reserves would be useful. The others looked grim and somewhat shaken.

"Same thing we did last time. Walking retreat up the trail. Now we have some low-level clerics to heal. Keep them behind the front ranks and they should be fine." Astrid said and Kat considered. That would allow her few remaining tanks a margin for safety. The mortals still had to make it through the meat grinder.

As the rest of her raid moved up the cliff the mortal army moved in. Kat retreated halfway to below the castle walls. She barely had time to drink a few blood potions before the humans were on them. The mortal came towards her almost timid in his attack. The lance he held was held across his body defensively. He thrust out several times. Kat raised her shield easily blocking the random jabs he threw at her. Then she stepped into his space cutting him across the arm. Kat blocked a strike from a second fighter before stepping back. She outclassed these level thirty fighters. Kat felt somewhat confident about this battle, that was until she stepped back. She tried to get into line but it had moved. The defenders were ten feet further than she expected.

"What's going on?" Astrid asked suddenly. Kat dodged a lance as the humans advanced. She was forced to throw herself towards her troops. She wanted to know that as well.

CHAPTER FORTY-THREE

Climax

"He who knows when he can fight and when he cannot, will be victorious."

— Sun Tzu

A female vampire standing next to Kat vanished, and for a few seconds, she stared at the empty space. Then another fighter was taken. Gaping holes began to appear in her defensive line. Kat and her undead forces were going to get overrun if this continued.

"Retreat," Kat said turning to run up the trail. The humans moved with them, advancing quickly after. "Get inside the keep!" Its broken walls seemed to offer the only protection against whatever was happening. Liam waited just inside.

"Astrid just disappeared!" A young zombie member said nervously. This wasn't how the battle was supposed to go.

"Why did you retreat? What's going on?" Liam asked quickly.

"It's the GM! He's teleporting people away." She hissed flashing her blade as if she could use it against the power targeting them. Kat raised her other hand tapping at the air before her. She accessed her system menu and saw both Sarge and Folken were missing. "Look at the guild page, they're all offline."

"Contact Walter fast," Liam said.

"I'm already on it," Kat replied typing with one hand. More

382

and more vampires ran out of the keep before disappearing.

The mortals moved forward until their archers were in range, and began picking at the undead army. The low-level players ran, while others charged forward, and still more started to flee. Liam did the only thing he could think of. Targeting several nearby dead bodies Liam cast [Raise Dead], then sent the new pets charging at the mortal archers. The humans backed up, retreating partially down the bluff, and behind a row of tanks. More zombies vanished. Every time an undead player started to get the upper hand they were immediately teleported away. They had to hold out until Walter got there. Her tiny brigade was getting decimated though. The mortals again crested the bluff and started to fire into his army. Not knowing what to do the noobs blindly ran towards the enemy to be cut down. He would at least make it hard on them.

"Retreat inside the keep!" Liam called to the troops. He and Kat stood near the entrance herding people inside.

"I don't know why we are still here, but let's portal away," Kat said.

"We can fight them inside, near the stairs. They can't stop us from running into the private rooms and teleporting away. We need this keep." Liam said turning towards the advancing army. Before stepping inside he controlled another set of five pets to follow them. Next he cast a [Black Briar] root and a [Grasping Hands] to keep the army from running inside. Kat though impatiently dragged him through the doors.

Sarge was sitting on the rubble but looked unconscious. His armored body was draped over the crude throne like a drunken rag doll. If they didn't hold the humans back they would kill the Guardian a second time tonight.

"You messaged Walter?"

"Twice," Kat replied pulling Liam along. It took the mortals ten minutes to clear the courtyard of undead pets. All the while undead players continued to vanish and after ten minutes it was over. Everyone was gone, a thousand undead disappeared, like so much smoke. Liam was genuinely annoyed. So much of his effort had been wasted by some cheating bastard. The front doors pushed open, and a man wearing shining plate mail stood silhouetted by the moonlight. Then the mortals moved inside attacking Liam's meager defenses. Kat refused to let the lich get close enough to help, so Liam was forced to watch as his last troops were annihilated. All he had left was four zombies that had followed him to the stairs. The mortal army moved in a group towards Liam, and leading the force was a man in shining plate. He carried a shield and holy mace as weapons showing they'd come prepared for the fight.

Wait, that wasn't quite right. The weren't so many mortals anymore... They looked confused as their numbers dropped by at least half. Outside the army was vanishing in even greater numbers, and in less than a minute, a single man remained. The plate wearing leader started to laugh. Reaching up he took off his helmet revealing radiant blue eyes. He dropped the helm to the ground like a useless toy as he strode forward.

"So you're just like me. That's why I couldn't get rid of either of you." The man said in a commanding voice. He didn't seem to realize that another GM was present. Walter was nearby or he wouldn't have been able to ban those players. As a higher level admin he could remain invisible even to Orenthal.

"Bloody cheater, we're nothing like you." Kat spit raising her crimson blade. The action made Orenthal smile.

"I'd hoped not to resort to such crude measures, but I suppose this will make things more simple. I'll just kill you both then summon a guild member to sit on the throne. This world will be mine. Now that I'm truly immortal I have all the time I need. The human guilds will eventually follow me." Orenthal said smiling.

"You'll never get away with this. The admins will have to step in." Kat said to the man.

He laughed in response. "The GM's are so inept. So long as I lay low they'll just say it was a strange bug. It'll be mysteriously fixed with a hot-patch." He said rushing across the hall.

"Attack," Liam ordered and his remaining undead converged on the human. "Kat, keep him occupied," Liam ordered, but Kat glanced at him stubbornly. She wasn't about to step away from Liam. If she needed to she could push Liam upstairs to safety. At least if they weren't fighting a GM. "Just do what I ask for once, and trust me." He added pointedly. Pieces of one pet already lay on the ground, and Orenthal gleefully smashed another. The man seemed content in taking his time.

For a few seconds, she debated on whether to drag Liam away or fight. Kat gripped the blade in her hands with enough forced her knuckles turned white. Finally, she spun rushing the short distance toward Orenthal and [Shield Bashed] him. He laughed at Kat's childish attempt to knock him off his feet.

"Haven't you noticed by now I'm immortal. You can't kill me." Orenthal said striking out with his holy hammer. Black smoke rose from Kat's skin as the holy weapons slammed into her. She was forced back on the defensive, but Liam wasn't idle. Black and green fire formed a circle around him, and whispering lines of magic congealed as the lich cast his highest level spell. Kat tried again and again to press the attack, but the GM parried her like she was a novice fighter. Finally, she leaped back and tried using [Piercing Thrust] on the player. Oranthal knocked the blade away and smashed her face with his glowing mace. Kat staggered, and just barely raised her shield in time. Even mostly blocked, she was sent sliding across the floor from the blow. Orenthal smiled again, advancing and completely ignoring the zombie pets attacking him. Throughout the fight, the GM's health had remained stubbornly stuck at one-hundred percent.

Liam's spell finally finished, and he pointed at the mortal man. His voice was dark, and full of fury as he intoned the words, "Death's Knell." Behind Orenthal a huge door rose from the tiled floor. The pillars to either side of the wooden portal were made of ancient bone, and covered in grinning skulls. Slowly it creaked open, exposing the void within. Orenthal continued to laugh hysterically as he attacked Kat.

"I am going to enjoy killing you both." He said in gleeful passion. The holy hammer smashed into the shield, and Kat lost her grip on it. He stood triumphantly over the Blackguard as a

Grim Reaper appeared through the dark door. It's upper torso that of a black-robed skeleton. A scythe comes into view as it circled the GM's throat, and other skeletal hands reached out grabbing the admin. The final sound Orenthal made as he was dragged inside, was short gurgled laugh. Then the door slammed shut with a violent echoing boom, and within seconds disappeared into the ground.

"It worked?" Kat asked in astonishment.

"Back when Walter and I had our disagreement, I noticed my paralyzing grasp worked on him. As a ghost my powers affect even admins." Liam said rather smugly.

"Why did you do that?" Walter asked appearing above them, his aura already coloring toward crimson in anger. "That spell completely deletes the entity you use it on. You killed him." Walter said and Kat looked away from the floating rabbit. Shame filled her face, but Liam wasn't so affected. In fact, he felt rather good about killing the man. He'd been a thorn in Liam's side for months.

"What else should we have done with him? No jail could hold an admin, or do you think you could have changed him? Possibly taken his GM levels away without harming him?" Liam asked gesturing to the location Orenthal's demise. Walter flew down to the two players. His aura was less powerful but the stone tiles still broke at his approach.

"What were you doing while we fought for our lives? Trying to stop him, freeze him? Nothing worked am I right? Your powers work on registered players. Had I attacked him regularly, he would have known I could hurt him. Then he'd have just teleported away." Liam said looking down at the GM.

Kat looked around assessing the damage. Sarge was sitting on the throne, but he was logged out. Thankfully, Orenthal had been unable to teleport him away. She gathered her wits, and considered their next step. Just because one threat was gone didn't mean it was all over.

"What happened to my guild members?" Kat asked changing the subject.

"They've been banned for twenty-four hours, which will be easy enough to fix. The problem is this incident. The board is going to ask questions." Walter said glaring at Liam.

"Tell them it was a hacker, it's true enough," Liam replied with a shrug.

Walter rubbed his face and turned in a quick circle as he gathered his thoughts. "You should both return home. Get away from here before more GM's come to investigate." The rabbit said and floated upward. So long as they both looked like they were offline, everything would be okay.

"How come his power didn't work on me?" Kat asked after thinking about it.

"I placed a level five shadow lock on your account. Only someone of my level could affect your character. Go now, I'm going to call in more GM's." He said and started to type. Liam took out his stone, activated it, and within seconds was back at the palace. Kat followed his example then went so far as to log off.

Liam went to brood in his room. He had just killed a fellow ghost, but he wasn't guilty about it, not in the slightest. Orenthal had been trying to kill them both at the time. No... The only thing he was worried about was the repercussions. Or rather the fact, Liam had no little control over his life. It was vexing to think someone could just delete him like a piece of trash.

CHAPTER FORTY-FOUR

Kat - Ressurection

"The boundaries which divide Life from Death are at best shadowy and vague. Who shall say where the one ends, and the other begins?"
— Edgar Allan Poe, "The Premature Burial"

Kathrine Ines (Subject 4)
Homespace

Walter was in her living room, not the small rabbit but a middle-aged human avatar. The man's face was thin with brown hair and beard stubble. Even in human form he had mischievous almost impish eyes as he sat on the couch. Kat nervously picked up the virtual phone and dialed. It rang several times before being picked up.

"What can I do for you?" A smooth-voiced older man asked. It was Dr. Gedding, and she was glad he was still in the office.

"Ben, please come to my homespace," Kat said into the virtual phone.

"Is there a problem?" The older man asked.

"I'd like to talk to you face to face," Kat replied before purposely hanging up. It was slightly rude, but she wanted to make sure he showed himself. She brought the phone away from her ear and tossed it onto the table. Together with Walter she waited for the doorbell.

After ten minutes there was a chime. Kat stood moving to the front door. Ben was standing at her entrance with his bulging muscles and peppered hair. He had a slightly worried expression on his face as he came into the room. It changed to confusion seeing his old friend present. Especially when said friend was actually in his human form.

"What are you doing here Walter?" Ben asked.

"I'm here for moral support," Walter replied.

"Can I get you anything?" Kat asked into the awkward silence. "No," both men said in unison. She accepted moving to the couch where she sat primly. For a few long seconds she did nothing but straighten the folds her white sun dress. Again she glanced at the two men, mustering up her courage. The three sat looking to one another, Ben still in confusion.

"I want you to kill me," Kat said finally. Ben stood putting a hand before himself as if he was warding off an attack.

"Kat, if there's something wrong please tell me." He said coming towards her. He put a fatherly hand on her shoulder. "Suicide is never the answer," He added and Kat frowned.

"I'm already dead, Ben. My body has long been dissected in some second-year medical class."

"You're depressed about something, we can get you help." He went on ignoring her statement. Kat thought the man had something of a father complex. He treated her as a surrogate daughter, which was endearing but troublesome at the moment. She reached up taking his hand from her shoulder.

"I'm serious," Kat said.

"You've heard about the Digitized people, ghosts?" Walter said finally cutting in.

"That's just a vicious rumor. As soon they began, VRTek came to me for answers, and I told them it was impossible. The machines cannot send souls, or memories, or whatever they assume it is." Ben said stepping back. He turned glaring at Walter before he said, "How dare you put things in her head."

"It's real old friend. I should know as the head GM for Nigmus

Online. The place where it's all happening. I've met one, seen his data." Walter said his tone turning annoyed. He stood facing his old friend.

"You are mistaken," Ben said. Walter shook his head and opened his mouth to respond.

"Enough!" Kat cried. Both men turned to her in surprised. She took a second to smooth her dress then continued. "I don't care if you believe me or not. It's what I want."

"There has to be another way," Ben said but Kat stood as well. She approached the man and took his hands.

"I trusted you with my mind and my body. In return, I gave you eight months worth of data." She said looking into his eyes. "How long do I have to live?" She asked him. He seemed confused at her strange question. "You told me your first subject was on his twentieth month, so he should be almost three years without a body now. I've been sleeping longer lately and my concentration has been slipping. So how long do I have?" She asked again. Ben looked away refusing to meet the eyes of the young woman.

"You have years..." Ben said still avoiding her gaze.

"Years of what? Once again slowly dying?" Kat interrupted.

"You're throwing your life away on a gamble," Ben said before Walter jumped into the conversation.

"The ghost, Liam, is truly Digitized. The man in question hasn't been connected in four months. His account hasn't been accessed in all this time. The VR dive helmet is now being used by someone else." Walter said.

"What?!" Kat said looking past Ben. "Walter, how come you didn't tell the authorities about this?"

"As a ghost, I figured Liam didn't want the attention. If I did they'd wonder why I was investigating." Ben said before Kat stormed the short distance to him.

"Who is he?" She asked in a deadly cold voice. It was the one she used in game. The one she reserved for potential enemies.

"I'd have to look it up. All I know is the MAC Address for the dive helmet is no longer associated with Liam's account." Walter said taking a step back. She followed clutching at his avatar's shirt collar.

"You will tell me everything when we're done here." She said before turning on Ben. "Are you going to help me or not?" She asked and Ben started. He'd been watching the two with widening eyes, like a deer caught in a pair of headlights. "Don't make me get my mother involved. You know she never wanted this. She could make life very hard on you." Kat added twisting the knife in. The older man sagged in defeat.

"When?"

"Tomorrow evening at exactly midnight," She said moving closer to the older man. She poked him in the chest. "Midnight, not a minute sooner or later." She added and he nodded again like a lost puppy.

"I'll have to make the arrangements personally." He said moving towards the door. She stopped him though and wrapped her arms around his big frame in a hug. Kat then gave him a daughterly peck on the cheek.

"Thank you for all you've done." She said and he tried to smile. It was evident he didn't fully believe her. As Ben left she turned back to Walter. "I'm sorry for my tone earlier." She said to the gray-haired man.

"I can understand your emotions," Walter said in response.

"It's no excuse," She said then gave him a peck on the cheek.

"You're sure about this?" He asked her and she nodded.

"When do you leave for China?"

"Sometime tomorrow, I don't know exactly when." He replied. Kat considered this then followed him towards the door.

"If you're going Liam and I can't rely on your GM shadow lock. I want to be with him regardless of what happens. I love him." She said opening the door.

"Sorry I can't come to your wedding," Walter said with a more cheerful smile.

"You've helped us both enough." She said before giving him a hug. Walter left then and Kat turned back to her living room. It was empty save for the soft sound of seventies music playing in the bedroom. Everything was bright orange and pastel yellow. It was garish and ugly she knew but it wasn't hospital white. That's what had been important to her.

Walter would be in contact with her soon enough with the information she needed. For now though she wanted to talk to someone else. She moved to the couch and sat down. Kat picked up the phone and dialed.

"Hello Momma, I wanted to hear your voice." She said and her mother started to gush. Conversation flowed out of her like the Niagara Falls. Kat smiled and sat back in the couch. They were halfway through talking about her brother when she said, "I love you."

This made her mother pause not quite understanding the sudden announcement. Kat couldn't tell her about tomorrow, or the wedding. She wouldn't understand, but at least she could say this much. The conversation continued, but her mother knew something was different. Finally though they disconnected. Kat paused looking at the phone. When Walter sent the Dive Helmet information she could pass that along to the detective. She still wanted to see the person burn, whoever that murderer was.

***

KittKat - Level 50
Edoku'Kor - Necropolis Palace Gardens.

Kathrine stood in a black wedding dress, and a bouquet of blood roses were held in her grasp. Around her hundreds of vampires and zombies stood. The gardens had changed from the shriveled weeds, and rows of dead trees. Green plague brambles made up the hedgerows. Along the waterways death blossoms and vine reapers were in full bloom. Everything was a wonderful mixture of purples and reds. A blue plague mist was slowly leaking from the dire willows, and Mortals entering the gardens would be unable to regenerate their mana. To her though, it was a silvery shroud that rolled across the ground. The gardens were beautiful, exquisite in a dark gothic way. There would be tears in her eyes if she could cry still. She was overwhelmed by the sight. Finally she started forward down the rows of undead. The guild's top warriors were dressed in their best plate armor, and weapons of every description crossed overhead to form a long steel arch. Kat's wedding train continued to drag over the carpet of black rose petals.

Liam stood with Josh in the small gazebo. The cleric was in a new set of black priests robes. Liam though looked like Death in his black suit, and his half-orc nature made sure he filled the costume. His green flaming skull floated above the necktie. Kat stopped before him.

"You look dashing," She admitted resting a hand on his chest. Kat couldn't help but straighten his tie a little.

"You're always exquisite, Kat." He said in reply before both turned to the priest. Candles around the small atrium flared to life glowing green with the eldritch flame. Josh withdrew his prayer book and held it aloft.

"Under this night sky and silver moon these two have come together for unholy matrimony. Let the forces of Darkness and the infernal power within consecrate this place." He said to the assembled people.

"These two desire to make this union a matter of record. So that their friends and all undead may bear witness and lend support." He continued. Kat smiled at Liam gazing up into his flaming eyes. "I invite the dark gods and infernal demons to come bless this union." He intoned, following this the candles began to flow into the air. Their flames circled the couple within the altar.

A hush fell over the assembled crowd. Even the violin paused as the sound of magic began to fill the air. Josh held out a new unlit candle. This one began to float between Kat and Liam.

"We call upon the element of Darkness to serve us. We call upon the flame of passion to guide us. We call upon the blood of ardor to bind these two together." Josh intoned. "Do you Liam, take this woman to be your lawful wife in marriage?" the cleric asked.

"I do," Liam said and a green wisp of flame slipped from his mouth. It floated down to the candle and hovered over the wick.

"Do you KittKat, take this man to be your lawful husband in marriage," Josh asked next.

"I do," Kat said doing her best to keep her voice strong. As she said this a cut appeared on her lip. A drop of black blood floated towards the candle mixing with Liam's flame.

"Hear me, you who watch and lurk in the shadows. Be mindful as I ask you. Do any present see reason these two souls should not be wed?" Josh asked next and a hush fell over the crowd.

"This bond I draw between you; when you are parted in mind or body, there will be a call in the core of you, one to the other, to which nothing and no one else will answer. By the secrets of the fire and shadow is this bond woven, unbreakable, irrevocable. By the gods that burn and lurk is this bond written in your souls." He said as the green flame and red drop came together.

"By the powers vested in me, I pronounce you husband and wife." He said next. The flame had changed to be a red and green mixture of color. It dipped to the candle before flaring and catching.

"This candle shall burn evermore. It will burn in the night when no one watches and when peril threatens. Liam and Kat stepped forward and grasped the small holder between their hands.

"You may now kiss the bride," Josh said at last. Kat smiled raising up on tip toes as Liam bent. Her cold lips pressed against his teeth. A single tear slid down her right cheek as she parted with Liam. She felt so happy, so complete. Kat made no attempt to brush away the errant drop as it slid down her skin. Josh approached next with a pair of rings. They were black, dark as midnight. Folken had somehow found them somewhere in the Well of Darkness.

"The vows have been made before your friends, the forces of Undeath and all the Gods of the Dark. These rings, like your vows, are without beginning or end. They are the physical representation of your promises to each other's spirits." Josh said taking the first ring up. Kat held out her hand and the dark circle slid onto her finger. The ring slipped over his finger, and Liam lifted his hand to examined the item.

"All hail KittKat!" The crowd shouted.

"All hail Liam!" The crowd shouted.

"All hail the Lawful Dead!"

***

Outside the night sky was dazzlingly brilliant. Kat slumped resting her head against Liam's naked chest. She wasn't listening to his heart beat; both were undead. She, however, was enjoying the feeling of this elven body. Her hands slid over the smooth skin of his chest. They'd been making love for hours. Being virtual they were no longer limited by the stamina of their flesh. His long elfin fingers slid into her hair, caressing her. The other drifted to her chest. He massaged her scalp with one hand while his other slowly played with one of her breasts. His cool fingers quickly made her nipple stiffen.

"I love you," He said and she sighed again, happy, content.

"I love you too," She said glancing at the bedside table. The candle was there burning away. The wick hadn't moved in the slightest. It continued to burn a green and blood red flame. The eddies in the air making it dance back and forth. "It's almost time," She said checking the system time. She continued to straddle Liam but sat up. The blankets fell away from their naked bodies. Kat caressed his chest once more.

"I want to be with '*you,*' at the end." She said and Liam nodded. Kat slid off so he could exit, and she watched his bare elven backside as he left the room. Liam wasn't gone long, a seven-foot tall lich entered the room. She smiled at the skeleton inviting him closer. Kat beckoned for him. Liam set his staff down next to the bed before embracing her. His bones were hard under the robe but she loved the feeling of his aura. It made all the hairs on her body stand up on end. She sighed pressing her cheek against his chest.

They settled together on the rumpled bed sheets. Liam wrapped his arms about her pulling her naked body close.

"I'm afraid," She admitted looking at the candle. It continued to flicker back and forth.

"It will work," Liam assured her. For a minute or two they lay together in silence. For once Kat wasn't fidgeting.

"It's happening," Kat said suddenly. She opened her mouth trying to take a breath but nothing helped. She felt like she was drowning. Oxygen, she needed it and no matter how much she inhaled it wouldn't come. Liam's arms tightened around her, holding her still. It took minutes but her eyes slowly closed.

CHAPTER FORTY-FIVE

Walter - Flight

Walter Nowel
California
4:46am

Walter was supposed to be going at work in an next hour, except he'd finally gotten the message. For half the night he'd been awake, too keyed up to go to bed. Walter stared at the screen of his laptop, reading the email for the hundredth time.

"The yacht ticket came through, leave for work like usual." It said, which floored Walter. That ambiguous sentence severely lacked information. Where was he supposed to go? No instructions followed other than when he should leave.

He decided to get up and shower, which was the only thing he could manage. Walking into the bathroom, he turned on the water. Undressing he got into the lukewarm spray, which quickly warmed as he applied soap and shampoo. Walter was feeling a strange melancholy like he was experiencing homesickness already. The apartment had been his for the last fifteen years, and he was leaving it today, never to see the faded marble tiles of his bathroom again. Angrily he shut off the water, stepped out of the stall, and toweled off. He shaved then brushed his teeth. It was almost time to leave, so he activated the format software on the laptop. He knew he wouldn't be taking it with him. While a new operating system was installing, he drank a glass of water.

Finally, he left the apartment and walked down to his car. He carried nothing except the data drive in his shoe, which was as safe a place as any to keep it. However, Walter made sure there was an encrypted copy posted online. That was just in case though.

It was early spring, and a light morning fog had settled over the ground. In a little while the sun would rise chasing the mist away, but for a few seconds, he was reminded of Nigmus Online. The view was strangely beautiful, almost like a scene within game. Withdrawing the key fob from his pocket he disengaged the alarm. The driver side door popped open at his approach and he slid inside. It was nearing six o'clock as he started the car up.

"Destination?" The vehicle asked in a cheerful female voice. For a second he said nothing afraid his voice would crack. He was growing increasingly nervous. The message had told him to leave at the usual time. He could only hope new instructions would arrive.

"Work," He said to the empty vehicle.

"Autopilot engaged," It intoned backing out of the stall. Walter waited as the slowly exited the parking lot, turned right as usual, and drove towards the freeway. He took out his mobile phone and set it into the drink carrier.

"Radio," He said hoping the music would distract him. It came on as classical techno, something written nearly a century ago. For a few minutes he waited as the car drove down the street. He was about to check his mobile when his car beeped at him.

"Proximity Alert, Proximity Alert." The female said in a cheerful tone. The car was bumped hard from behind. The electric vehicle automatically corrected as it fishtailed slightly. In the rear view mirror, a delivery lorry was already pulling to the side of the road. "Collision detected, activating safe stop procedures." It continued as his car automatically slowed and pulled over. Walter's hands grew sweaty as he tried to take the wheel but it wouldn't let him.

"Contacting emergency services, do you require aid?" His car asked as if reading from a script.

"No," He quickly said. An ambulance was the last thing he needed. A gloved fist knocked on the driver side window. He turned to see a vaguely Asian man standing there. Another was using a flashlight to look into the passenger side. The man spoke but Walter couldn't hear him through the glass. Noticing this he made a rolling motion with his hand.

"Walter Nowel?" The man asked after the window was down.

"Yes?" He asked nervously.

"Your car is being tracked, it's best if you come with us." The Asian man said.

"I've never heard of such a thing," Walter responded and the man laughed.

"Of course not, Mr. Nowel. That would defeat the purpose." The man said stepping back.

"Emergency Services are on the way, we should leave." The second man said straightening. The flashlight flicked off. Walter wondered if he could trust these two. He could just wait for the police to arrive, then everything would go back to normal. If he went with these men he would end up in a shallow grave.

Swallowing his fear he got out of the car. The female voice politely suggested he remain in the vehicle and await help. Instead he walked back to the delivery van. They patted him down before tossing his phone into the bushes. The three got into the van and it pulled away. Walter ended up crammed into the middle between the two men.

"Where are we going?" He asked nervously.

"San Fransisco Bay," The driver replied. Instead of heading north the lorry took the south exit. It was no wonder the agents wanted him in a different car. Especially if his vehicle was being tracked by the US government. For thirty minutes or so they traveled in near silence. Neither man spoke much which left Walter to wallow in his anxiety.

Eventually the lorry stopped near a pier within the bay. About two dozen small boats were tied to the dock. A Hispanic man came out of the cabin of the third ship. A boy no older than ten followed him onto the dock.

"Usted necesita un paseo?" The man asked in a rough accent.

"Sí, es mejor salir pronto," One of the Asian men replied. It was barely considered Spanish.

"Pagar?" The man asked holding out a hand. A large envelop was dropped into it. For a few seconds the Mexican flipped through the bills. Within the envelope was a small map. This he took out and studied in the morning light. Then he handed the cash to the boy, presumably his son who took off running.

"Get in," He said and Walter nervously boarded. The Mexican unlashed the rope from the dock then went into the cab to start the engine. Neither Asian made an attempt to get onto the boat.

"You're not coming?" Walter asked.

"The money is only for one occupant, Mr. Nowel." The Asian said stepping away from the pier. This left Walter feeling very lonely. In the past half hour he'd come to feel attached to the silent pair.

The dawn light was coming over the horizon, though the sun had yet to make an appearance. Slowly the boat backed away from the pier before it shot away from the shore. As soon as they were on the water the Hispanic man became far more jovial.

"Hey Gringo," He said in a heavy accent. Walter grunted in response. "My name is Jose," The man said poking himself in the chest with a thumb.

"Walter," He replied.

"You want to hear joke?" Jose asked with a grin.

"I would love that," Walter said with some sarcasm.

"A hundred years ago my people try so hard to come to America. People like me made a lot of money getting others across the border." The man said in far better English than he'd shown before.

"Now I make money taking people like you out of the country," Jose said with a laugh. He thumped the steering wheel of his powerful boat.

"Funny, yes?" He asked after a second.

"I'd say there's something ironic in that," Walter admitted and Jose laughed again. It seemed to Walter that the joke had been told before, more than once. The boat got into a crude line going under the golden gate bridge. The fast little tourist boat began passing most of the other craft. Soon they were past the golden gate bridge. The man removed the piece of paper he'd been given and looked at it. He made an adjustment to the steering wheel then nodded to himself. Walter continued to sit watching as the sun rose up ahead of them. The radio crackled to life.

"This is Captain Steehl of the US Coastguard. You will cut your engines and prepare to be boarded." Came over the ship's com.

"Uh ooh," Jose said with a grin. "That was fast, you hot potato gringo." He continued with a smirk.

"Are you going to get into trouble?" Walter asked and the man laughed.

"I am American Citizen, they can't deport me. I break no law for giving ride. They might try and fine me but that is no trouble." Jose said then glanced back at Walter.

"You however, you in trouble." He said before a new player entered the picture. Something ahead of the boat breached the water. It was the conning tower of a real life nuclear submarine, and Walter leaped to his feet. Jose however didn't seem surprised at all. He turned the boat again aiming it directly at the dark ship. The thing was huge and he was surprised to see it so close to shore.

"Maybe God does smile on you," Jose said in perfect English. Walter looked at the man out of the corner of his eye. Funny how his accent kept coming and going. Mostly Walter was fixated on the giant Submarine before them. Sailors rushed out of the tower lowering ladders. In the distance a coast guard boat was burning towards them. Walter was grateful the radio was off. He could only imagine what was being said over the airwaves. Jose's little boat bounced lightly against the sub.

"Off you go," Jose said helping Walter up the rope ladder. Awkwardly he climbed up the side of the boat. He only hoped no water had gotten into his shoe. Hands reached down and hauled him onto the deck. A tall Chinese man barked several orders. He had considerably more flair on his uniform than the rest.

"I hope you are worth the fallout," the Chinese officer said.

"Considering this looks like a nuclear sub, that might be a poor choice of words," Walter replied.

"At least you can keep a sense of humor about you," he said as both descended the tower hatch. A sailor came in last locking it behind them. The captain shouted two Chinese words down the hallway. Almost immediately red lights along the deck flared. A warning alarm blared as the submarine descended below the waves.

"This sailor will take you to a private room. You understand space is limited on a ship like this, another is giving their bunk up."

"Thank you," Walter said and the Submarine Captain turned away. The sailor that closed the hatch tugged on his sleeve. He was led to a very cramped cabin where he sat on the simple cot. Without really meaning too he fell asleep. Several hours later he awoke to someone knocking on the hatch. For several seconds he was completely confused as to where he was. He'd almost forgotten the wild escape. The hatch opened as he rose to reveal the captain.

"I have been ordered to retrieve the package. I do not think they meant you." The man said rather pointedly. Several sailors were standing in the hall. Walter sat again on the cot. Picking up his right shoe he remembered he'd put some super glue on the seal.

"Do you have a knife?" He asked. A sailor behind the captain held out a Leatherman. Walter managed to work the blade around the hole, popped it open, and held out the data drive. Briefly, he wondered if this was the part in the movie where the spy was betrayed. Would they flush his corpse from the torpedo tube? The captain took the stick, and continued to eye Walter like a tiger appraising a meal.

"Breakfast will be served in an hour. You may dine with me if you wish." The captain said at last. Walter nodded rather dumbly.

It took almost a week for the submarine to dodge American patrols. Finally though he was brought into a military port. Walter never thought he'd be so happy to have two feet on dry land. The isolated, stale, and claustrophobic submarine had started to drive him batty.

Ji Chisan was there. He smiled seeing Walter come down the plank.

"Mr. Nowel, I have good news," Ji said meeting Walter at the edge of the dock.

"It's nice to see a familiar face," Walter admitted and Ji beamed. "What's the news?" Walter asked.

"The asylum is official, you are a Chinese citizen now that you stand on our soil." The man said proudly. He gestured to the spot they were standing on. Walter's emotions were still up in the air about that topic. He smiled though and extended a hand.

"I hope that I can help," He said as Ji shook.

"You have already. The source code is what we desperately needed. Still you are right, I have a place on my team for a man like you." Ji said still beaming. He looked into Walters still slightly green face.

"An apartment as been arranged near the facility. Would you like to rest for today?" Ji asked taking pity on the older man.

"I'd rather start working. I've slept enough the last few days." Walter said making Ji grin again.

"I told them you were passionate," Ji said before guiding Walter to a waiting car. In the distance the submarine was being refueled and prepared for launch.

"Yes, things were changing," Walter thought.

CHAPTER FORTY-SIX

Epilogue - Karma

"When karma comes back to punch you in the face, I wanna be there. Just in case it needs help."
— Dank Meme

KittKat - Level 50
Tramin Continent - Dragonfall City - Griffin Wing Tavern

It was still early in the evening, and the sun outside colored the sky in a canvas of colors. A human with bright green eyes pushed open the door for Kat. He held it for her and she passed into the tavern. A few steps into the main room she stopped to scan the crowd.

"Is that him?" She asked pointing with her chin. A corpse stopped next to her looking to the distant group. Five adventurers were sitting around a mug and plate strewn table discussing their dungeon plans. A blond man laughed tapping the map laid out. He had chiseled good looks, and a maxed out human build. For a long second Liam said nothing. The group continued to talk but the din of conversation was loud tonight as each group was trying to overpower the next table and the live band on stage.

"I only saw him the once, and I didn't know his name," Liam said still staring at the man across the tavern. Judging by the armor and weapons, the man was mid-thirties. Obviously a character who'd been playing a lot lately. "That seems like so long ago," Liam admitted after searching the fighter's features.

"His name is KingKole," Kat said sourly. She too was looking at the human, remembering the face of the player. Above his head a red gem was visible to her.

"That sounds like him," He replied with a snort. "Let's go say hello," Liam suggested but Kat put a restraining hand on his arm.

"Don't spook him. We don't want him to log out and toss the evidence." She warned and Liam nodded. They moved together weaving a path through the tables. The music on stage ended as the band climbed down allowing another to set up. The drummer tested his equipment by smashing out a quick solo. A guitar added its own sound to the mix. Soon a song was playing. Kat and Liam both sat as "Dance with the Devil," started up.

"What do you say Doug, Fungus Grove?" Cole said before the six noticed the two new additions.

"Good evening gentleman," Kat said keeping her tone light. She would have killed the fighter where he sat had combat not been forbidden. Kat had spent considerable money tracking the player down. She smiled instead.

"What the hell is a vampire doing in this bar?" A robed man accused. He must have recognized the red eyes or noticed her teeth. Kat's fangs must have been showing.

"I enjoy a good wine as much as the next person. Though I prefer a nice blood flavored tea." She said purposely flashing her long fangs. Everyone knew the vampires worked for the undead faction though none recognized her as the guild leader of Lawful Dead.

"I'm here recruiting actually," she said and the six laughed.

"You're joking right, why would we want to be a cold fish?" Doug asked.

"It has its advantages. You see I'm looking for bad people. Thieves, rapists, tax evaders…" She said then paused. "Murderers," she added with heavy emphasis, Kat couldn't stop herself.

"I'm a murderer," Liam offered and Kat turned to him in

surprise. "The guild leader, I killed him," Liam admitted in an even tone. Oh yes, Orenthal. She'd frankly forgotten him in all the after battle excitement. The fight itself hadn't been that memorable. Kind of a sad pathetic end for the man.

"Yes, but he deserved it," Kat said touching his leg under the table. Liam wasn't above taking a jab at Cole either.

"Speaking of murder did you know all humans have a habit?" Liam asked in return.

"Oh?"

"A trophy, after killing your enemy. Humans have a compulsive need to take something as a reminder. It's hard-wired into our nature. A heart, a scalp, some trophy." Liam said.

"You don't say?" Kole replied dryly.

"Are you sad you didn't get anything from Orenthal?" She asked Liam in response.

"I would have liked his corpse. An invincible bodyguard would have been useful." He said and Kat sighed. Liam was ever the practical man, and she patted his leg again.

"So what do you all think? Are you interested in joining the dark side?" Kat asked turning back to the table. Cole stood angrily grabbing the map from the table.

"You two are a couple of freaks. Coming here and talking about murder, fucking psycho's." Kole hissed pushing the paper into his bag. He shoved from the table and glared at them both. "Let's get the hell out of here, there are plenty of other bars." He said moving towards the doors. His friends tossed their cups to the table and followed. Liam and Kat both turned to watch them go.

"When do you think the cops will get there?" Liam asked in a distracted voice.

"No way to know exactly," Kat replied in a whisper. She'd had a long conversation with the detective last week. It had taken some convincing on her part to get them to reopen the case. Then the time needed to get a search warrant. The gears though had slowly started to move.

The six adventurers neared the exit. Cole was in the lead and had his hand pushed out like a football player. The door slammed open as he barreled through the exit, and they moved down the busy street. Kat glanced underneath the table they were sitting at. A shadow was there slightly darker than any other.

"Follow them," She ordered the shade. The darkness retreated slightly as Folken leapt into the shadow realm. A waitress appeared to clean the table and take their order. "Would you like anything?" The NPC asked.

"I want blood... that murderer's blood," Kat said absently looking towards the door.

"I'm sorry ma'am I don't think we serve that here." The waitress said in a chipper tone.

"Wine then, elven cherry port," Kat replied looking to the NPC.

"And you sir?" The girl asked turning to Liam's corpse.

"Dwarven Stout," Liam said setting his elbows on the table. "I haven't had a beer in ages." He admitted after the waitress had departed.

"We might as well settle in for the wait," Kat said scooting closer to her husband. She slid a hand across his leg. Kat loved Liam in all his forms, though he had a habit of picking handsome corpses to possess. In response, he wrapped his arm around her waist.

***

[Fungus Grove]

"You alright man?" Doug asked Cole for the tenth time that night. He just seemed so distracted.

"Yeah, those two freaks just got under my skin." He admitted after wiping off his sword. The creepy fungoid warriors always made a mess when they died.

He moved towards another group of fungoids with his shield ready. As he passed into aggro range the enemies charged at him. Soon he was able to lose himself in the fight. A fireball lit up one of the creatures as he attacked the second. Most of them would level soon, then it was onto forty. They were just getting ready to pull another group of monsters when KingKole collapsed to the ground.

"Shit, did he disconnect?" Doug asked the group. They'd have to wait for him to log back in to pull again.

"I don't think your friend is coming back." A female voice said from the shadows. The vampire from earlier emerged from the gloom.

"What the fuck did you do?" Doug asked angrily.

"I didn't do anything," Kat said in faux shock. "You, however, should pick your friends more carefully." She continued. As she spoke a new player appeared from the dark passage. It was a seven-foot tall lich. Not just a necromancer, but 'The Deformed Lich' that everyone had heard about.

"Fuck!" The group said loudly. Liam ignored them and approached the disconnected player.

"What do you think?"

"The detectives did strongly believed it was suicide," Liam said toeing the body on the ground. The five adventurers growled at him in response. He turned to Kat with a thoughtful look.

"They were told of a certain stock purchase a month before the incident. Then there were eyewitness reports of an ongoing feud at the location. The victim also had verifiable proof he was online at the time of his death. He'd be unable to pull the trigger, figuratively and viscerally. Lastly said dive helmet is currently being used by the son of the factory owner. A damning train of evidence." Liam said ticking off points on his hand. The five adventurers were staring at the corpse now. Their eyes filled with disbelief.

"You're lying," Doug said. Moving closer despite knowing it was fruitless, he tried blocking the necromancer.

"You always were a stupid fuck, Doug. Cole's little lap dog. Did you ever stop to question where he got his dive helmet."

"He said he bought it," Doug defended.

"It was a sixteen thousand dollar developers helmet. He didn't buy it, I did." Liam said poking the rogue with his staff. His aura was causing enough damage that the player was forced to retreat. He easily picked up the limp body of KingKole and brought it towards Kat.

"You said you wanted his blood," He said offering the vampire a snack. Kat eyed the unconscious murderer coldly before sinking her fangs into his neck. She didn't stop drinking until his health had reached zero.

"Do you want his corpse?" She asked her husband. He casually checked the now deceased human's level.

"Thirty-Eight..." Liam mused and shook his head. "Not useful." Kat lifted the bloodless body up and tossed it down the fungus pit. They'd likely find the corpse a good source of food. The five friends watched passively as this went on. All could see they were outclassed.

"Let's say we believe you. What does it matter, he was just a fat fuck." Doug continued.

"I don't care if you believe me. Also in a way you're right. I should thank that idiot for what he did." Liam said moving closer to Kat.

"You'll let us go?" One asked.

"It would be a waste of energy for me to kill you," Liam admitted walking away from the group. Kat too turned moving up the passage. She stopped though about fifty feet away. Undead began to emerge from the shadows. Vampires and zombies of every description. The group was surrounded by the dead, almost all of them higher level. Several necromancers stepped forward from the group. Skeletal mages that carried dark staffs and tattered robes.

"I told you before. You should learn to pick your friends more carefully." Kat said to the group.

"Kill them all, raise them as pets." She said turning away. Behind her the guild descended on the group. Kat was only sad she couldn't reach into Real Life and kill Cole herself. At least she'd ensure the murderer did his time. At the cave exit she caught up with Liam.

"I'll see you back home?" He asked.

"Yes love, I think I might return tomorrow. Since I'm here maybe recruiting some people would be useful." She said leaning over. Kat gave him a peck on the cheek bone.

"Thank you, I admit I enjoyed that quite a bit."

"You're welcome," She said as the lich began to cast a teleport spell. The magic took hold of him in its blue and golden light. Then he was gone.

Down below the guild necromancers were raising the mortals as pets. They'd be put to good use leveling her guild members. Was it vindictive of her to kill off KingKole's friends? Absolutely and she smiled a wolfish grin.

"Some days it felt good to be bad." She thought to herself.